Family Plots
Love, Death and Tax Evasion

Family Plots

Love, Death and Tax Evasion

Mary Patrick Kavanaugh

iUniverse, Inc.
New York   Bloomington

Family Plots

A Story of Love, Death and Tax Evasion

iUniverse books may be ordered through booksellers or by contacting:

iUniverse
1663 Liberty Drive
Bloomington, IN 47403
www.iuniverse.com
1-800-Authors (1-800-288-4677)

ISBN: 978-1-4401-0466-4 (pbk)
ISBN: 978-1-4401-0467-1 (ebk)

Printed in the United States of America

There is a fine line between fiction and nonfiction,
and I believe Jimmy Buffett and I snorted it in 1978.
--Kinky Friedman

Family Plots is a novel based on the facts of my life. Many events are drawn from actual experiences; however, I have collapsed time, conflated characters, invented dialogue, and rendered some fictional scenes and characters purely for dramatic impact. Because I am not the first or last writer to sensationalize the verifiable data of my personal life, I think there should be a genre recognized for this category of work. If it were up to me, I'd call it Pulp Faction.

To my beloveds…
∾ Tom, Mary & Ray, for giving me a story,
∾ Ashley, for being my most perfect creative expression,
∾ And Reggie, for never once asking when this book would be done.
I am eternally grateful for all you've taught me about love.

Loving the Wrong Person

From *Daily Afflictions* by Andrew Boyd

We're all seeking that special person who is right for us. But if you've been through enough relationships, you begin to suspect there's no right person, just different flavors of wrong. Why is this? Because you yourself are wrong in some way, and you seek out partners who are wrong in some complementary way. But it takes a lot of living to grow fully into your own wrongness. It isn't until you finally run up against your deepest demons, your unsolvable problems—the ones that make you truly who you are—that you're ready to find a lifelong mate. Only then do you finally know what you're looking for. You're looking for the wrong person. But not just any wrong person. It's got to be the right wrong person, someone you lovingly gaze upon and think, "This is the problem I want to have."

Affirmation
I will find that special person who is wrong for me in just the right way.

Prologue

Experts claim that the secret to a happy relationship isn't sex, children, money or even love. It has much more to do with the power of self-deception—a belief that your spouse is wonderful, even when evidence starts pointing to the contrary. Of course, if you happen to learn that Mr. Wonderful is making extracurricular whoopee with a woman who is, say, thinner or more successful than you, you can't pretend that your love life hasn't just splattered in your face, like a bug on a windshield. But there are trickier, more elusive marriage malignancies—such as lies of omission, financial infidelity, or a dogged refusal to change *anything*, be it a behavior, an opinion, or even a zip code. These may be easier to ignore.

The story that follows involves marriage and money, death and deception. There is also some messy business regarding an unresolved murder. It was the last decade of the twentieth century, when Big Brother wasn't watching people so closely. I was a budding private investigator and young single mother in love with an attractive criminal attorney who, it turned out, was committing a few crimes of his own. Through much of our marriage, I managed to disregard my better instincts—even as I slid into a world of pseudonyms, fake weddings, hidden bank accounts, and unexplained cash. It all made perfect sense to me at the time.

Looking back on the bizarre chain of events that changed the course of my life, I've concluded that there's no blaming my husband for what happened. He never forced me to lie or cheat or to commit ridiculous fiduciary crimes just to keep up with him. He certainly never asked me to stick my nose into the dark business of his past. Being immersed in this drama was like diving into an ice-cold lake—shocking and exciting at first, but then I became used to it. It never occurred to me that this could be dangerous—that hypothermia could lead to incoherent, irrational behavior.

But if happiness is the goal, perhaps denial is underrated. Especially so when you are trying to hang onto something you desperately desire. Though my former life is not one I would ever choose again, I'll never regret how I let love pull me along the slippery path that eventually landed me a permanent place in this secretive family plot.

Part One

Chapter 1

October 17, 1989

The day was unusually hot and clear. Without the relief of clouds or haze, the world took on the exaggerated brilliance of hard candy, the landscape packed with jaw-breaking colors. The flowers were too red, the streets inky black beneath a sky of over-saturated blue. Pausing next to our mailbox, I stared across the street at the water in the neighbor's wading pool. It looked eerily still, as if it had been replaced with shiny green glass.

Our apartment building was tucked into an upscale neighborhood in the wooded foothills of Oakland, surrounded by charming Craftsman bungalows. I often played a game where I pretended to switch lives with the people who lived inside them. My favorite house was directly across the street, a renovated white Spanish-style bungalow encircled by flowering purple ivy. A sprawling magnolia tree stood in the middle of the front lawn, and a grassy side yard held a swing set, sandbox, and yellow slide. Some weekends I'd see the family outdoors, the mom pruning the flowers that bloomed in the shade of the tree while her daughters and husband romped on the bright play equipment. I imagined this couple had a steamy sex life, fascinating and well-paid careers, toddlers who slept through the night, and no student loans or credit card debt. If she'd been home with the kids all day, he'd rub her feet and take her out to dinner, and he insisted on paying for a housecleaner at least once a week. In between all the great sex and family time, they made each other laugh. They were responsible and respectable and didn't have to spend this hot October

3

afternoon preparing for a meeting at Consumer Credit Counselors. That was for people like me, who had no idea how to be people like them.

I slammed the mailbox closed, and walked back toward the apartment, my hands full of bills, late notices, and a new issue of *Good Housekeeping*—the subscription courtesy of my mother. The front cover pictured a young housewife with shoulder length brown hair, blue eyes, and a wide, warm smile. She was holding a platter of frosted clown cookies next to the headline, "A-Craft-a-Day Keeps Boredom at Bay: 365 Creative Ideas!" It occurred to me that this good housekeeper and I were about the same age with similar features. Add the right hairstyle, professional make-up, some diet, exercise, airbrushing, and a sunny outlook, and it could have been me.

Rifling through the mail, I stopped to squint at the return address on a light blue airmail envelope, and groaned. It was a letter from Grandma Hazel, my Dad's mother, in Kalamazoo. When it came to me, she only had one subject on her mind. I unfolded the small, typed page.

> Dear Mary,
>   I am very sorry to hear that you still haven't set any kind of wedding date. You surely must want to give your darling Rachel a family name, or just what is it? Are you one of the turncoats of today? There is just no morality any more and soon the United States will be a mess, as you probably will live to see. I thought you said your college boyfriend Kevin was a wonderful man. Also you told me that he was a Catholic. You are twenty-seven years old and a mother! What on earth is wrong with you? Get yourself married and be decent. You'll be a lot happier.
>   Love and prayers, Grandma Hazel

I thought about showing the letter to "my college boyfriend Kevin," also known as The Impregnator—a nickname I'd invented recently, after struggling to find a proper title when asked if he were my husband. In our last raging fight, I'd told Kevin if he didn't get his act together, I was going to find someone who saw the upside of being a responsible husband and father. His response was, "You'll never do any better than this." I folded the crinkly vellum and stuck it in my pants pocket.

Back in the apartment, I opened Rachel's bedroom door and peeked in. Wearing only her Big Bird underwear, she snoozed on the bed, her silky blond ringlets moist with sweat, one pudgy arm draped across a stuffed white rabbit. Rachel was one thing Kevin and I had done well. I gazed at her and sighed. Maybe Grandma Hazel was right. After six years together, Kevin and I might as well be married; it would take us at least a lifetime to unravel our problems. And it would be a step towards giving Rachel, now three, the normal upbringing I wished I'd had.

The twangs and screeches of Kevin's guitar riff vibrated through the door of the attached garage. There was a lingering odor of marijuana.

"Damn him," I muttered, moving toward the noise. He'd *promised* not to smoke when he was on kid-duty. I opened the door to the humid garage. The sound abruptly stopped and Kevin stared at me. I scowled, waving away the smoke, and pressed the garage door opener. Sunlight filled the room. I handed Kevin the letter, moved the sticky bong from a stool, and sat down.

"What's this?" Kevin frowned, staring at the letter far longer than necessary, while I silently rehearsed a half-hearted speech about why we should grow up and get married. He looked at me, glassy-eyed and haggard, his shoulder-length blond curls sagging like limp coils.

"We need to talk," he said.

"I know. I don't think we can avoid it any longer."

Kevin glanced away; he looked like he might get sick.

"You're going to get a call," he said.

"A call? What do you mean, a call?"

"This computer lady is going to phone you." Kevin stared at the ceiling, loudly exhaling. I could smell the pot on his breath. "But believe me, it was nothing."

My heart beat harder. "Kevin, what are you talking about?"

"She's pissed at *me* so she's going to call *you*. Shit." Without making eye contact, he mumbled something about his drummer's cousin, a computer consultant. "We met at a gig. She's a skinny, uptight groupie, actually. She's not even my type. Hairspray, briefcase, you know. We were buzzed. I didn't even want to. *Shit.* She practically threw herself at me."

By now, his tone was indignant, as if he'd been somehow violated. "There," he blurted. "I've said it, okay?" He ran his fingers through his sweaty hair.

"You've said *what*, Kevin? You've said *nothing*." I couldn't seem to stop my voice from quivering, but I forced myself to keep it low. I didn't want Rachel to wake up to another screaming match. During the last one, right before we made the appointment with the debt counselor, she had pressed her hands to her ears and cried, "CALL 9-1-1! CALL 9-1-1!"

"All I am saying," he murmured, "is that I had a little fling." He nervously picked up his guitar and started to tune it.

"A fling?" I hit the side of Kevin's guitar. He grimaced and set it down. My body stung with prickly needles. "Are you having sex with her?"

"No. Yes. Well, no."

Bright heat filled the room, blurring my vision. I stared at Kevin, but he wouldn't meet my gaze. He sat crumpled over, rolling his head back and forth between his hands. I had the urge to help him twist it all the way off, to hear it *thunk thunk thunk* down the driveway like a bowling ball.

"We didn't have sex. She doesn't mean anything to me, we just—"

"You *just* what?"

"It was just, I don't know, just a blowjob or something."

I sat perfectly still.

"It was a mistake." Kevin shoved his hands in his pockets and stared at me.

"You mistakenly let some skinny woman suck your penis?" I pulled my tee shirt down over my lower belly bulge. My jeans felt tighter by the second.

"She had crunchy hair," he offered, as if this odd fact made the whole thing too unreal to take seriously.

"Get the hell out of here so I can think," I snapped.

"You said I had to watch Rachel."

"You do, dammit." I lurched off the stool, pointing my finger. "Because I've got that damn debt counseling appointment—where you should be, too."

"What am I supposed to do?" He threw his hands up. "I work every day, and I've got a gig tonight. Whatever they end up saying, we'll need money to pay these bills, right? Someone's got to hang out with Rachel, right?"

The phone rang. Kevin jumped up. "Don't get it," he said.

We both rushed through the door, my shoulder smashing against the frame as he tried to lunge ahead. I beat him into the hall, yanked the phone off the hook, and barked, "Hello." Kevin twisted the receiver from my hand, put it to his ear and hissed, "I told you not to call here." He listened intently, his free hand pulling at the fuzzy goatee he'd recently sprouted, then said, "Sorry. Yeah, hey. Wait a sec." He held out the receiver. "It's your little sister. Now in two fucking seconds your entire family will know, right?" Shaking his head, he lumbered down the hall, back into the garage.

"I called to make a huge confession," said Jamie. "But what the hell was that?"

"You want to hear about confessions?" I blurted, feeling the first sting of tears. "How's this: Kevin's been out shopping for STDs with some little band groupie."

"Kevin gave you an STD?"

"We'd have to be having sex for that, right?" I quickly told Jamie what had happened. "Can you believe it? And now I've got to deal with the debt counselor. How great is my life?"

The sun followed me like a hot spotlight as I cut through the back of Mountain View Cemetery. Hundreds of weathered granite tombs were perched on the manicured green hills, each plot hiding the duplicity and secrets of the dead buried below. Storming along the deserted, tree-lined paths, I inhaled the scent of cut grass, pine and eucalyptus baking together in the stagnant heat, trying to calm myself down. Sparrows, mourning doves, and thrashers clung to branches, stiff and sneering.

"How can this be happening?" I yelled at the birds. How could my life be playing out like the lives of my parents?

Growing up, my family was the picture of the American upper-middle-class dream—a doctor, his wife, and three children, settled in a house on a hill in La Jolla, one of the most expensive cities on the California coastline. Then Dad started having an affair with a psychiatric patient, who was an heiress. When my mother confronted her, she offered to let Mom sleep with her husband. This foray into the 1970s free love lifestyle ultimately sent Mom on a detour to a psychiatric hospital on her way to divorce court. I'd always sworn I'd never be in a relationship that would result in such messy love ethics, because I was certain I'd choose a man who would be faithful.

Reaching the section of the cemetery referred to as "Millionaires' Row," I passed a plot that was marked with a huge volcanic boulder. Its owner had been disgusted with the egotism of the men who erected grandiose monuments, so in an ostentatious display of simplicity, he'd had a gigantic rock dragged in from Yosemite. Usually I stopped to pat the stone, stretch, and enjoy the view of the San Francisco Bay. But today I kicked it hard enough that it sent me limping the rest of the way to the bus stop.

Consumer Credit Counselors was in a stately downtown Oakland office building, but inside, the furniture was scratched and dingy. A perky, lip-glossed receptionist told me to take a seat to wait for Nora, the debt counselor assigned to review my embarrassing financial situation. Nora, stern and stocky, appeared immediately. She motioned me into her office.

I sat in a stiff orange plastic chair and felt my toes crunch up inside my tennis shoes. It was a nervous habit I'd had since I was eight, when my psychiatrist dad hypnotized me to get me to quit biting my nails. His suggestion was to squeeze my toes instead. Now whenever I was nervous I bit my nails *and* squeezed my toes—and the somber, unblinking gaze of Nora inspired an urge to do both.

"How can I help you?" Nora said.

"I'm here to get out of debt." I paused, blushing. After some optimistic promises made by a local promoter, Kevin and I had convinced ourselves that his band would one day strike it big, and he would make hefty fees and royalties. Since I'd become pregnant with Rachel, almost four years earlier, we'd paid for everything we couldn't afford with plastic. Prenatal and postnatal care, crib, stroller, diapers, sometimes even groceries—all had been charged at double-digit interest rates. Now we were maxed out on our credit cards, still owed thousands on our student loans, and had even borrowed ten thousand dollars from my dad, at a lower rate, supposedly to help get us out of debt. Kevin's job and my tiny childcare business barely covered our rent, utilities, and weekly night out at Zach's pizza. And now there was the uncalculated cost of the blowjob.

"You're fifty thousand dollars in debt?" Nora frowned at my application. "That's a mighty high number." She let out a whistle.

I squirmed in the hard chair.

"What's this ten thousand dollar loan?" said Nora.

"That's a loan from my father."

"Let's set that aside. I assume your dad will wait on payment, so we can focus on—"

"NO." I cut her off. "No. I need to stay current with that."

After my parents divorced, they had remarried and resettled in upscale suburbs where they proceeded to live beyond their means. We barely scraped by in the exclusive neighborhoods of California, with my parents constantly worrying and fighting about money behind closed doors. We never went hungry, but my little sister Jamie claimed there was a time in high school where she had only two pairs of underwear, requiring her to wash one each night. My brother Hank recalled Dad bursting into tears when he was accepted to Stanford, having no idea how he was going to pay for it. I dealt with the pervasive cash flow worries by going to work as an Avon Lady at age fourteen. So that I could maintain product inventory, my mother co-signed on my first credit card, and I'd been charging ever since, a habit that infuriated my father. My whole life seemed to function in a world where there was always more debt than income—yet somehow things worked out. But lately, even I couldn't make the leap of faith necessary to believe things were going to change without my participation.

Nora squinted at the application. "Wait a minute. Looks like there are two people listed. Is this for you and your husband?"

"He's not my husband," I mumbled, studying my chewed up nails. "Just the father of my child."

"You have a child? Do you have life insurance?"

"Yes, some." I knew we had a policy through Kevin's work. "Why?"

"Can you cash it in?" asked Nora.

I let out a chortle, thinking she was kidding, but she remained somber, waiting for a reply.

"Wouldn't he have to die?"

"Depends. Is it term or whole life?" said Nora, clipping the paperwork inside a used manila file folder.

"It's the cheap kind."

"Term," she muttered. "Won't help."

Sitting quietly while Nora pounded numbers into an adding machine, I became uncomfortably aware that the thought of Kevin dead had actually elevated my mood. If Kevin had a tragic accident, I could use the proceeds to eliminate our debt and might still have enough left over for a down payment on a house, or at least a decent condo. I could forget about Kevin's thin, crunchy-haired tattletale. Rachel could attend some upscale daycare facility that had gymnastics, art and music, and organic snacks. I'd join a gym and finally lose the ten leftover pregnancy pounds, after which I'd buy some cute suits and launch an exciting career as...*as what?*

I watched Nora quietly, the room feeling smaller each time she struck a key. I wasn't going to win a life insurance lottery, and there was no quick fix to my problems. Feeling trapped and restless, I was desperate to flee from this small, claustrophobic room, into a new life with my daughter.

Nora laced her fingers together and cracked her knuckles. "You've dug quite a hole for yourself," she said.

"Too bad I can't hide in it."

Suddenly the room lurched and a mug full of pens rattled on the desk. I paused for a second, confused.

The room lurched again. There was a thundering crackle. I looked down at the grungy shag carpet to determine why the floor seemed to plummet.

"Get under the doorframe," shouted Nora. "We're having an earthquake."

The room bounced. I gripped the sides of my molded plastic chair while it jerked around like a carnival funhouse ride. Chunks of wall plaster crumbled to the carpet; I sucked in my breath, tasting a chalky residue. Nora pulled me to the door, where we faced each other as the earth tossed us around. With one hand gripping my shoulder, she yelled, "Are you okay? Are you okay?" for the fifteen elongated seconds of shaking.

Am I okay?

Before I could stop myself, I spewed details about grandma's letter, Kevin's pot smoking, blowjobs, and my desire to raise Rachel in a happy fling-free home.

"I hate my life," I said.

"Well, I hate my job." Nora glanced over, shook her head. "I never know how to help you people."

My tears welled.

"Come on. Let's get out of here," she said.

We scrambled down two flights of stairs and ran outside, where groups of people milled around, dazed, looking at the damage. A woman ran toward us, her cheeks flushed. "There's an old guy over there, bleeding. Something fell from that building!" She pointed across the street at a six-story medical complex, its windows broken and a deep fissure running down its side. Loose bricks and glass were still falling into the parking lot as the paramedics appeared.

"Help me, please," I said. "I've got to get to my daughter."

"Hop in. I'll give you a ride," said Nora.

Nora swerved up Broadway, dodging people and cars. Traffic lights were broken and sirens blared in the distance. A radio announcer reported that the Bay Bridge had collapsed, and a portion of the Cypress Freeway had fallen, flattening cars and trucks into metal pancakes.

The radio station received a report that apartment buildings in the San Francisco Marina District had crumbled. A few had burst into flames.

"Oh my God." I wanted to leap out of the car and run home. What if something actually had happened to Kevin? I quickly made the sign of the cross—*name of the father, son, and holy ghost*—and whispered, "Forgive me, please, forgive me."

Involuntary genuflection was an odd habit I'd acquired shortly after the birth of Rachel. Given that my parents had consciously removed us from the Catholic Church when I was five, I could only attribute it to genetics.

Nora stepped on the gas. "Everything will be fine. Everything will be fine," she repeated like a mantra. As she pulled up in front of my apartment, I noticed our car was gone.

"Maybe they went to get me," I said. "Can you take me back? We should go back."

"If you don't mind?" Nora's eyes bulged like blisters. "I've got my own family," she yelled, before her car shrieked away.

I ran inside and tore through the rooms. Piles of Legos were scattered on the living room carpet. Puréed carrots were smeared onto the face of a prissy porcelain doll perched in Rachel's highchair in the kitchen. Not a dish was broken, all of the books remained on the shelves, there were no cracks in the wall or debris in the fireplace, and both bedrooms were empty. I grabbed the phone and stared at it blankly, not knowing what number to dial. The electricity was off, so I fumbled with my portable radio until I heard a reporter announce in a wavering voice that a young mother and baby had been crushed to death in an apartment in the Marina, which was now in flames.

"Oh no, oh no, oh no," I covered my mouth with a shaky hand. Panic seeped through me as I pictured Kevin stoned, driving Rachel through the falling debris. I used to think unexpected death couldn't happen in my world, but that had all changed when my fifteen-year-old stepsister died suddenly of meningitis five years earlier. *I just wished Kevin dead. And he's got Rachel.* All I'd ever wanted was to provide a safe, secure life for my daughter, but how could I do that? I pulled at the cuticle on my thumb until it was long enough to rip out, taking a hunk of skin with it. A drop of blood immediately filled the hollow, spilling over in a tear that looked black when it hit the wood floor.

Please God, let them be okay. Let them be alive. Please, please, please. I'll do anything. Be responsible. Be a better parent. Clean up my act. Pay my debts. Jump start my life.

"Mama! Mama!" The light patter of small shoes echoed in the entryway. Rachel flung herself into my arms. I squeezed her tight, tears blurring my vision as Kevin entered the room. For a brief moment, the three of us stumbled into an awkward family hug.

Later that evening, once Rachel was asleep, I lingered in the kitchen to avoid the inevitable conversation Kevin and I needed to have. I poured myself a tall glass of wine and took it into the bedroom.

Kevin sat on the edge of our bed. He looked miserable as he watched me through the same clear blue eyes that I used to find sexy and charismatic, but now just reminded me of our daughter.

"I thought you quit drinking," he said.

"I did."

I'd come from a long line of binge drinkers and pharmaceutical drug fans, and had my share of overindulgences. Lately I'd sworn off all mind-altering activity because I wanted to be a better parent, but also because I wanted to be able to lecture Kevin with impunity. These, however, were extreme circumstances. I stared at the glass for a minute, then took a gulp and handed it to Kevin. He drained the wine in one long guzzle. We sat and stared at the faded bedspread for a long time.

"You can't stay here," I said.

"I know." Kevin picked up his tattered backpack and slowly stuffed it with clothes. Watching him wrap his frayed toothbrush in a plastic sandwich bag, I suddenly felt as sorry for him as I did for myself.

As Kevin's car pulled out of the driveway, my temples throbbed. Lifting Rachel's tiny flannel blanket from the floor, I draped it across my eyes. It smelled sweet and calming, like baby lotion. I breathed deeply and tried to slow the blood that whacked against my skull. The only thought I had was, *I want my mommy.* Even though we'd already spoken after the quake, I dialed the phone again.

"Earthquakes." Mom let out a long sigh. "They certainly shake things up. You know, I've always said you two seemed more like siblings than a couple. Even the way you fought."

"Mother, I feel awful—like I have a nest of termites gnawing at my gut."

"I know that feeling, dear," she said. "It was like that when your father was screwing around. Except when I fell apart, it was like *I* was the termite with my gut full of pus."

I hung up the phone, and called Dad. "I don't really hate him, Dad, I hate myself for being in this position."

"Always hate the other person, honey. It's more economical," he said. "You might try taking some Ativan until the worst is over. Want me to send you a few?"

I had an informal policy against scoring pharmaceuticals from my dad, even though our family always had easy access to his inventory of free samples. At Dad's sixtieth birthday roast, my brother Hank joked that in our household we were never spanked, just medicated and sent to our rooms. The crowd roared, but it wasn't that far from the truth.

Hanging up the phone, I called my sister, Jamie.

"Tell me why you called earlier," I said.

"Forget it. It pales under the circumstances," she said.

"Come on, it'll help me get my mind off my hideous life." Jamie knew I loved juicy details. The least she could do was offer up a few.

"No. I can't talk about it now."

"Fine," I said, annoyed. "Then Fed Ex me the rest of those old tranquilizers I gave you in August. I need them back."

"You don't need tranquilizers," said Jamie. "You need a job."

Chapter 2

October 1989

The day before Halloween, I awoke with pressure in my head and chest; my mouth was dry and mossy. It reminded me of waking up after drinking heavily, when I had the fuzzy recollection that I'd done something pathetic the night before. But I hadn't been drinking. *Oh yeah,* I thought. *Last night I was pleading with God.* "What am I going to do?" I'd prayed over and over. "Please, God, just tell me what to do."

There had been nothing left to do but pray, because after telling Dad I was broke and needed help financing the move, he'd announced that he was done bailing me out. DONE! "It's only allowing you to repeat the same destructive behavior cycle, which I've determined undermines your self-esteem."

Being homeless would undermine my self-esteem, too, I thought. But I kept quiet. I didn't want to create an opening for Dad to analyze me. The hard part about having a shrink for a father was that paternal disappointment was usually delivered with unsolicited insights into my psychological flaws. My dad had diagnosed most of my personality problems before I'd turned thirteen. I had an avoidance complex, didn't take enough risks with romance, and was glib, he said, "like your mother." He wanted me to seize romance, exploit opportunities, and feel my feelings—things he wasn't allowed to do in his own strict Catholic childhood. But hard as I tried, I couldn't get it right. Boys didn't go for me, my classes were overwhelming, and I spent most of my teens truant, staying out late, smoking cigarettes, binge drinking and taking cheap diet pills to keep my spirits up while avoiding having any feelings about my whacked-out home life.

Some things never changed. I still wanted to avoid feelings about my whacked-out home life, especially since I didn't know where it would be and how I'd pay for it. But the luxury of denial was impossible now that I had a wide-eyed toddler looking to me for survival. I had to quit whining and find a solution.

A few days after the earthquake, I'd managed to locate an affordable one-bedroom apartment off Piedmont Avenue in Oakland. But on this particular morning, the prospect of packing and moving induced an overwhelming fatigue. I poured myself a large mug of coffee and clumsily slammed the pot back on the stove.

"That's too loud, Mommy." Rachel frowned from her spot between packing boxes on the sticky linoleum floor, where she was drawing on a piece of paper. She was wearing overalls, a fleshy baldheaded cap, and thick Groucho Marx glasses, fastened in back with a rubber band. In an effort to persuade her that the move would be fun, I'd convinced her to dress up like a moving man for Halloween, and this is what we'd pieced together from the dregs of my costume collection.

I surveyed the boxes, books, and laundry that were strewn across the apartment. Somewhere inside I knew that Kevin had done us both a favor, but there were too many sad and expensive problems to solve before I could access any gratitude. I wondered how many couples continued to endure a mismatch because a break-up was outside their meager means. Couples who got to fight over actual assets didn't know how easy they had it.

The doorbell rang. I looked out the window and saw Jamie waving.

"Aunt Jamie!" Rachel jumped up and, holding her baldhead steady, ran to the door, almost knocking Jamie down with her enthusiastic embrace.

Jamie was twenty-three, four years younger than me, and five years younger than our older brother, Hank. I still felt the same pride around her that I had when she was the five-year-old joke-cracking mascot whom I dragged everywhere. By the time we were eleven and fifteen, I had her trained to cut across our back canyon to buy me packs of Marlboro Lights from the gas station vending machines. Still doing me favors, today she had taken the bus from UC Santa Cruz to help me move.

Rachel pulled at her aunt's backpack. "Did you bring it?" she whispered.

"Bring what?" I said, slightly taken aback.

Jamie's petite, bronzed body was draped in Santa Cruz organics and her worn backpack was covered with a layer of pro-gay, anti-establishment bumper stickers—the most prominent one reading, "Daddy's Little Bull

Dyke." Bleached blond spikes shot from her head as if she were a lit sparkler. She had golden-brown eyes, deep dimples, and was the only family member who could tan.

"Aunt Jamie got me something that's *pretty*," Rachel giggled. "Right, Aunt Jamie?"

"Tell Mommy that you aren't wearing that ridiculous moving man costume when you can go dressed as..." Jamie crouched down and poked through her backpack, yanking out a colorful plastic bag, "...A FAIRY PRINCESS!"

Within a few minutes, Jamie had Rachel re-dressed in a sparkling pink chiffon gown, sheer fairy wings, and a rhinestone tiara. "I'm going to do a princess show. I'll make a stage and audience," said Rachel, spinning toward her room. Rachel enjoyed giving live performances, turning her stuffed animal collection into a captive audience, sometimes even drawing tickets for each one.

"A princess?" I said, offering a sly smile. "From daddy's little bull dyke?"

"Whatever. She's three. Shouldn't she be able to have a real costume?" Jamie's tone was defensive. "And it's a teaching opportunity. I already explained to her that you'd have to be brainless to make it your life's ambition to seek happiness by marrying a prince—like that poisonous villain, Cinderella. Besides, I'm her aunt. I'm supposed to give her what she wants, right? It's not my job to—"

"Okay, okay. Calm down. I didn't accuse you of *being* a princess," I said. "So. Did you bring me a costume, too?" I began to rummage in Jamie's backpack, when she yanked it away.

"Get out of there, snoopy. You're probably looking for my journal. And just so you know, I didn't bring it. Fool me once, shame on you. Fool me twice, no fucking way."

"Oh, *please*." Jamie was still touchy whenever I went near her things, something that started after I'd read parts of her journal in high school. Around her seventeenth birthday, she planted fictitious entries about illicit sex and drug use, and I'd confronted her, blowing my cover.

"You're sure enjoying the evasive act," I said. "When are you going to tell me what's going on?"

"When and if I'm ready, nosy," she said. "Not today."

"Jamie, I would *never* read your journal again. Especially after what Dad did to me." During his second divorce, my father had used my journal entries as evidence to my stepmother that she'd done a crappy job as a parent. I was horrified when she called me in tears.

"Tell yourself whatever lies you have to so you can sleep at night," she said. "All I know is that as soon as Rachel's old enough to write, I'm warning her." Jamie pulled out a tiny bottle from her back pocket. "Here. I took two when I flew to New York last summer, so there's only two left." She held out the tranquilizers. "You know we could easily get more."

I pushed her hand away. "Oh, keep them. I'm cleaning up all my acts. No drinking, no drugs, no debting. From now on, I'm going to be a better mom and a better citizen."

"Have you also given up your obsession with grooming?" Jamie pulled back and studied me, her expression serious. "No offense, but you look awful."

"Vanity is overrated."

"Not when I'm the one who has to look at you," she grinned.

I pulled up the corner of my t-shirt, and wiped the shadow of yesterday's mascara from my eyes.

Jamie was scanning the newspaper, and now turned to the horoscopes. "Listen to this," she said.

"Expect a past romantic problem to unkink itself as an upsy-downsy month moves toward a—dare we say—climax? Write 'fini' to what's not working. Then reward yourself with something you've wanted for a long, long time. Someone or something from your past holds the secret to your future. But it's up to you to decide if it's a life of cloak and daggers or gowns and flowers. For some of you, it may be both."

"Interesting," said Jamie, looking wistful. Our birthdays were just a week apart, and we were the same sign. "It's like they have a camera in the bedroom."

"You must mean *your* bedroom," I said.

Jamie tuned back in, but ignored my comment. "What have you wanted for a long, long time?" she said.

"An interesting career. An exciting lover. And ever since I had Rachel, a normal, stable family."

"Well you *need* a career," said Jamie. "Mom and I were talking about it. You used to talk about that private investigation thing. Why don't you pursue it?"

"Mom's already called three times this week." My mother had forced each of us to take expensive career aptitude tests when we'd graduated from high school. Each time she called she reminded me that I had tested high in the field of investigation. "Mom said I had Dad's snoopiness and her high tolerance for inappropriate behavior—both of which are assets for private dicks."

"Well?" Jamie eyed me quizzically.

I didn't answer right away. The truth was, I had been thinking of contacting someone from my past, and maybe this horoscope was a sign—or an answer to last night's prayer. Ever since I'd taken that test, I'd had fantasies of a slick career solving mysteries. But all my ambitions got scrambled when my teenaged stepsister Lizzie died, just as I was finishing college. Then I got pregnant and plugged into Kevin's fantasy of fame and fortune, instead of seeking my own.

"Remember my old boss, Dan Murphy?" I said.

"Yes. The International Man of Mystery."

"He was always hiring investigators. I was thinking I'd call him, see if he could give me some leads, help me get started."

"Hey, good idea. He was into all that secret cloak and dagger stuff—kept everything in his office locked up, right?"

"He was a criminal attorney. He had to."

Throughout college, I'd provided part-time administrative support at the executive suite where Dan operated his law practice. I'd always snooped around his office, just for fun, to see what I could find. I imagined his locked file cabinets were filled with damning evidence from his criminal clients— forged documents, blood encrusted knives, smoking guns. Once, when I worked late, I frisked the private nooks and crannies of his desk, looking for hidden keys, but came up with nothing.

"He did other things too, right? High finance, investment stuff?"

"That's right. He was always a very busy guy."

"A good looking guy, as I remember," she said. "Thick hair, square chin, soft lips, a nice ass."

"Well said for a woman of your persuasion. Especially since you only met him once."

"What can I say? The guy makes an impression. And you had such a crush on him."

"I did *not*." I turned away from Jamie and began packing books into a box. "I just thought he was so kind. And cool. And clever. Whenever his wife called, he always interrupted what he was doing. And he ended all conversations with 'I love you.' He's my role model for the perfect husband."

"You told me that he had gorgeous hands—that you loved to stare at his elegant, capable hands."

"I would never say that."

"Cloak and daggers, gowns and flowers…what does it all mean?" chided Jamie.

"It would be great to work with him again," I said.

I'd always preferred working with Dan to the other characters in the office, especially because he assigned me to organize special community service projects for animal shelters and halfway houses. Once he asked me to rent a private cable car to usher friends on a Christmas caroling trip to local nursing homes. Dan had me fill three huge Santa sacks of candy, perfume, lotion, slippers, even portable radios. He said that countless petty thefts occurred in nursing homes, and he wanted to replace the missing items. Once I finished college, we'd kept in touch for a while, but I hadn't seen him since I'd invited him and his wife to dinner after Rachel's first birthday.

"I'll pack. You call," said Jamie.

"Unbelievable!" said Dan. "It's goddamn *unbelievable*! I've been thinking about you since the earthquake—meaning to give you a call myself. I heard about the freeway collapse in Oakland. Wanted to make sure you guys were all right, among other things."

At forty-five, Dan was eighteen years older than me. When I worked for him, he was always generous and protective, lending me the company car for night classes, asking about Kevin and my family, and giving me time off during final exams. It was comforting to think that he still took a big-brotherly interest in me.

"We're okay. More or less," I said. "Hey. What other things were *you* calling about?"

"I see you still have that heightened sense of curiosity," Dan laughed. "Okay, I have a proposition for you."

I perked up immediately. Maybe there was something to this praying business. Maybe Dan wanted to offer me a job.

Dan told me that his wife had left him for a guy from the gym and he wanted to invite Kevin and me to dinner to reciprocate for the nice meal we had made for them.

"Your wife left you?" I turned to Jamie; she slipped on the Groucho Marks glasses, forcing the fuzzy eyebrows up and down. "Dan, I'm so sorry."

"Don't be. She never wanted to socialize," said Dan, sounding chipper. "Now I can finally take your family out to the eating establishment of your choice."

"Here's the thing," I said. "We're not much of a family anymore. Kevin and I just broke up."

"No kidding?" he said.

"And I need some good solid career advice." My toes cramped in my slippers. "Why don't you just take me out to dinner?"

There was a brief, awkward silence.

"That could work." Dan made a cheerful clicking sound with his tongue. "How funny that everyone's breaking up."

"Who else?"

"Someone I want to you meet, in fact," said Dan. "An old friend of my brother's. He's divorced. Just moved out here. We're working together. I thought I'd introduce him to you guys. But looks like it will be a swinging singles party," he laughed.

Hanging up, I turned to Jamie, smiling. I felt ridiculously pleased by this small bit of progress, as if a curse had been lifted.

"He asked you on a date," she said.

"No. Not a *date* date. Dan's too old for me. And I'm sure he's not interested. He's just reciprocating."

"You're going to let him reciprocate his 'elegant, capable hands' all over your body, aren't you?" she smirked.

"Shut up," I whacked her arm. "Don't make me nervous. I'm not sure I even remember *how* to 'reciprocate.' No, Dan's going to provide me with guidance for my career as an investigator."

"There's your cloak and daggers," said Jamie.

"But it seems like he might be thinking of fixing me up with a friend of his brother's. Anyway, considering the shape I'm in, romance is not high on my list of priorities."

"But the horoscope said, 'cloak and daggers, gowns and flowers'—perhaps bridal gowns?" she sang. "What do we know about this man you will marry?"

"Jamie, stop it. He said he and this guy were working together, so I assume he's also a criminal attorney. I didn't even know Dan had a brother. If he was going to fix me up with anyone, I'd much rather it be someone who looks and acts like him. *Shit.* Now I'm going to be sick with nerves all night."

Chapter 3

November 1989

The following Saturday night, Dan arrived dressed in a starched white shirt, silk tie, and a soft cashmere sports jacket. His larger-than-life personality always had me remembering him as quite tall, but when he walked in, he was still a lean, muscular 5'10" or so. In my four-inch heels we almost stood eye-to-eye.

"Aren't you dapper, Dan. Hot date tonight?" Dressed-up, made-up, and perfumed, I was feeling free to flirt, especially knowing Dan was a safe target.

"You're not so bad yourself," he said, winking.

I caught myself thinking how young he looked. Except for the silver near the temples in his jet-black hair, he could have been in his mid-thirties. He leaned in for a hug, reminding me how much I liked that spiced soapy scent that used to arrive in the office with him each morning.

"What, no Rachel?" he said.

"She's with her dad." Dan's disappointment at Rachel's absence oddly pleased me. Despite his two marriages, he had no children, but he seemed to love kids. Rachel and Dan had become instant friends on the night he and his wife came for dinner. Usually shy in front of strangers, Rachel toddled right over to Dan in her fuzzy pink footie pajamas. Batting her lashes, she handed him the Gumby she was chewing, still dripping with saliva. He plopped her on his lap, and the two were inseparable for the rest of the night.

Dan led me to his car, where I sank into the leather bucket seat and pulled the seat belt across my chest. The silver Lincoln Town Car, a tank-like luxury sedan he'd driven since I worked for him, felt safe and solid, a sharp contrast to the battered old Toyota Kevin and I shared, and were still fighting over.

On the way to dinner, I forced Dan to spill the beans about his wife and her affair with the muscle man, and then I gave him the entire blowjob story.

"This is what I've decided," I said. "Part of Kevin's punishment is that I tell as many people as possible about his sexual transgression. What do you think?"

"Why punishment?" Dan glanced sideways. "Half the guys in the state want to thank him for putting you back on the market."

Dan was always quick with compliments, so I couldn't tell if he was flirting, flattering, or flat out making fun of my situation. And I had no snappy come back. I was still smarting over the whole ugly affair.

"I'm sorry. You're right," said Dan, somberly. "Given his sentence, I think that when we get to the restaurant, we should split up. I'll tell the hostess and anyone waiting for a table—that'll free you up to inform the waitresses and busboys."

I laughed and hit him gently on the shoulder.

Dan took me to Petar's in Lafayette, a quiet suburb outside of Oakland. I was a little surprised that he, a San Francisco native now living in Marin County, was whisking me to the suburbs—to the sprawl of ranch-style homes, backyard pools, tidy lawns, and shopping malls. Maybe his friend, Richard, lived out here.

"Are we meeting him at the restaurant?" I said.

"Who?" said Dan.

"Your brother's friend. The guy you work with."

"Didn't I tell you? I thought I'd keep you to myself. And you had some questions for me, right? I rearranged the itinerary. Richard said he'd show up at the bar later."

Then he wasn't thinking of fixing me up? The relief was tantamount to unzipping tight jeans after one too many trips to the buffet.

The restaurant entrance was radiant with twinkling white lights; the scent of roasted garlic and grilled meat greeted us as we entered. We followed the host to the dining room, and Dan held my chair as I sat down. The place was packed with couples his age or older. Just as I suspected, this was a restaurant for suburban grownups who looked like they had jobs, bank accounts, and garages filled with new model cars, not murky bongs and rock band paraphernalia.

The waiter arrived, and I asked for the filet mignon, medium well, with a baked potato topped with everything except bacon bits. I wanted the salad, but liked both blue cheese and vinaigrette dressings mixed and no tomatoes. Dan flapped his big leather menu closed, and said he'd have exactly the same thing.

"And what about the salad dressing, sir?"

"Exactly the same thing," he repeated while looking straight at me, smiling.

I had never noticed how intensely blue his eyes were.

"Wine, sir?"

"What are you in the mood for?" asked Dan, picking up the wine list.

I squirmed. I wanted to stay on the wagon, but wine could take the edge off.

"None for me," I said. "Go ahead, I don't want to spoil your fun."

"No, I'll skip it too." Dan smiled and handed back the list.

"No, go ahead," I insisted. Kevin always got testy when I suggested we curtail the drinking, especially if we were out on the town. "I'll have a glass, too, if you don't want to drink alone."

Dan laughed and patted my hand, causing me to twitch and pull away, embarrassed. Was he fixing me up with *him*? My pants felt tight again.

"Truthfully, I'm not much of a drinker, either," he said, appearing bemused. Dan's comfort with an alcohol-free meal had a soothing effect, but still, I couldn't quite relax.

"Tell me stories about the seedy criminals you've represented," I said.

"If I thought they were seedy, I wouldn't have had a successful practice. Besides, I don't want to have to sully your innocent Irish mind with tales from the criminal underworld."

"I'm already sullied," I said. "In high school I hung out with a fashion crime syndicate."

"Is that a new kind of girl gang?"

I explained that I'd transferred into a new high school for my senior year so I could live with my father. As a new student lost in a foreign high school social hierarchy, I let a group of blond-streaked, popular girls befriend me, even though I knew their motive was to gain access to my cute brother, Hank. Our first outing was a shopping trip to the mall.

"And by 'shopping,' it turned out they meant '*shoplifting*,'" I said.

Dan laughed and raised an eyebrow. "Did you rat them out?"

"And screw myself out of a social life? No way. I left the scene—waited for them in the get-away car."

"Then there's still a future for you in crime?"

"Too afraid of getting caught," I laughed. "Besides, I'm more interested in starting my private investigation career. Think you can offer some advice on the subject?"

"Perhaps I can." Dan appeared to give this some thought. "My advice is this: Be patient," he said, pointing at me with his fork. "I'm telling you I know exactly—*exactly*—what you're going to do with your life."

"Does it pay well, start soon, and have onsite childcare?"

"Yes, and I predict you will be wildly successful. Especially if you wear anything like this beautiful blue blouse." Dan reached across the table and stroked the silk sleeve. "Very flattering."

I blushed down to my roots.

The check arrived, and Dan reached into his pocket and pulled out a chunky roll of cash, which I found both thrilling and reassuring. The last time Kevin and I had a date at a nice restaurant, he took one look at the menu and told me he needed to run to the ATM. Our credit cards had already been maxed out, he hadn't brought enough cash, and he wasn't even sure there was any in the bank.

Dan peeled off two crisp fifty-dollar bills, tucked them into the leather folder for the waiter, and suggested we go into the bar to see if Richard had shown up.

"You've got to meet this guy, Mary. He's like a brother to me."

"That's what you always said about Johnny Curtain." Johnny was a wheeler-dealer type who shared office space with Dan when I worked for him. Apparently Johnny, who was at least twenty years older than Dan, had known him since he was a kid, but I never knew the exact connection. Dan always referred to Johnny as his "client *and* partner," and often said he was like a brother to him.

"That's because Johnny and Richard were both friends of my brother, Jimmy. My brother worked for Johnny, actually. But Richard was always hanging around. Years later, he fell off everyone's radar after serving in Vietnam. Then I ran into him a few months ago at the airport. It was like a miracle."

"Dan, I never realized you had a brother. Where does he live?"

"Jimmy's dead." Dan's tone was flat; he cleared his throat. "Murdered. Years ago."

"My God, I am so sorry. How?"

"You know what?" Dan took my hand and gave it a squeeze. "Let's not get into all that tonight. I'm celebrating the fact that Richard's back in my life. He's been gone a few decades, had a hard time reentering after Vietnam. I've been getting him out, forcing him to socialize a bit. Johnny, Richard, and I are doing a major project together, so you may be seeing a lot of them. I'll let Richard give you the details."

"So he's an attorney too?"

"Hell no. His background is in finance."

"But you're still working for Johnny?"

"Nope," Dan stood up. "Working *with* Johnny. We're partners in a real estate deal."

And I may be seeing a lot of them? It looked like this might be a job interview after all.

We entered the smoky bar, and Dan left me at a table so he could search for Richard. I was glad Johnny Curtain wasn't expected tonight. Johnny reminded me of a leprechaun—short and spry, with alligator green eyes, ruddy cheeks, and snow-white hair. He was always soaked in a grassy aftershave that made him smell, I imagined, like a field of shamrocks. Johnny was charismatic and funny—qualities that served him well because he was such a liar. He'd often have me tell bankers, investors, and bill collectors that he was out of the office when he was standing right next to me. When some of them cleverly popped in to surprise him, he'd slip out the back door. He had bilked so many investors in my years working there that it seemed mighty convenient that he was sharing an office with a criminal attorney.

"Doesn't look like Richard's here yet. How about a dance?" Dan took my hand and led me to the dance floor. The music was slow and jazzy. Dan pulled me close, placed his cheek next to mine. It almost felt like I'd never danced cheek-to-cheek with a man. Of course I had slow danced, but the feeling of Dan's smooth cheek next to mine was both foreign and familiar. He smelled good, like sweet cloves and citrus, and his steps were sure and strong. As he led me around our small corner of the crowded dance floor, blood pounded at my temples.

The song ended and Dan brushed the back of his fingers down my cheek, softly pinched my chin, and smiled. I was relieved that it was dark and he couldn't see me blush.

"Hey, look who's here," said Dan, pointing toward a pale, puffy man who stood at the back of the bar, a lit cigarette hanging from his mouth. He looked much older than Dan, and was dressed in rumpled pants and a dark v-neck sweater.

Dan gave Richard a backslapping hug, grabbed his shoulder, and guided him to me. "So, here he is, Mary," Dan yelled over the music. "Meet Richard Harding. He's the best. Like a brother. Loyal. Honest. We'd do anything for each other. Right Richard?"

"I do whatever it takes," said Richard, expressionless.

Richard offered his spongy hand, and I tried to meet his gaze. Although he smiled toward me, his eyes checked out the room, his shoes, the dancers, and Dan—landing anywhere but on mine. Through the hazy smoke I saw an oily glaze on his forehead and thin upper lip. Although he was both business partner and surrogate brother to my dinner date, I felt a powerful urge to grab Dan and run. Instead, I remained cheerful and attentive because that was my nature—and because I really needed a job.

"I got us a table back in the bar," said Richard, looking directly at Dan. "Too fuckin' loud in here."

"You two sit," yelled Dan. "I'll get drinks. Vodka, Richard?"

Richard grunted in the affirmative.

"Mary?"

"Just coffee," I hollered.

Richard and I slid into opposite ends of a leather booth. He crushed out his unfiltered cigarette and immediately reached into his pocket to take another. Usually when I sit with smokers, I long to join them, but Richard looked like the poster boy for the anti-smoking crusade. His skin had the ashy pallor of exhaled smoke and his fingertips were stained a dingy yellow. Perhaps it was the low lighting, but when he picked a piece of tobacco off his tongue, it appeared to be coated with a thick gray paste.

I fixed my eager, smiley expression across the table. A long silence ensued.

"Dan told me you served in Vietnam. I just read an amazing book about that war, called *The Things They Carried*," I said. "I'd be happy to pass it on."

Richard stared toward the dance floor. He took a long drag off his cigarette, blowing two white streams out of his nostrils.

"Why would I read about something that I hate to even think about?" he said.

"Right," I mumbled. My toes crunched into my shoes. "So. Dan says you were friends with his brother? He must have been a pretty great guy—if he was anything like Dan."

No comment.

"Anyway, I guess you remind Dan of his brother."

"I hope not. He was an idiot. Owed money to everyone in the world."

Just then, Dan appeared. I almost wept with relief. A waitress followed on his heels, carrying a tray of drinks.

"You getting to know this guy?" said Dan, smiling toward Richard.

"Sure am." Mr. International Man of Misery.

"I swear to God, he arrived in my life at just the right time. I don't know what I'd do without him." Dan explained that Richard was in charge of guarding assets and managing a coastal development "deal" that would make them all rich, if things went well with the "zoning politics."

"Mary's looking to go back to work." Dan smiled at me; I glanced down. "She's hoping to get started in private investigation. But in the meantime, who knows, something may turn up in our project?"

"Doubt that." Richard folded his arms, shook his head.

"We've got the backlog on the financials," said Dan. "You've done some bookkeeping, haven't you, Mary?"

"Got that covered, Dan. Up to date," Richard said, sitting up like he'd just snapped out of a trance. "Investigation, huh? Been doing it long?"

"I wish," I said. "No, I'm just thinking about it. I've been at home, taking care of my little girl the last three years."

"So you have a background in law enforcement?" said Richard.

"No. Apparently it's helpful, but not required. I'm hoping to train with a reputable firm."

Richard gazed past me, staring at a mute TV in the corner of the bar.

"I see nothing but success for this woman," Dan said.

We finished our drinks just as the check arrived. Dan and Richard both pulled out bulky wads of cash this time, but Dan insisted on paying. I liked that he was quick to pay the tab—not the kind of guy who shirked responsibilities. We said goodnight and left Richard alone in the booth, smoking. There was no more discussion of my career path. As we wandered out to the restaurant parking lot, I was still unemployed and now I was confused as well.

"Just a sec," said Dan, popping the trunk. "I have a tape I want to play for you. Wait till you hear this."

In the trunk were at least thirty long, shiny boxes of Reynolds Wrap aluminum foil.

"Wow," I said. "Did Costco have a sale on tin foil?"

Dan looked into his trunk, raised his eyebrows, and then slammed it closed.

"No, it's this other deal—you can't believe the number of sons-of-guns I face in this litigious world. I keep that around for protection of sorts."

"Tin foil? You could probably do more damage with a baseball bat."

Dan laughed, but offered no further explanation. He reached into his coat, pulled out paper and a pen, and made a quick note.

"What are you writing?"

"Oh, just this deal," he said, opening my door.

On the drive home Dan opened the moon roof and popped in his tape of Roy Orbison singing with k.d. lang.

"It cracks me up to think of a lesbian country singer performing a duet with old Roy. Listen to her, will you? Have you ever heard of her? Have you? Just listen," he said, reaching to turn up the volume. "Can she sing? *God!* She sure as hell can sing. *Unbelievable!*"

I smiled, remembering how Dan used to come bounding into the office to boast about his latest discovery. It could be anything from an old joke to a new ice cream flavor—but whatever it was, he embraced it like he was the first person on earth to stumble across it. He was like Columbus claiming to discover America, while all of us natives back at the office wondered where he had been. "Well, sure—we've heard a bit about Ben & Jerry's. And we've tried that chocolate chip cookie dough ice cream, Dan. But you're right. Great stuff. Really amazing."

I closed my eyes and sank into the leather seat of the car as we wound through the quiet streets. Kevin usually drove like a maniac. It had been a long time since I'd felt this safe in the passenger seat of a car.

"Richard sure is an edgy guy."

"Yeah, he's obviously been through a lot. Did I tell you he was a Green Beret? God only knows what that war was like for him. I can't tell you what it means to me to have him back in my life. I haven't seen him since I was a kid, since before Jimmy died."

"Where did he go after the war?"

"Somewhere in Southern California. He's got a son, but hasn't seen him much since the divorce. I'm encouraging him to get back in touch."

"That poor kid," I said, not even aware I'd spoken out loud.

"Richard's just a little rough around the edges. My brother was like that. Down on his luck. Well, the difference was my brother had a great personality. Everybody loved Jimmy—he just took people as they were. That made him a lot of friends. He and Richard had a regular Friday night poker game."

I wanted to ask Dan more about his brother—maybe even mention that his loyal, trustworthy, child-abandoning surrogate brother and business partner, Richard, had called his brother an idiot. Most of all, I wanted to know about the murder. But I didn't have the nerve to trot out any more potentially touchy subjects. Maybe I'd hone some of my investigation skills by looking into it on my own.

What was his name? Jimmy Murphy. James Murphy?

"How old is Richard?"

"I don't know, late fifties, I guess."

"So your brother was about fifteen years older than you? How old was he when he died?"

Dan suddenly changed the subject and recounted a story about some piece of Russian art he'd purchased when he was running a diamond investment company. But I was too distracted to listen. Why did he refuse to talk about what had happened to his brother? Why had he introduced me to his churlish friend? And did he even want to hire me? Or date me? I couldn't decide which option I preferred. Was he going to make a move? Was *I* supposed to make a move?

No wonder people avoided being single. This was exhausting.

I watched Dan talking, thinking how happy I was sitting alongside someone who was smart and kind and handsome. He smelled good, made me laugh, adored my child, and kept rolls of cash in his pocket. How could his wife have ever cheated on him?

Maybe my dad was right about some things. Maybe I didn't exploit enough opportunities, or take enough risks in romance.

During a pause in Dan's story, I laughed and said, "Oh you," setting my hand on top of his, which was sitting on the armrest between us. He turned his hand into mine, clasping it so tightly that I could feel his pulse beat against my wrist. After a moment he softened his grip and we lightly stroked each other's fingers until I could hardly breathe.

"Mary?"

"What?"

He squeezed my hand firmly again. "How is Kevin taking this?"

"You mean me going out with you tonight?" I said, still holding his hand. "Because, you know, so far it's been pretty innocent—"

Keeping a firm hold on my hand, Dan pulled the car over and parked it under the glow of a street lamp. He turned to me and said, "Mary, there's nothing innocent about my feelings for you."

"Oh."

We stared at each other.

"Maybe you and Kevin have unfinished business. I don't want to be the East Bay homewrecker."

A nervous laugh rose in my throat; Dan's expression remained serious.

"Really. If you need time, take it. I'll wait and see what happens. Not forever," he said. "But I'm in no hurry and I've thought about this a lot. I always felt we were kindred spirits. Something about you seems so familiar."

I was suddenly embarrassed. I pictured the chaos back at my apartment, and in my life: the pile of unpaid bills, the absence of any clear idea of my next career move. "Dan, I'm an unemployed, overwhelmed single mom—"

"Don't be ridiculous," said Dan, gently cutting me off. "Those are just temporary circumstances." He was silent for a moment. "Remember when you took a trip up the coast after your sister died? Just to read your books, be alone? That whole week I kept thinking how much I wished I could be with you. Just hang out. I even said something to Johnny at the time."

"You did?"

"I knew how bad it felt to lose a sibling. I wanted to do something, make it easier for you."

I thought about the day my sister Lizzie died. When I got the call at work that she had a dangerously high temperature, Dan lent me the company car to go to the hospital. I didn't think it was serious. She was fifteen with a fever—how bad could that be? It felt like a free day off; I even stopped at the store for cigarettes and magazines. When I arrived at the hospital, the doctor was explaining to my dad and stepmom that Lizzie had bacterial meningitis and "for all intents and purposes" was dead.

Lizzie was the youngest in the family, and everyone adored her, including my mother. I stood with my family as they pulled the plugs. The *blips* and *bleeps* of machinery ceased, and in the screeching silence, we watched her beautiful young body bloat like a ghoul because the fluids were no longer pumping through her veins. After Lizzie's funeral, I returned to my apartment in a daze. There were several messages from Dan. He had offered condolences, asked if we wanted him and the office staff at the service, and if he could help. I hadn't gotten the messages until it was too late. And I hadn't known at the time that this wrenching experience was something we had in common.

"And I love that you're Irish," said Dan. "It's like we're from the same tribe."

I nodded. All of that was true. Something about Dan did feel like family.

"Listen. Who knew we'd both be single at the same time, same place, anytime this lifetime?" he said. "No. I'm not about to back off unless you tell me to."

Dan's certainty filled me with a pleasant sensation, like champagne bubbles rising through my body. As we listened to the hoarse whisper of the wind scrape through the autumn leaves, he pulled me closer, stroking my hair until we fell into a soft kiss that went on long enough for me to know that I wanted it to go on a lot longer.

Chapter 4

November 1989

I exited the Embarcadero BART station in downtown San Francisco and checked my watch. It was 2:45 on an icy November afternoon, and I still had forty-five minutes before my appointment. The sun shone brightly but the temperature was in the low teens. The weather shelter at the bus stop was useless in this cold; it was like being trapped in a freezer with the lights on. With extra time on my hands and a need to warm up, I decided to forget the bus and take a brisk walk along the water to the small, crowded offices of Paine & Savage Criminal Investigators, where—thanks to Mom's push and Dan's advice—I'd landed an interview for a job as an "operative."

Operative! I wondered if they'd put that title on a business card? My teeth chattered as I walked. I wasn't sure if it was the temperature, my nerves, or both.

Earlier that week, Dan had suggested I go to the Yellow Pages and start calling investigation firms to see if they were hiring trainees. I even called the FBI to ask about their training program. The personnel clerk said she had to ask me a few qualifying questions before I could apply, and when I answered "yes" to her inquiry about previous illegal drug use, she scoffed and told me I wasn't qualified. "But that was in college. I don't *still* use drugs," I said, surprised at the rigidity. "That's not the point," she snapped. "How do you find people who have never used drugs?" I asked, incredulous. "Easy. Most people don't," she said, hanging up.

"That woman did you a favor," said Dan. "Hypocritical lawbreaking parasites."

After I'd made a dozen or so calls, a gravelly voiced man named Harry Paine told me to come for a visit. He and his partner, Simon Savage, were so backed up with cases, they didn't even have time to place a want ad. "You've got great timing," he said.

Doing my best to appear calm, I knocked on the locked door of the dank waterfront office near China Basin. The brown paint was peeling, and there was no company sign or logo—just a rusty metal suite number dangling from a nail. A small, jaunty looking receptionist ushered me in, sitting me in one of the gunmetal gray chairs pressed up against the wall.

"Hang tight," she chirped. "They'll be right with you. I'd chat but they're on my ass about this report."

The reception area, if you could call it that, was furnished with a beat up desk, a couple of gray file cabinets, and a water cooler. Almost as if staged, there was a half bottle of Jack Daniels on the sill of the open window, which let in cold salty air that left everything inside smelling fishy.

Thirsty from the walk over, I said, "Mind if I have some water?"

"Sure, sure. Help yourself," the receptionist answered, typing into her computer at a furious pace. Wearing pigtails, a beret, and rimless granny glasses, she looked like an urbane Pippi Longstocking. Several times, while typing, she burst into laughter, shaking her head at the small plastic radio that was playing robust classical music.

"Must be a funny report," I said, wondering if Pippi had taken a few slugs off the JD.

"It's not the report," she explained. "This conductor is doing a hilarious spin on this Mendelssohn piece. It cracks me up every time I hear it."

I didn't know that conductors could do comedy with classical music; I was lucky to recognize a selection at all. This made me suddenly desperate for the job.

"Mary? You out there?" A man's voice yelled from the back office. "What are you waiting for, a formal invitation? Come on back."

I picked up my water and my purse and headed toward the voice. Harry Paine stood smiling in the hallway and motioned me into the back office, where I took a seat. He was a short, gray-haired man with a smooth boyish face that engendered trust.

"Mary, meet my partner, Simon."

Simon entered, gripped my hand, and gave it a tight shake that bordered on excruciating. I looked back and forth at the unlikely pair. Harry had a refined, well-groomed professional look that seemed incongruous with the surroundings. Simon, on the other hand, looked like an extra from

31

"Gunsmoke" who'd wandered onto the set of "Moonlighting." He had a handlebar moustache and wore a plaid shirt, jeans, and scuffed cowboy boots.

"So, what can we do for you today?" said Harry affably.

Dan had suggested that I be prepared to ask questions. Alertness and curiosity are important traits in an investigator, he said.

"Actually," I smiled, "that's what I planned to ask you guys. How can I help you?"

"We're looking for someone to do background checks on convicted murderers due for sentencing. The information is used to convince the courts to give them life in prison instead of the death penalty," said Simon, who appeared to have a copy of the resume I'd sent in his hand. "I see you've got writing experience and you've worked for a lawyer, but can you stomach that? Letting killers live?"

They both watched me intently. Harry leaned forward, looking interested; Simon tilted his chair back, folded his arms, and studied me from head to toe.

My mind raced, searching for a true answer. Though I understood the inclination toward exacting "an eye for an eye," my clear aversion to any form of premeditated killing—even state-sanctioned punishment for a heinous crime—made this seem like worthy, interesting work. But did I want to be directly involved in helping killers?

"How is that done, exactly?"

"Mostly by looking for mitigating evidence—positive relationships, contributions to society, good deeds in the community, even decent grades. Something to show it's a life worth salvaging. If you even think it is."

"I guess it's safe to say I think all lives are worth saving," I said.

"Then you're vegetarian?" said Simon.

"No," I laughed, shifting awkwardly in my chair.

Harry shot Simon an impatient look.

"What? I was joking." Pointing a thick finger toward me, Simon turned to Harry. "I'm thinking she's got that Catholic-girl-next-door look that makes people comfortable."

Other than the occasional urge to genuflect, I hadn't been an active Catholic since I was five, when my parents left the church and became suburban hippie swingers. But I didn't announce this. I couldn't think of one other time where my looks had paid off, and I wasn't going to correct any assumptions that might help me land a job.

They both looked me over until I felt color warming my cheeks.

"Your particular style, it's true, it's an asset," said Harry. "Especially when trying to get ex-teachers and neighbors of murderers to remember random deeds that might prove the killer had a non-homicidal side, too."

I smiled and folded my hands primly on my lap.

"I just want her to be sure she knows what she's getting into," said Simon.

"Then quit talking about her like she's not here," said Harry, winking at me.

"Tell us why you want to be an investigator," said Simon.

My mouth was dry; it was impossible to pick up my water and take a sip because my shaky hands would give my nervousness away. "Of all the work I did in college," I said, "investigative journalism was the most interesting. I love digging up background information. And I did once work for a criminal attorney."

"Oh yeah," said Harry, glancing down at my resume. "Daniel Murphy?" He frowned and scribbled something on his desk pad. "Sounds familiar."

"Starting pay is low," said Simon.

"We would try to get you as many hours as possible," said Harry. "And you could do public record searches for us as filler. Not exciting, but it pays the bills."

"Sounds interesting," I inserted. "In fact, I was just doing a public records search for a friend. An old murder case." After making a few calls, I'd learned I could get a death certificate for Dan's brother, James Murphy, through the County Department of Vital Records. I planned to use the date of death to then search for obituaries or other newspaper articles about the murder. My idea was to hone my research skills *and* get the unpleasant details of Jimmy's death without ever having to traumatize Dan with unnecessary questions.

"I had to eat a lot of Campbell's Soup before I earned enough hours to get my license," said Simon. He went on to explain that since I had no background in law enforcement and my degree was not in criminal justice, I'd need to earn six thousand hours of investigative time to be eligible to sit for the statewide exam, which translated into three years of full-time work. "You have to be patient, willing to work hard and live on a budget."

"We have medical insurance, but not until you're full time, and you'd have to pay half," said Harry.

"Not a good path for anyone with debt," said Simon.

I glanced down at my bag, thinking I had a late notice from Visa poking out of my purse. Or maybe they could read body language and tell that I was thinking about the red ink in my portfolio. Simon, I figured, was on to me. But how were people supposed to get out of debt if they couldn't get a job? I took a deep breath and blurted, "I work hard and I'm a quick study. I know I could be good at this. I hope you two will consider giving me a chance."

They both watched me for a few seconds.

"You give it some thought, and we'll give it some thought," said Harry, standing up and offering a manicured hand.

"Thank you." I shook each of their hands with my sweaty palm, turned around and walked into the wall.

Harry chuckled. "Let's hope that's not an omen."

I let out a snorting laugh that only made the moment worse, and exited quickly.

Outside I heard a light *honk honk*, and Dan's Lincoln pulled up next to me. I got in, eager to get out of the icy glare.

"Perfect timing," he said, putting his hand lightly on mine and squeezing. "How'd the interview go? Are they going to pay you to snoop?"

I recounted the details, groaning when I came to my embarrassing exit. "But *whatever* the pay is, at least it would be a foot in the door."

"Versus a foot through the wall," said Dan.

I crossed the fingers on both hands and held them up.

Dan grabbed my hand and planted a kiss on the crossed fingers. I leaned over and rested my head on his chest, letting him stroke my hair while I inhaled the scent of his skin and clothes. Jamie insisted that my obsession with the way Dan smelled had nothing to do with his shaving products. "It's pheromones," she said. "His hot hormones are drawing you to him like a moth to flame."

I had no idea if that was true, but couldn't figure out why I'd never noticed how strong and sexy he was until recently. Had I been blind? Or maybe it was because he was not a casual flirt, like Kevin. I lifted my head and slowly kissed him, feeling delighted to be pressed up against such an honorable man.

"You know what I think?" said Dan. "They'd be fools to let you get away." He pulled away from the curb, driving along the gleaming water at the Embarcadero. "You'd make anybody proud."

"Wish that were true." I thought about the time, at sixteen, that I'd lied about trashing my father's car with spilled beer and cigarette burns. When the truth came out, my enraged dad stood by his open dresser drawer throwing rolled socks at me while yelling, "Why can't I have a daughter I can be proud of?" Not much had changed since then: In a recent conversation, Dad had told me that I needed to "grow up"—that I was too old to keep turning to my father for help. Thinking he was right, I wasn't sure what an older man like Dan saw in me, but being with him felt like confidence replacement therapy.

Dan parked his car in the garage on Sutter and Stockton, and we walked up the hill through Chinatown, swerving around newspaper and produce stands, bus stops and take-out restaurants with windows displaying roasted ducks and chickens dangling by their twisted necks. I couldn't stand to look at them, but they gave the noisy street a cozy, home-cooked aroma.

"How are things with Kevin?" he said.

"Tense." Kevin had rented a room in a rundown Victorian filled with cats, dogs, artists, and musicians. Rachel loved visiting him there, where she had her own "art gallery," but he often brought her home late, tired, and covered with fleabites. "Our two-household family is wearing her out," I said.

"I hate to hear that," said Dan. He gently guided me inside a long, narrow store, lined with mailboxes on each side. "I wish I could do something about that."

There was no one else there, not even a clerk. Grabbing me playfully, Dan turned me around, pressed me against the wall, and gave me a lingering kiss that left me feeling hungry and full at the same time. My heart raced against his chest as he moved from my mouth to the side of my neck, pushing my turtleneck down to expose skin while pinning me harder against the wall, one hand teasing its way up my shirt. A loud eruption of Chinese conversation and laughter interrupted the tryst, leaving both of us looking rumpled and feverish.

"I can't believe I'm making out with my ex-boss in Chinatown," I whispered, straightening my shirt and smoothing down my hair.

"Your ex-boss would like to do more than make-out with you." Dan smiled, arching an eyebrow. "How about I whisk you off on a romantic getaway?"

I hesitated. Dan and I hadn't had much time alone. With all the upheaval, Rachel had only just begun to spend an occasional night with Kevin, and I still wasn't comfortable with it. Maybe Dan was getting impatient.

"Hey, hey—come here. Don't worry." Dan took my hands and looked directly into my eyes. "I heard what you just said about Rachel at her dad's. That's got to get squared away first. I just wanted you to know that I appreciate you. *All* of you." He pulled me against him again. "It will happen when the time is right."

I felt myself smiling, inside and out. Dating a grown-up was good for me.

Dan put a key into the lock of a large box, opened it, and pulled out a thick stack of mail.

"Why do you have a mailbox here?" Dan now worked from his home in Marin. Even if he'd wanted a San Francisco address, this busy, congested part of town seemed a ridiculous inconvenience.

"Gotta keep the wolves from my door." He set the pile down on a narrow Formica counter and shuffled through his mail.

What wolves? I wondered.

"Isn't it a hassle?" I snuck glances at some of the letters. There was a thin blue airmail envelope with a return address in what looked like Portugal—or Pakistan or Panama.

"Yeah," he said, focused on his pile. "But the easy thing isn't always the best thing." Dan tapped the mail into an even pile, then reached into the inside pocket of his sport coat, took out a pen and paper, and scribbled a note.

Each time Dan and I had gotten together since our first date, he'd made some kind of note. Whenever I asked about it, he said it was some "thing" or "deal" he wanted to remember, but he never gave me details.

"Besides, my parents live in the city so I'm here often. Oh, hey—" he said, looking up. "I wanted to drop in on them today." He tucked the mail and the note inside his jacket pocket. "I haven't seen them since the earthquake. They're getting old and my father doesn't drive anymore. I was hoping you wouldn't mind?"

"I'd love to meet them." Remembering how devoted Dan was to entertaining the elderly around the holidays, I wondered if it had something to do with his parents. "Are they in a nursing home?"

"Oh, hell no," said Dan. "Doubt that'll ever happen. They're way too excited about getting to the cemetery."

"What do you mean?"

"You're the investigator. You figure it out."

Chapter 5

November 1989

Dan's parents lived on Rockaway Avenue, in a residential area of San Francisco called Forest Hills Extension. The neighborhood was named for its location at the edge of the fancier Forest Hills, where houses were stately and expensive, with red brick walkways that rolled through manicured lawns up to polished front doors. Unlike these, Dan's childhood home was squeezed tight on its lot, landscaped with a thin strip of balding grass and a bloomless camellia bush. The three-story house was sturdy, its faded paint an odd pinkish-tan that reminded me of scar tissue.

Dan parked the car, but made no move to get out. "This is it," he said, pointing to the house. "One of the two great plots of land my father worships."

"Where's the other one?"

"The cemetery in Colma," Dan laughed. "And I'm not sure which means more to him."

"You guys have a family plot? So *that's* their interest in the cemetery. Dangit, Dan," I reached across and cuffed his shoulder. "I wanted to figure it out myself."

I always wondered about the kind of people who owned family plots. Did they buy them before any of them started dying or did some tragic event—like a murder—precipitate the investment?

"Have they got room in there for you?" I nudged him.

Dan released a heaving sigh. "Believe me, I have no intention of spending an eternity with the people buried in that hole. And I'm not referring to the ones there now. Just some of my father's more recently invited guests."

"Your dad issues invitations into the family plot?" I was intrigued by this idea. It aroused my competitive spirit, making me wonder if I would ever be eligible—or even *want* to be eligible—for a permanent place in this family.

"Oh sure. It's quite an honor to be included. Get this: about ten years ago, my parents threatened to disinherit me if I didn't join them at a family party at the cemetery, where they were celebrating the signing of paperwork to allow my loser—not to mention violent—cousin into our family plot. Not even a first cousin, just the son of one of my dad's relatives. For this they would disinherit their only living child. We actually stopped speaking for six years over the subject. And *not* because I wanted anything from them." Dan's tone had shifted as he told the story; now he sounded genuinely furious. "Anything other than loyalty, anyway."

"It was all because you wouldn't go to their graveside party?"

"Actually, it's more convoluted than that." Dan adjusted his collar, and brushed some lint off his sport coat, obviously trying to retrieve his lost composure. "But trust me, I wouldn't be caught dead in that cemetery plot."

I cracked up; Dan looked pleased.

"Come on," he said. "They're probably waiting by the door."

The first level of the house held a garage and a basement. As we climbed the steep stairs to the front door, I asked, "What are their names?"

"Mary and Ralph," he said, ringing the bell.

"Your mom's name is Mary, too?"

There was a knock and a shuffle, like the sound of small animals trapped in a wall, and the door opened. Dan's father stood in the dark entry, smiling. He had cloudy blue eyes, a strong chin, and a handsome face stained with age spots. Dan's mom, a small woman with bright green eyes, stood behind him, holding her purse like she was ready to walk out the door. Both looked older and frailer than I had expected.

"You're Mary?" his mother said, smiling. "I'm Mary. But call me Minnie, hon—with all the Marys running around, it's easier that way." She took my offered hand and squeezed, using both of her warm little hands. She was pert and pretty, with a shellacked beauty salon hair-do and frosty pink blush and lipstick, liberally applied.

Dan leaned over to hug his father. Ralph was wearing a faded wool cap over thick white hair, and a mismatched suit—tan and brown jacket with pastel yellow and green plaid slacks.

"What the hell is this outfit?" said Dan. "You look like a clown." He whispered to me, "He usually dresses nice—I don't know why he's in this get-up."

"What? What's that?" said Ralph, who was clearly hard of hearing.

Minnie frowned and shook her head. "For godsakes, Dan. He can barely see. He's lucky to get anything on at all, at 81 years old."

Ralph perked up when he heard his age. "Hey Dan. Had me a check-up and the gal said I had the—Dan, Dan," he said, noticing Dan was turned toward his mother. "You'll want to hear this. The gal at the Kaiser said I had me the body of a 65-year-old." He stuck out his chin and did a little Tarzan drumming on his chest.

"See that, Dan? You come from great stock," I said loudly.

Ralph smiled, stood up a little straighter.

"Ma, why are you standing there with your purse?" said Dan. "You going to invite us in?"

"I thought we were going to the cemetery," said Minnie. "Then we'll go out someplace nice—to the Chicken Coop, or—you like Marie Callender's, don't you, Dan?" She turned toward me, took my hand, and squeezed. "Or you pick, honey. Marie Callender's has a beautiful cornbread, but I also love Chinese."

"Let's take them to Joe's," said Ralph.

"No, Ma," said Dan. "I said I'd come over to check up on you. It's late. I don't have time to drive you to the cemetery."

Minnie's face fell. She turned to me and said, "We thought we were going to visit Jimmy, Dan's brother."

"Not this time, Ma," said Dan, corralling his parents out of the entryway and into the living room. "I've got to get Mary back to Oakland, and there's all those detours with the bridge down. She's got to get back to her little girl."

My eyes widened. *Why pin this on me?*

"Oh honey," said Minnie. "Don't worry. Maybe next time you could bring her along?" She smiled and a triangular net of laugh lines fanned out from the edges of her eyes, like tiny fairy wings. "I bet it's so nice to have a little girl."

"Let's all just sit down for a minute and relax. Can we relax a minute?" asked Dan.

"What?" asked Ralph.

"We're not going to the cemetery," Minnie said loudly.

"We're not seeing Jimmy?" said Ralph. "What's the problem?"

"There's no problem," Minnie said, rubbing her hand up and down my arm. She leaned toward me and lowered her voice. "Jimmy was Ralph's first son, and oh! little Danny adored him, just worshipped him. He was like a second father." She nodded. Her voice dropped to a whisper. "You never get over these things. Such a terrible accident."

"Accident?" I said.

"Believe me, it was no accident," said Dan, glaring at his mother.

Minnie bit her lip and looked away.

"Okay, okay, Ma," said Dan. "Let's not get all worked up." He turned to me. "My brother died in 1953. You'd think we could get through a discussion without the tears."

Bingo—the exact year of death. Now I could go to the library and check out old 1953 newspapers on microfiche. But I almost hoped they wouldn't drop more facts during the visit—I didn't want to be deprived of further investigation.

"What are you saying, Dan?" said Ralph.

"We'll go see Mary and Jimmy another time," said Minnie.

I thought about asking who this other Mary was, but kept quiet.

"Goddammit, was I talking to you?" growled Ralph. "I was talking to Dan."

Minnie's lips tightened; she looked sideways and made sighing and clucking sounds, clutching her pocketbook as if she might collapse from the weight of it—or else use it to whack Ralph. She shook her head and her anxious expression seemed to settle, her face rearranging itself into a smile. It was like watching time-lapse photography capture fifty years of marital struggles in the time it took to twitch.

"Dad," said Dan. "Mary has to get home to take care of her little girl. We're just having a short visit. I've got to pick up that stuff we talked about."

"That's okay, then. That's okay." Ralph gave me an understanding look, but his eyes had dimmed slightly. My toes crunched; somehow I felt this was my fault.

"Got it right here, Dan." Ralph motioned to the hall off the entry, where a ladder leaned next to a box filled with duct tape. "Mary was my grandmother's name," said Minnie.

"Mary is *my* grandmother's name," I said. "I was named after her."

"Oh, no!" Minnie slapped my arm. "How's that for a coincidence? See how much we have in common already?" She held my gaze, smiling warmly. "Ralph, get the kids something to drink. Dan, can you help him? There's some nice cold beers in the Fridgidaire—"

"I don't need you to boss me—I was just going to offer." Ralph shuffled toward the kitchen.

"I'll be right back," said Minnie, to no one in particular. Still clutching her purse, she opened a door off the entry where stairs led down to the garage. She caught my eye and shook her little fist up at Ralph, who was walking away from her, talking to Dan. She held a wrinkly finger over her lips then feigned smoking to let me know she was sneaking downstairs for a cigarette.

I zipped my lips, locked them, and tossed the imaginary key behind me.

Minnie laughed, and our eyes snapped together like two magnets. If I lived in the Wonderful World of Disney, this would be when Tinkerbell zipped over and tapped our heads with her wand—*Ping! Ping!* —sending sparkles cascading around us to illuminate the magic of the connection.

Minnie reminded me of my sweet maternal grandma and namesake. Grandma Mary loved bingo, horse racing, and her grandchildren. She stuffed me full of jellybeans at church services when I was a bored kid, and let me smoke freely in her apartment when I was a miserable teen hiding from my mother, the hippie turned career woman who worked as a counselor at the Schick Anti-smoking Clinic. Even when I reeked of stale smoke disguised by Grandma's favorite perfume—"Intimate," by Revlon—she would hotly deny any wrongdoing on my part, and remind my mother that I shouldn't be punished for something I probably wouldn't have done if she had just stayed married to my father. "You're just my sweet little jellybean girl," she'd say, winking, once we'd won the battle.

Still smiling, I joined Dan and Ralph in the aging pink-and-yellow kitchen. I walked over to the sliding glass doors and looked out.

"I built that deck," Dan said.

"You did? When?"

"I lived here with Mary, my first wife—the one before Julia."

Ralph was opening and closing cabinets, seemingly unaware of our conversation.

"You've been married twice?" I whispered.

"Mary and I married young. We moved in here when my parents were living for a little while in Santa Rosa." He dropped his voice. "Didn't I tell you that?"

"No, I had no idea," I answered. "Is that the Mary at the cemetery? With your brother?"

"No, no, no," said Dan. "That's my dad's first wife, Mary. She died in a terrible fire. After Jimmy. She was smoking in bed, drunk." Dan winced. "Godawful way to go."

"You and your dad were both married to Marys the first time and now they are both dead?" No wonder I seemed familiar to Dan. The only other place I'd heard my name so often was at a spiritual retreat populated mostly by ex-nuns.

"No, my first wife isn't dead. She lives in Phoenix," he said. "She still comes out here once a year to visit my parents. Everyone loves my parents," he added, sounding annoyed.

Pulling some glass tumblers from the cupboard, Ralph shuffled to the freezer, scooping big handfuls of ice into a bowl. "Will you have a Manhattan?" he asked. "I make a mean one."

I had no idea what a Manhattan was, but accepted, even though I was currently on the wagon and had told Dan that I didn't like to drink.

Ralph rattled around the kitchen pouring bourbon, sweet vermouth, and bitters. He wrestled open a jar, then plopped a maraschino cherry into each glass and put them all on a large brown tray adding a candy box. "I'm going to crack open the peanut brittle, just for you," he said, grinning.

Dan took the tray, navigating his way through the dining room to the living room. Some natural light had filtered into the kitchen, but the rest of the house looked dark and lifeless, as though most of the rooms hadn't been used since the time the furniture was in style. Heavy gold curtains hung on the windows and wall-to-wall green and gold carpet hid what were probably beautiful wood floors. Under a layer of dust, the furniture was upholstered in shades of avocado and mustard.

As I started to follow Dan, Ralph pulled me back and explained that the cherry dining room set, including the eight chairs, buffet, and china cabinet, all came from Lachman Brothers, the furniture store he had managed throughout his entire career. "I had the whole place professionally decorated by the interior designers—drapes, carpet, and all—top of the line." Ralph gestured toward Dan, who was in the living room unloading drinks. "The house, the furniture—it'll all go to him, of course," he nodded, eyes distant. "When I'm gone."

I wondered what it would be like to have married parents living in the original family home. No divorces, no home-based sex parties or primal scream therapy sessions. No revolving door of stepmothers, stepsiblings, changes of address, and new schools. Dinner every night at the same time, at the same polished cherry dining room table. It seemed so solid and permanent. Even if his dad had once threatened to disinherit him, he obviously hadn't meant it. A few days earlier I'd told my dad that I couldn't keep up the payments on the loan he'd given me when Rachel was born. His first reaction was to tell me I was a loser. Maybe a six-year break would be good for our relationship, too.

Ralph insisted I take a house tour. I followed him up the stairs, passing a grandfather clock on the landing. The upper floor had a lonesome smell, a mix of stale peanuts, mothballs and instant coffee.

"This is the master," he said, flipping on the light. The room was so quiet and tidy, it seemed as if it should be cordoned off like a museum display of a 1950s bedroom.

"Your room is much cleaner than mine," I said.

"Oh, I don't sleep here—got this for guests," said Ralph. "Not that we get many visitors anymore." He escorted me down the hall, where there were two smaller rooms. "That's hers. This is mine."

Ralph's room was set up with two twin beds, one piled with clothes, the other made up with a brown bedspread. A TV tray set in front of a chair held an interrupted game of solitaire and a pile of toothpicks on a plate. "Can't really see the TV anymore so I like to play my cards," he said.

I studied the pictures on the wall: Ralph receiving various awards, a photo of him with Minnie on vacation, a childhood shot of Dan, portraits of Jimmy and of Ralph's first wife, Mary. There was a contemporary shot of Ralph standing arm-in-arm with a portly middle-aged man with unusually large ears. "Who's this?" I asked.

"That's my nephew, Mike." Ralph looked nervous.

"Does he live nearby?"

"He does." Ralph shoved his hands in his pockets and stared at the photo. "Dan hates him. Won't come over if he's here. But I don't care. He gave me this here framed photo and goddamn it, I put it up. Can't tiptoe around Dan for the rest of my goddamn life." Ralph faced me and held up a bent and blotchy finger. "If you know what's good for you—or really," he paused and chuckled, "what's good for *me*—don't you bring it up either."

Ralph opened his top dresser drawer. "Lookee here. Nobody better'd mess with me." With a shaky hand he moved back some socks, exposing the handle of a handgun.

I stepped back. *Jesus.* Old, deaf, half blind, shaky, cranky and armed—it was like Mr. Magoo with a deadly weapon.

Dan yelled upstairs. "What are you two doing up there?"

Ralph slammed the drawer and put a finger over his lips to indicate, I assumed, that this was classified information. The secrets in this household were starting to pile up.

Downstairs, Minnie emerged from the guest bathroom, trailing a cloud of smoke and perfume. She sat down on the sofa, patting the cushion next to her. "Honey—sit here on the Chesterfield. Take a load off."

Dan moved to the window and pulled the drapery cord. A slice of white sunlight cut across the room, and tiny dust particles swirled and collided around us. I suddenly wanted to rip out the carpets and drapes and furniture, throw open the windows, let in some fresh air.

"You have a lovely home," I said.

"Oh honey, thank you. You know, we bought this house just to get Dan in the school on the corner. Didn't we, Ralph?"

I braced myself for Ralph's reply, but he just smiled and nodded. His sharp edges seemed to have melted like ice cubes in bourbon.

"We've done pretty well for ourselves. The house. The furniture. We've got a nice Chrysler in the garage. It's in great shape, isn't it Ralph?" She leaned in, whispering. "He doesn't drive anymore. Not since he almost mowed down Father Sproul by St. Brendan's."

"It'll all be his someday," said Ralph, grinning. "Even the RCA." He pointed to a heavy walnut veneer console that sat like a closed coffin between the windows.

"Everything we did, we did for our boys," said Minnie.

"Enough, already," snapped Dan. "Can we talk about something else?"

Minnie glanced sideways; Ralph's smile faded. I picked up my drink, contemplated taking a sip, but instead inhaled the sweet fumes, keeping a tight grip on the glass. The grandfather clock announced the long silent seconds. I thought about eating a piece of peanut brittle, but held off, afraid it would make too much noise.

"Would you excuse me?" I stood and set down my drink. "I have to use the powder room." Dan stood and motioned toward the guest bathroom near the front door.

As I flipped on the light switch, I noticed Minnie's purse sitting on the back of the toilet. I rested onto the seat, relieved, mostly, to be out of the palpable tension of the living room. I never did well when I got caught in the crossfire of festering family feuds. Once, in college, my best friend's parents started bickering at dinner and I started to cry, worried they were headed for divorce. They all found this hysterically funny.

Reaching for the toilet paper, I found an empty roll. *Dangit.* Quietly, I creaked open the cabinet under the sink, and found nothing but a can of air freshener. I quickly scanned the room for any kind of paper goods that would do the job, but there was nothing. *Shit.* Praying she carried a travel pack of Kleenex with her, I guiltily picked up Minnie's purse and thumbed through the contents, pulling out the quilted black wallet, a clear plastic bag full of lipsticks, and a pack of Merit Menthols. There was a small side pocket sewn into the lining. I unzipped it carefully, my heart lifting when I spotted what appeared to be a thin folded napkin. But it wasn't tissue; it was just a folded letter. I pulled it out, opened it, and glanced at the date: August 10, 1987. It was written over two years earlier and she was still carrying it around in her purse? Well, she'd certainly never miss this. But if I flushed it and caused a major toilet overflow, what then? I'd just have to drip dry. While doing so, I let my eyes graze the flowery handwriting of the letter. Must be a woman, I mused. I checked the signature: Maureen McDonough. *Good work, Sherlock.* I considered how wrong it was to read someone else's mail; I used to hate when my father did that to me. But I didn't even know these people, and this looked like it was all superficial news, anyway. Maureen rambled about the Pennsylvania weather, how she was getting ready to plant her bulbs, the bingo club, how she wished Minnie would tell Dan the truth about Jimmy's death once and for all—

What? I reread the last sentence.

I pray each day that you will tell your Danny the truth about Jimmy's death, once and for all. Please— it's only fair that Milton should be set free so he can find happiness.

Who the hell was Milton?

Shaking, I quickly reached back and flushed the toilet, somehow believing the sound would offset the loud hammering in my chest. I pulled up my pants and turned on the water faucet full blast, letting it run as I slid the folded letter back into its compartment and returned Minnie's personal items—hopefully, just as I'd found them. I tried to compose myself as I left the bathroom, but I felt as if I'd been hit in the head—and so ashamed that I couldn't bring myself to sit down next to Minnie again. Instead, I took the small stool next to Dan, who was now laughing.

"My mother's telling jokes," he said. "Go ahead. Give us another, Ma."

"Okay," she turned to me with a mischievous grin. "How about the day Frank Sinatra went to the retirement home to make a few bucks?" Minnie blinked flirtatiously, took a big gulp of air, and motioned me to the sofa. "Frankie was hired to woo the ladies, pick up their spirits with a couple of his hit tunes. And I'm telling you, honey," she hit my arm, "Old Blue Eyes sang his heart out. He was so well received, he was covered head to toe in lipstick stains. He was feeling pretty good about himself, until he sees this old babe in the lobby, giving him a long blank stare. No smile, no request for autograph, no kiss—*nothing*."

Minnie whacked my arm again, hard. For an instant I imagined she suspected me of foul play—but this was just her version of a punctuation point.

"Old Blue Eyes says to her, 'Hey lady, DON'T YOU KNOW WHO I AM?' She looks up at him and says, 'No, I don't. But if you ask them at the front desk, they'll tell you.'"

We all burst into laughter, mine more shrieking than normal.

"Good one. Ma! That was really good," Dan said, smiling broadly. "My mother is always good for a laugh."

Minnie giggled and shook, throwing her hands up like a champ, clapping them together before pulling them to her face.

Ralph, stood up—wobbled slightly—and said, "How about another round?"

Dan stood. "We can't stay—this was just a quick visit."

"Oh, no," said Minnie. "You can't go yet—you just got here."

"We had some laughs, Ma. Let's not ruin it now," said Dan.

"Does your baby like candy?" Ralph asked. "I love the little ones—always wanted me a baby girl, too." He whispered to me. "Would have named her Mary—after my first wife, not her," twitching his head toward Minnie.

"Actually, she's three years old." I stood and followed Ralph, while Dan moved onto the couch next to his mother. We smiled at each other as we passed, and he leaned in, rubbed his hand up and down my back, and whispered, "We'll leave in a few minutes."

In the kitchen Ralph opened and closed cabinets, muttering about the "sweets" he knew were there somewhere. In one large cabinet, he pulled out three heavy glass vases and some wild plastic salad bowls, patterned with tropical fruit and palm trees. "We never use these goddamn things, so I don't know why we keep them," he said, waving one in front of him. "I'd give them to Dan—but he doesn't want them. They'll go to him anyway," he muttered. Suddenly he perked up. "You know, if things work out between you and my son, these will be yours."

I started to laugh, but then I saw the desperate look on his face. I wanted to remove his funny cap, kiss his head, and assure him that someday Dan would put his tropical salad bowls to good use.

"I don't know why he gets involved with so many crooks," said Ralph, continuing in low motorized tones. "Can you give me just one good explanation?"

"Maybe because he's a criminal attorney?"

"Well, he ought to represent the bastards," he barked, "not do business with them." This statement felt like another sudden smack to my head. "Have you met some of these clowns?" said Ralph.

I pictured Richard's face, Johnny Curtain's smile.

"Hell, he's got a law degree. He's smart, could do anything he wanted. You seem like a nice girl, you ought to talk to him." Behind his watery eyes, Ralph's expression was intense, worried. "Now he's up to no good with that Richard. Thinks he was a friend of Jimmy's. Well I'm telling you, he was *no* friend."

Dan walked in. "Ready to roll?" He was holding the box of duct tape. I patted Ralph's shoulder; he turned back to fill a baggie with wrapped caramels and peppermints for Rachel.

"What's this for?" I asked Dan, tapping on the box.

"Long story—a tedious home improvement project."

Repair by duct tape? I never seemed to fall for the guys with tool belts.

We said our goodbyes amidst pats and kisses. Dan picked up the ladder. "Ladies first," he said, and followed me down the front stairs. We pulled away with his parents waving to us from the stoop.

"Wow. What a couple of characters," I said.

"Yeah," said Dan, fiddling with the vent. "They're a real kick in the pants. As long as you do things their way."

"What are you talking about? They're devoted to you. All they talk about is what they want to give you."

"They don't have anything I want."

They have the truth about Jimmy. But was that something Dan wanted?

"What is it you want?"

"Loyalty, for one thing. Unconditional love." Dan reached over, taking my hand in his. "If it exists."

"Dan," I hesitated slightly. "What happened with your brother?"

"Half-brother. We had different mothers. Mary the first was his Mom, my godmother. She and my dad married real young." Dan let out a long sigh. "Jimmy was shot. Through the head. By my cousin—an intellectually challenged asshole from my father's side of the family."

Milton.

"Mike was a rookie cop."

"Mike? Who's Mike?"

"My cousin. The cop."

Mike was the big-eared man in the photo in Ralph's bedroom.

"He lived with Jimmy in a flat in the Richmond. Jimmy got along with just about everyone, but he and Mike were always fighting. Mike was a holier-than-thou type, always trying to get Jimmy to give up gambling, to reform. I guess that last time Jimmy really pissed him off because Officer Mike finally sent a shot flying through Jimmy's skull. Killed my brother and his career with one bullet."

"My God. I am so sorry. How old was Jimmy?"

"About twenty-three, twenty-four. I barely remember it," said Dan. "I was only eight."

"Was there anyone else involved?" I tried to sound casual. Certainly Ralph would have to be a saint to keep a picture of Mike—his son's killer—where he could see it every night. And why would he let this Milton take the blame for Jimmy's death if Mike was the actual killer? It didn't make sense.

"No, it was just Jimmy and Mike. Mike's word against a dead man's. There was an investigation. They ruled it an accident. But I'll never forget the look in Mike's eyes right after it happened. Every time he tried to talk to me, I could tell he was lying. Why else would he quit the force? It was no accident."

I wanted to ask about Milton, but there was no reasonable way to bring it up. I racked my brain, trying to remember the last name of the woman who signed the letter. It was Scottish or Irish. Mc-something? McDougal? *Dammit.* I needed to start packing a pad and pen like Dan, take some notes.

"What was Jimmy like?"

"Jimmy? He was great—the best. He was fifteen years older than me—worked for Johnny Curtain, back when Johnny first started out."

"Jimmy worked for Johnny too?" This surprised me.

"Johnny owned a couple of buildings in the Richmond. He had a bar, a little back room numbers racket. Infuriated my father. Low radar stuff, but my father didn't want Jimmy tarnishing his civic reputation. He wanted Jimmy working for him, delivering furniture, working his way up to management one day. That's the kind of low ambition dear old Dad held for his firstborn. But Jimmy was too smart for that," Dan gloated. "Plus he had the ladies to impress. His girlfriend Rusty in particular. God—she was beautiful. I swear, she smelled like peaches."

Dan told me that Jimmy and Rusty always included him when they went to the Saturday night drive-in. They let him sit between them in the front seat and fed him hot dogs, popcorn, and orange soda.

"Sounds like you were in love with her," I said.

"Yeah." Dan laughed. "Mostly I wished that she was my mother and Jimmy was my father. But Jimmy was a gambler and a bit of a ladies' man—that wrecked things with Rusty. In fact, she'd heard about some indiscretion and ended it once and for all a few days before he died. I don't know who was more crushed about the break-up—Jimmy or me. I was so pissed at him. I wouldn't let him come to some scouting event at the school because I wanted Rusty with me. That was the night he was killed."

"Oh. Ouch." Dan's profile looked handsome glowing in the dash light. Stoic. He had a strong chin, a straight aristocratic nose, and those thick black lashes and brows enhanced the already natural intensity of his face. I'd always felt an indefinable mystery shrouding Dan, but it made more sense to me now.

I suddenly wished I hadn't seen that letter, and vowed to keep my curiosity contained to my job—which I needed more desperately than anything. Maybe keeping a few secrets wasn't such a bad idea. I might have turned out much better if my parents had kept their let-it-all-hang-out sex and drug drenched personal lives better hidden.

We were silent as Dan drove through the heavy traffic.

"Dan, did you know that your dad has a gun?"

"Yeah. Sure. He loves to show it to people. I doubt it's loaded."

"He sure is obsessed with wanting to leave you his house and things."

"I told him I didn't want his damn house. He should give it to charity."

I had never seen Dan be as testy as this with anyone, at work or socially. I found it odd that a guy so devoted to helping the elderly could be this snippy to his fragile old parents.

"How often do you take them to the cemetery?"

"About once a month, but they go more than that. Hell, if they can't get a ride, they'll take three buses to get there."

"I love cemeteries," I said. "I'd be happy to take them to the cemetery with you sometime."

"Really?" Dan laughed and squeezed my hand. "If they ever find out you like to visit the cemetery, you'll be in like a burglar."

Chapter 6

November 1989

On a sunny Saturday morning, just over a week after my visit to Dan's parents, I met Jamie at our favorite cafe near U.C. Berkeley, where she was doing research. Bette's Bakery was located on chic Fourth Street, a few blocks from the bay. Dan was going to pick me up afterward for our first night away, and I was feeling anxious. It hadn't helped that when I'd called to tell him where to meet, his wife's voice was still on his answering machine, despite my explicit instructions on how to change the message.

In the café the muscular counter boy smiled at Jamie and threw open his arms. "She's back!" he said, in a singsong voice, prompting two other young pierced types to start a mock fight over who'd take her order. We took our coffee and scones outside to sit on a bench underneath a droopy oak.

"Let me ask you something." Jamie's expression was serious. "Do I look like a lesbian?"

"You *are* a lesbian," I said. "What's going on with you lately, anyway?"

"Nothing." Jamie reached up and ran her hand across the tips of her spiky blond hair. "I just think this haircut makes me look too butch."

"That's probably why all the counter boys were panting at you."

"They'd pant at you, too, if you wore normal clothes. What's up with the *Little House on the Prairie* look?" She lifted a piece of my long flowery skirt, sending a breeze underneath. I was wearing it with a light blue cardigan with a lace collar, buttoned to the top.

"Good-bye Morticia Adams, *hello* Laura Ashley," I said. "Dan loves the innocent, girly look. And I like it because it hides all my excess."

"Since I've been with Alison, I've put on seven pounds." Jamie bit into the scone. "Careful, that's what monotony does to you."

"Monotony?"

Jamie laughed and shook her head. "I meant monogamy!"

"I like the hip, electrocuted look." I pinched one of her spikes between my fingers. "But I didn't think Santa Cruz lesbians were allowed to bleach their hair with anything but sunshine."

"I didn't bleach it." Her expression was of mock outrage.

"Right."

Jamie smiled. "Well, Alison doesn't know it's bleached, so don't say that around her."

"I think Dan dyes his hair. His sideburns are silver but his hair is jet-black. I asked him, but he denied it. He said it was this other '*thing*.'"

"What other thing? Paint? Shoe polish?" Jamie let out a snorting laugh. "Maybe it's a rinse. But what difference does it make?"

"I like gray. I think it's sexy."

"If he's going to hit on young chicks, he's got to do something, right?"

I thought of mentioning that Dan didn't even know how to operate his own answering machine, but didn't want to give Jamie more material for age-related jokes.

"Tell me the truth; do you like him?" I said.

"Sure." She lit a cigarette, took a long drag, and blew it out slowly. "I think he talks a lot, but—"

"But what?"

"You seem much better lately. You know, nicer. Did Dad give you a prescription?"

"I'm not dignifying that with an answer." Rifling through the newspaper, I pulled out the classified ads. I hadn't heard anything from Paine & Savage after more than a week, and was losing hope.

"So, what do you think?" Jamie gave me an exaggerated wink. "Is this the big night?"

"Let's just say I'm packing birth control," I said, patting the overnight bag sitting next to me.

"I still can't believe you've been with him over a month and you've never done the deed. How does that happen?"

"Let me explain something to you, my young and loose lesbian sister. It turns out real men aren't so desperate to get laid that they'll insist on doing it with a three-year-old in the next room. Plus he's been traveling, and I've been moving. If you can believe it, I haven't even seen him naked."

"You'll finally have a chance to investigate his natural hair color," said Jamie.

I laughed. "Speaking of investigations, remember how I told you about his brother?" I'd filled her in on my visit to Minnie and Ralph's, and explained about Dan and Minnie's conflicting viewpoints on the cause of Jimmy's death. "The only mention of it in old newspapers was a long obituary that had as much about Dan's dad as it did about his poor dead son. I thought Ralph was just some retired furniture salesman, but he was quite the mucky-muck in his day." I'd also scanned the paper for some mention of a Milton, but I omitted that part of the story. It would only set her off on a tirade about my snoopiness.

The obituary mentioned that Ralph had served in World War II, overseeing operations at Fort Mason after he returned from overseas. Later he was the president of the San Francisco Merchants Association, worked tirelessly on two successful mayoral campaigns, ran an annual charity drive for St. Ignatius High School, and was a "loyal donor" and "community leader" in events supporting both the police and fire departments.

"Did it say how Jimmy died?"

"No. That always pisses me off about obituaries. That should be a required fact. That's what everyone really wants to know."

"I'm just happy you're focusing your nosy high beams somewhere other than on me." Jamie dropped her cigarette into the dregs of her coffee, sending out a thin trail of smoke. "Which reminds me, Sammie Spade. I have a present for you." She pulled a book out of her backpack and handed it over. "Check out the title: it sounds like a sex manual."

It stood out in big red letters against a glossy white cover: *A Nasty Bit of Business: A Private Eye's Guide.*

"Jamie, this is so cool." I skimmed the pages. The book was written by a saucy high-heeled private investigator called Rat Dog Dick, named—it said—because she could sniff out secrets like a rat dog finds rodents. In her first chapter, "Portrait of a Scoundrel," she listed the traits of someone who might have something to hide.

We hunched over the book, reading together. The bulleted list included people who always paid in cash, let their machine answer all calls, and received mail at a P.O. box.

"Oh my God. That's Dan," I laughed, even though I also had a queasy feeling in my stomach. I pointed to a sentence that said, "Just because a person does one or more of these things doesn't mean he or she is a scoundrel, but put them together and the odds are, here comes trouble."

Dan pulled over in front of the cafe and honked. I jumped, and my heart raced as if I'd just been caught red-handed with illicit evidence. As he jumped out of the car, I shoved the book in my purse.

"Okay gorgeous. Ready?" he asked.

"Dan, you remember Jamie?" I glanced at Dan's car. The sturdy old Lincoln looked like a dad-mobile.

"Nice to see you again." Dan smiled and shook Jamie's hand. He walked toward me and took my bag. His natural stride carried a bounce that made it seem like he was walking on a trampoline. He leaned in for a quick kiss, tossed my bag into the trunk, and we were off.

"You look handsome," I said. He wore a loose black crew neck sweater over a creamy turtleneck, producing a look that resembled a clerical collar. "I feel like I'm running away with a priest."

"Turn you on?"

"You know it." I stroked his sideburns, then gently pushed his hair behind his ears so it framed his face more angularly, the way I liked it. Dan grasped my hand, gave it a squeeze, and moved it to the armrest, freeing his hand to readjust his hair so that it covered the tops of his ears again.

"Don't get carried away, young lady," he said. "A weekend away means nothing—*zip zero nada*—in the scheme of things. Have you heard my theory about that?"

"No, but something tells me I will."

"It's called 'The Romantic Weekend Sham,' because so many people go off for a weekend in the early stage of relationships. They come back, claim they're soulmates, and get married. But any couple of idiots can survive a weekend. Everyone's on their best behavior—they look good, smell good; they're charming, full of new jokes and stories. But can they survive the return? The tedium of day-to-day living? Can they learn to fart, cough and make a budget together?"

"So our relationship means nothing until we pass gas in front of each other? That should be a great relief to everyone. Especially Rachel—she's lactose intolerant."

Dan eyed me sideways, amused. "On second thought, some things are better kept to ourselves. Which reminds me of another theory," he continued. "I think the secret to a successful marriage is privacy—meaning each party has his or her own office, bathroom, and closet."

"I'm all for that. Everyone needs a room of one's own."

"I didn't have it in my first marriage, so I insisted on it the second," he said.

"There goes that theory."

Dan smiled, reached over and opened the glove box.

"Look what I brought," he beamed, holding up a cassette. "Neil Diamond." He stuck the tape into the car stereo.

Neil Diamond? *Oh no, oh no.* First Roy Orbison and now Neil Diamond? Two musical heroes with similar yet equally awful hair. I liked Roy's music, but Neil Diamond? I never understood the passion that man evoked. And it was definitely old fogy music. I looked over at Dan, who was singing along to *Longfellow Serenade.* What if Dan played this at a dinner party in front of my friends?

"*Sheeeeeeee* was a lady, I was a dreamer," he crooned. Dan took my hand, and belted out the final chorus: "Ride, come on baby ride...Let me make your dreams come true!" The song ended, and Dan turned down the volume and said, apparently in all sincerity, "I'm going to make your dreams come true, honey. You know that?"

Corny, I thought. Yet exactly what I wanted to hear. I closed my eyes, feeling a smile linger on my lips. I was picturing myself, Dan, and Rachel living in that pretty house across the street from my old apartment, surrounded by flowers, a swing set, and two shiny new cars parked in the driveway.

"You can't know how appreciative I am that you're so loyal and understanding. I've had so much goddamn betrayal in my life—with my parents, my ex-wives. I'm ready for that to change."

I had no comment. I'd never thought of myself as loyal. Not that I thought I was disloyal, either—it just wasn't a quality I'd ever paid much attention to.

"I couldn't get my first wife interested in supporting my business ideas. She was always so insistent that I stick to my law practice. But when they paid off, she was ready and willing to take the money and run after our divorce."

"What about Julia?" I asked, referring to his second wife. "She seemed like quite a sport. And you still have her answering your phone."

"Yeah, got to fix that," he said. "She was alright, sometimes, but—" Dan rolled his eyes and told me that when he'd been on trial on unfair charges having to do with a diamond investment company he'd founded in the seventies, all she could think about was herself. "One night the phone rings. I finally get this elusive sonofabitch that I need an affidavit from on the line, and you know what she does?"

"What?"

"She rips the phone out of the wall and throws it across the room. Couldn't offer an ounce of support while I was fighting for my life."

"Why were you fighting for your life? What did you do?"

"What did *I* do?" Dan turned, briefly taking his eyes off the road, and said, "You have no inkling, Mary, how corrupt our government is. At *every* level. What I did was fight like hell to prove my innocence."

I didn't know what to say. I didn't even know what to think.

"They say anyone who represents himself has a fool for a client, but you know what?" he asked.

"You won?"

"That's right. I thought you knew all this?"

"How would I?"

"I thought some of it was still going on when you worked for me. I guess it was before your time. The State of Missouri indicted me for fraud—said it was against the law to sell diamonds as investments. I was back and forth on planes, didn't know which way was up. It was pretty traumatic. In the end, all charges were dropped. And the jury was so disgusted with the way the prosecutors treated me that they pooled money—*pooled their own hard earned cash*—and flew me out for a weekend to show me that the people of the State of Missouri were nothing like their corrupt, vindictive prosecutors. I'm still untangling from that fucking fiasco." Dan's expression was self-righteous, proud.

"Hey, I've got to make a quick stop at the IHOP up here. Richard's meeting me so I can sign a few papers, pick up some cash." Dan moved across the freeway lanes to exit at a sprawling shopping center in Novato. He was an excessively precise driver, always using his turn signals and never speeding, to the point where sometimes he went below the limit. This embarrassed me, but that was offset by how safe I felt in his car.

"You want to come in?" Dan parked, switched off the ignition. "Or you can listen to music. I've got another Neil."

"No, no. That's okay, I'll read." I reached into my bag and pulled out my new book.

"I shouldn't be long." He grabbed his briefcase and gave me a kiss.

I rolled down the window. A cold breeze filled the car, making me feel more alert. I reclined the leather seat and opened my book.

- *Scoundrels deal only in cash.*
- *They receive their mail at P.O. boxes or mail drops.*
- *Trouble is their middle name—they are constantly the victim of schizophrenic ex-wives, card-eating ATM machines, and unreasonable S.W.A.T. teams.*
- *They make friends easily.*
- *They're secretive.*
- *They're new in town.*

Dan's certainly not new in town, I thought.

I opened his glove compartment. There was sunscreen, various maps of California, and more cassettes, including ABBA's Greatest Hits.

ABBA? How could this ever work?

Looking up, I saw Dan walking toward the car, smiling. I slammed the glove box closed. In the next instant, Dan looked angry; his eyes fixed somewhere just beyond the car. He made a beeline toward a fat man in a sweatsuit who was pushing a cart and waving. The man had a thick gut, thinning gray-brown hair, and large meaty ears that were so much redder than his pasty complexion that they looked detachable. He looked familiar, even beyond his vague resemblance to Mr. Potatohead. Dan appeared to be speaking at him sharply. I couldn't make out the words, but the man looked stricken. He turned his palms up and muttered something back to Dan, who just turned on his heels and bounced toward the car.

He yanked open the door, and dropped into his seat, exasperated.

"What was that?" I said.

"Oh, Christ. What did I do with my briefcase?" Dan hit the steering wheel. "Shit. Hang on, I'll tell you when I get back." He hopped out of the car and jogged back toward the IHOP.

Mr. Potatohead suddenly appeared at my open window.

"I won't belabor this," he said, breathing heavily from the short walk. He smelled like Aqua Velvet aftershave and Scope—but despite the minty freshness, I could smell alcohol on his breath. He handed me a card. It said, "Mike Murphy, Shamrock Investigations. P.I. License # 8876779."

Mike? Dan's cousin? That's why he looked familiar. I'd just seen his photograph in Ralph's bedroom. The murderer—or accidental killer—who was keeping the mysterious Milton from being set free was a private investigator?

I looked from the card to Mike. He appeared so harmless, pathetic even. I couldn't detect a Murphy family resemblance in any of his features, but there was an ineffable quality that reminded me of Ralph—perhaps in his gait or facial expressions. It was the kind of bizarre likeness one might notice between a pet and its owner.

"Dan is in trouble. Besides that, he's keeping the wrong company. I can help him. Even with the IRS. Maybe you can convince him to give me a call?"

I looked back toward the IHOP, but couldn't think of a thing to say. Why would Dan need Mike's help with the IRS?

"Do you two live around here?" he asked.

We two? Did Mike think I was Dan's wife?

"Aren't you his cousin?" I said.

"Mike." He stuck his large hand in the window. "How do you do?"

I started at the sound of Dan's voice.

"Leave her alone." He yanked open the driver's side door.

"Dan, we're family." Mike flipped his palms over again, pleading.

"Leave, goddammit. Now."

Mike straightened up, turned, and slunk away. Dan's rejection had been so uncharacteristically cold; I had an almost irrepressible urge to run after Mike and comfort him.

"Jesus, honey. I am so sorry you had to experience that. I was afraid this would happen." Dan slid into his seat, and slammed the door. "He lives around here; I usually avoid Novato because of that. Shit. So there you have it. Cousin Mike—the man who arrived on this planet to make my life miserable."

"God, Dan. You think that was a little harsh?"

Dan looked incredulous. "Mary, I may not know exactly why he killed my brother. But accident or not, I know he's lying about it."

"I'm sorry. It's just, he doesn't look dangerous. And he's got the biggest pair of ears I've ever seen. Record breaking."

"Jimmy used to call him Dumbo." Dan chuckled, but his voice still sounded strained. "Listen, that bastard caused a six-year rift between my parents and me. And now he's harassing you. Maybe I wasn't harsh *enough*."

"*He's* the relative your Dad invited into the family plot?" Ralph might have forgiven Mike enough to hang a picture—but would anyone elect to spend an eternity with his child's killer?

"Right. It was his fault we needed to buy the plot to begin with. Now he's an invited guest. But like I said, not over my dead body. Or next to it, or even under it. Goddammit, why won't he just leave me alone? What was he saying to you?" said Dan.

"He said he could help you with the IRS. Then he asked me if we lived around here."

Dan tensed up imperceptibly. "What did you tell him?"

"First of all, you may recall, I've never been to your home. Second, give me some credit, please. I didn't say a thing about you, me, or we." I was feeling more and more agitated. I held out Mike's card. "Why didn't you tell me you had a private investigator in the family?"

"I wouldn't refer my worst enemy to Mike. And not just because of our history. The guy's a drunk. Probably has to drink to live with himself. He does slip and fall cases, spies on people to see if they're really injured. Photographs adulterers and helps break up marriages. But from what I hear, he usually passes out before finding any evidence."

"He said he wanted to help you. Help you with what?" *Maybe Mike knows the truth about Jimmy's death. Maybe he knows Milton?*

"He thinks he has some big insight into solving some old tax issues I have from the diamond company. I think it's some twisted need to make good with me. He's told just about everyone I know he wants to help, but the last thing I need is some drunk running around discussing my private business. I only agreed to see my parents again if they swore on Jimmy's grave not to give Mike any news about me."

Dan had an explanation for everything, and all the pieces of his story fit neatly together. So why was I was feeling so overwhelmed and confused?

Dan opened the briefcase and took out a thick pile of twenties, which he folded in half and stuck in his back pocket. "That guy ought to look in the mirror. He needs to help himself."

"So what, is Richard your personal ATM machine?"

"Something like that." Dan's eyes swept across the parking lot; he checked his rear and side mirrors, then started the car. "He manages my money."

"Why can't you manage your own money?"

Dan gave me a wary look, then pulled out on the road. He kept raising his eyes toward the rear view mirror—looking, I assumed, for Mike.

"Here's a little education, Ms. Private Eye. And one of these times I'll give you more detail, but let's just say everyone—*everyone*—needs a few layers of protection. You've got to protect your family from a greedy government and a suit-happy society. The best way to do that is with *irrevocable* trusts—you technically give up your rights to your assets permanently, which is a lot different than the popular revocable trusts. Richard happens to be my trustee. Do you know what that means?"

A familiar glaze formed over my eyes. When I worked for Dan, some of his answers to the most straightforward questions had trapped me in his office as he detoured through four or five subjects before arriving at an answer. *What am I doing with him?* His life was so complicated. I never knew what he was talking about. His business partner was spooky and rude. He drove an old fogy car. He had ex-wives and tax issues. He couldn't operate a simple answering machine. *And he listens to ABBA?* I should be at home getting my job hunt organized, figuring out how to take care of my daughter and myself.

Ten minutes later we turned off the main highway onto a smaller, winding road that led through the Sonoma countryside. Cows, sheep, and llamas dotted the brown hillsides. Amber and plum leaves dangled from near-bare branches, the slightest movement sending them fluttering to the ground below. There was a tinge of smoke in the air that made me feel anxious, as if a small, hidden brushfire might be at risk of igniting out of control if the wind kicked up.

Dan glanced at the book I'd left beside me on the seat.

"What's that you're reading?"

I picked it up and turned the cover toward him. "Jamie gave it to me. To help me with the P.I. stuff."

"Is she a lesbian?"

"That's one of the things she is." I gazed out the open window, letting the wind blow across my face, forcing me to close my eyes. "And just because someone is attracted to women, doesn't make her a lesbian." I clutched the book harder.

"You think?"

"I've been attracted to women plenty of times. When Kevin read that in my diary, he freaked."

Dan twitched slightly and made a clicking noise that sounded like a turn signal. He gently pulled his hand off mine, adjusted the vent, and put it back on the steering wheel.

"Kevin read that? I wonder how much that affected his behavior?"

"He shouldn't have read my journal—it was private."

"Well, I agree with you there. I'd be furious if someone invaded my privacy. Furious," he said, eying me sideways.

My toes crunched hard in my shoes.

"All that aside, this is good news because I've always said I was a lesbian in a man's body."

I shot him an obligatory smile, closed my eyes and pretended to doze.

We reached the Sonoma coast just before dusk. The light mist over the ocean looked like cool steam wafting up from a pool of dry ice. Dan pulled onto a gravel driveway bordered with trees that had dropped shiny, gold leaves into thick piles. It made the roadway leading us to our romantic hideaway look as if it was lined with pirates' booty.

We parked in front of a large white Victorian farmhouse called the Old Milano Hotel. Dan checked in while I stayed outside on the wraparound porch, overlooking a lawn that sloped down and ended abruptly at a cliff above the sea. I tried to avoid being around when Dan paid for things. Dealing with money on dates always unnerved me, especially when I didn't have any.

A few minutes later, the screen door squeaked. Dan nestled behind me. "I'm so happy to be here with you," he said.

I shivered and stiffened. "I'm kind of cold out here. Maybe we should settle in."

"We've got the garden cottage in the back. Very private. They'll deliver dinner right to our door. And get this—there's a private Jacuzzi above the cliffs, over there, behind that fence. I signed us up for an hour at ten."

We followed a winding brick path to the back of the house. The air smelled mulchy and sweet, and the mist was starting to coagulate into a thick coastal fog that crept up the cliff.

Our cottage was cozy and charming, with French doors that opened to a garden where a few straggly pink and lavender roses still bloomed. A wide feather bed faced the garden, and off in the corner were a loveseat and coffee table by a wood-burning stove that was already set up with wood and kindling.

"I guess I can't impress you with my Eagle Scout fire-building skills."

Dan rattled on about how he'd had to keep a fire burning all night in the woods to earn his merit badges. I half listened as I tucked away my bag, then sat on the loveseat and watched the fire start to smoke and crackle. Dan opened the bottle of Cabernet that was sitting on the coffee table next to a vase of fresh daisies. He handed me a glass.

"Why are you giving me wine? I told you I'm trying not to drink," I said. The room was chilly; the fire Dan had lit wasn't making much progress.

"Oh. Right. Well, we don't need to drink." Dan put down the glasses and joined me on the loveseat. "You can simply relax and be beautiful."

Dan told me I was beautiful a lot, and I liked that. From the time I was in seventh grade I'd worried I was fat and hated my freckly Irish skin. One day, Reid Remmington, the popular sapphire-eyed surfer I obsessed over, walked toward me in an empty junior high hallway. I did a mental check: *Outfit? Okay. Hair? Brushed. Pimples? Puttied with Clearasil that morning.* Reid had no clue who I was or that I spent hours locked in my bedroom, secretly listening to the Carpenter's *Close to You*, over and over, pining for him as I sang along. As he passed me, something inspired him to say, "Hey you—white girl. You're uglier than Popeye's chick, Olive Oyl." He guffawed, clanging his skateboard across a row of metal lockers. I ran home, locked myself in my room, and cried for the rest of the afternoon, taking solace only in the fact that Olive Oyl was thin. The next day I took a shortcut through the elementary school. A lone sixth-grader was slumped on a bench, waiting for a tardy parent to pick him up. I felt sorry for him so I smiled as I passed. "Fuck you, ugly," he said. This couldn't be coincidence, I decided.

Once I decided I was ugly, I found lots of evidence to support it. By the time I was seventeen my self-esteem was low enough to send me into the slimy arms of my alcoholic, womanizing old boss, Rod—a creep I worked for during a summer secretarial job after graduation. Falling in love with Kevin in college was a big step up because he treated me like I was smart and pretty.

So far Dan had treated me like a beauty queen. But now that I was alone in a cottage with him, knowing the direction we were supposed to go, the fog outside seemed to invade my senses and I was fuzzy about what I wanted to happen. Especially after that scene in the IHOP parking lot.

Dan sat down next to me, putting one arm around my waist and the other hand gently behind my neck.

"Ow. You're pulling my hair," I said, drawing back.

He looked surprised. Hurt.

"You caught my hair." I didn't look into his eyes, but sidled away, pulling a few long brown strands out from under my necklace.

Dan stood up and shoved his hands deep into the pockets of his slacks. "Mary, is something wrong? Are we okay here?"

I was trapped in the loveseat, unable to speak or move, a heaviness filling me like sand.

"What's wrong?" he said, sounding alarmed.

"I don't know," I barely managed to whisper. It would be much easier if I could just drink and get this over with, I thought.

Dan started pacing. He always paced when he was on the phone, negotiating, or whenever he was telling an emotional story. His frenetic movements made me feel even more immobile. Watching him cross the room drew my attention to the forced romance of the setting—the flowery fabrics, candles, wine, and two fluffy robes set on hooks near the enormous bed.

"Do you not want to be here?" he said.

"I don't know," I whispered. A sharp pain hooked into my throat. I wanted to sink underneath the cushions, or slip outside into the fog, but I knew Dan was going to keep questioning until he pulled something out of me. Since I wasn't sure what that would be, I was afraid to say much of anything.

"It's just—I don't think I'm ready for all this yet."

Dan abruptly stopped pacing and looked at me.

"By 'this,' what do you mean? Do you mean spending the night together? Making love? Sex?"

I flushed, looked away. Dan sat by my side, his voice slow and stern. "Are you wanting to wait longer? Is that what you're telling me?"

I wasn't sure what I was telling him. But I answered, "Yes."

We both sat quietly.

"Unbelievable," he said, shaking his head. "This is unbelievable."

I figured I should stand up, get my bag, and head for the car before he exploded, but the heavy feeling in my limbs held me down.

Dan jumped to his feet. I began to think of things to say to stop him from being angry. Should I pay for the room? Of course, I couldn't afford it. Offer to drive us home? Wash and gas his car?

"Do you know how great this is?" Dan looked like a Little Leaguer who'd just knocked one out of the park. "This is exactly—*exactly*—the kind of thing that makes this relationship special. *I knew it.*" He was pacing again. "Half the world engages in premature fornication, locking into commitments based on hormones instead of love. But we're going to wait, take our time. It's perfect. *Perfect.* It's like—in some twisted way—we'll be virgins again, for each other."

I let the fact that Dan was excited about not having sex sink in. I felt like an hourglass that had been flipped over.

"You don't mind being patient a little longer?" I said.

"Don't you see? I've never felt this patient—this willing to wait. Isn't it great?"

"Okay counselor," I nudged, "You might want to sound a little less gleeful about holding off."

Dan noticed my change in demeanor and smiled. He emptied the wine down the sink and rejoined me on the loveseat.

"I'm happy to hold off, as long as you let me give you a taste of what's coming soon, to a theater near you."

I laughed, rolled my eyes. Dan slid closer and pressed his lips lightly against mine. This time I didn't resist as his fingers slid through my hair, down my neck, and in circles across my back, where I felt the warmth of his hand through my thin cardigan. I relaxed and let my hands roam over Dan's chest and back, then up to his head. I crushed handfuls of his thick black hair, messing then smoothing it, fixing it back behind his ears. I flashed him an appreciative smile and said, "Why can't you always be this cooperative?"

Dan leaned in to kiss me, but was interrupted by a knock at the door. He opened it, but no one was there, just an oversized brown wicker basket on the stoop, stuffed full of food. As he lifted it, a gust of wind blew into the room. The smoldering wood in the stove flared, finally setting the resistant log on fire.

We unpacked the carefully wrapped plates and bowls, and sat down to a green salad, garlic bread, and linguini tossed with grilled chicken, red peppers, zucchini, and olive oil. After dinner we curled into opposite corners of the loveseat, separated by a tray that held a carafe of coffee and two pieces of flourless chocolate cake that we were too full to touch.

"Time for our Jacuzzi," said Dan. "You still game?"

I went into the bathroom to undress and wrap myself in one of the thick white robes. Dan undressed in the room. When I came out he stood holding a leather toiletry bag.

"If you'll excuse me a moment," he said. "I've got to do my ablutions."

"What's that?"

"Wash up. Clean my teeth," he said.

Dammit. I hadn't brushed my teeth. Dan went into the bathroom and closed the door. Ablutions. What kind of word was that? When I had worked for him, whenever he wanted something inserted in a document, he'd ask me to "impregnate it into the text." The bookkeeper and I made all sorts of cracks about that behind his back. I held my hand in front of my mouth, huffed out and took a whiff. Garlic. I sipped some water, swished it around, and swallowed.

Outside, the cool night was roaring with sounds of the surf. We jogged across the wet lawn to a gate hidden behind the redwood grove. The Jacuzzi sat in the middle of a small deck, surrounded on three sides by a tall fence. The fourth side faced the churning ocean below—which was easier to hear than see through the clouds of steam. I was grateful for the cover it offered because I wasn't quite ready for Dan to see me naked. He slid off his robe and sat on the edge of the deck, dangling his feet into the hot water. I paused, calculating how I might get in without exposing myself.

I stole a shy look in Dan's direction. I had never seen him completely naked, either, and given how private he was with bathroom and grooming rituals, was surprised that he seemed so at ease. He was only a few inches taller than I was, lithe and compact, with a broad chest and muscular shoulders. I wanted to sidle up behind him and let my hands make their way to the dark hair on his chest, bury my face in his back, and ignore the voice in my head that was telling me to run for my life.

"Are you coming in?"

"In a second."

"What are you waiting for?"

"I feel modest," I said.

"Why? What don't you want me to see?"

"Oh, my lower belly. My freckles. Stretch marks on my ass—to name a few." I let out a sigh. "Will you just look away?"

He laughed and slid into the Jacuzzi, under the bubbles, where he remained long enough for me to slip in next to him.

We soaked with our heads tipped back, staring into a pearly sky that was broken only by the bony white glow of the hidden moon.

"I don't know if it gets any better than this," he said.

Hot air bubbles tickled my thighs, stomach, and breasts as they rose, fast and furious. After a few minutes the heat was so forceful, I wished I could somehow dive into the icy ocean to cool off.

"I can't stand it anymore—too hot." Dan said, raising himself out of the water to sit on the edge. Steam rose off his skin, floating into the muted moonlit vapors.

"I know," I moaned, staying put.

We sat quietly for a few minutes. I licked some salty water off my lips and realized it was sweat.

"Can you hand me the robe?" I said. "I want to get out too."

"Honey, are you really that shy about being naked in front of me?"

I didn't comment.

"I wish you could see yourself through my eyes," he said. "Come on, come here. I will look *only* at your eyes. I promise."

The tub was bubbling like a pot about to boil over. "Okay," I said. I took his hand and raised myself into the soothing chill of the night, collapsed onto the deck, and closed my eyes, keeping one foot dangling in hot water.

Dan stretched out and faced me, making a point of keeping his eyes pinned on mine while he stroked my cheek. I reached my hand around the back of his neck and pulled him closer until I could feel his warm breath on my mouth, his moist skin against mine. The sweet scent of him seeped into me, clouding my senses, until he pressed his mouth against mine. With one hand cradling my head, and one on my rear, Dan pulled me toward him. I felt him pressed hard against my thigh. Slowly he stroked my shivering body until my heart seemed to pound with the same rhythmic force as the rolling, crashing waves below. The excitement of being out there alone with him, wet and naked, hot, then cool, feeling the vibration of the surf beneath us, so dangerous and inviting—made me forget everything we had agreed upon earlier that evening.

The next morning, I felt a heavy sleepiness and dozed off as we drove.

"Hey, lover girl," said Dan, gently nudging me. "What time is Kevin bringing Rachel home?"

"Not until six." I yawned, stretched and smiled at him. "What did you have in mind?"

"We could take a short hike in the Marin headlands. It's got a great make-out spot."

"If we're going to Marin, I know an even better make-out spot," I said.

"Where?"

"Your place. I bet it even has a bed." I batted my eyelashes.

"This isn't the day for that," said Dan.

"Why's that?" I sat up straighter.

"The house—it's going through this deal. You'd love the spot on the headlands. Then we could grab a bite before I take you home."

Dan still lived in the house he had rented with his second wife in a sparsely populated section of Marin County, hidden between the coast and the stark, grassy hills. We would be passing right by the exit on our way south, so it made perfect sense to me to stop there.

"What do you mean, the house is going through a deal?"

"I'm having to do some tedious redecorating—it's a mess. It'd be better another time."

"I'm too wiped for a hike. And I don't care about messes."

"You want to go to a matinee? There's a multiplex in San Rafael."

Dan's responses were making me squirmy. Why the resistance? *Scoundrels are secretive.* My mind raced as I thought about all the reasons he had given me for always meeting me in Oakland or San Francisco, never at his place, even when Rachel was with her dad. Then I thought about his wife's voice, still on the answering machine, and it hit me. Jesus, I was such an idiot!

"Julia hasn't moved out yet, has she?"

"What? Of course she moved out!" Dan looked horrified. "Is that what you think? Is that what you *really* think?"

I gaped at him. Anything was possible.

"You don't believe me? I'll goddamn prove it to you—we can go to my house. I can't believe you'd *think* that."

We were both silent. I crossed my arms and leaned against the passenger door, as far away from Dan as I could get. His jaw was tense, and for the first time since I'd known him, he was exceeding the speed limit.

Dan slowed in front of a boxy redwood house, surrounded by overgrown grasses, a few random eucalyptus trees, and a deck. As we approached the driveway, he opened the automatic garage door and parked in the cool darkness. He waited for the garage door to shut completely before getting out of the car. Neither of us said a thing. I was starting to feel like an ass.

"Alright. Come on in and check it out for yourself," he snapped. "Be my guest."

"I don't need to check it out. I just don't understand why you never want me over." I slammed my door and followed him up some stairs.

Dan was right. His house was a mess. In the living room there were scraps of paper on the couch, the coffee table, end tables, and floor—each with some note scribbled on it, some even covered with a thick layer of dust. Ticker-tape parade meets windstorm—that's what it looked like. If he weren't standing next to me—walking, talking, clean, and clothed—I would be certain that a crazy person lived here. I looked at Dan, who was standing in the middle of it all, looking vindicated.

The kitchen opened onto the living area and was clean, but file folders and books were scattered across the dining room table, along with the familiar boxes of Reynolds wrap and some scattered rolls of duct tape.

"That's what I was telling you," Dan said, following my gaze.

Suddenly I realized that the front windows and the large sliding glass door to the deck were draped with foil, sealed along all sides with duct tape. At midday, the living room was dark.

"I'm covering the windows," he said.

"Why are you doing this?"

"It's just temporary. I need to block the light so I can work here."

If he was so loaded that he needed a money manager, I thought, why didn't he just shell out for some sun blocking mini-blinds?

"Go ahead, go room by room—see if you can find her." His arms were folded, his tone indignant. I was exhausted, embarrassed. I sat on a barstool. "I'm sorry. I'm just freaking out. This is all really new. Last night was great, it's just—I've got a lot on my mind."

He didn't say a word, but I could tell he was starting to soften.

I let out a long sigh. "Can I use your phone? I want to call for messages."

"Sure, honey. Sure," he said.

In the next minute, everything changed. Harry Paine's gravelly voice was on my machine, telling me, congratulations, I had the job.

"I got the job! I'm an operative!" I no longer cared if Dan was mad, hurt, or offended. I didn't care if he was a slob, crazy, or still living with his wife. I didn't even care any more about Mike, Milton, or murders. The important thing was, Rachel now had a working mother.

Chapter 7

April 1990

Rachel and I stood in the kitchen of our tiny apartment, the sunny one-bedroom that I had rented six months earlier. Scanning the food in the refrigerator, I tried to figure out what to make for dinner.

"I had a very exciting day at work, honey. Wanna know why?"

"Yep," said Rachel, now almost four.

"They gave me new responsibilities," I said.

That afternoon Harry had assigned me to interview a young man who had at one time worked for an insurance executive. The executive had been convicted of paying two homeless men to murder his wife. For a fee of five thousand dollars, they ran her off Skyline Boulevard and stabbed her to death. I needed to collect evidence that would humanize the husband for the penalty phase of his trial. According to his attorney, he was a generous employer, offering to pay for this young man to attend the local college.

I thought about calling to tell Dan about my assignment, but decided to wait. I was feeling conflicted about him lately. Almost every time we went out he had to do some sort of work with Richard, who lived on my side of the bay. That meant I saw Dan more often, but it also meant I saw more of Richard than I could take. The man gave me the creeps, and I was tired of having him interrupt my love life.

And that was the other thing that bothered me. I spent way too much time having steamy fantasies about Dan, which was out of character and confusing. Following Rachel's birth, sex had about the same appeal as housecleaning. I did it, but only because things got messy if I didn't. And, of course, things got messy anyway. But when I'd observed that Dan had strong, capable hands, I hadn't known the half of it. Dan was competent with nearly every part of his body, and was constantly introducing me to hidden but extremely responsive parts of the female body. Forget the obvious G-spot; we had A-spots, B-spots, F-spots, and my favorite, the XXX-marks-the-spot spot, which required a tricky three-point skin-to-digit contact that always left my heart thumping and legs trembling. His creativity, generosity, and wild abandon in the bedroom made me, in turn, eager to reciprocate. With Dan, I found myself wanting to do things that I'd only read about—and he was always happy to oblige. This was exciting, but it was also throwing my concentration off balance. In front of the mirror that morning I stared at my pink, whisker burned chin and—stopping just short of slapping my face—ordered myself to *snap out of it*. I imagined that getting my mind off sex was why things were taking a turn for the better at work.

"Rachel, do you know what a 'new responsibility' is?"

"Nope." She climbed onto a chair and fiddled with the crayons inside a plastic cup.

"A new responsibility is something you get to do because you learned a new skill—like how you tie your shoes by yourself now. My boss wants me to do things that are harder and more interesting."

Rachel looked at me and smiled. "You should be proud of yourself, Mommy."

I laughed at her remark because she was mimicking me. I had recently read *How to Talk So Children Will Listen, And Listen So Children Will Talk*. It noted the importance of saying, "You should be very proud of yourself," instead of, "I am proud of you." That way kids learned to look inward for validation.

"How about I give you a new responsibility tonight? You can grate the cheese for the macaroni."

Rachel jumped out of her chair and went to the kitchen drawer where we kept the grater. She was dressed in polka-dot leggings, a yellow shirt, and a fuzzy pink bathrobe that she insisted on wearing every day. I'd tried to get her to give up the robe in favor of a stylish jacket from Gap Kids, but getting my choice of an outfit on Rachel was like attempting to hold onto a wet bar of soap with slippery hands—except it also included high-pitched wailing. When I apologized to the director of the daycare for sending Rachel to school dressed as a frump, she looked at me patiently and said, "Relax. It's preschool."

But I was worried about her fitting in—or me fitting in. She was at her new expensive school, I was at my new low-paying job, and I had no clear indication that this was a recipe for our success—especially since my rent was due, I had to pay Rachel's school fees, and I was still responsible for my half of the debt that I'd inherited when Kevin and I split.

"Wait, Mommy. We forgot to change outfits." She jumped off the stool, and skipped into the bedroom. "Come on!"

Since we became "roommates," Rachel and I had established an after-work routine. I'd take off my work clothes and put on a bathrobe and she'd take off her bathrobe and put on one of my big tee shirts. She would "help" me make dinner by sitting at our wooden kitchen table to draw, sing, and chatter while I chopped and cooked.

After dinner I would soak her in a warm bath filled with bubbles, ducks, and her collection of decapitated Barbie dolls. We'd pass the time decorating one another with bubble beards, jewelry, and new hairstyles until she popped out of the water, moist and pink as a poached prawn. That was my cue to bundle her in a towel, carry her to our room, and bounce her onto her bed. Sometimes we'd stand up in front of the full-length mirror and recite the affirmations out of another self-help book I was reading. The list of affirmations was called "I Love Myself," and it put a positive spin on money (*I make money easily*), health (*I trust myself to take care of myself*), love (*I give and receive love easily*), and our favorite, the affirmation about body image. This one required that you stand in front of a mirror, naked or in your best underwear, take a good look at yourself, and announce, "I *love* my beautiful body."

That night I was excited. My cranky bosses finally trusted me enough to send me on an assignment that involved interpersonal skills, instead of sentencing me to the courthouse to dig through dreary public records—where I'd usually be bored silly, even when I went off the clock to sift through the infinite number of 1953 criminal records filed under the letters "Mc," trying to turn up something on the mysterious Milton Mc-*something*. I knew it was like trying to find a seed in a sand pile, but I had a romantic notion that I might someday be the one who helped uncover the truth about Jimmy's death, the one who would do something to "free Milton so he could find happiness." Now it was clear that my luck was changing, and my career was turning a corner.

My cheerful mood was rubbing off on Rachel. "Are you ready, Mommy?" She wiggled in front of the mirror in her Winnie-the-Pooh panties. I was wearing a pair of Dan's boxers and an old tee shirt.

"I'm ready!" I said.

"I *looooooooovvvve* my *beeeeee*-yuuuu-teeee-fulll   BODY!" we chimed together, running our hands from mid-calf, right up our sides, until our arms spread up and open into a "V" over our heads.

"Remember, honey," I said. "This is our little secret, okay?"

"Don't worry, Mom. I won't let anyone tease you."

Since I was in such a good mood, I read Rachel three bedtime stories. "Now go to sleep, honey." I tucked in her covers, kissed her goodnight, and crawled into my own bed, which was in the opposite corner of the room. I propped myself up to read *How to Get Out of Debt, Stay Out of Debt, and Live Prosperously,* the self-help book I needed most of all, though it also made me drowsy. After a few minutes, I felt Rachel's eyes on me. She was perched in her bed, reading my copy of *The Seven Habits of Highly Effective People,* making a point to turn a page each time she heard me turn one.

"Honey," I said. "Did you know that you're reading that book upside down?"

"It's okay, Mommy." She extended her open hand like a flipped starfish. "I don't know how to read."

Seconds later, the phone rang. I was surprised at how happy I felt to hear Kevin's voice. The one thing I missed most since we'd separated six months earlier was being able to share funny stories about Rachel. Dan always appreciated her antics, but Kevin and I knew her so well that we could acknowledge nuanced shifts in her behavior just by shooting one another a knowing glance. I was starting to tell him what she'd just said when he broke in to inform me I had to make other arrangements for her pick-up tomorrow. He planned to work late.

"No way, Kevin. You need to figure it out. I can't pick her up. I have to work too."

"Can't do it. Do you realize if I miss this gig, my whole job is at risk? I've got bills to pay. *Your* bills to pay."

Fury crackled through every cell in my body; it took all the restraint I had not to react to the taunt.

"Kevin, it's *your* night with her."

"I'd like to help," he said, dismissively. "I just can't."

"You'd like to *help*? Now being her dad is doing me some kind of favor?"

"Here we go," he said.

"I have an important assignment at work." I looked over at Rachel, who was lying flat on her back, immersed in an intense game of "Itsy Bitsy Spider."

"Get your boyfriend to pick her up," he said. "If he wants to steal my family, let him do some of the driving."

"Dammit, Kevin." I hung up on him. Now I'd have to rush through my first witness interview so I could make it back in time to pick up Rachel. The daycare charged a late fee of two dollars per minute. And I didn't want her waiting, anyway.

"Honey?" I whispered, realizing Rachel had heard my half of the conversation.

She didn't answer.

"Honey?" I slid out of bed to snuggle her and explain the change of plans, but she wouldn't open her eyes.

After a few minutes, I moved into the living room and dialed Dan.

"I wish I could," he said, "but I have a late meeting myself. I don't want to promise you something and not come through, especially where Rachel's concerned."

"It's fine, I'll just call—"

"Wait a minute," Dan perked up. "I've got it. Richard can pick her up, then I'll meet them—"

"Dan, are you insane?"

Dan was silent. I had never spoken to him that way. But what was he thinking, sending that crazy-eyed ex-Green Beret to fetch my little girl? I couldn't even imagine the horrific acts of torture, murder, and maybe even baby killing he had encountered during his stint in Vietnam. And he'd clearly never gotten over it. Where was Dan's common sense? This was the problem with dating a man who didn't have his own kids. Lately it had occurred to me that he might not be able to have kids, given his two childless marriages. Infertility was great for uninhibited sex, but I wondered if I could really have a future with a man who would never give me more children.

"Sorry, Dan. I know he's your friend and your partner."

"Mary, he's family. He's like a brother—"

"Rachel's only met him a few times," I said, cutting him off. "It would be too weird for her. Don't worry about it. Sorry I overreacted." Dan needed some help, I decided—some therapy about his dead brother. Then maybe he wouldn't be so fixated on finding so many odd sibling surrogates.

I hung up and called my mother in Southern California to grouse about Kevin, and then Dan.

"At least you're having great sex," said Mom.

"How do you know? Did Jamie tell you that?" What a big mouth. And she accused *me* of not minding my own business.

"Honey, I only bring it up because a shrink once gave me some expensive, life-altering advice. You get it for free because you're my daughter." She paused for effect. "Are you listening?"

"Yes, yes. Go on."

"When there's great sex, sometimes we work too hard to create a relationship that's worthy of it."

I was silent. I had to admit, given how I'd been feeling lately, this did warrant careful reflection. Dan was a lot older than me. He probably couldn't have children. What did he really know about raising kids, being a family? He already had two failed marriages. He'd stopped speaking to his own parents for six years. Maybe he was just supposed to be my rebound affair.

"But of course if that were true," rambled Mom, "I would have created a better relationship with my personal shower massager. Remember that thing? We had one installed right after they came out. I swear to God, that piece of hardware was better than most of the men—"

"Mother." I interrupted. "Please. Stop."

The next morning I was up before the alarm went off. The warm April day held a sweetness like the inside of an old lunchbox—a blend of banana, peanut butter and jelly, and sour milk that conjured up a nervousness that buzzed around me all day. I told myself to stay calm and focused. *Calm and focused.* That was my mantra.

I called the parents of one of Rachel's classmates. They offered to bring her home with them if I was late. I was free to focus on the task ahead: I would find evidence that would save a man's life. Even if the guy was a creep who paid poor people to do his bloody work, I accepted our role helping criminals avoid unnatural, premeditated, taxpayer-sponsored deaths that ended up, after all the appeals, costing more than a lifetime in prison.

My new employers had asked me to tell a little white lie to get the interview. Since budgets were tight when working for criminals, my bosses didn't want to pay me to drive all the way out to the interviewee's suburban house if he wasn't going to be there, and they didn't want me to make an appointment. We had a better chance of getting good information when we caught people off guard.

Okay, I told myself, a little fib to preserve a life? No problem. I had certainly mastered the art of lies by omission. My main concern with this assignment was that it always felt like my nose lit up when I told a blatant fabrication, and I was terrified of getting caught. But given the stakes, I was willing to do anything to prove myself.

I called the home of the young man I needed to interview, and when his mother answered, I asked if he was home.

"No, who's calling?" She sounded intrigued, making me think that girls didn't call the house often.

"Wendy. From school," I said, in a high-pitched voice. "Do you know what time he'll be home?"

I drove out to the beige ranch house at the hour his mom said he'd be there. She answered the door and I started to perspire. The mother was a short, cherubic woman with an open face. Her maternal looks immediately relaxed me. Handing her a business card that identified me as an operative with a private investigation firm, I got right to the point.

"I need to speak with your son."

She studied the card and frowned. Within seconds the light in her eyes dimmed and all kindness in her expression drained away.

"Did you call earlier and claim to be a classmate of his?"

My toes crunched; my nose got hot.

"Did you?"

I smiled sheepishly and started to explain.

The whites of her eyes swelled as her shrill voice cut through my explanation. "You *lied* to me?"

"I am so sorry, really. So sorry—"

"You liar! Get off my property—you *liar!*"

"It wasn't—I didn't—I'm not usually—" I started to back across her tidy green lawn, and with each step, my heels sank deeper into dirt.

"Do you want me to call the police?"

"Listen, please. I have my own child. I know how you must feel. You can stay in the room. Just let me have the interview."

My brazen persistence in the face of her rage surprised even me. But as scary as she was, I was even more terrified of leaving without the interview.

"GET OFF MY PROPERTY! I'M CALLING THE POLICE!"

I jumped in my tattered blue Toyota as she yelled at me from her cement walkway, shooing me away with such force that her loose upper arms swung like hammocks. *Oh no, she still has my card!* I pictured her running into her house to call my irritable new bosses.

They were going to kill me. Only six months into the job and it was already over. Oh God. I made the sign of the cross. Please don't call, *please don't call.* Maybe I should call them first?

I stopped at the nearest payphone. Simon answered, and by his terse tone, it was clear he'd already heard from the woman.

"But you told me to lie," I said.

"I told you to lie, not confess. I'll have to clean this mess up myself," he grumbled, slamming the phone down hard.

How would I ever be a private investigator? *Dammit.* Why did this have to happen? How was I going to pay rent?

"Shit. Shit. Shit. Shit. Shit." I hammered the heel of my hand on the steering wheel until it was sore and bruised. I looked at my watch. If there was any good news, it was that I still had plenty of time to get Rachel. Goddamn Kevin, I thought. This was the one night I could have used some time off.

It was hot and muggy when I arrived home with Rachel. The sunset, which should have looked beautiful, instead seemed streaked and messy. Rachel was perched on my hip. My overstuffed purse hung over my other shoulder, and I fumbled with the keys, desperate to get into the cool apartment. Rachel chattered about a new game she'd learned in circle time. Each kid got a chance to go in the middle and demonstrate a special dance move. I wasn't listening because I was sweaty, my feet hurt, and I was sure I was going to get fired from my job. I wanted to take a bath, an aspirin, a nap—anything, to relieve the dread.

"And this is what Henry did, Mommy, like this, *look*!" Rachel had her hands around my neck and was leaning backward, tilting my brittle body so I couldn't slip the key into the lock.

"Honey, stand up like a big girl." I tried to plunk her down on the porch.

"Noooo! I'm tired," she wailed, clinging tighter.

"Rachel, come on. Get down. I need to get us in the door."

"Henry made this face, Mommy. Look. *Look!*" Rachel put her hands on my face to pull my attention in her direction. She puffed out her cheeks, making it look like she was sucking on a baseball.

"Rachel, I need you down."

"*Nooooo*! I don't want to." She reattached herself to my neck with a tighter grip. My heavy shoulder bag slipped and I dropped the keys.

"*Dammit*, Rachel!"

I wrenched her off my side, hard, then felt her go limp—like a pacifist under arrest—slipping through my arms into a boneless puddle of flesh, landing right on top of the house keys.

"Rachel! Stand up right now. You're on the keys."

Tears blurred her red-rimmed eyes. She started whimpering. "You owe me a quarter." Rachel was referring to our deal where I paid her twenty-five cents for each profanity I let slip within earshot.

"I know." I adjusted my bag and took a deep breath. "I'll give it to you when we get inside."

"No."

I leaned over to pick up the keys. She pushed them aside.

"Rachel—*shit.*"

"You owe me for two bad words." She kicked the bracelet of keys toward my feet. "You *owe* me!"

Rachel's cheeks were flushed and droopy. Her tongue washed across her upper lip like a pink sponge, wiping away the fluid that trickled from her nose.

My heart raced and I knew I had to calm down, pull myself together. It felt as if Rachel and I were attached by an invisible cord that fed my emotions right into her. I walked through the front door and turned to Rachel, who remained pasted to the porch. "Come on, honey. Get in the house."

She glowered.

"Fine, stay there if you want." I dropped my bag and keys on the floor. The phone rang.

"It's my daddy." Rachel pounced through the door.

I picked it up.

"I wanted to answer. I WANTED TO ANSWER!" Rachel dropped back down into a heap and started to wail.

"Rachel. *Shhhh!*" Dan was on the line and I was trying to explain what happened. "I fucked up so badly today," I whispered.

"Oh, it's probably not as bad as you—"

"No. Dan, it's bad. I went to that interview I told you about, and this woman chased me off the property and—*wait*—Rachel is screaming… Rachel! *Shhhh*, just wait, just one minute—" I covered the mouthpiece. "Do you want a time out? Do you? You are going on a time out young lady."

"How 'bout I bring dinner over?" said Dan.

"NOOO TIME OUT," yelled Rachel.

"I'm bringing you dinner, honey."

"Mommeeeeeeeeeeeeee!" Rachel jumped up and grabbed at the phone.

"I'll be there in a bit." Dan hung up.

"Rachel!" I slammed down the phone. "You're on time out." I picked her up, stomped into our bedroom, and deposited her on the bed. "You are on time out for ten minutes, and I don't want to hear a peep from you."

I left Rachel sulking, and decided to take my own time out on the couch. But as soon as I sat down, I heard a *thunk* and then the *clop clop clop* of Rachel's feet as she slid off the bed and came marching back out to the living room.

"It's dinner time! I want to help make dinner!"

As she stood by the bedroom door demanding to make dinner, I hesitated. Our routine of dinner, baths, affirmations, and reading helped steady us as we navigated the rapid changes of the last six months. I knew she was trying to find her footing, but I didn't think I should let her skate on her time out, especially since I was so rattled.

"Let me help," she said.

I took a deep breath, trying to suck in my temper.

"Rachel, Dan's going to bring dinner. You're on a time out—"

"You owe me two quarters. You said you'd give them to me."

In a loud exhale, two streams of hot air burned down my nostrils. Rachel was never a cooperative prisoner, and I didn't want to fight her now. I wanted to figure out how to salvage my job and pay my bills, and the best way to create enough peace to think was to calm her down.

"Okay. How about a bath?" I walked past her to the bathroom. I dumped the mesh bag of toys into the tub, turned the water on full blast, and squirted in a long stream of Mr. Bubbles.

"No. Bath is after dinner, Mommy."

"Rachel, you're taking a bath."

"No."

"Yes." I yanked her in the bathroom and pulled off her bathrobe and Velcro tennis shoes. She wiggled away. "I mean it, Rachel. I want you in the bath." I pulled her back into the bathroom, undressed her, and lowered her into the water.

"Mommeeeeeeee! No, *no*, it's too cold, too cold," she squealed, curling her legs up and clinging to my arms like a kitten being forced into a pool. I stuck my hand in the water. It was tepid, but not cold. "Let go of me and get in this water now."

"*Noooo*, it's not bath time."

"Rachel!" I pushed her away with one hand, pulled the other hand back, and slapped her across the face.

I froze as I watched the outline of my four fingers deepen on her cheek, developing like a Polaroid photograph.

Rachel dropped into the water with a thud. She looked away from me, wide-eyed and silent, as the bath water lapped back and forth from the force of her fall. I shut off the faucet, knelt by the tub, and heard the raspy whisper of her shallow breathing. I had never hit her before, and neither of us knew what to do next. Eye contact seemed inappropriate, embarrassing. I wanted her to cry or scream, but she was silent. Her frozen, distant expression looked painted on, like she was trying to blend in with one of the bright plastic ducks that bobbed next to her in the dissolving bubbles.

"I told you to sit down so I could give you a bath." I scooped some water from a little bucket and poured it over her back and shoulders. She winced. When I looked down at her, she glanced away, her eyes filled with tears. I lifted her out of the water, set her on the bath mat, and wrapped a towel around her. She still didn't make a sound.

"You were supposed to be on a time out." I picked her up in a bundle. She felt smaller, withered from the bath. This would be the time when she'd usually run to the mirror and start singing, "I *looooooooovvvve* my *beeeeee-yuuuu-teeee-fulll* BODY!"

I pulled a flannel nightgown over her head and threaded her arms through the sleeves. She stared at the ceiling. Between pounding the steering wheel and slapping Rachel, my heart and hands felt like they had been tenderized with an ice pick.

I jumped when I heard the chime of the doorbell. "I'm going to let Dan in," I said. Rachel turned toward the wall, curling around her Wile E. Coyote doll.

Dan held out two bags of Chinese take-out. He whisked past me and set down the food, telling me that he thought my employers did a goddamn lousy job at training. Then he turned toward me and stopped mid-sentence.

"You look awful," he said. "You know, it's probably not that bad—besides, if they can't see what they've got with you, then they're idiots—"

"Dan," I whispered. "I hit Rachel."

He stood watching me.

"What?"

"I hit Rachel."

"You spanked her?"

I sank into the couch and whispered hoarsely, "No. I slapped her across the face." It felt like there was cotton filling my mouth. I wanted to explain but no sounds came. My eyes blurred; I had to concentrate to see.

"Kevin said he couldn't take her tonight and—"

"That's fine. Hell, let's take her every night."

Let's take her? I couldn't speak.

Dan looked toward the bedroom. "Is she okay? Where is she?" He gently squeezed my shoulder and then, making the soft clicking sound with his tongue, walked into the bedroom and closed the door.

Through the wall, the low vibration of Dan's baritone was interrupted by the lilt of Rachel's voice, liquid and tinkling, like wind chimes fluttering in the rain. I couldn't make out the words, but the voices—low and high—harmonized into a soothing, watery music. Hearing it gave me enough momentum to move into the kitchen. As I started arranging chicken fried rice and broccoli beef onto plates, I thought about what Dan had said. I had never wanted Rachel to feel bounced around like I had, like my siblings had; and yet that's what Kevin and I fought about—whose turn it was to be on parent duty. And look where it had led tonight. This had to change. Had Dan really meant it when he said, "Let's take her every night?" Were we in this together?

After I set the plates on the table, there was a *thunk* and a shuffling sound from the bedroom. The doorknob turned and Rachel stood in her pink nightgown, peeking at me from the doorway, swinging the squeaky door open and closed. Dan sat amidst the pile of stuffed animals populating her bed, watching.

"Mommy?" she said meekly.

I wiped my hands on a dishtowel, walked over, and picked her up.

"Yes, sweetie?"

Rachel looked down. All I could see of her eyes were the wet lashes clumped together like rows of soft black feathers.

"Mommy?" She played with my hair. "Can we be friends again?"

"Oh honey." I pulled her damp head into the crook of my neck. "I'm so sorry. Of course we can."

Dan looked steadily at the two of us, the slightest smile starting to brighten his deep blue eyes.

"Come on you two," I said. "We're having a family dinner."

Chapter 8

May 1990

Helium balloons in bright primary colors waved from tree branches against the backdrop of a clear blue sky. Dan and I were surrounded by Rachel's preschool classmates, their parents, family and friends, hot dogs, potato salad, and a big bakery clown cake. There was plenty of bird food for the squawking ducks that splashed in the gunky brown pond at Montclair Park. I also had silly string, squirt guns, and goody bags filled with Pez dispensers and Bazooka. But there was still no sign of the birthday girl.

"Where's Rachel?" I'd been asked twenty times.

"With her dad. I guess they're running a little late," I answered casually, even though I was sure they were in a car wreck, dead. The party had started at 11:00 a.m. It was already close to noon. Dan was mingling like a champ, organizing the kids into games of duck-duck-goose and red-light/green-light, and making sure the parents had cold drinks. After emptying another bag of ice into the cooler, he approached, wrapped an arm around my shoulder and whispered, "Relax, you're scaring people. And you have to go talk to your father."

I arranged my mouth into a crisp smile. This was the first time I'd seen my dad since we'd had words over my default on his loan. I had begun making regular payments to him, but they barely covered the interest. I was sure he was still disappointed. And I was still hurt about his remarks.

"He didn't mean what he said," said Dan. "He was just worried about you. He drove all the way up here, just go talk to him."

My dad was standing with Jamie and a few parents of the young invitees. His new wife was relaxing on a blanket under a tree with my mother and her doting husband, chatting amicably. Always well dressed and groomed, Dad looked young and fit for a man in his sixties, his trimmed brown beard hiding any possible signs of wrinkling underneath.

I moved beside Jamie, who caught my eye with a mischievous expression that set off an internal alarm. Dad was fully engaged, recounting an experience he'd had trying to get a therapeutic massage for his bad back in San Francisco at a place that offered, he said gregariously, "many, many, *many* more services."

There was a freeze-dried look of horror on the face of a petite mother in a tennis skirt and lots of gold jewelry. I reached behind Jamie and pinched her. She smiled sweetly toward Dad, ignoring me.

"Have you heard of what they call, a 'Happy Ending'?" said Dad. "The little Oriental gal says to me, *You want Happy Ending? You want Happy Ending?* And I say, sure, who the hell doesn't want a happy ending? Of course I had no idea what I'd just ordered."

The three men laughed incredulously, but the tennis outfit turned away, her eyes panning the park, I assumed, for a safe spot to relocate. Despite the mild weather, I felt myself begin to perspire. There was nothing I wanted to say that would help Dad and me patch things up. As I excused myself, I heard Jamie patiently explaining to Dad why the term "Oriental" was racist and unacceptable, as if that was the only offensive nugget in the story.

Dammit, where are they?

Glancing up the hill, I saw Kevin's car approaching. Ignoring the manicured pathway, I raced up a tangled ivy embankment, threw open the passenger door, and unbuckled Rachel. Pulling her out with one arm, I shoved the middle finger of my free hand in Kevin's face, shaking it centimeters from his chin and nose.

I felt a firm hand on my back. "Hey Kevin," Dan said.

I turned around, cringing slightly at Dan's outfit: a tennis shirt, blue shorts, and bright white sports socks pulled all the way up to his knees. Why would someone with such great legs do that to himself? "Men don't wear knee socks unless they are hidden under pants," I'd told him when he arrived at the park. I'd convinced him to push the socks down into a more casual bunched-around-the-ankle look. But he must have pulled them back up under his knees when I wasn't looking.

"Can't anyone do anything I ask?" I growled at Dan, who lingered by Kevin. I lasered Dan a look, indicating I wanted him to follow me. He patted me on my fanny, said he'd be down in a minute. As I stomped down the path carrying Rachel, she grabbed my face, stared right into my eyes, and said, "Why're you mad, Mommy?"

"I'm not mad, honey." I kissed her, smiled, and held her closely against me so I could breathe in the familiar sweetness of her skin. She looked so serious that I forced myself to loosen my grip and relax. I adjusted her floppy sunhat and held her above my head, letting the breeze fill her flowery party dress like a sail as she swirled to the ground. Once down, she ran toward the waddling ducks and the toddlers who were feeding them. A gust of wind stirred the rotting scent of old eggs, either from the duck pond or one of the guest's training pants, but everyone cheerfully ignored the stink.

I passed a rowdy group of picnickers by the baseball diamond. A tall, pale woman clad entirely in hot pink was waving wildly.

"Hey babe! I know you!" she sang.

It was a teller from the local Wells Fargo. I should have known by her wiry shape and signature color. Nails, lipstick, hat, socks, shoes—all hot pink. She looked like a cartoon.

"Hey!" I smiled, waved. "Haven't seen you at the bank."

"That your new guy?" she yelled, motioning up the hill.

I smiled and kept walking, pointing toward the group of toddlers I wanted to reach.

Dan and Kevin remained by the car. As always, it looked like Dan was doing a lot of the talking, but then I noticed Kevin gesturing as he emphasized his words. Dan was a big talker, but he was also a careful listener. He worked hard to understand what someone was trying to tell him and often pulled out the capped pen and paper he kept in his pocket to make notes about someone's concerns, something they might like, or something they reminded him to do. He and Kevin remained deep in conversation as we tossed water balloons, taped the cottontail on the rabbit, and sang happy birthday. After I scooped out the last piece of gooey cake and placed it on a Tweety Bird party plate, I looked toward Dan and Kevin. They were hugging.

Jesus, I thought. That jerk brings Rachel to her own birthday party an hour-and-a-half late and now Dan is standing there in his knee socks hugging him.

I walked to Jamie, handed her some cake, and pointed up the hill. "Watch Rachel, would you? Curiosity is eating me alive."

By the time I made it to Dan, Kevin was in his car, pulling away from the curb and waving goodbye.

"Why are you up here hugging my ex?" I asked, suspicious.

Dan put his arm around me and asked if I was feeling better. Then he started impersonating my earlier red-faced fury by shoving his middle finger in the center of my face, the way I had with Kevin. He found his imitation very funny; I didn't laugh.

"Stop it, those parents will see," I said.

Dan pulled back, made a note, and before he could tuck it into his pocket, I snatched it.

"Hey!" he said.

The note had the date, "May 14, 1990," next to the words, "Mary is unusually cranky. Check her cycle." Below that there was another scribble that said, "Ask Richard to see reconciled bank statements. Originals, not copies." My first thought was that it was odd for someone to write reminder notes out in complete sentences. Usually a word or two would trigger the idea.

I frowned at Dan. "You're writing about me? I'm unusually cranky?"

Dan sighed. "Give it back, please."

"You track my menstruation cycle?"

"I chart it out. Yes. You may not realize it, but you get testy."

I took a step back and stared at him.

"Hey, I wouldn't chart it if you would," he said. "You know, you are a little over-the-top anxious today. And I've noticed coffee makes it worse."

"Really? And you think there's no other good reason for my anxiety? Do you realize what a sexist, dismissive idea that is? If there's nothing to be upset about, what the hell was that big bonding session with Kevin?"

"I've been way overdue to have a conversation with Kevin about my role in the break-up. I've made a lot of notes, given it a lot of thought. It had to happen." Dan said he had assured Kevin that he didn't want to create any unnecessary tension in our family. He knew things between us had happened quickly, but Kevin must have known that sooner or later I'd wind up with someone else.

"I said that at least with me, he'd know who would be influencing his daughter's life, that I would never try to take his place with Rachel. I even said I'd always try to promote him to Rachel, speak highly of him, and treat him with respect." Dan paused, grabbing my hand. "I also asked him if he'd be kind enough not to make it difficult for Rachel by badmouthing you or me, or by directly or indirectly being disrespectful."

"Like bringing her to her birthday party an hour-and-a-half after it starts?"

"Right."

"And he took all this well?"

"Yes."

"You're so mature."

"And patient, too. Don't leave that out," he winked.

We held hands as we walked back to the birthday party. My tension almost evaporated—at least until I heard Dan bragging about our relationship to Jamie, my mother, and the parents of Rachel's best friend.

"Aren't you two the lovebirds," said Mom, clapping her hands together.

"That's an understatement," said Dan, approaching the group as I went to tidy up the picnic table. "Because you know what I've determined?"

They looked politely attentive.

"Our love," he said, "is the emotional equivalent of a perpetual motion machine that sparks energy and excitement back and forth until it reaches explosive—*explosive*—levels."

Jamie caught my eye, raised a brow, then whispered something to my mother. They both suppressed giggles. I sprinted over, interrupting his speech.

"Hey, how about some help folding up blankets and chairs?"

Everyone eagerly pitched in.

This wasn't the first time Dan had trotted out this speech about our deep love. At a recent dinner party with his friends I'd wanted to kick him under the table. I appreciated the enthusiasm, but as he spoke, I worried that someone might get an urge to stuff his mouth with a dinner roll, just to shut him up.

"Not everyone is excited about 'our love,'" I said, "especially if theirs is in the crapper."

"Are you kidding?" He was genuinely surprised. "I think it inspires them."

"That's right," hollered Mom, overhearing us. "We're all inspired that you found a way to calm Mary down. She can be edgy, you know."

Dan beamed and nodded his head vigorously. "*Please!* Don't say anything that will set her off, I've done all I can for today."

Dan squeezed me close; I grimaced.

After we carried the last load to our cars, Dan yelled, "Hey, look who's here!"

Richard headed down the pathway carrying a gigantic gift-wrapped box and a dozen colorful balloons. Lately he seemed to be making a greater effort at bonding, but it was having little effect. He was dressed in a tee shirt and army fatigues. This annoyed me, especially after that terse remark he'd made to me the first night at dinner, about not wanting any reminders of the war.

"Where's the birthday girl?" he said in his irritating, nasal voice.

Rachel ran up to him, Dan by her side.

Richard aimed a wan smile toward me and then turned his attention back to Dan and Rachel. They tied a yellow balloon to her wrist and the rest of the bouquet to our cooler. We watched her rip the bright red paper off her gift. It was a deluxe home Karaoke machine, complete with cassette tapes and two microphones. Dan was explaining what that was to Rachel, while Richard fumbled for his cigarettes.

"Richard, would you mind not smoking around Rachel?" I said. "She's allergic."

"Should be okay, we're outside." Richard lit his cigarette, tossing the match onto the grass.

I glared at Dan. "Will you pack up the rest of the gifts in your car? I'll meet you back at my place." I picked Rachel up and perched her on my hip.

"Hey, stay a sec," said Richard. "You can check out my new car. Got a Jag."

"You what?" Dan looked floored.

I glanced to the street and, sure enough, there was a shiny new silver Jaguar parked along the curb.

"Come on, I'll show you," said Richard.

"Next time," I said. "Thanks for the gift for Rachel. Say thank you, honey."

"Thanks Richard!" Rachel beamed.

Thanks asshole.

As I was about to start the car, a lurid pink shadow filled the side window. Jerking my head around, I saw the Wells Fargo teller tapping her hot pink fingernails on the glass. I lowered the window.

"Sorry babe, didn't mean to startle you." She was out of breath. "I usually mind my business, but that man?" She motioned to where Dan and Richard spoke. "I'll swear on a stack of bibles I never said this, but that man over there? He's no good."

"Dan?"

"Dan? No honey, the one in the fatigues. Richard. Richard Harding."

"You know him?"

"Dated him, but worse than that—I handled his banking." She flashed Rachel a sugary smile. "It didn't come from me, but watch out. He's a gambler. And a liar, too. Okay?" Tapping her hands on her puckered lips twice, she said, "Kiss, kiss," and left.

An hour later, Dan arrived at my apartment. When I opened the door, he bypassed me and headed straight to Rachel, who was sitting on the rug, arranging her new birthday blocks around a stuffed white rabbit named Lover Bunny.

"How's my birthday girl?" said Dan.

It used to confuse me when, upon arrival, Dan always greeted or focused on Rachel before me. "Hey," I'd said. "Who are you dating—me or the cute little blond?" Dan explained that he didn't want Rachel to see him as someone who took her mother's attention away from her. He wanted to be someone who added something to Rachel's life.

"Richard is a bad man," said Rachel, looking worried. "The pink lady said to watch out."

"What?" Dan looked up at me, puzzled.

I told Dan what had happened, and he started to laugh.

"Rachel, Richard is not a bad man," said Dan, still chuckling. "And I know he likes to play a little poker. Hell, he and Jimmy had a running game back in the day."

"Maybe he won the car in a poker game," I said.

"Mary, he leased the car. Put a few grand down, and leased it. He has a showy side, apparently. But he's not a high stakes player. And, Ms. Investigator, consider the source. Do you know who that lady-in-pink is?"

"You can't meet her and not know her. She's not exactly wallpaper," I said. "What do you know about her?"

"Richard dated her. She's a nut—practically forced herself on him. In fact, he saw her at the park and had to hightail it to the men's room and hide. Afraid she'd stalk him."

"Stalk him?" Dan said he didn't know the entire story, but this woman's erratic temper was what had prompted Richard to want to move their accounts to another bank.

"Richard banks at my Wells Fargo?"

"He's got our business account there. But he's making some changes."

That's probably why Dan had made that note to ask for the bank statements, I thought. Originals, not copies.

Dan turned toward Rachel. "Meanwhile that bad pink lady isn't allowed to touch our money. She'd want to dip it into pink dye, turn it pink like everything else in her life. Her clothes, her house, her poodle."

"Her pee-pee," Rachel giggled.

"Whoa now. That's taking it too far," laughed Dan, who was downright prudish when it came to potty humor.

I enjoyed the sight of Rachel and Dan chattering and playing on the rug as I tidied the house. Fiddling with the television, I noticed it wasn't getting a picture.

"Shoot," I said, "It looks like the TV's busted."

Dan and Rachel were busy playing. I was worried about missing the next episode of David Lynch's creepy new serial, *Twin Peaks,* the following night.

"Looks like we're going to have to watch it at your house," I flopped on the floor next to Dan.

"Can't do that," he said, not looking up.

"Sure we can. Rachel is with Kevin tomorrow, remember?"

"It's not that, it's this other thing."

Rachel turned her big eyes onto us. Her finely tuned tension meter was picking up static.

"What thing?"

"Why don't you see about getting the TV fixed?" he said.

"Objection, the witness is non-responsive," I said. "What's this *thing* you speak of?"

"It's not because I'm hiding a wife there." Dan shot me a sharp look. "It's this other deal. We have to stay away from my house for a while. It might be better to fix your TV."

I was learning that whenever Dan used the word "thing" or "deal" there was a lot more to the story. But when I pressed for information, the longwinded and intricately complicated explanations of *things* and *deals* always wore me down. Last time I had asked, it was related to the "trust thing" he had with Richard. After forty-five minutes of tedious details about tax law, I still didn't understand. Sometimes it was easier not to ask.

"Dan, fixing the TV is not an option right now." I didn't mention how strapped I was for cash, because I didn't want Dan to offer a financial rescue. This time I was succeeding on my own. Never again would I hitch my wagon to someone else's star, as I had with Kevin. Nor would I borrow money from loved ones, as I had from Dad. I'd learned both those lessons the hard way.

Besides, except for the wad of cash Dan carried in his pocket and a lot of talk, I didn't see any real evidence that he had piles of money to spare. He rented his house, drove an old car, and complained about the cost of wine by the glass. When I made some extracurricular inquiries while searching public records for Paine & Simon, I'd even learned that he'd never owned property in any of the Bay Area counties. In the meantime, he served up generous portions of romance, kindness, loyalty, and a belief in my abilities. I needed that as much as anything. That, and an operating television.

"So what do you suggest?" I asked. "See if *you* can get a clear picture."

Rachel whined and rubbed her eyes. I put her into a bubble bath to soak off the leftover grime from the party. Later, she nodded off, snoring lightly under the down comforter as I read *Green Eggs and Ham*. I leaned over and kissed her cheeks, rosy and warm from too much sun, thinking how much happier she seemed, especially since I'd found a more stable job.

After the interview debacle, Harry had talked Simon into giving me another chance. But the problem was, they really didn't offer enough hours for me to make ends meet. Harry pulled me aside and told me about another possible job opportunity at a fire investigation firm that often hired him to do background checks. They needed someone to do research, marketing, and assist the arson investigators with reports. Harry mentioned this to me in confidence, informing me that his partnership with Simon wasn't going to last, and when he went out on his own, neither of them would be able to afford me.

"This job ought to land you on your feet for now," he'd said. "They've got the whole benefit package, too. They're expecting your call." He handed me a business card.

"Wow," I'd said. "I don't know how to thank you."

"Don't mention it. Really." Harry smiled. "Especially to Simon."

We shook hands, and off I went. My new job had structure, potential growth, a decent salary, and a bonus plan. I had my own office, and a boss who focused on training. And the company's ranking as the premier fire investigation firm in the Bay Area meant there was always something interesting for me to do, from visiting fire scenes to setting up test burns. Everything in life had seemed to operate more smoothly after that.

Except for the TV.

When I returned to the living room, Dan was sitting on the floor with the TV, studying it from various angles.

"I'm sure it needs a picture tube," I said. Even if I could afford it, I knew I couldn't get it fixed fast enough for tomorrow night. "I don't see why we just can't go to your house, Dan."

"I told you," he said. "You can't believe the crap I'm dealing with. I was named in another damn lawsuit because my client committed suicide and now they need another deep pocket. I want to feel sorry for him, but he left me in this mess."

Dan explained that some greedy bastards were after him—trying round the clock to catch him so that they could serve him with the lawsuit papers.

"Sooner or later they're going to find you home, Dan. Why not just deal with it."

"I'm not going to sit around holding a Sunday open house for process servers for something I shouldn't even be involved in. It's just another goddamn false accusation. I won't do it." Dan jumped up, startling me. "I tried to reason with these people, sit down and sort it out, but they only care about the dough. I've had to organize my entire life around a series of false accusations, and I'm sick of it."

Dan's cheeks were flushed, his normally flawless hair loose and messy. Aside from the panicked flash in his blue eyes, I liked this look: it was wild, sexy. Until he revealed why he'd used his lifetime supply of Reynolds Wrap to cover all of his windows.

"You said it was to block out glare from the sun."

"What? No I didn't," he said. "It was to make sure no light could be seen inside or out. I've got to make damn sure anyone looking for me will think I'm gone. And after all the precautions I've taken I'm not taking any chances by having you come over to watch TV."

I stared at him, mute.

"Well say something," he said.

"You covered *all* your windows with tin foil?" I felt suddenly stupid, duped. "To hide from servers?"

"That's right. I refuse to spend one more second defending myself over things I didn't do. First there was the Missouri deal, then the tax thing, now another frivolous lawsuit?" Dan launched into another rant about how impossible it was for an attorney who was not with a big firm to protect himself from litigious clients when the cost of liability insurance was prohibitive and spurious lawsuits forced him to spend his time defending himself so that he couldn't even find time to bill hours. There was no point in even practicing law anymore, he said, and that's why he was going to turn all his attention to developing this deal with Richard, which would make him enough money so that he could retire.

"And don't even get me started on the IRS," he railed, by now sweating from the pacing. "They've got me tied up with ridiculous allegations about taxes I couldn't in a million years owe."

"Whoa, whoa—what?"

"It's this other deal—a long story," he said.

I already felt as if I'd had a lethal injection of chaotic financial information. I was also stunned to realize that I—who had tested high in investigative skills—had overlooked the glaring red flag of tin-foiled windows. Why did he have to make his life so complicated? And by extension, make my life so complicated? But truthfully, I was tired and didn't want to think about it. Instead, I chose to focus on the small picture. Literally.

"What are we going to do about the TV?" I sounded shriller than I'd intended.

Dan looked at me, arms crossed.

"We can't go to your tin foiled house, there's no time to get someone to fix it, you don't know how to fix it yourself. Just what do you want to do? What?"

He was quiet. I knew he was trying to think of a strategy, but his speechless patience made things worse. I could hear my heart thumping in the silence.

"Who the hell am I to you anyway?" I screeched. "You're here all the time. You tell me you love me but you won't let me go to your house for a TV show I really want to see? We're acting like a little family but then you pick up and go back to your hideaway. I'm sick of not having a normal family. Dan, Rachel's getting attached to you. She needs a house, a mother and father. She needs stability!"

"What do you want from me?"

"We've been going out over eight months. What do *you* want from *me*? For godsakes," I shouted, whacking his shoulder, "do you ever plan to marry me?"

Dan looked like he'd been punched. "Marry you?"

I flopped down on the couch with my arms across my chest and looked out the window. We were both quiet. The moisture from my palms seeped into my shirt.

"Are you proposing to me?" he said. "By God, you are proposing to me, aren't you?"

I scowled. I was in no mood to be teased.

"I've always wanted someone to propose to me." He sat down next to me and took my squishy hand. Dan was not smiling but he looked amused. "I just think you should ask nicer."

I pushed his arm and he grabbed me, pinned me gently on the sofa, and looked into my eyes. His soft kisses calmed me. I didn't want to think about the process servers or the Reynolds Wrap or the IRS. All I wanted was to have a family—safe and loving, healthy and monogamous—under the roof of a house with clear glass windows.

By the time we rolled off the couch, giddy and disheveled, we'd replaced the tense subjects of tin foil and televisions with talk about our future.

"But I'm not changing my name to Murphy," I told him. I had never really liked his last name, not to mention that his mother and first wife were already named Mary Murphy.

"Right. It's probably bad luck when the first wife has the same name as the third wife," he said.

"I'm not going to be your 'third wife,' buster. I'm going to be your *last* wife," I said, pulling him closer to me.

"We should both start with a new name," said Dan, perking up. "I always thought that would be a good idea—the most fair, non-sexist way."

We finally settled on taking Dan's middle name, Patrick. It was snappy and Irish. But then we decided to lop off the "k" like the actor, Jason Patric. Dan thought it looked cool, even though it made the name sound French.

"I can hardly wait to tell everyone about the night you first popped the question," said Dan, "with those sharp teeth and foaming mouth—squeezing my neck and shaking me until I finally screamed *YES! YES!* I'll marry you."

"Just so you know," I pulled back. "If you're not up for this—I mean if you're not really, really sure—then I don't want to do it. Last week when I told Rachel my dad had been married three times, do you know what she said?"

"Tell me."

"'That's silly, Mommy. I'm only getting married twice.'"

"I was kidding, honey." He stroked my cheek. "I hate when couples make jokes at each other's expense. Let's always treat each other with the most tender love and respect. When we make that commitment—until death do we part—that's the only way either of us is getting out of this relationship."

Chapter 9

July 1990

"When we get married, let's do it outside when the light is soft and pink like this," I said to Dan.

"Somehow I can't see you up that early—even for our wedding," he said.

It was the first weekend in July, and we were driving down Highway 5 toward Los Angeles, headed to my brother Hank's wedding. We'd left home when it was still dark, but now the rising summer sun cast rosy shadows across the gas stations and fast food malls that dotted the endless stretch of road.

"I was thinking dusk, not dawn." I poured a cup of hot coffee from the thermos.

"Go easy on that stuff, honey. We don't need you cranky," said Dan.

"Just give me my coffee, and no one gets hurt," I said, swallowing a mouthful of the creamy dark roast.

Even though we hadn't made it official, we enjoyed referring to our wedding. We'd agreed that we would move in together sometime within the year, and that marriage would follow, but not until I promised to perform a more tender and romantic version of my proposal.

"Did you tell your mom?"

My eyebrows shot up. "Don't you think we should wait awhile?"

"There are a couple of ways to approach these things." Dan revved up for what I now recognized as one of his philosophical discourses on human communication and behavior. I had accepted the fact that he was incapable of keeping his comments brief. If ever I asked him to stick to the headlines, he explained it was impossible and that we'd have to discuss the matter—whatever it was—when we had more time. Since Dan lived outside my area code, his loquaciousness made for some hefty phone bills. But we were on a road trip, staring straight into hours of flat farmland and freeway underneath a dull blue sky. With Rachel dozing in the back, I settled into the cupped warmth of his leather seats, sipped my coffee, and let him talk.

"Sometimes it's best to take a live lobster and drop it into boiling water, so it doesn't know what hit it. Other times you want to lift it gently, ease it into a pot of tepid water, and turn up the heat slowly—so by the time it starts to feel uncomfortable, it's already half cooked. Either way, they're goners; they have no choice but to accept their fate."

I was of the mind that we should go for the gradual approach. I knew my family was still getting used to the idea that Kevin and I were no longer a couple. I wanted to give them a chance to get to know and love Dan, to see that I had finally found someone solid, someone with whom I could find true commitment, build a family. And by the eager expression Dan wore whenever he met one of my relatives, I knew he wanted the approval of my family, too. Given his tension with his own parents, he seemed excited about finding an extended family with mine.

"I'd love to tell Grandma Hazel I've finally got a live lobster cooking, but she's not even going to be there. Plus, we don't want to steal Hank and Paula's spotlight. It's their wedding."

"You sure?"

"Our day will come. Let's hold off any announcements. And I don't want to freak out Grandma Mary. She loved Kevin. She always hoped he and I would have a real wedding some day."

"I can't believe she agreed to that wedding sham—and that she still wanted you to be with him."

Five years earlier, Kevin and I had held a fake wedding to placate Grandma Mary. After I got pregnant, Grandma Mary was worried about what she would tell her old friends and relatives on the East Coast if a baby arrived before a wedding announcement. So on a sunny Saturday morning during my first trimester, my mother went to the trouble of staging a fake wedding photo opportunity and party at a grassy park above the cliffs of the Pacific Ocean in San Diego. I dressed in a lacy white prom dress that made me look like an exploding wad of gauze, and Kevin wore a conservative blue suit. We posed together and with the miscellaneous family members we rounded up for the ruse. The resulting photographs solved Grandma's dilemma, so she happily participated in the charade. But it was something we had to keep secret from my devout Grandma Hazel, who would have gone apoplectic at the thought of simulating a holy sacrament.

"Well," said Dan, "Your Grandma Mary's going to love me."

"Why's that?"

"Because I'm the guy who's going to make an honest woman out of you, and make sure your life is exciting."

"I'm having second thoughts about 'Patric' as a last name. Maybe we should keep the 'k'? Otherwise I'll be back having to spell my name for people."

"Well, do you want it to be convenient?" asked Dan, tweaking my side, "or unique?"

"Good point," I said.

"Mary and Dan Patric," he said, reaching to hold my hand. "I like it."

Last time I'd had a fake wedding and kept my real name. This time I'd get a real wedding, with a fake name.

We pulled into the parking lot of the Ventura motel.

"There's Aunt Jamie!" squealed Rachel, wriggling in her car seat, trying to unlatch the belts.

I stepped into the white glare of the afternoon sun and greeted my sister, who was jogging toward the car. She wore an orange cotton dress and looked much more girly than usual. "Is everyone here already?"

"The whole freak show," she said, waving to Dan. "And don't be pissed."

"Why?"

"I told mom that you and Dan were pretty serious," she said, cheerfully. "That you guys might have the next family wedding."

"Dammit Jamie," I growled. "You want me to start mouthing off about your love life?" I looked around. "Where is Alison, anyway?"

"At home. Don't ask me about it."

"Jamie, what aren't you telling me?"

Jamie gave me a sly Mona Lisa smile. She lifted Rachel into her arms and moved toward the herd of relatives who were chattering and laughing in the sunshine.

"I'll check us in," Dan said. "I need to see if there are any messages from Richard."

"You have to do that this second?" I said.

"Are you nervous about seeing your dad, honey?" Dan held my shoulders, gave me a serious look. "You want me to speak with him? Tell him what an amazing job you are doing, clearing the debt?"

"God, no, Dan," I said, aghast. As much as I wished Dan could wave some magic wand to ease my rift with my father, Dad would find public relations from a new lover strange and annoying. "I just don't see why you have to rush into work stuff."

"It's the damndest thing—I can't seem to catch Richard at home."

Dan had been distracted about Richard on our drive down. He had even stopped to call him from a pay phone.

"Maybe the pink lady had him killed."

"Can we not make jokes right now?" Dan sounded genuinely worried. "I'll be back in a second."

I joined the family under the palms beside the mint-green pool. My mom, step-dad, and father were all there, as was my dad's second wife. His third and current wife, sporting a bright green t-shirt that said, "My next husband will be normal," was being photographed between my mother and ex-stepmother, both pointing to the shirt and giggling. Hank and his fiancé Paula were sitting with Grandma Mary under striped umbrellas, with the rest of the family milling close at hand. Jamie brushed by me and whispered, "Grandma keeps asking about Kevin."

"Hi Gram," I said, leaning over to kiss her.

She grabbed my hand and said, "Can't you fix things with Kevin, Mary?"

Before I could respond, Dan approached and in his best stage voice said, "Is this the beautiful, the elegant, the famous Grandma Mary, who I've heard so much about?" He took Grandma's hand in both of his, and she gave him a half-hearted smile.

"Is this the famous Dan?" cooed Aunt Maggie, as she slid her hand around my waist and kissed me. "Mary, introduce us to Dan."

"Gram, Aunt Maggie, this is Dan." I smiled.

"Hi Aunt Maggie," said Dan, shaking her hand.

"Oh, call me Maggie."

My mother waved at us from her huddle with dad's other wives. She looked elegant. Mom had a heart-shaped face, large breasts, and a soft cushiony lap that Rachel sought out whenever she was in the mood to cuddle. The laugh-lines around her hazel eyes made her appear perpetually amused. "Come here, Mary," she called.

As I left to join her, Dan turned back to Grandma Mary and Aunt Maggie. "Have you beautiful women heard the cat-on-the-roof joke?"

Ah geez. Not that old joke Dan.

My toes crunched hard inside my shoes. While Mom listed our wedding responsibilities, I tried to keep an eye on Dan, whose arms waved as he worked his little audience. My aunt smiled warmly at him, but Grandma's blue eyes looked like two bright but distant stars. Halfway through his performance, Dan realized this was the wrong joke to tell, given that the punch line included someone's old, dead mother. I saw a wave of anxiety creep across his face, and he began fidgeting like someone trying to keep his balance on shifting sand. Desperate to rescue him, I excused myself from the mothers and rejoined him, teasing, "I was just telling Dan it might be time to retire some of his material. What do you think, Gram?"

"No, that was a good one," said Aunt Maggie, smiling with warm encouragement. "Funny!"

"Thanks Aunt Maggie," said Dan.

"Call me Maggie," she said, gently squeezing Dan's shoulder. "Otherwise people might think I'm old enough to be your aunt. I mean, we're just about the same age, right? You might even have a few friends I could meet, hey?"

An avid runner, Aunt Maggie was a more youthful, hard bodied, thinner version of my mother. Divorced and a notorious flirt, she had a knack for putting people at ease.

"How's the attorney business?" interrupted my dad, shaking Dan's hand vigorously, and then planting a kiss on the side of my mouth.

"Not practicing too much law these days," said Dan. "But what about Mary? How about her big job with the fire investigators?"

"Dan." As much as I loved it in private, I didn't want Dan launching into a cheerleading session about my career in front of my family.

Dad perked up. "Perfect place for her. My guess is she's paying off my karmic debt. Did she tell you my brothers and I used to set brush fires when we were kids? We'd set them, call the fire department, then offer to help put them out with brooms."

"Psychiatry was the right career choice for you, Phil," said Dan, laughing. "Otherwise I could've made a fortune representing you boys."

"You still representing that crook—Jackie or Johnny—what's his name?" asked Dad, who had visited me many times when I worked with Dan and Johnny Curtain. "That guy who bilked the investors?"

"No, I've got another deal going now, Phil. Not practicing much law—"

My brother joined us. Hank had been quite a heartthrob in high school— tall, athletic, and dark-haired, he was a younger version of my father. It hadn't been unusual for Jamie or me to catch an occasional friend sneaking from our room into his during some of the rowdier high school slumber parties held when our parents were out of town.

"Not practicing law? What are you doing, then?" said Hank, who had clearly been eavesdropping.

"What am I doing? What are you doing, Hank? Taking the big step, huh? Congratulations. How's it feel?" Dan clapped Hank on his back.

"Expensive," laughed Hank. "But I guess you know that. Been around this block a few times, haven't you?"

I shot my brother a sharp look. I was hot and tired and wanted to get out of the suffocating smog and check into the motel room, to rest and hide for a few minutes.

"Mama! Dan! Look!" squealed Rachel, as Jamie twirled her around like an airplane. I leaned into Dan, then felt him suddenly stiffen.

"I'll be damned," he muttered. Dan excused himself, and strolled over to shake hands with a newly arrived guest, the husband of my mother's closest friend from high school. I assumed Walter, a successful attorney in San Francisco, knew Dan from their work in the legal community. But when Dan returned, he told me they went farther back than that. Their parents had been friends.

"My dad arranged for me to get a job at his father's law firm, but I didn't want it."

"Why not?

"Davidson, Riley and Sons is a big firm. Stuffy. Uptight," he whispered. "Not my style. They do wills, estates, family law. At the time, I wanted to do criminal work exclusively. Half the associates at that firm worked for their daddies. I just wanted my father to butt out of my career."

Later, at the pre-dinner cocktail party, Dan and Walter made polite conversation, comparing notes on colleagues and old cases. I looked around to see if any of my family noticed that Dan was already acquainted with people we knew. Somehow this connection to Walter was comforting.

Late the next morning I showered and slipped into my blue satin bridesmaid dress, swept my hair up, and put on my makeup to prepare for the pre-ceremony wedding photos. Dan sat at a small writing desk doing paperwork as Rachel went wild, leaping across from one synthetic green bedspread to the other. "I get to do this! I get to do this!" she squealed, because I had waived the "no jumping on the bed rule."

"So, what are you wearing?" I tried to sound casual.

"Don't worry, we'll match," he said, without looking up.

I wished I didn't worry about what Dan wore, but I did. Sometimes he got it so right with his tailored business suits or a classic button down shirt tucked into soft, pressed slacks. Other times I just wanted to cry *no, no, no* and march him right back to his closet. On those days he'd either pop up the collar of his polo shirt like he was Elvis, or wear his too-short red cotton pants with a black suit belt and polished business loafers. One time he had even combined the two styles.

How to Help a Self Published Author

If you like the book...

- Tell everyone, or give it as a gift.
- Get it read at a book group, writer's group, family holiday, work group, women's group, cooking group, or group therapy.
- Invite the author to do a reading at your local independent bookstore, reading group, writing group, or community group.
- Put a review on Amazon or Barnes & Noble.com.
- Spread the news on Myspace, Facebook, and blogs. Link it to your website.

If you don't like the book...

- For god's sake, keep that to yourself.

Not that Dan always approved of my clothing choices. He often dropped me hints about wearing appropriate undergarments and lower heels, and keeping my blouses buttoned up a little higher.

"Shouldn't you wear a bra with that?" he asked, zipping me into the slinky dress.

"It's strapless," I said. "I don't have a strapless bra."

"Isn't it a bit revealing?"

"What does it reveal? I'm not that well endowed," I said, leaning over and flashing my chest.

Dan shook his head, helped me into the little matching jacket, and said, "Just keep yourself under wraps—I don't want anyone to see those except me."

I swished diluted peroxide around my mouth for the third time. My brother, his fiancé, and their Southern California friends all bleached their teeth a bright white semi-gloss. I didn't want mine to look dingy in the photos. Turning to Dan, I curled my lips back. "What do you think? Dazzling?"

Before he could respond, the phone rang. Dan mouthed, "It's Richard," and waved me away. I could forget about getting him away from his work, even for a few days. Shaking my head, I kissed him on the cheek as he frowned into the phone. Then I tickled and kissed Rachel, who was still jumping up and down on one of the beds, making faces, but no noise.

"Brush your teeth really well, honey. I'll see you guys at the church."

The steamy mid-day haze was way too hot for a satin polyester dress and matching bolero jacket. Within seconds, my makeup was melting and I could feel perspiration trickling down my chest. By the time we had finished with the photographs, my red face felt like it had been glazed and baked. When the afternoon ceremony started, as the other bridesmaids and I moved slowly down the aisle to Pachelbel's Canon, I had to resist an urge to dunk my head into the cool holy water, lap it up like a dog. I smiled stiffly at Rachel and Dan, who were waving at me from the second pew.

Dan looked good: dark blue shirt, yellow and red silk tie, light slacks. The two-tone shoes were a little showy, but all in all, dapper.

When my future sister-in-law hit the bridal runway I was too distracted by my growing sweat stains to appreciate the moment. Someone needed to run around the church and blow out the votive candles; sacred or not, we couldn't take the extra heat. The musty church smell made breathing difficult, and my feet were puffing up like bread dough, making me seesaw from one foot to the other.

Paula was radiant as she glided down the faded gold carpet toward my brother. He was the most well adjusted sibling in the family. He had graduated from college before getting married and was getting married before having children. I was happy for them—envious, really. Except for holding the wedding in a kiln, they were doing everything just right.

Paula's father kissed her before passing her hand to Hank. On the bride's side of the church, rows and rows of familiar faces smiled and shifted and fanned themselves on the squeaky wooden pews. Hank was marrying a woman who came from a big family, but her big family consisted of one mother, one father and seven brothers and sisters. On the groom's side, our expanding numbers came from my father and mother and their many marriages, children, and stepchildren.

As the priest spoke about commitment, I looked at Dan. He suddenly reminded me of Captain von Trapp from *The Sound of Music*. I'd fallen in love with the Captain when I was six years old. It was during the scene where he joined in to sing with his children, after years of treating them coldly because they reminded him of his beloved dead wife. Fraulein Maria stood in the doorway watching and listening with such heart-swelling emotion that I could almost see the love gushing from her misty blue eyes. I turned and aimed my own version of a gushy blue-eyed gaze toward Dan to see if I could catch his eye, and—*bingo*—it worked. He looked over at me and winked, Rachel cuddled by his side. I sure love that guy, I thought, my heart swelling like Fraulein Maria's.

My brother and his beautiful new wife swept up the aisle, and I followed the line of blue bridesmaids back toward the church door. Squinting in the sharp sunlight. the guests pelted the new couple with a shower of rice, and we all walked back to the motel for the poolside reception.

"*Ahhhhhhhhhhh*," I said, slipping into our chilled motel room. I collapsed onto the chair next to the vanity and said, "My god. I hate hate *hate* smoggy Southern California heat."

"Well, I love love *love* you," said Dan, patting my arm.

"Yeah Mommy, I love love *love* you, too," said Rachel.

I smiled as I dabbed powder on my sweat-shiny face. Who would have thought my life would've changed so much for the better in less than a year?

"Honey," said Dan. "I have a little problem with this thing with Richard."

"Yeah," said Rachel, with authority. "He's leaving and you're going to be sad so we got gas and washed the windows."

"What?"

"I have to fly back late tonight, but you can stick around—relax with your family—then drive my car back up with Rachel on Sunday. "

My face burned. I slapped my compact closed, shoved it into my purse, and eyed Dan crossly. I wasn't going to lay into him in front of Rachel, and he knew it, but I was furious. Dan's business deals followed him everywhere.

The explanation this time was that Richard needed him right away to release some money. Apparently Richard had found a new house in the East Bay that he wanted to lease so he could be closer to the neighborhood where Dan and I were planning to rent. He needed Dan back to finalize the deal.

"Richard's going to be our neighbor?"

"Looks like it." Dan seemed distracted.

"If it's his lease, why does he need your money to pay for it? He had enough money to buy a Jaguar. Besides, he manages your money, right? If he needed it, couldn't he just take it?"

Dan made the clicking sound that accompanied deep thought. But something was different. Some of his confidence seemed to have seeped away; it made it difficult to maintain my annoyance.

"Dan? This doesn't make sense—why do you have to leave the wedding early? Can't it wait a day?"

"Richard said he's coming into an inheritance but needs me to front him some funds to secure this house. All the money I've got is locked up in time deposits. He needs me to pull a few strings with the partnership, free up some cash for him. And he has to leave town to deal with the estate. I'd been having a hard time finding him—apparently that's where he's been."

"Who died?"

"I think he said a great aunt. I don't know, he's never mentioned her before. I don't think they were that close."

I was getting more and more concerned. Dan came to my side.

"Having him live closer means I won't be far from you for all our business meetings." He gently stroked my arm, flashed me a flirty look. "As soon as I close this deal with Richard, we're going to be set." Dan smiled, pulled me to his chest. "I'm doing this so we can have more time together."

"Yeah," said Rachel, nuzzling at my legs.

I said nothing as we walked to the reception, where flushed and smiling guests mingled in a lounge that opened out to the pool, eating skewered pineapple and teriyaki chicken and sipping fruity tropical drinks topped with paper umbrellas. But the drinks weren't cold enough and the food was too warm. The band kicked off with a Beach Boys hit, and Dan whisked me onto the dance floor.

"*Nooooo*," I whined, "Wait for a slow one. It's too hot. I'm the half-cooked lobster."

Dan ignored me, pulled me in, then twirled me twice under his arms and scooted us around the floor. He loved to dance and I loved to dance with him. I tried to loosen up and enjoy the movement, but I couldn't shake my irritation.

My mother rocked wildly with Jamie and my stepmothers. "I want you next, twinkle toes!" she yelled at Dan. I shoved him her way and went searching for an icy drink.

I made my way through the crowd, breathing the dense mixture of body odor and perfume. Dan was causing a slight commotion with his disco gyrations mixed with swing moves. It's those two-toned shoes talking, I decided, as Dan twirled. He finished his dance with my mother and then slid across the floor with my new stepmother, just as the bandleader started cajoling the non-participants up and out of their chairs to do the hokey pokey.

Off on the side of the dance floor Grandma Mary was smiling and swaying slightly. She looked thin and tired. Her hair was carefully coiffed into a halo of toasted orange that circled her pretty face like the afterglow of a sunset, but her frosted coral lipstick was smeared, one end of her false lashes was tilted and sticking to her upper lid, and her white suit hung loosely on her shrunken body. I walked to her side. She wasn't wearing the sweet perfume I expected. Instead she had a slightly sour smell that made me sad.

"Come on, Gram. Hokey pokey with me."

"No, no, hon," she said, trying to pull away from me. I kept ahold of her, making sure our movements stayed gentle and easy. The bandleader burst out with enthusiastic instructions,

Put your right foot in,
Put your right foot out,
Put your right foot in,
And you shake it all about…

As the rest of the crowd *"turned themselves around!"* I stood in front of Grandma and playfully poked and tickled her on both sides of her waist, trying to get her to smile.

And you…do the hokey pokey!
POKE POKE
And you… turn yourself around!
TICKLE TICKLE

"No, Mare, *noooo…*" Grandma stared at me with frantic blue eyes as urine gushed down her skinny legs.

"Oh, no Gram…I'm so sorry, " I yelled, as a puddle formed on the dance floor.

Stupid, stupid, stupid, I thought, feeling my throat constrict.

The music was loud and tinny and the air thick and pungent. I guided Grandma toward the lady's room, looking back just in time to notice Dan spinning my stepmother through the drippy puddle. The bride and groom were heading in that direction and as my brother spun his new wife around, her short white train smeared the floor with pee, stretching the wet hazard out further. I turned away, unable to watch anymore.

Grandma was ashen and weepy. After I settled her in the ladies room, I ran off to find my mother to help me clean her up.

In the reception hall, Rachel bounced in her seat, as Dan tried to eat a piece of sugary pineapple wedding cake. I explained we had to get Grandma back to her room.

"Can I go swimming?" whined Rachel. "Dan's taking me to the pool, okay Mommy?"

"Sure, honey." I was relieved that I wasn't getting resistance about leaving the party.

Mom was huddled by the bar with Aunt Maggie and her attorney friend, Walter. As I approached, Aunt Maggie caught my eye and elbowed Walter. He abruptly stopped speaking. It was as if she pressed the pause button on the remote; when I walked up, they were frozen into a stiff set of blurry-eyed smiles.

"Mare," said Maggie. "Did you hear? Walter knows your guy?"

"Yeah, Dan mentioned that. You're both attorneys?" I turned to my mother. "Mom, I need you to come with me."

"That, and I went to school a few years behind his brother, Jimmy," said Walter.

"Really? I guess you know he died." My voice was clipped. I needed to get back to Grandma.

"Terrible accident," he said, staring into his empty drink glass. "My father was actually handling some of the family legal matters at the time, back when Milton appeared on the scene."

"Milton?" I lit up and spun around. "Who's Milton?"

"God, I don't mean Milton." Walter appeared flustered. "His cousin, the one who was there when he died? What's his name?"

"Mike. But who's Milton?" I knew I sounded overly eager.

"Mike, that's it. Sorry, I misspoke. Listen, give his parents my regards." Walter maintained a stiff smile, patted me on the back, and quickly turned toward the bar to refresh his drink.

"Mom, Grandma has a female problem. Help," I pulled her away from the bar. I was distracted by Walter's obvious gaff, but needed to get back to Grandma.

"It's not your fault, honey," said my mother, after I'd confessed what I'd done. "Sooner or later everyone pees at a wedding," she joked. Neither Grandma nor I laughed.

"I just want to die," whimpered Grandma, as we shuffled her into her room. "Oh, I just wish I could die…"

"I'm so sorry, Gram," I said. "That was stupid of me."

"It's okay, doll," said Gram, barely audible, patting my arm with her splotchy, perfectly manicured hand.

I watched Grandma as my mother helped her out of her dress.

"Mare, let's just have Mom here," said Grandma, turning to me.

I kissed her goodnight and walked outside. Under the glow of the amber porch light, three frantic moths careened into each other as they fought to find a spot of warmth. They all wanted the same thing; there was plenty of it to go around. Why did they keep getting in each other's way?

On the way back to my room I ran into Aunt Maggie in the hall.

"Hey sweetie," she said. "You look exhausted. Want a cup of tea?"

I followed her into her room, kicked off my shoes and collapsed on the extra bed.

"Mom said Dan was going back early—something about his work? I know he's not practicing law." She handed me a cup of chamomile. "What does he do again?"

I let out a dramatic sigh. "Development. He and these guys own a huge piece of property on the San Mateo coast and they plan on developing part of it into houses and condos. They just have to make a deal with the city about turning some of the land into a nature reserve. It's some kind of trade off, but they're about done with it and Dan's handling the legal end. Why is everyone so curious about his work? Why aren't you asking me how much help and sanity and romance he brings into my life?"

"Well honey, you know what your mother says. Given the childhood you kids had, she's afraid you might have developed a high tolerance for inappropriate behavior."

"Mom's the one who's inappropriate. Just look at her life," I interrupted. I was sick of the intrusions and innuendo, especially when it seemed like things in my life were finally going well. Where were all these concerned busybodies when I was exhausted from a day of work and Rachel needed to be fed and put to bed? Dan was the person who was standing by me, and I was going to stand by him. "I thought *you* of all people would be supportive."

"Of course I support you. It's just… *Damn*, how did I get this job?"

"What are you talking about?"

"Well—and don't yell at me—I'm just asking because your mother's friend Walter knows Dan from way back and he told us some things."

"What did he say?"

"That maybe you should be careful about getting involved with him."

I set my tea on the nightstand and shoved my foot back into one shoe.

"I told your mother I didn't want to be the one to say anything," said Maggie.

"Is that it?"

"He mentioned some shady business deals—and an old criminal indictment? He said Dan had a history of starting businesses with guys who'd served hard time—guys he'd met through that Johnny Curtain. He just wanted to make sure Dan wasn't hiding anything from you. The criminal indictment was all over the papers so it would be easy enough to check, if you wanted."

"Well, I know about it," I snapped. "Dan's told me about the indictment more times than I wanted to hear it." I didn't mention that the delivery of these facts usually included some rant about the corruption of our government. Or that he'd also mentioned his former partners had some legal issues, but hadn't been specific. "It was in Missouri for a diamond investment company that no longer exists. Whatever the charges, he fought it and won, by the way."

Aunt Maggie's jaw tightened. She looked like she was losing enthusiasm for her task as messenger.

"Did he say anything else?" I said. "Anything new?"

"Walter said that after Jimmy died, rumor had it that Johnny Curtain had something to do with it. And given that, everyone finds it odd that Johnny and Dan are so close."

What? My body felt like rigor mortis had set in. I couldn't cram my rigid foot into the other shoe.

"Maybe you should look into this. Given your profession, it should be easy enough."

"Why would I check him out? He answers every question I ask, usually with more than I need to know."

My aunt raised her eyebrows and muttered, "Now, Mary. It's not that I don't like Dan—don't think that."

"You want to know what I think?" I was suddenly admiring how tight-lipped Jamie had been recently about her personal life. "I think everyone in this family should keep private matters just that—PRIVATE. Why do we have to talk about everything? Do you think I *like* knowing who my father and mother screwed throughout my childhood? Would it kill us to keep a few family secrets?"

My aunt exhaled loudly, opened her paperback and started reading. Obviously, we weren't going to discuss it further. Besides, what difference would it make? I loved Dan and couldn't imagine not being with him. I'd gone too far to turn back now. I really was the half-cooked lobster.

I limped out of her room, one shoe on my foot and one in my hand, feeling undressed and off balance.

In our room, Dan was reading on the bed next to Rachel, who was asleep. His bag was packed and sitting by the door.

"I was going to start calling around to find you." He scooted off the bed and embraced me. "I've got to get going."

I told him about my conversation with my aunt, but before I could finish he was shaking his head and pacing. "Walter told your mother that? Jesus, that's completely out of context."

"*Shhhhh*, you'll wake Rachel." I said.

"That two-faced sonofabitch, smiling and talking to me while he runs around spreading rumors to my future in-laws." Dan was speaking in a harsh whisper.

"Dan, he also said some people blamed Johnny for Jimmy's death."

"He said that?" Dan ran his fingers through his hair. "Just so you know, that's not news. It's gossip." He looked disgusted.

"Why would anyone think that?"

Dan sighed. "Jimmy owed Johnny money when he died. Gambling debts. Johnny was letting him work it off. My father wanted Jimmy to quit working for Johnny, go to work for him. There were rumors that Johnny was squeezing Jimmy for the cash, but it was bullshit. My dad put Mike up to the task of convincing Jimmy to change careers. Said he'd bail Jimmy out if he'd leave Johnny. Jimmy told them all to go to hell. That's supposedly what Mike and Jimmy were fighting about when the gun went off. I'm sure Mike was only too happy to shoot Jimmy. He was jealous."

"Of what?"

"Of the fact that Jimmy had a father, and he didn't. My dad's cousin Maureen raised him alone."

"Dan, who's Milton?" I knew I was pressing it, but I couldn't let the opportunity pass.

"What?" Dan looked puzzled.

"Who is Milton?" I figured it was safe to mention it now that the information had come to me innocently enough. "Walter said he was doing legal work for your family when Milton first arrived. Around the time of Jimmy's death?"

"What are you talking about?" Dan's expression was blank.

"Have I met Maureen? What's her last name?"

"I don't know. Murphy, I assume. I haven't even met her. Other than Mike, we have no contact with that side of the family." Dan looked at me oddly. "Why are you asking me these questions? You're not buying into this crap from Walter, are you?"

"Of course not." I couldn't tell if he was angry, wounded, or both.

"Goddammit. I can't believe Walter's dredging up this ancient history. Do you see why I could never work with the Walters of the world—such inbred society gossips? Christ, it's like he's still in high school." Dan shoved his hands in his pockets and paced. "Goddamn him. I'm going to straighten this out as soon as I get back. Give me your mother's home number."

Dan's fury pleased me for more reasons than I could count. Up until now, I was the one who had to clean up the messes. With Kevin, I was the one to fix flat tires, pay parking tickets, and negotiate with landlords and creditors. Dan's insistence on taking charge was such a relief that it didn't immediately occur to me to ask whether any of what Walter had said was true.

"Yes I was indicted," said Dan. "But I wasn't *convicted*. Did Walter mention that? My partners were imprisoned, that wasn't *me*. Did Walter mention that? And what does that whiny busybody know about my family business? Insinuating Johnny had something to do with Jimmy's death? People latch onto one little fact about someone, and they invent insane stories." Dan ranted for another five minutes, stopping only when the concierge called to tell him his taxi had arrived.

I was glad when Dan had gone. I didn't want him under the family microscope anymore—and it gave me time to think. If Jimmy had owed Johnny money, could Johnny have been involved in his death? If Mike hadn't done it, and there was someone named Milton who was locked up, was there a cover up? And how had I overlooked the obvious? I hadn't even thought to check criminal records under the name Milton *Murphy*. Maybe he had been prosecuted somewhere outside of San Francisco. In California, criminal records were kept only on a county-to-county basis, and I certainly couldn't drive around and check every one. In any case, something told me it was also time to check out Richard.

As I made the long drive home the following day, my head throbbed with thoughts that ended in question marks. Foremost in my mind was one question that just might offer answers to some of the others: How could I access the company database to do complete background checks?

Chapter 10

August 1990

A few weeks before Labor Day, I spotted a "For Rent" sign in front of a charming white colonial surrounded by redwood trees in the Oakland hills. I knew instantly that we had to live there. There was a big, shady yard with a tree swing. The lavender and rosemary bushes lining the brick pathway spiced the air, and the deck in the back sat above a row of flowering plum trees, the kind that exploded each spring with puffed pink blossoms. Rachel called them the Jiffy Pop popcorn trees, and was gleeful at the prospect of having a view of them from her bedroom window. Beyond the trees there was a clear view of the bay stretching across to San Francisco. The house was set back from the street, private and quiet, and included a separate office and bathroom downstairs for Dan—all very important features to him. Deer and squirrels visited the yard, which delighted Dan and Rachel, who were both passionate about all things furry. I thought the bright white cottage looked sweet and fresh and cheerful—the perfect place for all of us to make a clean start.

Family furor over Dan's past quieted down after Dan made personal calls to my aunt and each of my parents. He even called Walter to clarify what his role had been in the dismantling of his investment company. "Yes, my partners behaved badly. But I was the one who stuck around, took all the heat," he'd said. "That's why I was battling the indictment, not to mention every other lawsuit we were hit with."

Besides, I wasn't interested in the drama around Dan's former career when there were so many more pressing questions floating around. About Richard. And Milton. Of course I couldn't bring them up with Dan without threatening the peaceful family life we were creating together. But knowing I planned to spend a lifetime with him made some prying into his past reasonable. Necessary, even. How could we live happily ever after if there were secrets eating away at our foundation?

Back at work, I'd made some inquiries into accessing the background checking databases, but it turned out that our firm mostly outsourced that type of research. I would have to take time off to go check the county records, unless I could figure out a more efficient strategy. Meanwhile, I kept my attention on moving in together.

Lydia, the property manager for the rental, told us to fill out the applications. "We'll run a credit check, and then we'll discuss details of the lease," she said.

I cringed, but smiled and took the applications. Every place I had rented before had come through friends or acquaintances. Credit had never been an issue. Before I had a chance to process my worries, Dan snapped open his small leather satchel and pulled out some papers.

"Lydia, not a problem. I have a clean copy of my credit report here and would like to talk about the lease now."

"Oh, I see," she said, taking his report. Lydia was dressed in a prim gray suit, very formal for a Saturday. Her tightly coiffed hairstyle made her look as if white carnations were embedded in her head. "Actually, we have a procedure." She lifted the bifocals that hung from a chain around her neck, and studied the papers, frowning.

A few weeks earlier, when I was trying to get more background on Milton Murphy at work, I'd attempted to get a copy of Dan's and my credit reports, too. It turned out that getting that kind of information was more complicated than I had expected. Now that I was working with fire investigators, unless arson was suspected, we rarely conducted background checks. Once in a while we subcontracted work to Harry Paine, my former boss. When I got the new job, I learned that I'd been lucky to be recommended by Harry. He was highly respected, well known for his incisive reports, insatiable curiosity, and brash remarks. His innocent, boyish expression camouflaged a shrewd ability to see through anyone or anything with something to hide. This used to make me nervous, but after he'd helped me land this job, I relaxed, and we'd developed a friendly rapport. He knew I was eager to earn my own investigator's license and wanted to help, so when he was in my office a few days earlier, I had asked a casual question about how technology was impacting the business of background checking.

"Is it getting any easier? You think it's something a lowly beginner can do?"

"Why?" he said. "You wanna check out your boyfriend?"

I was appalled, like he'd just yanked down my pants.

"*Aha!* You do, don't you?"

"Jesus, Harry. It's a simple question. Can you just educate me without analyzing?"

"Give me his name," he gloated. "You know you want to. Come on. Cough it up."

"God, you're nosy," I said.

"Guilty, your honor." He chuckled. "That's why I'm so good."

"You're nosy and you're wrong." I shuffled the papers on my desk into neat, nonsensical piles.

"You should already know this," he said. "The best way to get stuff legally is still the old fashioned way—public records."

"I thought there were online searches now," I said. "Can't you get credit reports and criminal records that way?"

"It's not that straightforward. You can't get credit reports period. Not without a release. Get your boyfriend to sign a release and I'll help you out." He winked. "You can get info online that directs you to the more interesting stuff—the stuff at the courthouse. If you find someone's divorce file—and it was ugly—that's pay dirt. Whenever I can afford to get you to come to work for me, I'll show you how to find what people are hiding." Harry put his hand on his hairpiece and lifted the front up as if he were tipping a hat.

I sat down at my desk and pretended to concentrate.

"Alright. Give me lover boy's name and I'll show you how to get his divorce files. What better way to get a quick peek in his shorts—"

"Hey, Harry? Give it a rest. I don't need to check out my boyfriend," I said, slamming a drawer closed harder than I meant to. "I've known Dan over five years—I worked for him, for godsakes."

"Oh, come on," he said. "You aren't seriously pissed off. I'm only kidding."

Harry plopped into the chair facing my desk, aimed his eyes at me, and blew out a long stream of air.

"Okay," he said. "What is it? What do you really want to know?"

"Nothing," I mumbled.

"Come on," he said. "I'm sorry. I want to throw you a bone. No questions asked."

I looked back at him for a few seconds.

"Okay," I said, scribbling a name on a piece of scratch paper. I wasn't about to give him the name Milton Murphy; I was sure he'd recognize Dan's last name. If he were to turn something up about the family, it would make things tense and embarrassing. "Check out this guy. The name's Richard Harding."

The mounting benefits of using Patric as a fake name crystallized for me. If no one knew Dan's real name, there'd be no way to track the connections between Dan and his past—or the pasts of any the Murphy's, for that matter.

I wondered if Dan had realized this. Then, for a moment, I wondered if Dan had planned this.

Now, as I saw Dan showing his credit report to Lydia, I felt relieved. Despite the nasty accusations about his business associates, he obviously had a legitimate financial pedigree.

Lydia studied the documents for a few minutes. "This isn't the reporting company we generally use," she said. "We use Equifax, and can get it done fairly quick." Her voice was dry, like the sound of paper being ripped.

"I understand," said Dan. "How long does it take?"

"Just a few days," she said.

Dan paused, put his hands in his pockets, and started to make his clicking sound.

My wooden table would look so cute in this breakfast nook, I thought. And I could take my china cabinet out of storage and finally get to display Grandma's teacups.

"Well," he sighed. "That might cause a slight glitch, Lydia. There's another home—in Alameda. I have to commit to it—one way or the other—this evening. I don't want to let it go unless I have some kind of guarantee."

My heart sank.

Rachel was outside building a leaf fort in the warm puddle of sunlight that had spilled between the trees and the house. A light gust of wind fluttered through the flower boxes, sending a swirl of loose blossoms airborne.

"Mama! Mama!" Rachel twirled around, arms thrown high as she tried to grasp handfuls of the soft, papery shower. "Look! It's snowing!" she said, leaping up and waving at us through the window.

"I appreciate your problem, Lydia," said Dan. "It was nice meeting you."

"Honey?" I said, trying not to expose my panic. "Can I show you something?"

Dan waved at Rachel, and then shot a look that was meant to silence me. It was easy to remain mute; I didn't know what to say anyway. My credit was embarrassing; I couldn't afford the seventeen hundred dollar monthly rent on this place alone, and while I assumed Dan could, maybe he wasn't ready for us to live together.

"I'll tell you what, Lydia," he said. "I can tell my girls are taken with this place." He made his clicking sound again. "I'm prepared to give you a large deposit to hold it for us, if that would address your concerns."

"Well, our procedure—"she looked down. "I'm sorry, I don't think that would make much difference."

"I understand." Dan smiled, then gazed back toward Rachel, who was now climbing the tree. He resembled an oversized version of the altar boy I imagined he'd been in Catholic primary school. His blue eyes were earnest, and his tone respectful—even apologetic, as if he felt guilty about unnecessarily taking up Lydia's time.

"It would only take a few days," she said, softening.

"But you understand my predicament? I don't want to give up this other thing where we are first in line."

"Honey?" I said again.

"I'm sorry," said Lydia. "We almost never make exceptions."

"Very good then," said Dan. "I understand and appreciate your professionalism. There isn't enough of that going on these days, Lydia. Sorry about the timing, but I've got to think of my little family here." Dan reached out and shook Lydia's hand, his expression somber. "The place is beautiful— I'm sure you'll have no trouble renting it. It's a wonderful home and a fair price. Thank you. Really. And good luck."

The tiny seed of panic I had felt earlier hardened into a thick lump of disappointment, but before I could make a sound, I glanced outside to Rachel in the plum tree, on a branch that looked ready to collapse under her weight.

"Hey! Hey! Get down from there!" I yelled, just as she tumbled from the tree. Dan bolted out the door, swooping her from the pile of mulch where she'd dropped on her face.

Rachel coughed and spit as Dan helped brush mulch and leaves off her jacket. Dan whispered something into her ear. She punched his arm and giggled.

"Looks like she'll live," said Lydia, laughing. Her wide smile spread vertical crinkles along both sides of her face, like curtains being opened.

Dan lifted Rachel and she buried her face in his chest. He stroked her hair, saying something that caused her to grab his cheeks.

"He sure is sweet with her, isn't he?" Lydia shook her head and gazed toward Dan like he was her very own grandson. "We could call the owners," she blurted. "Tell them about your time constraints, see what they say?"

Within minutes, Dan was engaged in an animated conversation with a couple from Atlanta that included chatter about the view of San Francisco, the neighborhood schools, and how lucky they were to have found the professional services of someone like Lydia in this dog-eat-dog real estate world. When I saw him jotting down instructions about how to maintain their hardwood floors, I wanted to leap into the tire swing and hoot. The place was ours.

We drove to the post office, where Dan used cash to purchase the two-thousand-dollar money order that we hand delivered to Lydia. By the time we returned to her office, Lydia had transformed into someone sweet and pliable, as if she'd been soaked in hot sugar water.

"Man, you're good," I said, as we drove away.

"There are two secrets to successful negotiations," he said.

"Let me guess. Charm and bullshit?"

"No," he said. "You've got to be fair and you've got to be willing to walk away. If you're not willing to walk, your opponent will know it."

"I wasn't ready to walk. I was ready to whack you upside the head. I have to admit, smart idea bringing a credit report."

"Christ, I have to. One of the reporting agencies has false information. I've got to gear up for that fight now."

"What false information?"

"I told you about it."

I almost argued the point, but decided to keep quiet. I had what I wanted, and didn't want to get sucked into a long tedious war story. Turning to Rachel, I sang, "*Our house, is a very very very fine house, With two cats in the yard, Life used to be so hard…*"

"Hey you guys," I said, interrupting myself. "Did you see that built-in pet door in the family room? We need to get a cat!"

"Yay!" said Rachel.

"Yay," I echoed.

"Nay!" said Dan.

"I want a new kitten or another baby," I said.

"Let's think about a cat," said Dan, driving us down to Barney's to celebrate over hamburgers and fries.

Dan looked pale but happy, as we raised milkshakes in a toast to our new life.

"All right my darlin' Irish lasses," said Dan. "I have something very special for each of you." He reached into the pocket of his jacket and pulled out two small boxes. "One for my big woman; one for my little woman."

Rachel and I unwrapped the boxes, and before I could pop mine open, I heard her squeal, "A ring! A beautiful ring!" She put the little ring on her index finger and held it up so we could admire the shiny glass stone.

My heart raced as I opened my velvet box. Inside there was a pile of small, glistening diamonds.

"I didn't want to presume to know what style ring you wanted," said Dan, taking my hand. "But there are twelve diamonds in there, one for each month of the year that I plan to love you. You can pick out a setting that you like—design it yourself."

I was speechless.

"I thought it would be nice to give these to you now, and marry you on Valentine's Day," he said. "I know how much you love that holiday." He leaned in and gave me a lingering kiss. "So I guess this makes it official? One big happy wedding, coming soon, to a theater near you!"

"We're getting married," I clasped Rachel's ringed finger and held it up.

"Yeah. We're getting married," said Rachel.

"Buckle your seat belts, ladies," said Dan. "Our love is going to take us on a wild ride—I can feel it already."

Chapter 11

December 1991

The excitement of the move and upcoming wedding sent us into a romantic haze that seemed to agree with all three of us. Every morning while I got ready for work, Dan got Rachel moving and made my coffee. He set Rachel up on the kitchen barstool with her Cheerios and kept her company while she ate. When we were ready to depart, she raised her arms, and Dan would lift and carry her up to my car, kissing the loopy curls on her head before settling her into the back seat.

"She's almost five. How long do you think she'll get you to carry her?" I said, one morning.

"At least until junior high," he said, "Right, Rachel?"

Rachel smiled, looked away. She knew how to milk a good deal.

Most days Dan worked in his home office, or dashed off to meet Richard for meetings. Since we saw him regularly, I felt a little guilty about attempting to pry into his past. Harry had never gotten back to me, so I let it drop. I was even surprised how little interest I had lately in pursuing the mysterious Milton. Digging up Dan's past was much less important to me than working to build our future. Any time I had off from work was spent on other, more conventional family-building activities like cooking with Dan and checking out wedding venues.

Richard, meanwhile, was acting like the Publisher's Clearinghouse Prize Patrol. He kept showing up at our door with expensive gifts. By summer we had a new high-tech stereo system, plush patio furniture, and a gift certificate for three nights at a swank resort in Lake Tahoe.

"Don't you think it's weird that Richard's giving us such big presents?"

"No," said Dan, shaking his head. "He's so happy to be reunited with his son, he's just going overboard with appreciation. And you have to admit, it's great stuff."

Recently Dan had acted as a mediator between Richard and his ex-wife, to resolve the rift that kept Richard from seeing his ten-year-old. He had impressed upon Richard the importance of his presence in his son's life, and urged him to get more involved. Dan even planned daddy-child double dates at the Exploratorium. I wasn't thrilled to have Rachel getting more exposure to Richard, but wasn't going to interfere with any venture in improved parenting.

When Richard gave Dan the gifts, he said he did it because Dan hated to spend money on himself, which was true. Dan still had a stereo system that contained an eight-track tape player, and a rust velour sectional that he'd purchased in the early eighties. When we moved in together, I refused to let it into our house.

"Maybe the bank teller is a nut. But remember? She said Richard liked to gamble," I said, after he'd dropped by with his latest gift. "You think he made a big killing recently?"

"When would he have time to gamble? He's working with me all week and has his son most weekends. He's obviously just making an effort," said Dan. "And it would mean a lot to me if you would return the favor."

I was willing to do any number of favors to maintain the happy family life I had finally achieved. These days, I never worked late or made plans with friends, because I could hardly wait to pick up Rachel from childcare and get back to our cottage in the hills. Dan often had dinner waiting when we returned home. The only events I liked to attend outside family outings were PTA meetings and an occasional class. With Dan's encouragement, I signed up for the financial fitness class my father had suggested. I diligently did the homework, learning how to set aside a certain amount of money every month for debt repayment and upcoming expenditures—like my wedding dress and flowers, my areas of responsibility for the big event. I signed up to contribute to the retirement fund at my job and called an insurance broker to investigate life and disability plans, so Rachel would be protected if anything happened to me, Dan, or Kevin. It felt very grown-up and responsible, and Dan told me regularly how proud he was of me.

Dan and I used the forms distributed at my class to set up an official family budget to which we each contributed. We decided that he would pay the rent and I would pay the groceries and utilities, and then there would be no need to have a shared checking account. Even though he hadn't legally changed his name and we weren't married yet, I put the phone and electric bills in our new name so we wouldn't have to change it after the wedding. Each month the bills came to "Mary and Dan Patric." The utility companies never asked for any proof and I loved seeing our names merged that way, it seemed so solid and permanent and connected.

It was easy for me to change my name because it was something our culture expected women to do. My first stop was Wells Fargo Bank, where I waited until Darlene, the famous pink-clad teller, was free. "Guess who's getting married?" I grinned and proudly wiggled my fingers on the counter.

"What?" She squealed and pulled my hand close to her pink cat glasses. Examining my diamonds, she made a happy clucking sound.

"I need to do a change of address on my checks, but I'll have to update the name in February. Should we do it all at once?" I showed her the utility bill with our new made-up last name.

"Absolutely, *Mrs.* Mary Patric. Let's do it now!" she said, neatly printing the new name on the check order form, and never once asking for a marriage license. After she finished, she raised one over-plucked eyebrow. "Just please tell me your fiancé isn't still friends with that turd bucket I dated."

"Worse than that. They work together. I've actually been instructed to make more of an effort to *like* him."

She shook her head and made *tsk tsk* noises, her pink teardrop earrings swinging like pendulums. Despite the growing line behind me, I lingered at her counter.

"Hey Darlene, how did you know he's a gambler?"

"Baby, I invited him to Tahoe. And do you think he spent an instant in the hotel room? That I paid for? I couldn't pull him away from the casinos. If I even tried, he got buggier than a wasp."

"He's a testy guy." I lowered my voice. "It may be because he spent some time in Vietnam. Special Forces. I guess that can cause all kinds of post traumatic stress."

"You're kidding me. Special Forces?" Her wrist bangles clattered as she put her hands on her hips. "If that man was in the Special Forces, then honey, we need to fear for our country. He didn't even know how to swim. Couldn't ride a bike. He couldn't even read the trail map when we tried a simple hike."

She had a point. Richard didn't strike me as someone to whom I'd trust the care of our national security, let alone any of my business affairs. But it was probably the violence in Vietnam that turned him into such a jerk.

When my new checks arrived, I took them to the DMV along with my utility bills and used those for proof of my fake married name. With the new driver's license, I was able to change my name on my social security card. No one ever asked to see a marriage license or legal documents.

"When are you going to change your name?" I asked Dan.

"That's tricky," he said. If he went to court to change his name, then there would be a public record on file. That would be like leaving "gourmet breadcrumbs" right to our front door for the "greedy lunatics" who wanted to sue him and tear down everything he'd spent a lifetime building. He said he was working on a plan and took out some paper and made notes.

Of course I knew this desire of Dan's to remain invisible or untraceable on public records was a multi-layered problem that I'd eventually have to address directly. But I was also feeling protective. Living under the same roof and connected by a new name, we were starting to feel like an established family. Even my mother seemed pleased. When she arrived for a visit and noticed that Rachel was calmer and happier than she had ever seen her before, she complimented Dan on his good influence.

"I don't care what he did in the past," whispered Mom. "He's working magic on you girls."

One quiet Sunday morning, I began to work on setting goals for myself. A repetitive message delivered in my financial planning class was that couples needed to be "clean and clear" with one another regarding money issues. I mentioned this to Dan, who was reading the Sunday paper in his blue La-Z-Boy.

"Couldn't agree more," he said from behind the sports section.

"Well," I paused. "There's still some stuff I don't get."

Dan lowered the newspaper so I could see his face.

"Why aren't you practicing law anymore?"

"Don't need to. After I close this development deal, we'll be set. Our partners will be paid off. No more late night calls or meetings. We'll live happily ever after."

"What partners are those?"

"Me, Johnny Curtain. A few of Johnny's associates. If all goes well, we'll give Richard a cut."

"Should you be doing business with Johnny? He was your client. He was a crook. You said so yourself."

Dan folded the paper and sat it down. "First of all, I never said Johnny was a 'crook.' Secondly, I haven't made a living exclusively practicing law for a long time. What you don't understand is that it's a gargantuan hassle to be a sole practitioner these days. I don't want to pay the exorbitant malpractice insurance rates and I'd have to spend half my life defending myself."

"Defending yourself from what?"

"Governments, jealous partners, people looking for a deep pocket. Do you know how many lawsuits I've been named in, for no other reason than someone wants some dough? Right or wrong, once it's filed, then you've got to defend the goddamn thing. I'm sick of the entire commercial world—it makes me just want to go underground."

I sat quietly while Dan explained that he wanted to remove his name from the bar association directory—in fact, he didn't want his name listed anywhere.

"It's a nuisance and an invasion of privacy, and with these ridiculous lawsuits multiplying like cockroaches, I don't even plan on keeping a bank account anymore."

"What? Why not?"

"Then any idiot can go after me for the sole purpose of stealing my money, no questions asked. All they'd need is a default judgment."

Dan's particular financial strategy had not been covered in class.

"How does anyone get a default judgment?" I said.

"Listen," he pointed a finger at me. "In this litigious world, anyone who thinks you have a bank account can sue you, and then, like it or not, you have to pay to defend yourself. If you're unwilling to do that, then WHAM-BAM, you lose."

"How do you function without a bank account?"

"You've got to be willing to be inconvenienced," he said. "Most people aren't willing to do what it takes to protect themselves because it's inconvenient—"

"Is it legal?"

"Legal?" Dan stood and tightened the tie on his black robe. "Let me explain something to you." He was winding up for a big speech. I wished I had brought my coffee from the kitchen. "It's these specious lawsuits that should be illegal. It's the arbitrary IRS practices that should be illegal. It's the over-bloated government and self-serving legal system that's breaking the law—"

"Honey," I said, trying to head off one of his anti-establishment speeches. "Seriously, how can you function without a bank account?" I retrieved my coffee as the question hung in the air. "Please," I said when I returned. "Couples need to be clean and clear with each other about money. Explain this so I get it."

"It's not that complicated." He sighed, sat back down, and spoke slowly. "When you are sued, your liability for accidents or injury extends only as far as the value of your assets. If you don't own it, you can't lose it. By divesting yourself of all personal ties to property you protect that property from liability and vulnerability. I don't own my assets anymore. They are owned by a common law entity—a trust."

Dan explained that Richard ran the trust, in order to protect our future. Each month Richard withdrew and gave Dan a fresh pile of cash, some of which he shared with me so I could pay the rent.

"Are you sure this isn't illegal?"

"Yes and no."

Silence.

"Irrevocable trusts are commonly used by the wealthy to protect assets," Dan continued. "It's downright unfair, if not immoral, that the same privilege isn't extended to everyone because they don't know about it."

"So how do you track your income? Pay your taxes?"

"I don't pay taxes any more," he said. "Don't need to."

I felt a sharp pain between my eyes. "Isn't that illegal?"

"Illegal? The money in the trust is after tax money," he insisted. "I paid taxes on every dollar I've ever earned and I'm not going to roll over in ignorance and let all my assets, money I made and saved and paid taxes on, be stolen. Do you think that's fair? Why should *that* be legal?"

I had no idea, but I had temporarily lost interest in that particular subject, anyway. Knowing that Richard was intimately involved in our financial life was making my brain hurt. I took a sip of my coffee. It was cold and bitter.

"None of your money is in your name? What if something happened to you? What would we do?" Outside the window, all I could see was fog.

"You don't need to worry about that stuff, honey."

"Of course I need to worry, Dan. I'm a mother." I shook my head. "I guess I'd better hop to it on getting us that life insurance. You'll have to have a full physical, because of your age. Can we get you an appointment?"

"Not to worry," said Dan. "Life insurance is great, but it's for people who don't have significant assets. I've told Richard to take care of you if anything happened to me."

"Richard?" I was stunned. "You're trusting *him* to take care of *us*? With all the things he's been buying lately, how do you know he's not spending your money?"

"What?" Dan popped up like a rocket. "What the hell do you mean by that? Of course I trust him. I'd better—I let him control everything I own. I told you, he even fronted some of his inheritance to our project. Do you know how far we go back?"

His next sentence had become so predictable; I was tempted to join along in a lip-sync.

"Richard's like a brother to me."

Despite his ghastly personality, the man had somehow earned permanent placement as Dan's surrogate sibling. And Dan was so blinded by loyalty, it was clear that he would never be able to handle criticism of Richard.

"Think about what you're accusing him of. Just because you don't like him." Dan snatched pieces of newspaper and crammed them into a pile.

I glared at him, arms folded.

"What? Nothing's going to happen to me," he said. "I'm working my ass off to make sure that we have a solid future. I'm working around the clock for our family, can't you see that?"

It was true. When not doting on Rachel or me—leaving hidden love notes, planning weekend adventures, or delivering breakfast in bed—Dan worked around the clock. And each month, without fail, he handed me my pile of cash.

Fine, I thought. That's the last time I'd try to have a clean and clear financial discussion with him. I'd just buy the damn life insurance.

The day after our tense financial discussions, Dan finally agreed that I should get Rachel a Christmas kitten. I took it to be an apology for overreacting to my comment about Richard. Rachel was going to be thrilled. Although she had quit verbalizing her desire for a cat, she regularly put her cereal bowl on the floor after breakfast, dropped on all fours, and lapped up the remaining milk, then licked her paws clean.

"We either get her a kitten or raise her as one," I'd said to Dan.

That following day, I took the afternoon off to go to the animal shelter to select our furry new family member.

"I'm sorry," said the kindly woman at the animal adoption center. "But it's not kitten season."

"Kittens have a season?" I stared through the dirty glass window at the abandoned cats, and spotted two adolescents. One was gray with a long tail; one was black with a stub tail. I reached for the long tail and she hissed and scratched, slicing a thin red gash into my hand.

"Ouch," I said, wiping the blood on my jeans. "Let me hold the one with the stub tail."

The little black cat relaxed into the crook of my arm and started purring as I nuzzled her. That's when I caught wind of the odor. It was sour, rotting crab shell, cat poopy awful. Santa did not deliver things that smelled like this. I started to put the stinky cat down, but then I looked into her round, yellow eyes. She was the closest thing to a kitten they had, and getting Dan to agree to this new addition to our family had been exhausting; I didn't want to have to start all over again. I packed her in a transport box, prepaid for her spaying, and purchased a bottle of deodorizing shampoo. I buckled the box into the backseat, unrolled the windows, and listened to her mee-yew, scratch, and thrash.

The gash left by the other cat was nothing compared to what our new kitty did when I shampooed her. But she greeted Dan and Rachel at the front door all shiny, clean and wearing a red Christmas ribbon.

"What are you doing, Puppies? Huh? What are you doing?" cooed Dan, getting down on the carpet with the kitten. Dan referred to all small animals and babies as "Puppies." Sometimes he even used the term with me and Rachel. It always surprised me to see him reduced to this state of gooey baby talk.

"Oh. Look. Look!" squealed Rachel, as the cat slipped the ribbon over her neck.

After we spent a few minutes wrestling with the kitty, the phone rang. I went into our bedroom to answer it.

"Mary? Harry Paine."

"Hey," I said, sounding surprised.

"They said you took the afternoon off."

"Yeah. Did they give you my home phone?"

"Hell no."

"Because I'm unlisted—"

"Who do you think you're talking to?"

"Oh," I laughed. This made me nervous. "What's up?"

"I got something on your friend Richard."

Rachel and Dan were crawling on the living room floor, dragging the ribbon for the cat to chase. I quietly closed the bedroom door and readjusted the receiver in my sweating palm.

"Mary, you there?"

"Yeah. Sorry. I thought you'd forgotten."

"I did forget, until I came across my notes again. If you thought I'd forgotten, why didn't you ask about it?"

"It wasn't that big a deal," I said, trying to sound breezy.

"Okay, we can skip it. Sorry to get you on your day off—"

"Wait, wait. What did you find?"

"So it is a big deal?"

"No, it's not that important, but—*come on*—now I'm just curious."

"Well make up your mind if it's a—"

"Harry, you sadist, just tell me. What is it?"

"Too soon to know exactly, I have a runner going to the courthouse. It's some kind of felony conviction in Los Angeles County. I'll know by Friday. Wanna do lunch? I've got a couple other things I want to cover with you."

We arranged a meeting and I returned to the living room. Rachel and Dan were debating the cat's new name.

"Hey," said Dan. "Let's ask Mommy. Should we call her Puppies?"

"Puppies? Okay," I said, without really listening.

Felony? Murders and rapes and brandishing weapons were felonies. Had he returned from the war, freaked-out, and killed someone?

"No!" said Rachel. "She's not a dog. She's a little kitty." The words poured from Rachel in a syrupy drip. She was starting to sound like Dan.

"Honey, pay attention. You're not thinking about work are you?" said Dan, mimicking one of my constant complaints to him. "We're trying to come together as a family, name this cat. You need to learn to compartmentalize," he mocked.

"Okay," I said, snapping to attention. "How about Stinky? Morning Breath? Pepe Le Pew?" *Or we could skip the euphemisms and call her Richard.*

"Goody! We'll call her Goody!" said Rachel. "Cause she's a Good Kitty. *Aren't you?*"

How the hell was I going to wait until next Friday?

In Goody's first week of residence, she returned to our deck to shred three birds as they fluttered and gasped. She gnawed on their heads, then she sat next to them to preen, sometimes with small bloody feather pieces still hanging from her lips. At least twice that week she eviscerated a lizard and left it on Dan's desk. One sunny afternoon she trotted up to the door five times, dropping a punctured, wiggling, bald baby mouse on the mat at each visit.

"How can such a cute little kitty be so vicious?" said Dan to her in his gooey voice. He crouched on the floor to rub her belly.

"How can you get cozy with something so vicious?" I said.

If Goody wanted to sleep on Dan's desk, he worked around her. If she was asleep on his office chair, he stood while taking calls. Together they struck a handsome pose—especially when Dan held her while wearing his black terrycloth robe.

"You two sure are a good looking couple," I said a few nights later, as Goody sat curled and purring in his lap. "I might be getting jealous."

Dan gently put her on the floor and then pulled me onto his lap, letting his hands move up my neck and behind my ears, where he softly scratched.

"You think I'm petting her more than you?" He kissed me. "That's just a figment of your very active imagination."

After a few minutes I stood up and took his hand. We stopped in Rachel's room to watch her sleep for a few minutes, surrounded by a heap of her favorite stuffed animal friends. Back in our bedroom, we undressed and curled together in the darkness, letting our bodies melt into one another as we made love. For a long time afterwards, I couldn't settle down. I watched Dan breathing softly beside me, his tattered old baby blanket covering his eyes. "I just use it to keep out light," he'd explained the first time I found him napping with it. "This is the only thing that seems to work."

I lay awake as my happiness collided with worry about what Harry had unearthed. Dan was right; I did have an active imagination.

Chapter 12

December 1991

"Dan, I can't believe you're telling me this now. We had it all planned." I dropped my purse, flopped onto the blue recliner, and crossed my arms.

"Honey, I just can't get away. You and Rachel go—have a good time, and of course I'll still kick in some dough. But I'm under ungodly pressure right now—*ungodly*," said Dan. "We'll plan another trip—as soon as things settle down." There were dark smudges under his eyes.

"It's okay, Mommy," said Rachel. "We'll do it again." She patted my arm, her expression somber.

It was Friday morning and I was already stressed. I was having lunch with Harry to learn about Richard's felony charge. After work, we were supposed to drive to Monterey to visit the new aquarium and finish Christmas shopping at the outlet stores in Gilroy. I'd figured that the timing was good: Dan would be relaxed when I broke the news that his surrogate brother Richard had run a prostitution ring or operated a methamphetamine lab—just some of the less violent scenarios I had imagined. I still wasn't sure how I'd explain knowing about it; I doubted Dan would be thrilled that I'd asked an investigator to check out Richard.

"I can't drive my old car down to Monterey—I doubt it would make it," I said.

"That's right." Dan paused, clicking. "Take my car—I'll drive yours this weekend."

Goody bolted through the cat door with a bloody lizard hanging from her mouth.

"Goody. Bad kitty!" said Rachel, hiding behind Dan's legs.

"Oh no, little Puppies! What did you bring?" said Dan.

"Come on, you guys. She's a hunter—it goes with the territory." I opened the French doors, picked up Goody—dangling reptile and all—and tossed her on the back deck. She dropped her lizard and looked up at the three of us.

"Fine. We'll go without you." I quit arguing. When Dan was like this, there was no point. And maybe we'd be better apart, after all, while he processed the news about Richard. "Do your thing. Rachel and I know how to have fun, don't we sweetie?"

"I promise—I'll make it up to you." He leaned in to kiss my cheek. "I promise you—we have a lifetime of traveling together. I'm going to show you the world. I just need to get a handle on things right now."

"He's taking you on more trips, Mommy."

Dan laughed, leaned over, and picked Rachel up. "That's right, I am," he said. "And I'm taking you on lots of trips too—starting with a free ride to the car."

She giggled but kept an eye on me as I followed them out the front door and up the brick path to our driveway.

Christmas was a busy time of year for fire investigators. With so many dry trees coming in contact with frayed light cords and festive candles, we could count on facing a pile of residential fire investigations every morning in December. I had reports to proofread and clients to call, but I arrived at my office that morning in no shape to work. I was upset with Dan and fidgety about what Harry might tell me. Instead of calling insurance adjusters, I called Baskin Robbins to see if they could make a chocolate mint wedding cake. Our wedding was in two months, and whenever I felt stressed about anything, I found that thinking, planning, or making actual arrangements for the event calmed me down. The person who handled cake orders wasn't in, so I left a message, then called around to find a pianist who could play "How Do You Solve a Problem Like Maria" for my walk down the aisle. I was on hold with the church organist when our receptionist appeared in my office and slipped a note under my nose. "Your mom is on Line 2—family emergency."

I punched the blinking light on my phone. "Mom. What is it?"

"Honey, brace yourself. I have sad news about Grandma Mary." My mother sounded faint and distant, like her voice was coming from under water.

"Oh no, Mama." My chest tightened as I swallowed.

"Gram died late last night. Her kidneys finally gave out."

Not Grandma Mary, I thought, remembering how her eyes looked like open wounds after the dance floor puddle. Grandma had always stood up for me, in any situation, using her influence over my parents to rescue me from punishment. But the last few times I'd seen her prior to the wedding, I hadn't known how to deal with her old age and anxiety. Once, at my mother's house, Grandma followed me around the kitchen as I made the morning coffee, hunching behind me crying, "I'm afraid to die, Mare. I'm so afraid to die." I didn't know what to do or say. I just wanted her to act like my Grandma again. Instead of comforting her, I sat her down, poured her coffee—careful to add hot milk, just the way she liked it—then lamely assured her she wasn't going to die. I left her alone at the table and fled to the guestroom, where I went back to sleep.

"Oh, Mom. She was so afraid to die."

"I know. She told me she didn't want to run into her first grade teacher, Sister Rose, the mean old nun who told Gram that if there were even one sin on her soul, she'd burn in hell for eternity. It scared the beejezus out of her. You should thank me for yanking you kids out of the church before you were damaged."

I made the sign of the cross to that.

"Was she scared?"

"It was peaceful, honey. Aunt Maggie and I were right by her side. In fact, I tried to go home but she got real squirmy, so I decided to stay—thank God."

"Mama, she won't be at my wedding." A lump grew in my throat.

"She will be, in spirit," said Mom. "She wouldn't miss it—none of us would."

Mom told me not to rush to Southern California. There wasn't much I could do, and they weren't sure what they were going to do for a memorial. She thought that they might even wait until after the wedding.

I hung up and called Harry's secretary to cancel our lunch. "I'll call him Monday to reschedule," I said.

All week long I had thought I'd explode, wondering what crime Richard had committed. I'd even confided in Jamie, telling her I imagined he was capable of anything. "Even murder?" she'd asked. "If I wind up dead," I joked nervously, "he's your go-to guy." But I didn't care about that now. I was taking the rest of the day off. And even if I had to forfeit our deposit on the hotel in Monterey, Rachel and I weren't going. After this news, I didn't want to be away from Dan.

It was about noon. As I fumbled with my front door keys, the door flew open. Dan faced me with a panicked expression on his face. I assumed he'd heard the news.

"Oh, honey. It's you." He looked disappointed. "I thought it might be Richard."

I couldn't speak. A new lump swelled in my throat.

"What're you doing home?" He absently stepped aside so I could enter. I walked past him, dropped my things in the hallway, and went into our bedroom to lie on the bed. Dan followed me.

"What's wrong?"

"Grandma Mary died." I put my hand over my eyes and started to cry.

"Oh, Jesus." Dan sat down on the edge of the bed. "I'm so sorry. Honey—what happened?"

I told him about my mother's call, that I didn't want to go to Monterey, that I just wanted to stay home—maybe make a special scrapbook or something, fill it with Grandma's pictures. It seemed like an empty gesture, since Grandma would never see or enjoy it. Still, it might be comforting to Rachel—and to me.

"Is your mom okay? Should I call her?"

Dan loved my mother. Even before they had met, he had seen some of her pictures and told me she had the kind of "timeless beauty" he admired. "And I bet she was the dream mom—loyal, affectionate." He was right. My mother was loyal and affectionate. Except for the times she was locked in the mental ward following a botched suicide attempt. That year she sent glazed ceramic vegetables from her hospital art class. Mom didn't rebound to her jovial self until the divorce was final.

Ever since Mom's pal Walter had made "those libelous remarks" about him at Hank's wedding, Dan had gone out of his way to compliment my mother, send her notes and articles, and arrange special family outings. During her last visit he took us all to the St. Francis Hotel for an English high tea in her honor. After that she'd joked that he might turn out to be the doting son she'd meant to give birth to, since Hank wasn't prone to spoiling her. Dan strutted around with a blown-up chest all day.

I grabbed a tissue from the nightstand and blew my nose. "You look wiped out, Dan."

Dan told me Richard was missing. He hadn't seen or heard from him in days.

"Have you checked his house?"

"Locked tight. We have our weekly conference call with the partners scheduled tonight at nine, but I have a bad feeling."

"What'd he say the last time you spoke with him?"

"That he's had a lot going on with his family. He promised he'd call back. He said he had something to explain."

"What does that mean?"

"I have no clue." Dan's face looked pasty. "But I don't want you to worry. Just rest. I'll pick up Rachel, I've got some errands to run anyway—I want to go by his house again. *Jesus.* I can't believe this goddamn nuisance—especially now that this happened with your Grandma."

He paced by the bed. I'd never seen him act this nervous. I was suddenly tempted to tell him about the mysterious felony charge.

Dan started to walk out of the bedroom. "Honey?" I said. "Can I talk to you?"

"Sure. You need something?" He shoved his hands in the pockets of his jeans. I could tell it was an effort for him to look concerned.

"You know how I was worried about Richard?"

"Yes."

"And you know how you taught me about the importance of due diligence?"

"I'm going to stop you right now, honey." Dan held his hand up like a traffic cop. "Please don't give me a lecture on due diligence."

"It's not that." Before I could stop myself, I told Dan about Harry's offer and how, on a whim—and in the spirit of due diligence—I'd had Richard checked out. I assured him that Harry didn't know or care who Richard was anyway, but he'd pulled up some kind of felony charge. "I was supposed to find out what it was today, but then Grandma died."

"Oh God." Dan sat down heavily. My mouth went dry. I heard myself swallow, then whispered, "Am I in big trouble?"

Dan stared at me. He looked dazed, shell-shocked. After a long silence, he said, "You've got to call this guy, Harry. Find out what it was." Dan's muscular voice was drained of its usual confidence—it even shook a little. "Under no circumstance tell him who Richard is to us."

Dan held his head in his hands and made the clicking sound as I got up to make the call. Harry wasn't in the office but I got his assistant, Debbie, who did a lot of his research. I told her Harry had done a criminal background for me, and before I could finish my sentence, she said, "I know—I've got the paperwork from the court runners right here. Let's see…Richard Harding. Felony embezzlement. Appears he skimmed about three hundred grand from an accounting firm he worked for, and went on the lam for a period before being apprehended to face charges. Time served: three years, Lompoc, 1967-1970."

I echoed each fact she recited so Dan could hear and then hung up the phone.

"The years he was in Vietnam," muttered Dan.

I was thinking of what Darlene at the bank had said about how Richard would make a sorry excuse for a soldier. It was apparent now that none of his time served was with the Army Special Forces, but seeing Dan's expression, I didn't need to state the obvious.

Dan started chanting, "Fuck me. Oh, fuck me."

Within seconds he was on his feet. "I've got to call the bank—see if I can find out what's going on." He bolted downstairs into his basement office, and I followed.

Dan's office was a mess: little notes and files piled atop dusty furniture, and the big black file cabinet that was always—*always*—locked tight as a crypt. He started rummaging through some of the piles until he came up with a typed report that listed bank account numbers. He looked over at me and banged out some numbers on the phone pad.

"Yes. Thank you. I'm the holder of a check in the amount of seventy-five thousand dollars for Account Number 0096-998768 and I'd like to know if there are funds available for it to clear today?"

We waited. A horsefly buzzed around the office. The sound was unnerving. It finally hurled itself against the window and fell on its back, frantically attempting to flip over. I picked up an old newspaper and smashed it.

"Very well, then. Thank you," said Dan. He dropped into his stained swivel chair and turned so pale that the whites of his eyes appeared grayish-yellow. "A check for seventy-five thousand dollars won't clear that account." He looked glassy eyed, stoned. I thought he might start to cry.

"You have seventy-five thousand dollars there?"

"I have well over half-a-million dollars there. If seventy-five thousand won't clear, holy shit—"

Half-a-million dollars?

"Of investors' money?" I said.

"What? No. *My* money."

"What do you mean, *your* money?"

"What do you mean, what do I mean? Money I've earned, saved, paid taxes on."

Dan had a half-a-million dollars in the account managed by Richard? And now it was gone? I didn't know whether to feel sympathetic or enraged. I'd had no idea Dan had access to that much money because he never liked to spend it, constantly complained about what things cost, and put me off every time I brought up my desire for us to buy a home. He'd told me that every penny he had was tied up in the property he was trying to develop. This new information made me momentarily furious, until it occurred to me that it was much easier to cope with than if I'd just learned he'd received a blowjob. Anything was better than finding myself in bed with another two-timer.

"Jesus Christ, he was like a brother to me—supposed to be the goddamn best man at our wedding! He *knew* how my past partners had screwed me."

I turned away. Why was he so desperate for a replacement brother? Why was this surrogate sibling wrecking our life when things were going so well? And why did I have to deal with all this when I'd just lost Gram?

"I've got to find that lying bastard," said Dan, the blood rushing back into his cheeks. He was up and pacing again. "I'm sorry for what you're going through, honey. I want to be more of a help, but you'd better get Rachel. I have to find out what the hell is going on." Within seconds, he was on the phone with Johnny Curtain. "You'd better sit the fuck down, Johnny. We've got a problem."

I picked up Rachel and told her the news about Grandma. We decided to celebrate Grandma Mary's life by having a dessert picnic next to our Christmas tree with lots of jellybeans and strawberry ice cream—Gram's favorite sweets.

When we returned home there was a cacophony of deep voices rising from Dan's office. I set Rachel up in front of the TV and quietly descended the stairs. It stunk like someone was smoking in the house. Could this mean Richard was here? I stood by the closed door to eavesdrop, but couldn't make out his distinctive nasal tone. I recognized the voices of Dan, Johnny Curtain, and a man named Larry, a thick-necked chain smoker who wore loopy gold necklaces and a discolored hairpiece. "Call me Blackjack," he'd said when I was first introduced to him.

I pressed my ear against the door. Expletives flew from their mouths like dirty flies. As far as I could make out, they were scheming to find that "mother-fucking, mud-sucking pig Richard who goddamn raped Dan—that's right *raped him!*—the low life ass-fucking coward that he was." Dan and his foul-mouthed posse were concocting a plan to hunt that "snaky sonofabitch" Richard down and make him show their "hard-working asses" where he stashed the money he'd stolen.

I heard Dan's voice get closer and quickly backed up. When he opened the office door, I was already on the stairway.

"Hey honey." My heart hammered in my chest. "I was just coming down to find you."

"We're on his trail," he said. "Don't wait up."

Johnny and Blackjack stopped briefly to greet me.

"Mary, darlin'," said Johnny. "I'm darned sorry to hear about your grandmother." He reminded me of the character Eddie Haskell on the old show "Leave It to Beaver"—talking trash behind closed doors, but unctuous whenever meeting me or other acquaintances. Sincere or not, his kind words still caused me to tear up again.

Dan embraced me. "You know I wouldn't leave now unless I had to. I'll be home as soon as I can. We'll think of something special to do for your grandmother."

I didn't reply, but followed them upstairs and watched as they jumped in their cars and caravanned down the hill. My body buzzed with anxiety. How could the same man who cooked our meals, took out our trash, and showed up for every one of Rachel's school events be involved with this questionable cadre of associates—lying, chain-smoking, cologne-doused men with lacquered hairpieces?

That night I had a dream of Grandma Mary yelling at me, her eyes two bottomless black holes, but I couldn't hear what she was saying. I kept screaming, "I'm sorry Grandma, I'm sorry." I was startled awake as if I'd been zapped with electricity. My mind spit out frightening images faster than I could absorb them. Grandma was dead and Dan was on a trail leading where? Didn't people kill each other over sums smaller than this? Richard was a liar and an embezzler, not a murderer, I kept telling myself.

The mid-December wind was wild, blowing pinecones and branches down off the trees so they cracked on the roof, sounding like footsteps. I thought I heard a noise inside the house and prayed it was the cat, but when I sat up, I saw her curled in a fuzzy black lump on the chair in the corner of the room. I got out of bed and went to check on Rachel. She was soundly sleeping under a blue quilt. Before I left her room I heard another loud *thunk* in the house. My heart lurched.

I walked down the hall. There was a light glowing from Dan's downstairs office and its warmth spread relief through my limbs. He was home. We were all home now—healthy and safe.

"Honey?" I said, in a whispery yell. "That you?"

I peeked into the room. The lights were on, but he wasn't there. The digital clock said it was 3:24 a.m.

I heard a groan and looked down. Dan was lying on the scratchy brown carpet behind his desk, staring at the ceiling, both hands holding his head.

"I'm here."

"Oh my God, are you all right?" I ran to his side.

He groaned again.

"What are you doing?"

Silence.

Dan's breathing was ragged; both hands were draped over his face. He was crying.

"Honey?" I knelt next to him.

"Go back to bed. I don't want you to see me like this."

I was speechless. He looked terrified.

"What happened? Are you hurt?"

"I'm begging you, honey. Please. Give me this time alone."

"I'm not going to leave you like this."

"Well, you were right. Okay? You were right. My life savings? He spent it. Gambled it away. All except thirty grand. He thought he'd pay it back by taking a loan on the coast development. Now that's completely fucked—it's encumbered with a two million dollar lien and is close to foreclosure." Dan started to ramble. "I thought maybe, just maybe, he might have hid some money. You know? Tried to steal it, and I'd get it back. How could anyone blow through that much, that fast? It's fucking inconceivable."

"He spent it all?"

"Pissed it away on nothing."

"You mean it was *your* money he spent on all that stuff he bought us?" I asked, incredulous. Even though I'd suspected this, I couldn't understand how someone like Dan could be so overtly bamboozled. "Are you sure?"

"With a gun to his head, he swore on his own life. You can say it. 'I told you so,'" he said.

"What do you mean, a gun to his head?"

Dan told me that he, Johnny, and Blackjack had gone to Richard's house. A large moving van was loading up furniture but Richard was nowhere to be found. Dan and Johnny decided to follow the movers, who led them to San Francisco, to a big Mediterranean style mansion inside the gates of Sea Cliff. That's where they saw Richard's Jaguar parked in the driveway. Blackjack met up with them after he had returned home to get his gun.

"Jesus Christ, Dan, are you all insane? People get killed over things like this!"

"No one was hurt," said Dan. "We needed it to protect ourselves, with Richard acting like such a goddamn criminal."

"How could you let a thug like Blackjack into our home? With Rachel here?"

"It's not like you're imagining." Dan assured me that no one ever was at risk of being shot. But Blackjack and the gun had acted like a truth serum on Richard, who had cried out the whole ugly story. Richard said he had been spending down Dan's cash, then passing off copies of monthly bank statements that had been doctored. When that money ran out, he took a short-term high-interest loan on the property for two million dollars. He used forged documents and his authority as trustee to complete the transaction. Though he meant to use the funds only to try to win back the disastrous losses, things started to spiral. Now that they were back in touch, his ex-wife was threatening to tell Dan that Richard was lying about his past. He'd shut her up by paying off the mortgage on her house. The Jaguar wasn't leased; it was paid for in full. He'd furnished his rental with imported Italian furniture, then got into a year-long lease, at ten thousand dollars a month, on a seven-bedroom San Francisco mansion above the surf in Sea Cliff, where he imagined he'd set up high stakes poker games and make a killing. Even the money he'd loaned to the project had come straight *from* the project.

"He's cannibalized the whole fucking deal," said Dan. "He was crying— Jesus, you should've heard him. 'I'm paying it all back,' he said. 'I have a plan,' he said. He put his fucking signature on papers that left us hocked to the hilt. He figured he'd pay it back when the development deal closed—that we'd all make a fortune and he'd be some kind of superhero. And you know what? I really think he believed it."

"And I really think *you* believe that you haven't put us all in danger," I said.

My entire body was shaking. If Dan was so out of touch with reality in this situation, I didn't know what to think about his crazy coastal deal. It had always seemed too good to be true—or at least too convoluted to be good. No matter how many times Dan explained it, I never understood Richard's role. The part that stuck was that Dan let Richard handle all the meetings and money, with Dan strategizing behind the scenes. They had legal documentation that made Richard a front man so that Dan could protect his assets. It was called an "irrevocable trust" because you couldn't revoke the trustee—Richard—at any time. Presumably these trusts wouldn't be abused because no one would put someone untrustworthy in an irrevocable position. This "asset protection" had allowed Richard to access the trust bank accounts and to authorize a loan on the property without Dan's knowledge.

"Thirty grand—that's all that's left in my account," said Dan, groaning. "I'll sell the Jaguar, and try to get out from under the lease. We don't know what he did with the loan money."

I sat there, stunned. Richard had spent $470,000 of Dan's money and all we got was some patio furniture, a stereo, and a weekend trip to Tahoe?

"Dan, can't you get him arrested?"

"Don't you get it? I can't. There's no way to prosecute Richard without implicating myself. I was unlawfully hiding money," said Dan, his voice straining.

"I thought the trust part was lawful? Asset protection?"

"Lawful as long as you're not sheltering it to avoid legal obligations." Dan appeared circumspect. "I was hiding assets from the IRS."

"I still don't understand. Can't you sue him?"

"Sue him for what? He doesn't have any money. Besides, I still need him to try to save the property."

Dan sat up and leaned against the wall. I wanted to reach out to him, but couldn't. This entire mess was too complicated, too unbelievable. I wanted to scream at him; but it seemed cruel and unnecessary, especially when he was already devastated. It didn't help that I had the absurd notion that it was partly my fault—that none of this would have happened if I'd just minded my own business, and the felony conviction had gone undiscovered.

Dan spent the entire weekend in a state of panic, talking on the phone, pacing, running off to meet Johnny and Blackjack. I tried to stay out of his way, taking care of Rachel, and checking in regularly with my relatives to gage how everyone was handling our sad news about Grandma. I had to believe that Dan would figure out some solution but I didn't ask for the details.

"Remember," I said, "It's only money."

Dan looked at me like I needed a brain transplant.

"I have a job," I reminded him.

He rolled his eyes.

Several times, Dan told me how much he needed "his woman" to be on his side. He hadn't felt supported by his mother or by his former wives, and that had upset him deeply. I did my best by making trite and reassuring remarks, but that was just to keep from screaming, "I TOLD YOU SO" over and over again. If there was any good news, with Dan and I now both despising Richard, I could at least trash him with impunity and still remain the loyal partner Dan craved. No sense kicking a man while he was down.

Sunday afternoon, while Rachel visited her dad, we took a long hike on one of our favorite paths in Redwood Park, which wound deep into the hills. Instead of the usual musings about our wedding, recipes we wanted to try, or whether the co-directors of Rachel's school were secret lesbian lovers, I listened to Dan rant and rave about how he was sick of the pervasive betrayal in his life by his ex-wives, his ex-partners, his good for nothing *sonofabitch* cousin Mike, his parents, and now Richard, the man who had been "like a brother" to him. He'd been ready to retire, but now he had to start all over again.

"And putting us through this right while you're grieving? When I should be totally available to you? I swear to god—if I didn't need Richard so badly— I can picture myself squeezing his fat throat until he chokes to death."

"Now you're scaring me," I said.

"Jesus, honey—can't I vent a little with my wife? In the privacy of our relationship?"

Wife? "I have to tell you, Dan. I've been a little nervous, thinking we'd have to postpone the wedding."

We walked silently for a few minutes. Dan stopped and grabbed my hand, startling me. He looked down towards the view of the San Francisco Bay emerging out of a thick cloudbank that pressed against the coast. A few misty fingers of condensation crept under the bridge, making it look as if a living creature was moving toward us from the shore.

"Do you want to postpone the wedding?" he said.

"Do *I* want to?" I said.

"Because, if so, I'd understand." Dan frowned, pulled a red bandana out of his pocket and wiped his forehead. His eyes were moist. Looking off into the distance, he said, "Sometimes I think I'm too much."

"Too much what?"

"Too much to deal with."

"Do you really think you're too much for me? Or are you just trying to get out of marrying me?"

He gripped my hand, said nothing. A peppery spray of black birds swirled overhead. We watched them fade into a dark smudge against the pale winter sky.

"I don't know what I'd do if I lost you—and Rachel, too." Dan dropped my hand and turned away from me. "I'm so sick of the commercial world—of man's inhumanity to man. If I didn't have our little family—" Dan finished his sentence with a loud sigh. He took my hand again, I squeezed it reassuringly, and we continued to walk along the rocky trail, each of us lost in our own thoughts.

Chapter 13

December 1991

"Harry Paine is in your office," the receptionist told me when I arrived at work the following Monday.

"Welcome to your work day." Harry lounged in a chair by my desk, sipping a cup of coffee. "How you surviving?"

"I'm okay. Sorry about canceling lunch."

"I'm sorry for your loss." Harry stared at me a minute. This always made me feel uncomfortable. "I hope this Harding fellow wasn't your Grandma's CPA."

I smiled at Harry's effort to cheer me up.

"No, it's this other thing." *God, I'm starting to talk like Dan.* "I promised the information to a friend. Thanks for digging it up." I shot him a grateful smile, hoping to shift the subject. "Now, to what do I owe the pleasure of your visit, Mr. Paine?"

"This ought to entertain you." Harry set his coffee cup on my desk, reached inside his suit pocket, and pulled out a brochure. "We just signed up with a new online search company." He studied the brochure. "Accurate Information Services. Bottom line is, they put out personal profiles of people; you can get names, address history, relatives, liens, bankruptcies and judgments. Listen, it says here, 'Find the data to inspect and protect, twenty-four-hours a day.'"

I took the brochure. "Inspect and protect? Cool. Want me to pass that info out to the powers-that-be around here?"

"Hell no. I wanted to give you a chance to play with it. They gave us a special password. We get six free hours of online searching—you can check out everyone you know and not pay a penny. It's a promo they give out so we can train people."

"Why would you want to train me?"

He grinned. "Because you know you're going to end up coming back to work for me."

"Maybe *with* you, but not for you," I said wryly.

"Whatever," he said. "I know you love this stuff—I've never met anyone nosier than you." He held out the brochure.

"What makes you think I'm nosy?"

Harry tapped his nose then pointed at me. "Takes one to smell one."

"I like my job, Harry." I grabbed the brochure and started to read it.

"Yeah, but you can only go so far here. I'm thinking of starting a new firm. You could do my marketing—"

"Everyone wants me to do marketing. I want to be an investigator."

"And if you'd let me finish my sentence. You could do my marketing *while* I turn you into an investigator. With all due respect, Nancy Drew, a little honing of the investigative skills wouldn't hurt."

"Okay. I know."

Harry cleared his throat, smiled. "Here, I'll show you how this works."

I stepped away from my computer and Harry took my seat. He pulled up a Web site and typed in a password. "See here? This is the temporary password. Now. Let's put in your name."

"Here's a better idea," I said. "Let's put in your name."

Harry squinted up at me, shook his head. "You drive a hard bargain."

"I'm sure you already have a secret dossier on me."

"Don't flatter yourself, sister." Harry hunted and pecked on a few more keys. "See? Here comes my profile."

We both stared at the screen as Harry's home address, office address, phone number, and P.I. license numbers popped up, as well as repeated references to his former partner, Simon Savage. I studied the report. The names of two different men, all sharing his address and phone number, appeared regularly.

"Who are these guys?" I pointed at the screen.

"Aha. See? Already you've learned something. One is an ex-business partner. One is an ex-lover. This program picks up names of anyone you've ever shared credit with. And so you know—this database is pretty sparse. It doesn't give criminal or civil records, but you can use it as a springboard to explore other areas. Interviewing exes, neighbors, knowing what county courthouses to search."

I eyed Harry carefully while he spoke. I'd always thought he dressed nicely for a guy who had never married—tailored suits, fancy socks that matched his slacks, hip shoes—but I hadn't figured him for gay.

He stood up. "You're loving this, aren't you? The next test is, can you keep a secret? Discretion is everything in this business." He lifted his coffee cup with his pinky held high, and strutted out of my office.

Could I keep a secret? That was probably the funniest thing he had said to me yet.

I walked outside my office and looked up and down the hall. It was very quiet this morning. Most of the investigators were out in the field. Maybe I'd check a few names, just for the hell of it. Mine, Dan's, and—did I dare? After the trouble that erupted after my last glimpse into Dan's world?

Quickly, I typed in the name Milton Murphy, and held my breath.

Forty-seven records for Milton Murphys popped on the screen. And this was just in California. Christ, I thought. Saved by sheer overload.

Next, I typed in Michael Murphy, limiting the search to the city of Novato. I thought that's where Dan said he lived.

Only one record hit the screen. I clicked on the profile, and almost spit coffee all over my desk.

Michael Murphy, aka Milton McDonough.

Mike *was* Milton? Milton was Mike?

My mind jumped around questions like a bird hopping from branch to branch on a tree. But this didn't make sense. If Mike was Milton, then Milton was already free. Did the letter from Maureen just mean he should be metaphorically free? If Mike *aka* Milton had shot that gun accidentally, then what was the guilty look Dan had seen in his eyes? Not that Dan had any innate skills at judging character; I still couldn't get over how he'd trusted Richard. Perhaps Mike's expression only reflected the natural guilt anyone would feel when involved in a fatal accident. But then when and why had he changed his name? Dan truly didn't seem to know who Milton was. I guessed I could try to ask Walter, but then realized it would be impossible to pull that off gracefully. Walter now held a permanent spot on Dan's shit list. Even Dan's desire to please my mother couldn't get that friend an invite to our wedding.

Was this the answer to the big mystery I'd obsessed over all this time? I'd had big ideas about a murder, even a cover-up, and a man named Milton hiding somewhere, unable to show his face. My fantasy went as far as discovering Johnny Curtain had been an accessory to the crime. Then Dan would have to drop kick him out of our life along with Richard, and start making some more trustworthy friends who had absolutely no connection to his poor, dead brother, rather than this set of shady characters who seemed to have congregated around Jimmy. It felt like my theories had been suddenly sapped of all life and color.

Almost without actually deciding to, I typed in Dan's name and waited. After a few minutes his profile popped up with all of his former addresses. I recognized his parent's home, the office in San Francisco, the names of his first and second wives, his license to practice law—all of it. I scrolled back and looked at his addresses again. His house in Marin didn't appear. Clever, Dan. There were a few listings for P.O. boxes, one in San Francisco and one in Pacifica. As I scrolled down again, I was startled by the intercom buzz.

"Mary, there's a call for you on line one. It's an old woman—sounds like she's crying."

"Thanks."

I picked up the phone, figuring it was an aging homeowner who had lost everything in a fire, probably caused by piling flammables too close to the space heater—another common winter fire starter. Maybe she wanted to know if our investigators were going to blame it on her, afraid she wouldn't get the insurance money. I was a pro at these kinds of calls. I would reassure her, explain nicely that insurance companies don't penalize people for accidents or stupidity, just arson, and then I'd refer her to the claims adjuster.

"This is Mary. Can I help you?"

"Mary?"

I could barely hear her.

"Mary? Is that you? This is Minnie. It's Minnie calling."

My fingers gripped the receiver. "Minnie? What's wrong?"

"It's Dan, Mary." She squeaked between sobs. "He…he…called and … said he wouldn't see us…he wouldn't see us anymore."

I didn't know what to say.

"Mary, we're old. Why is he doing this?"

"Minnie, calm down, okay? Explain this to me."

She sniveled a moment, said something to Ralph, who barked something that I couldn't make out. Then she blew her nose and explained that Dan had called and told her Richard had stolen his money, and because of this he wasn't able to be around people who had betrayed him. It was too painful.

"Mary, he can't get it out of his mind that his cousin purposely killed Jimmy. He still blames his father for bringing them together that night. Were we wrong to want Jimmy to get away from all of his troubles? To have a decent job at the furniture store, a future? Mike only tried to help. Dan insists we're betraying him because we want to accept Mike, let him be a welcome part of the family."

"God, Minnie. I'm so sorry."

"Mary," she squeaked. "He said he wouldn't be taking us to the cemetery this Sunday, and maybe not for a long, long time." Her sobs sounded like wet hiccups.

I knew Ralph was standing by Minnie, unable to comfort her. That wasn't something they did for each other. Besides, he was old and tired. When he couldn't figure out how to solve a problem, Minnie had told me, he would slump in his chair and say, "Take me God. I'm ready. Please just take me."

"Minnie," I said, "Is it possible that Dan just doesn't know the whole story about Mike and Jimmy? It's like there's a piece missing."

The line went quiet. Even the sobbing stopped. The soundlessness was so extreme, I thought I heard the ticking of their upstairs grandfather clock.

"Minnie? Are you there?"

"Yes." Her voice sounded small, terrified.

"Minnie, don't worry. We're coming over this weekend. I don't know about Dan, but Rachel and I are still coming over."

She relayed this to Ralph and I could hear the relief.

I hung up the phone feeling furious with Dan. I kept hearing the sound of Minnie's voice. I couldn't stop thinking about Grandma the last time I saw her at the motel, where those crazy moths were zigzagging back and forth, battling to find warmth around the glowing amber light, unable to stop their frantic search long enough to see that it was right in front of them. I pictured Minnie and Ralph sitting alone in their kitchen, old and scared and, like Dan, desperate for family.

I had put up with a lot of strange behavior on Dan's part, but this was too much. I wasn't going to let him leave his parents high and dry; this time I would figure out what to do. I had picked up the phone to call him when something caught my eye on the computer screen. Underneath the heading, "Bankruptcies, liens, and judgments," an IRS lien was listed in the amount of $2,173,645.

My eyes widened and I blinked a few times.

The intercom buzzed.

"Line three, Mary," said the receptionist. "Baskin Robbins for a cake order? Do you want to take the call?"

I stared at the computer screen and picked up the phone. "This is Mary. Can I help you?"

"Returning your call, ma'am," said a woman. "You wanted to place an order for a chocolate mint ice cream cake large enough to feed 125 people?"

"Right. I left you a message."

"For a cake that size, you'd have to special order it, ma'am. And we require payment in full."

My eyes had latched onto the screen. I couldn't think straight.

"Ma'am?"

"I'm going to have to call you back."

"Do me a favor," said Dan, holding up his finger. "Do not come in here accusing me of things I did *not* do." His face was reddening.

"I'm not accusing you of anything." I softened my tone. "I'm just asking about that tax lien."

"Honey, I told you I had tax issues."

"Dan, this is not an *issue*. It's a calamity. It's over two million dollars, for godsakes."

"Listen to me," Dan held my shoulders and looked me straight in the eyes. "At this point, the only calamity I can think of would be if something happened to you, me, or Rachel. This tax thing is just another problem that I have to solve." He let me go, and started sifting through some papers on his desk. "And I don't even owe that amount. The IRS just slapped that lien on me because they couldn't find my ex-partners."

Dan had mentioned many times that the large diamond investment company he'd founded a decade earlier continued to have unresolved tax issues. "They don't care that it's erroneous—they just want the goddamn money and then—and *only* then—will they look at the evidence that I don't owe it. Is that fair?"

"That's not the point—"

"Not the point?" Dan pushed his chair aside, and started to pace, needing to detour around our lounging cat. "What is the point then? Do you know what the IRS requires before you're allowed to file a complaint?"

Uh-oh. Here we go again.

We were in Dan's basement office. There was nowhere to sit among the clutter of books, files, newspapers, and countless notes. Despite the mess, it always surprised me that Dan could find whatever paper he was looking for, no matter what file or pile it was in. When I read the self-help book *Prosperity Now!*, it said we had "to clear our minds of old beliefs in order to make room for the good that we wanted to manifest in our lives. The best way to kick-start this process was to rid our environment of clutter." Based on this, I'd suggested to Dan that he might want to clean his office, and examine his fears about losing money. "Your belief that everyone is out to betray you might have been what created that result—I mean, it caused you to hide your money and then look what happened."

Dan just looked like he wanted to pop me.

"Can we go upstairs?" I said. "I can't think here." I leaned against the side of Dan's black file cabinet, casually resting my hand on the knob to see if it was unlocked. On occasion, I'd seen one of the drawers opened when Dan was in his office working. But whenever I entered the room, he would close it. In one quick shove, the open drawer would snap shut with a confident, metallic *clack*. In another deft move, he would slip the key from its hold, and press the lock button, *click*. From there, he would distract me with a kiss or strategic change of subject.

"What's in there?" I'd asked one day, careful not to appear too interested.

"Files," he said. "I'm done with them."

Clack.

Click.

Kiss.

But whenever I returned to his office alone, the keys were gone and the drawers locked.

Now, pretending to fidget, I played with the sliding release button on the top drawer. As usual, it was immovable.

"Honey. Can you leave that alone? I don't need that to break right now. Just give me a second. I have some notes about how to handle the tax stuff in relation to our wedding. I'll grab them and come up."

Rachel was with her father; we had all evening to talk. Upstairs, I kicked off my boots, pulled off my socks, and stretched my toes. Normally, I loved workdays like today. My boss, Kent, had taken me to a potential arson fire at a house in Berkeley. I had photographed, measured, and helped collect evidence samples in the grimy, wet remains of the kitchen. Within a few minutes, our canine assistant, Cinder, had picked up the scent of accelerant in three separate areas.

"You know," said Kent, "whoever set this fire could've just let something burn on the stove next to some flammables. Instead, he uses gasoline—like we're not going to notice that." He reached down and scooped up a pile of sludge and sniffed it. "Here. Take a whiff."

I inhaled and started to cough.

"I swear," said Kent. "Criminals are such idiots. They almost go out of their way to draw attention to themselves."

I blushed, but Kent didn't even glance in my direction.

Now I that was home in my sweet white cottage I didn't want to give any thought to idiotic criminals, but I had a tax lien to learn about. With Christmas just a week away, I only wanted to enjoy our first family tree—a fragrant Douglas fir that was missing its lower ornaments because Goody kept knocking them down. Dan had something cooking in the oven that smelled garlicky and sweet. I breathed deeply and some of my frustration dissipated. Bed made, dinner cooking, dishwasher emptied, plants and cat fed. For a guy who came packaged with such great homemaking skills, he sure had a lot of dirty laundry.

Dan came upstairs holding the cat. The two of them plopped down on the blue recliner. In his sweatsuit, he looked boyish and relaxed.

"Can I just jump right in?" I said.

"Yes." Dan scratched Goody's neck with one hand, and clutched a small pile of papers with the other.

"This tax lien? Will I owe the money when we get married? I mean, since it was your debt? I'm wondering, will it show up on my credit rating?"

"The short answer is, no, you wouldn't owe the money but we *would* be linked financially. Or, at least credit reports would cross-reference our names. And that begs the larger issue—"

Dan kept talking but I was lost in thought. I had been working diligently to clean up my finances. I had sent letters to each of my creditors stating my intent to pay. Even though I didn't have much to apply to debt at that time, I paid a small amount every month and kept up my list of affirmations, including my favorites: "I am debt free and prospering," and, "I am a money magnet." I wanted to own a home and figured, with the help of Dan—who still had plenty of marketable skills—we could do this. But not if his credit was shot, and it turned out that our legal union contaminated mine.

"So, short of doing anything illegal, immoral, or fattening, that's another option," said Dan, sorting through his notes. He looked at me expectantly.

"What's an option?"

"If you insist on a legal document, we could get married out of the country. In fact, honey, I have some business in Panama. We could have a short, sweet ceremony there, and stay for a honeymoon."

"Panama?" I pictured my family opening invitations to our wedding, relocated somewhere in the Canal Zone. "Are you crazy?"

Dan set Goody on the floor, and joined me on our new couch.

"Honey, I'm sick—*sick*—about being in this situation right now. I'm just saying we can have some kind of ceremony in Panama—make it official there. That'll get you your formal marriage license and I'm not on any public records here."

"Dan, I can't suddenly ask my family to go to a wedding in Panama. What about all our plans? We've reserved the church, I'm about to order an ice cream cake."

"Whoa—" Dan took my hand and aimed his eyes into mine. "We'd still get married on Valentine's Day in San Francisco. It's just that that ceremony will be more symbolic. We'd be married in the eyes of God and our family and the government wouldn't have to know a goddamn thing about it. We'd honeymoon in Panama—have a legal ceremony there. It will be the first of many exciting trips together, I promise."

Something told me that it might be a good idea not to have my name on any marriage license with him—here or in Panama. *Inspect and protect.* Forget his worries about being tracked down; I didn't want to fall into the hole he'd dug with that big fat tax lien. The more Dan brought up the need to stay off public records, the less interested I was in connecting any of my records to him. I tried to think of what actual advantages I would gain by being legally married to this man. I wanted a real husband and, license or not, Dan felt like a real husband. The financial planning teacher said marriage gives us the benefits of society, like getting your spouse's insurance or social security if he died. But Dan no longer paid into that system; he operated outside of society. So what benefits would marriage secure for Rachel and me? None. And anyway, if I tried to file for any benefits, wouldn't they go after me for his whopping tax liability?

"Dan, maybe we don't need any legal ceremonies. I mean, with your tax thing."

"I tend to agree with you," he said.

We both remained quiet for a moment.

"But I'd want a wedding."

"Of course."

"Oh my God," I said. "Do you realize that this would be my second fake wedding? What are the chances?"

"Listen, honey. I know how important it is to you to be married and you need to know how much I want to be married to you. I love you and Rachel so much. The *ceremony* would be a performance." Dan held my gaze. "Our marriage would not be fake."

Goody jumped next to me and started to purr. "So—how would it work?" I asked.

"Johnny can marry us in San Francisco, as planned, it's just that the certificate will be more decoration than legal document."

I had reluctantly agreed to have Johnny Curtain perform the ceremony. Neither of us were close to any clergy members, and since Grandma Mary was dead and Grandma Hazel too frail to attend, we didn't feel obliged to have a priest. Johnny had years of experience as a public speaker and sent away for a mail-order ordination—from some Church of Universal Love—that allowed him to marry people legally. Not that the legality of it was relevant now.

"But our witnesses will expect to sign a license, right? Jamie and whoever you get to replace Richard, won't they have to sign off, too? We'll have to make up a fake certificate."

It occurred to me that Jamie, my maid-of-honor, would love this charade. But I'd have to insist that she keep this a secret from the rest of the family. And Dan's best man—whoever that would be—had to be trustworthy.

"Dan, it would be a disaster if it slipped out that we weren't getting legally married. What if my dad finds out that he's spending ten thousand dollars on a wedding chapel, hall, champagne, cake, buffet—and it's all fake?" Thanks to Dan, Dad and I had recovered from the fight we had about the loan, which I'd almost repaid in full, and I was so far back in his good graces that he hadn't flinched at paying for my wedding. "This could cause a little set-back."

"Yeah. I've got to think about who to approach on this," said Dan.

"On the other hand, how serious can Dad be about marriage when he's done it three times?" It occurred to me that we were discussing how I, too, was also about to become a third wife.

Dan squinted, pulled a pen from the pocket of his sweatsuit, and scribbled a note.

The living room was getting dark. The bushes and trees outside the front window were formless shapes merging in and out of the thickening fog. I got up and turned on the corner light.

"Hey! Here's an idea. Make your dad your best man," I said.

Dan frowned and shook his head. "How would that help anything? I can't be around my parents now. No, I'll work something else out."

"Dan, your dad is old and depressed. He should get a special role in the wedding, to cheer him up."

"You know what? I think it's great that you love my parents. But that's not going to work." Dan got up and moved into the kitchen. He flipped on a light and opened the oven, sending out a steamy cloud of roasting aromas. I followed, with Goody trotting behind me.

"Can't you see?" I said. "This is the perfect solution. He'll sign the certificate. He's almost blind; he'll never notice a thing. Actually, he probably wouldn't even notice if we didn't have him sign anything."

Dan suctioned some juice from the pan and basted the baked chicken, Goody meowed at his feet.

"Come on, honey. It would be so great to include your dad," I said. "And your parents are old and scared right now."

"They're scared?" He slammed the oven door closed. "I'm so damned scared, half the time I can't breathe. I worked my whole life to build up a financial reserve and it just got ripped away from me, right under my nose—and frankly, their lack of loyalty is part of the problem."

"They're family," I said calmly. "I want them at our wedding."

No response.

"I know things are hard for you now," I said. "But your parents are upset and worried. I told them I would take them to the cemetery this weekend, as planned."

Dan stood in the kitchen, looking agitated. But the solution was so obvious that I knew he would come around.

Chapter 14

February 1991

The night before the staged ceremony, Aunt Maggie and Jamie slept over. After we returned from our "girls' night out," they giggled in the bathroom as they tried on their dresses. There was a loud rattle at my bedroom door and Rachel burst in, smiling in her flower girl attire. Jamie trailed behind wearing her bridesmaid dress—a black velvet top sewn into a cream satin skirt.

"I've only worn a dress this ugly two times in my life," she said. "The last time I was five years old. And, you know what?" She walked to the closet, looked in the full-length mirror. "I think it was the same dress."

"It's pretty, Aunt Jamie," said Rachel, twirling. "It's like mine." Her skirt spun out like a saucer.

"It's not like yours. You know why?"

Rachel stopped, waited for the answer.

"Because yours looks good on you. I look like a chocolate éclair with a human head. Ask that person you call your mother how someone with such fashionable siblings can make these terrible choices?"

"Very funny," I said. "Come on, you beauties." I lifted Rachel, propping her on my hip. "Bedtime."

"Hey," said Jamie. "Is Dan here?"

"No, why?"

"His stuff's sitting on the couch."

I looked into the family room. Dan's black tuxedo lay over his packed suitcase.

"Oh, no," I said. "Either my groom forgot his costume, or he's still downstairs in the dungeon."

A group of Dan's friends had planned to take him out for a celebratory dinner, then he was spending the night at Johnny Curtain's. His car was gone and I'd just assumed he was, too. It was almost eleven. I went downstairs, saw light glowing behind Dan's closed office door, and I peeked in. Dan was at his desk wearing his gray suit, shirt unbuttoned at the neck and red tie hanging loosely around his neck, like a noose.

"Why are you still here? Where's your car?" I walked to his desk, navigating around piles of paper.

"Honey, I'm still working." Dan turned around, gave me a brusque kiss. His cheeks were cold, eyes bright—he looked happy. "We had a break with the project. Johnny and I had to run some numbers. He's down at the copy place printing the settlement proposals."

"It has to be done now? The night before our wedding?"

"It looks like we're about to close the deal. This could be an amazing— *amazing*—wedding gift."

Dan would never recover the money Richard had spent from his personal account, but he was working furiously on a way to salvage the coast development deal. Apparently, when Richard took the loan out on the property, he'd dealt with an over eager lending agent. This agent may have known that Richard had forged signatures on the documents, but proceeded with the loan because he was greedy for a fat commission. I didn't fully understand the details, but I'd been told that as long as Dan could get Richard to verify that the loan agent knew he didn't have full authority to encumber the property, some kind of insurance policy would kick in and save it from foreclosure. Once that was done, Dan had buyers who wanted to take over the project and develop it themselves. Richard was now camped out at Blackjack's house so they could all keep an eye on him until after the deposition or affidavit or whatever it was they needed him to do.

Dan stood and spoke quickly. "If we can clear this up, we'll take the offer on the property. And it's only good until the end of the business week."

"Don't they know you're getting married tomorrow? They've got to know you're leaving for your honeymoon."

"Right. Well, it may work out perfectly. Remember that bank deal I told you about in Panama? That we could get a protected account? We're going to have to move on it right away. I need you to make sure you have your account numbers, and the address and manager's name of your bank." Dan packed papers in his briefcase.

"Why?" I had handled all the logistical details of the wedding; all Dan had to do was show up. I dropped into his office chair.

"It's an intricate deal," he said. "I'll give you the whole dog-and-pony show when we have time. But we need a letter from the manager of your bank branch verifying your accounts."

"You want *me* to open the Panama account? Why don't you open it in your name?"

"It will be in my name, eventually. But for now, the Panamanian banking system requires proof that foreign customers have accounts established in their native country. I don't have an account, you know that."

I frowned. "Is this legal? Can I get in trouble for this?"

"No, I'll make sure nothing—*nothing*—happens to you." Dan stopped and watched me for a minute. "Honey, if you are at all uncomfortable with this, there's another option."

"What's that?"

"I could set up the account in Johnny's name." Dan sighed. "The only downside is—given the timing, he'd have to come to Panama with us."

"Johnny Curtain?" I stood up, sending the chair slamming against the wall.

"Settle down, honey. Johnny's got the connections there. He's got his own accounts."

"You would actually do that *again*, put your money in someone else's name?"

"What would you have me do? I need to have proof of a U.S. account and you two are my only options."

"Why does Johnny have accounts in Panama?"

"He's fighting his own tax wars. Completely unfair."

"Don't tell me, I don't want to know." I held my hand up, imitating one of Dan's dramatic gestures. "Tell me this: If it's going in my name anyway, why do we have to open an account in Panama? Why not deposit it here?" I liked the idea of filling my bank account full of Dan's money. I could keep my eyes on it, and him.

"How would you explain that sudden influx of money?" he said. "No, we need this."

Dan explained that once we had an account established, the Panamanian funds could be accessed through a credit card that was attached to the account. He could pay for everything with this credit card, even access the money through ATMs, and there was no connection to the United States.

"Hiding in plain sight, you see? And here's the brilliance," he said. "Most people are hiding their money in well-known tax havens like the Cayman Islands, Antigua, the Bahamas. It's gotten so goddamn out of hand, the IRS is going to blow their cover any day now, you can bet on that. There are laws in Panama that make it less attractive to bank there, so nobody does it. Nobody does it, so our government isn't sniffing around. And the first payment from the sale may be coming through for a couple hundred thousand, so—"

Two hundred thousand dollars would be more than enough to provide us with a down payment on a house. And if I went along with the plan, Dan would certainly have to reward me by agreeing to get us a home, especially because I'd be in control of the cash.

"I have my most recent bank statement," I said. "Should I pack that? Is it enough proof?"

"No, that's not what I want. These bankers we're dealing with—if they don't see an existing high balance, they're not going to go for it. That's why we've got to get a letter from the branch manager—with just the account numbers—it'll buy me the time I need to complete this settlement. You'll need to get a letter from your bank on Monday, before we fly out." Dan moved around his office, collecting books, papers, and his calculator.

I sat back on his office chair and stacked scattered slips of Dan's ideas into a precarious tower of paper.

"Honey, leave that stuff. I know where everything is." Dan picked up his briefcase, sending the notes fluttering onto his desk. "Johnny will be here any second." He picked up his suitcase and tux and we stood out front, waiting.

"The fact that this thing is settling tonight? It's a great omen," he said.

A gust of wind rustled through the trees, making the leaves look like winged creatures squirming on the branches. I shivered and crossed my arms. Dan set down his bags and wrapped his arms around me.

"We should both be in bed, getting beauty rest," I said.

Dan pulled me close and whispered, "We should be in bed together. And you know what? Tomorrow night we will."

Headlights illuminated the trees, transforming them back into friendlier foliage. A car door slammed, and footsteps sounded at the front of the house.

"Glad I made it before midnight." Johnny Curtain's white hair and broad smile glowed in the darkness. "We don't want the groom to see the most beautiful bride in the Bay Area on her wedding day." Johnny kissed me on the cheek. "Did Dan tell you? We're settling this bastard tonight? The terms exceed everyone's expectations. You ought to be proud of him; it's Dan's brilliance that sealed this deal. Then you two are off to Panama for a great adventure!" Johnny reached over, pinched my cheek.

In every harrowing event of my childhood, my dad had attempted to comfort me by suggesting the dire situation was actually a "great adventure." He had said that on a family vacation when our rented waterski boat crashed against rocks and again when mom was hospitalized for a nervous breakdown, causing Dad to cancel my eighth birthday party and put us on a plane to stay with his strict mother in Kalamazoo. Even when he insisted the family dine-and-dash from a Thanksgiving dinner at the Honolulu Hyatt because they had lousy service, he'd told us to look at the crime as if it were "a great adventure."

That night, the logistics of the Panamanian honeymoon ran through my mind. The later it got, the harder it was to find the upside of having a secret bank account. This would be the first trip I'd taken away from Rachel. What if the plane crashed? I was risking my life and the future of my child so Dan could hide from his taxes? If Dan and I opened an account into which he poured his recovered fortune, and we were dead, Rachel had to have access to the money. I got out of bed and walked to my dresser. My life insurance and a letter to Jamie with details about my final wishes were there underneath my bras and panties. I found a pen, and scribbled a note on the back of the envelope: "Jamie, if I'm dead, check for bank account in Panama. Ask Harry Paine for help."

Two hours before the wedding I stood in my room in my bra and slip, doing deep breathing exercises. I couldn't get enough oxygen. My make-up was on, my hair neatly blow-dried, and I smelled like vanilla and rose—scents that were supposed to calm me. I rested on the bed until my breathing became normal. This was it—the day I had been dreaming about. I stepped into strappy cream pumps, and slipped my gown over my head. It was a simple, form-fitting lace dress with long sleeves and a scooped neck. It slid easily over the flesh colored slip I wore, but the fit was snug. The cozy meat-and-potatoes meals Dan regularly cooked had added weight to everyone in the family.

The veil dropped from a crown of white silk flowers, and as soon as I'd placed it on my head, the doorbell rang.

"Where's my first-born daughter?"

The sound of footsteps echoed in the house and my door flew open.

"Mommy? Grandpa's here. He wants you to come out and model." Rachel clasped my hand and pulled me into the livingroom.

"What a beautiful bride." Dad held out his hand. "How about giving your old man this dance?"

Looking sharp in his tux, Dad led me around the living room to Louis Armstrong's "What a Wonderful World," the song we had picked out for our father-daughter dance. I loved dancing with my dad. All his movements were fluid and playful, and offered me plenty of opportunity to spin and sashay in ways that showed off the gown. The tension over the money I owed him seemed to be behind us. When the song finished, Dad dipped me, while Rachel and Aunt Maggie applauded.

"Now get me to the church on time," I said.

My mom, former stepmother, and current stepmother were already at the church with Jamie, getting things set up for the reception. I was pleased by Dad's chummy relationships with his exes, but Kevin and I hadn't yet reached that state of grace. He wasn't invited.

The weather cleared, and the world looked clean and bright as we crossed the Bay Bridge to San Francisco. I cracked the window and let the crisp February breeze fill the car. It smelled like rain and sea, until we drove off the bridge into the noisy San Francisco traffic.

The Swedenborgian Church was located on a quiet corner in Pacific Heights, a stone and brick building surrounded by colorful, renovated Victorians. The church gates opened into a quaint, grassy courtyard. The air was sweet, with patches of red and white flowers and dainty trees wreathed in the palest blossoms. I had picked this site because the stone chapel was small and intimate. A large fireplace gave off warmth and a soft, smoky scent, and the only lighting came from windows and the hundreds of votive candles that were lit just prior to the ceremony.

Dan's car was parked up the block. Jamie ran ahead to make sure he was out of sight while I slipped into the bridal chamber. I knew Dan had picked up his parents. They must all be inside.

"Guess what?" said Jamie, bursting into the bridal room. "Mom's packing Grandma."

"What?"

Jamie cracked the door open, and pointed toward Mom, who was wearing a chic black suit and holding a black patent-leather case that looked like a cosmetic tote. One of Grandma's favorite scarves—an ivory and black paisley—was neatly looped and flowing from the handle. Mom spotted us and raised the shiny box with a cheeky smile. "I told you she'd be here."

"And she's wearing the wedding colors," I said, delighted.

"Look at Harry. He's flirting with a man who has a big organ between his legs." Jamie pointed to the organist I'd hired. "They're totally into each other."

It surprised me how happy I felt knowing Harry was there.

I scanned the guests milling in the courtyard, looking for Jamie's girlfriend.

"Where's Alison?"

"She's in the chapel," said Jamie. "Alone and pissed."

"Pissed about what?"

"Let's not get into it; it's your day."

"Jamie, I'm so sick of your evasive answers. If it's *my* day, then talk to me."

"Pissed about our sex life. Our lack of sex life. Pissed that she's paying for a hotel room tonight and there's little chance we'll put it to good use."

I stared at her for a minute; she truly did look absurd in that bridesmaid dress.

"Why is your sex life lacking?"

"Lesbian bed death, I suppose," she sighed. "Apparently it's common enough to have a name."

I took her hand, and gave it a squeeze.

"Mary, you're totally shaking." Jamie reached into the silk sack purse that was draped over her shoulder. "I know you're Miss Purity these days, but since you won't even drink, I brought a few Ativan samples if you need them." Jamie handed me two thin sample boxes, each smaller than matchbooks.

"I won't need them," I said, grabbing them anyway. "I don't plan on missing my own wedding." I tucked them into my bra.

Warm, buttery candlelight flickered in the chapel. As soon as the organist started to play, my smiling mother made her way down the aisle, one hand linked with Minnie's, the other toting Grandma Mary's remains. They walked to the front of the church and lit the unity candle before taking their seats, Grandma resting peacefully on her own chair. Sunlight streamed through a stained glass window spreading a prism of colors through the chapel. Jamie moved slowly, arm-in-arm, with Ralph, and Rachel followed, dropping rose petals to the tune of "My Favorite Things." Then the organist began cranking out an exuberant version of "How Do You Solve a Problem Like Maria."

Dad looped his arm through mine, and I took off down the aisle.

"Slow down, Fraulein," he whispered. "You only get to do this once."

I fell into step with my father, and kept my eyes locked on Dan, who stood smiling next to Ralph, his best man. Ralph, also in a tux, looked stiff, but happy. Dan held Rachel's hand, and his eyes were misting as I approached the front of the church. I kissed my father and Rachel, handed my bouquet of white roses to Jamie, and the church fell silent.

Johnny Curtain cleared his throat. He wore a white cleric's robe and collar and a huge, garish rosary hung around his neck. It struck me as overkill for a guy who hadn't stepped foot in church since his altar boy days, but I kept my attention on Dan until Johnny announced in his best stage voice, "I now pronounce you husband and wife."

Johnny turned to me solemnly. "Mary," he said, "you may now kiss the groom."

A loud round of laughter and applause rose from the pews and the organist played "Climb Every Mountain."

Click. Flash.

My stepfather followed with his camera as we entered a small anteroom where the fake certificate sat. Dan made a big show of getting his father and Jamie to join us. "Come on in witnesses. Let's make this legal."

I nudged Dan and whispered, "Don't be so obvious," then glanced around, to see if Harry or my boss, Kent, were within earshot.

Johnny signed the document, then handed the pen to Ralph, who was grumbling under his breath that the name "Patric" was "a load of crap." I glanced at Jamie. She rolled her eyes. I quickly looked away, leaning into my new husband, kissing his cheek.

"You look very beautiful, Mrs. Patric," whispered Dan.

Click. Flash.

We posed for the camera. Dan pulled me close, keeping one arm resting on my back as I leaned over to sign. The experience made me feel like a properly married lady who was having a torrid, secret affair.

We crossed the courtyard and entered the reception hall. Dad greeted us with big bear hugs. "You two sure put on a great show," he beamed.

Did he know? I squeezed my toes.

"Thank you, Phil. For your generosity, and so much more," said Dan, earnestly shaking Dad's hand.

"Thank you for making it necessary," said Dad. "And welcome to the family."

The party had been launched. John Coltrane played on the stereo, and people mingled around the buffet, filling plates with finger sandwiches, long stemmed chocolate-dipped strawberries, and a variety of other exotic spin-offs inspired by teatime fare. Waiters circulated with trays of champagne, wine, and sparkling cider, and there was a side room with couches, a fireplace, and even a basket of toys for Rachel and friends.

I joined Dan's parents, who were standing by the fireplace watching the children play. Minnie squeezed my arm as I kissed her powdery cheeks.

"Oh, honey," she whispered. "I told your mom, there's plenty of room for your Grandma at Holy Cross. She should go in with us. With all the Marys in there, we wouldn't even have to shell out for the engraver."

"I don't think she's homeless," I laughed. "Mom and Aunt Maggie have a plot for her with my grandpa. Too bad you didn't meet her before she died. You two would have loved each other."

"Well we sure love you." Minnie raised her voice and looked at Ralph. "I'm telling Mary how happy we are that she's our daughter-in-law, Ralph."

"Where's Dan?" Ralph eyes shot through the crowd. He looked nervous.

"You want me to get him?"

"No, no," said Ralph. "Minnie, give it to her." He stuck his thick pointer finger into the side of Minnie's purse. "If he doesn't have the decency to give you the Murphy name, by God, I will."

"Now Ralph? Where's Dan?" She scanned the room uneasily. "Let's wait."

"Oh I'll get it myself." Ralph started to pull Minnie's handbag from her. She yanked it back, fiddled with the latch, and pulled out a white envelope with my name scribbled across in blue ink.

"A little something from the two of us, honey. Just for you."

"Open it," said Ralph, his expression anxious.

"No wait honey. Slip it in your purse. You can open it when—"

"Goddammit, Minnie, just have her open it," growled Ralph.

The bickering continued until we all agreed I could open the envelope. Minnie and Ralph watched me eagerly.

The outside of the greeting card was covered with glittery stars and said, "We made a wish . . ." Inside it read, "...and there you were!"

I'd assumed they were slipping me a check for the honeymoon, but instead I unfolded a piece of paper bearing the letterhead of Holy Cross Cemetery. I skimmed the document and saw that my name had been added to a list of others who were granted access to Plot No. 1368, owned by Ralph and Mary Murphy, purchased August 1953.

Minnie and Ralph hovered closely, nodding and smiling, waiting for my reaction.

"Wow," I said, feeling as if I'd just been granted membership into an exclusive country club. "Can I really accept this?"

"Of course! Please don't deprive us of this pleasure," said Minnie, gripping my arm. "It'll be decades before you'll ever need it. A lot could happen."

"Need what?" Dan appeared beside me, glancing over my shoulder. His brow furrowed, and he snatched the document from my hands. At least his style of snooping was done out in the open, I thought.

Minnie, Ralph and I stood frozen.

"Do you see what I'm saying?" Dan said, turning to me. "On my wedding day? No matter what I tell them, they think we're all going to live happily ever in the afterlife together. Unbelievable."

Dan spoke as if his parents had dissolved into the carpet, which they may have. I was too afraid to look. What I did know was that these people had to resolve this nonsense soon so we could all rest in peace—dead or alive.

Jamie and Alison wandered over with my stepmother, in a flurry of chatter and congratulatory kisses.

"You snagged a hottie," said Alison, nudging Dan. "I've always said, Mary's a keeper."

"We think so." Minnie smiled, and with a jerk of her chin toward the paper that Dan still gripped, indicated to me that I should snag it back.

Ralph drained his champagne glass, slapped it down on the mantle.

"That's right," said Ralph. "Dan finally did something right." He stood with folded arms and a stony jaw, looking petulant.

Dan raised his eyebrows, and took a step back, addressing the larger group. "I guess you would know, Dad. With three under your belt, you're the expert on good marriages." Dan smiled, but his tone was curt.

Ralph shifted uncomfortably.

I might have pointed out that Dan also had three marriages to speak of, but I didn't want to further infuriate him.

"Well, Ralph should be an expert," I said. "He's been married to the best catch in the Bay Area—*besides me*—for almost fifty years."

More laughter. Minnie took my hand, squeezing it tight.

One of the waiters noticed that I didn't have a drink, and arrived with a tray. I picked up a sparkling cider. Ralph grabbed another glass of champagne.

"There you go, Dad. Have another drink," said Dan.

Ralph looked away, tilted his glass back, swallowing it in one slug. He teetered on his feet. Aunt Maggie grabbed his arm.

The *clink-clink* of a spoon against a champagne glass echoed in the room. The crowd settled down, turning its attention to Johnny.

"Everyone get a beverage," he said. "Let's toast the bride and groom."

Removing the cemetery deed from Dan's hand, I tucked it and the card back into the envelope and slipped it to Jamie as we moved across the room to stand by Johnny. "Keep this safe."

"Ladies and Gentlemen," said Johnny. "Your attention please. I want us to raise our glasses to my brother, Dan, and Mary, his bride, on their day of joy. I don't mean the joy that we get from things we own, or covet, but the joy that we receive from people, and especially the joy that we receive from those we love." Johnny raised his glass. "I know I'm not alone in recognizing the great love between these two special individuals. May the love that you, brother Dan, and, Mary, blessed wife, have shared, with us and each other, renew every day of your lives together as husband and wife. Cheers."

From the back corner, Jamie caught my eye and pretended to shove a finger down her throat.

"Hear, hear," said Dan. "Beautiful." He drained his glass and walked over to hug Johnny, leaving me with his parents. Blackjack joined Dan and Johnny.

"Look at those fuckin' clowns." Ralph gestured toward Dan, Johnny, and Blackjack. "Fuckin' circus clowns."

He had a point. Blackjack wore a cream wool suit with a wide, red and white polka dot tie. Johnny was in a priest costume. And in his tailored black and white tuxedo, Dan looked like the ringmaster.

"What's this 'brother Dan,' bullshit?'" Ralph slurred. "Dan's brother, *my Jimmy*, had more goodness in his pinky than that clown has in his big, fat—" Ralph's glassy eyes darted around the room. He looked like a sad, parched old toad. "You would've loved Jimmy. Everyone loved Jimmy." Ralph fixed his gaze on me. "You know, Jimmy's funeral was the biggest they'd ever seen at Duggan's Mortuary. Standing room only. The owner told me he never'd seen a man with so many friends. And I'm not talking about that bozo Johnny Curtain. I mean *nice* friends."

Harry waved from across the room. He sat next to the organist on a black storage trunk. Harry smiled, raised his glass and his eyebrows, and took a swig of champagne, glancing toward Dan and his gang. He seemed to be taunting me with his expressions. In that moment, my stupidity hit me. I'd put Dan's real name on the wedding invitation. Harry knew everything about him; I was sure of it. I looked back at Ralph, who was bleary-eyed and still talking, and felt a rush of blood fill my face.

The waiter leaned toward me. "Can I get you anything else, Mary? Food? Coffee?" I put my hand across my chest, letting it rest where I could feel the outline of the Ativan samples.

"I'd love some champagne." I lifted a glass off his tray, took a long sip, almost emptying it in one swig. It was my wedding day and, legal or not, I deserved to celebrate. I glanced back at Harry, who was listening to the organist with rapt attention.

It had been well over a year since I'd had a sip of alcohol and I felt the effect immediately. My head was giddy as I scanned the crowd. Everyone was behaving, more or less. Dad was tucked in the back corner, drinking champagne, flagrantly flirting with my boss's wife. Aunt Maggie held a champagne bottle in one hand and a glass in another. She looked flushed and bleary-eyed as she stood between Dan and Johnny, occasionally nuzzling Johnny's side, laughing uproariously at his remarks.

"Dan, you've been holding out on me," teased Maggie. "Quit hiding your good looking friends from me."

"Maggie, if you want, I'll make it my life's work to find you the perfect mate." Dan's face was arranged in his famous altar boy look.

"*Itzadeal*," slurred Maggie, pulling Johnny to the dance floor.

Dan was not a flirt and this fact grounded me like gravity. Kevin had liked to catch the eye of attractive women, offering winks and smiles. "I'm just being friendly," he'd say, acting surprised and indignant that I was bothered.

The champagne left me feeling more relaxed than I had in months. I was glad I hadn't needed to join a twelve-step program to give up drinking, or made a formal announcement. Then I'd be forced to do this in the ladies' room. I took another full glass from a passing waiter, and excused myself to find Harry. If he already knew about Dan, what would it hurt to get some help tying up the loose ends on the Mike/Milton mystery? I needed to make time to see him before we left for the honeymoon.

Maybe it was the booze, but I was warming to the idea of having a permanent spot in the Murphy family plot.

Chapter 15

February 1991

The café where I'd arranged to meet Harry was empty except for the tattooed teenagers who worked the counter. The espresso machine hissed and gurgled, filling the air with the scent of coffee. I folded and unfolded the letter signed by the Wells Fargo manager until Harry strolled in and plopped down at the table, causing it to wobble.

"Don't think you're the first woman who's preferred to spend the first day of her honeymoon with me," he said, pointing a finger at me.

"Harry, you're such a heartbreaker," I said, scooting his drink over. "One non-fat, decaf, extra-hot latte—per your request. When I ordered it, the kid at the counter said, 'One Burning Impotent, coming up.'"

"Tell that smart ass that a 'burning impotent, coming up,' is an oxymoron." Harry looked amused as he poured a packet of Sweet & Low into his latte. "I've given up sugar and fat. I'm getting a gut, which could have a more disastrous effect on my love life than impotence." He took a sip. "So. What's up?"

"I want to talk to you about Dan." I tried to continue, but no more words came. I reached for my coffee, realized I was shaking, and set it down abruptly.

"Come on, spit it out." Harry folded his arms, struck an expression of rapt interest, boring his green eyes into mine.

"You're not making it any easier," I said.

"I'd make it easier if I knew what the hell 'it' was."

"Oh, Harry. You know. Our fake name. The tax lien? Among other things." I was on the verge of crying. I hadn't expected it to be this difficult.

Harry's expression changed to one of concern. "Go on."

"You know what I'm talking about. Come on, you checked Dan out, didn't you?"

Harry looked amused. He scooted his chair back slightly. "You think I ran a background check, behind your back, on a man you planned on marrying? Someone I have no reason to deal with? Someone who's not paying me?" Harry shook his head and sighed. "You think I spend that kind of energy on your life? That's a classic diagnostic indicator of Narcissistic Personality Disorder."

I blushed. I had no idea how to respond.

"You know," he said, "there's a subtle power that comes with being a private investigator that also affects shrinks and psychics—certainly priests." Harry laughed. "People confess things because they think I know more than I do. Trust me, I don't check out everyone for fun. It costs me time and money."

"God, Harry. I'm so embarrassed—I'm sorry." I laughed and blew my nose. I'd just assumed you ran his name after you saw it on the invitation."

"Absolutely not." Harry looked offended.

I started chewing on my plastic stir stick.

"I checked him out way before that."

It was like a pie had just hit my face. "You what?"

"Yep. I ran it long before I gave you access to that database—back after your first job interview, when you told me you'd worked for him. But it's one thing to work for a guy, another to marry him. That's why I gave you a free pass to the database, though—because I *knew* you'd check out everyone you knew. And I just wanted to make sure you had a peek at his history. Didn't want to watch you blindly walk into another wall." He chuckled.

"But how did you—"

"The good news is, you trusted your intuition about me, and you were right," said Harry. "And I have a certain peace of mind knowing you walked into this wall with your eyes open."

I hit Harry on his arm, sending latte foam spilling down his pants.

"Serves you right," I said.

"I brought you something," said Harry, wiping his pants with a napkin. "For awhile, that scuffle with his diamond business was all over the papers. Have you seen this?" Harry fished a folded document from his jacket pocket. "It's from the *Wall Street Journal*."

"Really?" I grabbed the article from Harry and started to skim through, excited. "Wow, he was famous."

"He had his fifteen minutes." Harry shook his head. "We girls sure love our bad boys, don't we?"

"Dan mentioned there was some hideous story that ran in the papers. He goes nuts whenever he tells this part of the story. He wanted to sue for libel."

"That's likely what got him into trouble in the first place," said Harry. "The article says that his company used lawsuits like most folks use telephones. Not to get religious on you, but looks like he reaped what he sowed. Plus, his partners and executives traveled with some interesting baggage."

Scouring the article, I found that it confirmed everything Dan had already told me, and more. It said the company was the "largest marketer of investment-type diamonds," with annual sales of roughly $200 million. "Even its critics concede that the company has some powerful claims to distinction." The part Dan never mentioned was that his former company sued anyone and everyone they felt threatened them, from competitors to regulatory agencies to the State of Missouri. The article outlined the confusing and corrupt histories of key players in Dan's defunct company. One partner had spent three years in prison for defrauding investors using "false documents" and then diverting over $300,000 for personal use. The other once ran an air-charter business that was actually a dope smuggling operation. Johnny Curtain had referred these men to Dan's small law practice, and he'd represented them on criminal charges. After that they formed the company together.

"He sure gets into bed with some nasty people," said Harry, smirking.

"You don't know the half of it."

Recently, I'd read that one definition of insanity was doing the same thing over and over expecting different results. Immediately, I had thought of Dan. Jamie had a theory about his associations, which I explained to Harry. She believed that his brother Jimmy must have been a conman or a crook. Since Dan had worshipped Jimmy, and then lost him to an untimely death, Jamie thought he kept seeking out conmen and crooks because they were familiar, and he was still trying to complete the relationship he was never able to have with his brother. "Just the same old script with a new cast of characters," she'd said.

"This brings me to another topic," I said.

I gave Harry the entire background on the Mike/Milton mystery, even confessing to reading poor Minnie's mail. He listened patiently.

"I can't help but think there's a missing link here; something that will help Dan put it to rest. What do you think? What's the next step in the investigation, Master Teacher?"

Harry let out a whistle. "That's quite a tale, Mrs. –what's your name now?" He cleared his throat. "But don't you think that fixating on psychoanalysis and unfinished family business is missing the point?"

"What point?"

"That your husband's current problems are far from over. And *you* are sharing the same made-up last name? What is going on with you?"

The tears surprised me this time; I hadn't known how upset I was. I ended up telling Harry everything—the fake wedding, Dan's insistence that he stay off public records, the messed up coastal development deal, and how Dan lost everything because he was trying to hide. After my second or third spin on the explanation, Harry patted my arm and said, "Mary, I could care less. I have no opinion about people who live on the fringe. Some folks really have been screwed and see dropping out of the system as the only way out. Congratulations on not getting married. You need to look out for yourself, and it appears you are."

He explained that there were ways around a lot of our taxation and banking laws, and there was an entire subculture that ran to other countries, hiding assets, setting up offshore companies, operating only in cash.

"But you? I don't know," he said. "We both know you make a lousy liar. Plus you've got that Catholic confessional urge." Harry paused and closed his eyes for a second. "Listen, there's something I have to say. I watched Dan closely yesterday. He clearly adores you and your girl—what's her name, Rachel? That's obvious. And according to what I gleaned from family wedding gossip, you and the kid are happier than you've ever been. Here's the thing: Why haven't you convinced him to clean it up?"

"My mother says I have a high tolerance for inappropriate behavior."

"Not a bad thing." Harry laughed. "It makes you flexible, tolerant. But you can't let it get you in trouble by doing things you're not comfortable with. He'd probably make some changes if you stood your ground."

"How would I do that?"

"Threaten to walk." Harry looked more serious than I'd ever seen him. "And mean it."

"What? Harry, fake wedding or not, we meant what we said in the vows," I said, beginning to regret spilling my guts. "Right now Dan needs my support. It's pretty complicated."

"Looks to me like he's a pro at making things more complicated than they need be. At this point he's got nothing to lose, everything to gain," he said. "And it's obviously stressful as hell for you."

"Yeah, but I'm approaching it like an adventure. What other choice do I have?"

"You always have a choice." Harry fixed me with his penetrating stare. "Listen, if Dan doesn't deal with this tax lien, it's the kind of adventure that could eat him alive."

We sipped our coffees in silence. Outside, a siren blared. A growing crowd of confused drivers attempted to navigate around an enraged woman in a red Porsche, who was screaming, "It wasn't my fault!" at the officer who pulled her over.

"Harry?" I fiddled with the photocopy of the letter the bank manager had addressed to the Panamanian Bank, stopping short of handing it over. If he had all the details, Harry would probably tell me not to contaminate my finances with Dan's. And I didn't want to explain that it was probably my best bet at getting us a house, the next step in moving us toward a more normal life. "If anything happens to me in Panama, I've told my sister to go to you. She could give you information to check out if any of Dan's money was accessible to us here. You know, for Rachel."

"You may be too imaginative to be an investigator," said Harry. "Maybe you should write fiction."

"I don't mean to belabor this. But the Milton thing? I know it's not a matter of urgency, but how can I get more information?"

"I'm not going to insult you by suggesting the obvious."

"Check out civil records for the name change? Because I already did that and —"

"No, no, no." Harry looked disappointed, if not exasperated.

"Go ahead. Insult me."

"Do you know how often people call me because they want to track someone down? An old flame. Someone from college who owes them money. A high school friend. They want to pay me to find them. The first question I ask is, have you called 4-1-1? Nine times out of ten, the answer is no. Nine times out of ten, the number they're seeking is listed."

"Okay, I get it. I should call information services and ask them why they think Milton McDonough changed his name to Mike Murphy, and why no one told Dan about it?" I said cheerfully. "Why hadn't I thought of that?"

"Cute. No. But you should go to the most likely source of information. Just ask the old lady."

"Minnie? Forget it. Besides, I already asked her, more or less."

"If you ask cagey questions, you'll get cagey answers. Not to sound like a broken Biblical record, but you really do reap what you sow. That's it. That's all I have." Harry stood up to leave.

Considering he was such a sharp guy, I thought most of his advice was half-baked. Especially threatening to leave Dan on the eve of our honeymoon.

But how would a single, childless playboy have any idea what it was like for a mother of a toddler to find a faithful co-parent to devote himself to family life with the enthusiasm Dan did?

"Harry, Dan would kill me if he knew I'd confided in you. Please don't ever say anything."

"About what?" Harry made a face like a monkey, and used his hands to cover his eyes, his ears, and his mouth.

Chapter 16

February 1991

Panama City Airport: Honking horns, loud diesel trucks, screaming taxi drivers, and a high pitched banging from a nearby demolition zone. The late morning air was thick, warm, and smelled like cigarettes and gasoline. A gravy colored haze puddled along the horizon, shrouding the bright sun.

I held Dan's hand, squinting at a dusty blue sedan careening toward us. The driver waved wildly, looking as if he wasn't going to stop.

"Whoa!" Dan jumped in front of me and pushed me toward the curb, knocking me down. The car swerved, missing him by a fraction, before screeching to a halt. I watched, breathless, as the driver jumped out and started arguing with a security guard and two taxi drivers.

"You okay, honey?" Dan helped me up and gave me a long hug. I was too rattled to respond.

"Hey Dan!"

We turned and saw the driver of the blue car, a smiling middle-aged man with frizzy red hair, faded freckles and a bright Hawaiian shirt.

"Wow, sorry about the commotion. You two okay?"

"Hey, Frank, what are you doing? Trying to kill my wife before I even get to enjoy the honeymoon?"

"I'm so darned sorry about that," said Frank. "You've got to drive like a maniac to get anywhere on these roadways. Long time no see, buddy." He stuck out his hand and Dan relented, pulling in for a brief hug and slap on the back.

"Mary, this is Frank Ajax, an old friend and client. He's got us all set up, don't you, Frank?"

"Anything I can do for the honeymooners." Frank flashed a toothy grin.

An old friend *and* client? And he lived in Panama? I tossed aside my fantasies of having a romantic honeymoon free of ex-cons. I wished I had as much say in Dan's friendships as I did in Rachel's.

Frank clapped his hands together. "How about a little city tour before we meet Dudley?"

Frank had arranged a lunch for us with a prominent local attorney, Dudley Blanco, who was going to help us set up our bank account. From what I could gather, Mr. Blanco also had a business proposition for Dan and was under the impression that Dan might offer up investors as a quid pro quo. I'd hoped we could check into our hotel and take a nap before all the high finance, but at least we were getting it over with right away.

"You enjoying it here?" said Dan as we pulled out into traffic. "Business good?"

"Fantastic. Amazing. Beautiful," said Frank. "And trust me, this Kava-Kava thing? It's a great opportunity. Big money to be made."

I imagined that Kava-Kava was a code word for whatever drugs he was dealing, not entirely sure whether or not I meant the thought to be facetious.

"The question is, are you making it?" said Dan.

They both laughed uproariously, which, I guessed, could have meant yes *or* no without anyone having to provide details.

"Let me take you on the scenic route," said Frank. "We have amazing beaches. This place is truly paradise."

The deserted coastline stretched for miles. Water the color of mud washed up trash along the shore. Bottles, plastic bags, rusty cans, and an alarming number of tires littered the sand.

Looking in his rearview mirror, Frank noticed my expression. "These aren't the best beaches. You should see them closer to the Canal Zone, at the resorts."

He drove us through the old town, Casco Viejo, an area that jutted into the sea on the southwestern side of the city, and we got out for a brief stroll. The old colonial buildings were decayed, paint peeling off walls, balconies looking ready to collapse. Even with a coastal breeze, the air was heavy. Breathing was difficult and I was relieved to climb back into the air-conditioned car. We drove up some hills, into the "wealthy section," where the houses looked like bunkers. They were cement compounds with prison-like bars on the windows and doors. Many of the yards were landscaped with pink and gray rocks, and an occasional tropical plant. The tour ended when we got stuck in a loud, honking traffic jam in the middle of the commercial district, where high-rise buildings were aggressively crammed onto each block. Waves of people poured into the street, blocking intersections and causing a few angry altercations.

"We're a little early, but we can kill some time here," said Frank. He pulled into a parking garage.

We were at a mall lined with booths that sold roasted nuts, sweet drinks, fake designer wallets, and toys. The centerpiece of the mall was the brightly lit Casa de Carne, "House of Meat," a super-sized grocery store. Dan and Frank talked outside while I went looking for a cool escape. The store smelled like air conditioning and blood. There was a butcher shop spanning the full length of the building, displaying an endless selection of raw flesh. A chubby young man in blood-smeared clothes chopped up entrails. A smiling woman offered me a sample of a cold yellow beverage. I swallowed it in one long gulp. It was thick and sweet and left me thirstier.

Dan came into the supermarket. "What are you doing?"

I looked at him. "What are we doing at Casa de Carne, Dan? This is our honeymoon."

"Okay. Okay. This wasn't what I had in mind, either. I promise you, honey—*I promise*—there will be lots of romantic trips to make up for this one. Let's keep our eye on the ball, okay?" He pulled my chin up. "Okay? You know how goddamn hard I'm working. I'm so close to solving this problem, and it's coming together now. Stand by me, okay?"

"I'm sorry." Dan had given me so many motivational speeches about how terrific he thought I was, I'd momentarily forgotten that I'd decided in return to be the loyal trooper he desired.

We walked down the block, swept along by the crush of people. Frank stopped at a small Italian restaurant and held open a glass door leading to a dark air-conditioned lobby that smelled like garlic. The low buzz of conversation blended with the ringing and scraping of silver against china, as business people ate their lunches. Tuxedoed waiters bustled about the white linen-covered tables with big leather menus, trays of drinks, and steaming plates. Frank clasped the shoulder of a tall, elegant man. They shook hands and headed toward us, both smiling.

"Dudley Blanco, I'd like you to meet Dan Murphy. Dan Murphy Patric?" Frank looked flustered. "And his wife, Mary. Mary Patric."

Dudley took my hand in both of his. "Mrs. Patric. Congratulations are in order, are they not? And you are so gracious to allow us to intrude on your honeymoon with our business affairs. Please forgive us." His accent was light.

Dudley's eyes were dark and colorless. He had slicked back hair, an expensive watch and a gold wedding band on his finger. I thought he looked like the perfect attorney for a drug lord—charming, calculating, and a bit snazzy. I wondered if he was a criminal attorney, like Dan, or if he was an attorney who was a criminal—also like Dan. But of course Dan's crimes were only on paper—in illegal trusts and avoidance of process servers and tax bills. No one was ever really hurt. Then I thought of all the worry and hassles we were dealing with. No one was hurt physically, anyway.

Dudley fussed over me through the entire meal, pointing out the best dishes in the menu, offering me wine twice—which I accepted, surprising Dan and myself. I noticed that Dan drank none himself.

I began to feel as if we were in a movie—whether a mobster film or a dark comedy, I wasn't sure. Dudley, dapper and articulate, was outlining an investment opportunity for Dan to take to his clients back in the United States. *What clients?* I wanted to ask. Dan had given up his law practice years ago, and his current associates were scrambling to recoup losses. Dudley explained it as a sophisticated currency exchange, managed by a "brilliant financier" in Columbia. *Currency exchange? Doesn't he mean money laundering?* "Or you may consider the opportunity yourself," said Dudley. "The minimum investment is, of course, one million."

I looked from Dan to Frank to Dudley. They all had perfectly straight faces, nodding as if this were feasible.

"My dear," said Dudley. "May I offer you a cigarette?" He flipped open a gold case and held it toward me.

"She doesn't smoke," said Dan.

In this movie, I thought, I would smoke. "Maybe, just this once. Since it's a special occasion." I took a long, thin cigarette out of Dudley's case, and held it between my fingers. "Thank you."

"And you?" Dudley turned to Dan, offering the cigarette case.

"No thanks." Dan folded his arms and watched me for a few seconds, expressionless.

Dudley flipped the lid off his small, gold lighter. There were diamonds embedded in its side. I leaned in to let him light my cigarette. Nodding my thanks, I inhaled deeply.

Even though I hadn't smoked a cigarette in years, I was amazed at how easy it was to let the dry, sharp smoke fill my lungs. I exhaled the white stream and felt a familiar, pleasant dizziness swirling through my body.

The waiter left the check and Dudley immediately reached for it.

"That's not necessary." Dan reached into his pocket, smiling. "I know your country accepts American dollars."

"Please, Mr. Murphy, as you so graciously observed: You are in *my* country. Allow me to be your host." Dudley's gaze met each of ours, but I couldn't read any warmth or emotion. He opened the folder. I glanced at the amount and was surprised to see it was $367. That must have been some bottle of wine.

"Now, there is the business about your account?" said Dudley. "They are expecting you at the bank this afternoon."

I wanted another cigarette. Would it be rude to ask? His cigarette case was sitting on the table, but it seemed out of the question to just take one. And if I took another, Dan would definitely say something. Just as I cooked up the nerve to ask for one more, the men stood to leave, shaking hands. Dudley kissed each of my cheeks before we exited into the Panama City glare.

Dan, Frank, and I went to Banco Panama. When Frank was off making arrangements, I pulled Dan aside. "You've got a million dollars?"

"If I put together an investment group, yes."

"You're planning to invest the settlement money with *that* guy when we don't even own a house?"

"Relax," Dan whispered. "Just hearing him out, that's all."

Frank motioned me over to sign some papers. The euphoria I had felt at the restaurant was starting to settle into nausea. A pulsing headache reminded me why I stayed away from alcohol and cigarettes.

There was some kind of problem with our account. We had been given an introductory letter from Dudley, which we provided along with my letter from Wells Fargo, my passport, and one thousand dollars in traveler's checks to open the account. Three bank employees, all wearing drab gray shirts, studied the documents. Frank, our brightly clad interpreter, looked like a tropical bird getting pecked by a flock of pigeons. He called us over.

"Mrs. Patric," said a tall, thin, balding banker. "Please excuse us. All of the documents are in order, but Mr. Blanco had informed us that your deposit was to be significantly larger."

"Yes," said Dan. "But we want to establish the account first. We'll transfer additional funds when we return home."

Phone calls were made, the manager was stern and grumpy, and I needed a painkiller. Dudley was called, Frank spoke to him for a few minutes, and just when I was about to drag Dan outside to talk him out of this, the account was opened. We were handed a small leather passbook showing our balance in U.S. dollars.

Back in Frank's car, Dan explained that he was depositing the proceeds from a recent property sale directly into the Panamanian account.

"It's a very large sum, hundreds of thousands." Dan looked expectant, like he wanted Frank to be impressed.

Frank dropped us in front of a sign that said, "Luxury Hotel." When I looked up, I didn't know whether to laugh or cry. It was a dingy white high rise, glazed with the black smoke that gushed out of a factory down the block. The building had three fading billboards, including one for whitening toothpaste showing a smiling model with teeth pockmarked by a filthy layer of soot.

We checked in and were told that the elevator was broken. Our room was on the seventh floor.

"You've got to be kidding," said Dan.

"I'm not joking, sir. And you have a call." The somber desk clerk handed Dan a telephone message.

Dan unfolded it and looked at me. "Jesus." He put his hand on his forehead. "It's from Johnny." He turned to the clerk. "Where can I get an outside line?"

Dan handed me the message. It said, "Deal postponed. Call immediately."

The clerk motioned Dan to a private phone box in the back of the lobby. Dan was in there for a few minutes, his angry voice audible more than once. He hung up the phone, and pounded his fist on the wall before exiting the booth.

"What'd he say?"

"Richard's escaped. We're FUCKED." Dan's voice was loud and his tone sharp.

The desk clerk eyed me with concern, which caught Dan's attention.

"What do you mean, *escaped*?"

"Goddammit," he said, more quietly. "He's gone. He left sometime early this morning when Blackjack was helping his mother with some car emergency. He wasn't out of the house twenty minutes."

"Maybe he just went out. He'll be back?"

"No. No fucking way. He was supposed to give his deposition this morning."

"I thought he wanted to help you?"

"I did too. But it was bullshit. All bullshit."

The clerk was brazenly staring at us from his post at the desk.

"Let's just get into the room," said Dan.

Dan looked as exhausted as I felt. Lately I'd noticed that dark circles were spreading under his eyes. We walked wordlessly across the lobby's scratched linoleum, and followed the clerk outside and up seven flights of cement stairs. The doors to each room faced out to an open-air walkway, and the only air conditioner was a wall unit in the room, which wasn't on when we arrived. Dan tipped the clerk, closed the door, shut his eyes, and groaned.

The placed looked dismal, worn out.

"I'm guessing they didn't have a honeymoon suite." I walked over and fiddled with the air conditioner until it made a clicking noise.

"Bear with me, honey. I wanted to save a few bucks. Obviously I had no idea." Dan sat on the mattress. "I'm sorry. This is just goddamn embarrassing." He looked like he wanted to crawl under the bed. "Motherfucking Richard."

I sat next to him, held his hand. "You know, you don't need to keep promising me big money and big trips. What I want the most is to be at home—our home—with you and Rachel. I want a family. How's this: *Normal Family*—coming soon to a theater near you."

"That's what I want to give you. That's all I ever wanted, too."

"You know what I want you to give me the most?"

"What, honey?" Dan cupped one hand around my face. "Just name it."

"Come out of hiding. Clear things up with the IRS. You don't have any money, right? Richard's gone, the property deal is dead. As terrible as that all is, there's a silver lining, Dan. You can straighten things out with your taxes and start over. With me."

Dan was lost in concentration; I thought he might be coming around.

"See what I'm saying? You can make a deal. What do you have to lose?"

"What do I have to lose?" Dan was up and pacing, he looked like he might come unhinged. "I appreciate your advice, but you have no idea what we're dealing with here. The IRS doesn't make deals. It doesn't matter what I do or don't have. If I show up at their door, not only will they take what I have, they'll attach all future earnings. There's no way to approach them. And I didn't owe them the money in the first place."

"If it were me, I'd just want to face it—get it over with."

Dan stared at me, dismissively. "You don't know that," he said. "You don't know how far the IRS is willing to go to exact revenge. Trust me, if the roles were reversed, you'd be facing a huge helping of fear."

The roles would never be reversed, I thought. I'd never get myself into such a complicated financial jam. Then I remembered my credit mess.

"Dan, this is a terrible way for us to live. How are we going to have a normal life, a family, a house? I mean, look around. Keeping things hidden has only made it worse."

"I just have to clear a few things up, then—" Dan stopped and looked straight into my eyes. "Just bear with me, honey. A little bit longer. I'm still reeling from this fucking Richard fiasco—we have to pursue another angle. And the tax thing? I'm outlining a plan. I'll go over it with you at home. This will all be straightened out. I promise."

I went to the bathroom and rummaged in my cosmetic bag, looking for Tylenol. Inside a Ziploc bag was a varied sampling of everything in my medicine cabinet: Tylenol, Pepto Bismol, codeine, and the Ativan samples Jamie had given me at the wedding. I usually only took codeine for menstrual cramps, but my headache was bad, and my stomach sour. I grabbed one Tylenol, one codeine, one pink Pepto Bismol, and popped the tiny Ativan out of its shrink-wrapped nest, washing the drug cocktail down with a bottle of water.

Dan and I both stripped down to our underwear and flopped on the squeaky bed. I wasn't feeling very romantic.

"So much goddamn betrayal in the commercial world," said Dan, letting out a low, pained moan. "Sometimes, when I'm going to sleep, I fantasize that you and I live far away, in some bucolic setting—on the campus of a beautiful university, somewhere in Ireland, maybe. We live there with Rachel, writing and teaching. People come from all over the world to solve real problems, world peace, hunger—"

I curled into Dan and listened to him fantasize as the rattling air conditioner struggled to cool the room.

"There's this professor in Bangladesh," said Dan. "He started a bank that only lends money to poor people. It's brilliant. The average loan is about $150 and it's jacked up their economy—helped all these people make a life for themselves. That's what I want to be creating, not chasing money that was stolen from me. As soon as this thing gets settled and I get a couple more bucks in the bank, I'm calling it quits. I'm going to start a foundation that honors small acts of kindness, and innovative ways to empower the little people." Dan yawned, rested an arm across me, and his breath slowed down.

"Why not do it now?" I nudged him. "Let me help."

Dan didn't reply. His mouth relaxed; he'd dropped to sleep like a baby. Scooting quietly off the bed, I looked in his overnight bag, pulled out his worn blanket. I wrapped it around his head, letting it partially cover his eyes the way he liked it.

I gazed out the large window. The sun had just set. Water drops appeared like small, black smudges on the glass, blurring the view. I grabbed a towel from the bathroom, desperate to clean the grime off the window, but there didn't seem to be a way to open it from the inside.

Harry was right, I thought, watching Dan sleeping so sweetly. He had to quit all the running around trying to recoup his losses. First his brother, then his reputation, and now his money. Money, money, money.

Next to me on the nightstand was a beat-up Holy Bible. Staring at it a moment, I made the sign of the cross, tented my hands, and started to silently pray.

Dear God. First off, I know everyone says this, but I'm sorry about contacting You only when I'm desperate. And know that when I use Your name in vain, I'm not complaining, just explaining.

Thank you, God, for all I've been given. Rachel. Dan. Our health. And my family. All of them. No matter how inappropriate. For all of this, I am so grateful.

But today, I really do need guidance.

Eyes squeezed shut, I prayed for Dan to think clearly. I prayed for his cooperation with the IRS. I prayed he'd forgive his poor old parents once and for all. I prayed that I would make so much money that he would stop worrying and quit fraternizing with criminals. I prayed he would start a nice little foundation that honored good people. Do God's work. I prayed we would make it home alive so Rachel wouldn't be orphaned, and that she would grow up strong and healthy and happy. I prayed our marriage would always be a place of love. And I prayed for a sign.

God, I promise to do whatever You guide me to do to make sure that we never—never—have to worry about money again. Thank You. Thank You. Thank You.

Please say hello to Grandma, my sister Lizzie, and Jimmy. Tell them I'm open to any help they have to offer, too. In the name of the Father, the Son, and the Holy Spirit, Amen.

I stared out at the filthy view, looking, watching for my sign. Rain continued to drizzle from the murky sky. I curled against Dan and counted my breaths, anxious to relax enough for sleep to take me away. Perhaps the sign I craved would come to me in a dream.

What seemed like hours passed. Then an idea came to me. I opened the drawer in the nightstand and found the Bible. Shutting my eyes, I fanned through the light tissuey pages—sticking my finger in at the place I felt guided to. It was in the Book of Malachi. I had to read the passage twice to understand it. Smiling with recognition, I looked up, and whispered, "Thank you. It's a deal."

Chapter 17

September 1992

It was a sunny autumn afternoon, and everything looked sparkling and clean, especially my brand-new, freshly detailed company car. I pulled in front of our house and tapped on my horn, drumming out a cheerful staccato.

Unrolling the window, I inhaled deeply. The scent of new car mixed with the fresh air was invigorating. I had recited the affirmation, "I have a safe, stylish, and affordable new car," hundreds of times. And here it was—a deep green Ford Taurus, fully loaded with air conditioner, stereo, sunroof, automatic windows, locks, and seat adjustments, even an outside temperature gauge. "It's the color of money," I'd told Dan. "Which is perfect, you know, because I *am* a money magnet."

Dan had laughed. Once in awhile he was receptive to my New Age affirmations and philosophies. Since I'd just been given a car, a raise, and a big bonus, he was on the verge of becoming a believer. But I also knew that it was my honeymoon prayer six months earlier that was accelerating my success. I was taking my instructions straight from a Bible passage, and it was paying off in spades.

According to my interpretation of the Bible passage I was guided to, I had been instructed by The Book of Malachi to tithe—to make offerings wherever and however I could. Then God would "open the windows of heaven, and pour out a blessing that there shall not be room enough to receive."

This process of tithing was fun and exhilarating. With every paycheck, I took ten percent out in the form of small bills, and handed them to anyone with an open palm. Homeless men and women, teens looking for camp donations, girl scouts, boy scouts, bell ringers with Santa hats, and collection boxes for free clinics and soup kitchens. Rachel had great fun working with me on this project. Even with her own allowance she'd adopted the general policy that one should spend some, save some, and give some away, and she was particularly interested in making donations to benefit homeless shelters that had children's programs. I always saved five or ten dollars that I could fold up and put into the wooden offering boxes at random Catholic churches to buy candles. Each time I lit a candle I silently said, "I am a money magnet. Whatever I give is returned to me heaped up, pressed down, and running over. Amen."

I honked again. Dan and Rachel came bounding out of the house. Dan threw open the passenger door and smiled. "Who's the successful woman with the hot wheels?"

I flashed him a big grin. My boss, Kent, had given me a promotion that required a company car for visiting clients. Jamie had been appalled when she'd heard I'd picked out a Taurus, "For one thing, it's a gas hog. And what are you thinking? It's so *square*." But Kent had insisted I drive an American car since I was promoting his business. That afternoon, when he'd handed me the keys, I'd wanted to leap up and kiss him. Quite a change, considering that just earlier this week I'd wanted to quit. I'd been bored and frustrated because I was getting more marketing responsibilities, but fewer opportunities to dive into the mess and excitement of unsolved cases. "I want you to focus on business development," Kent had said. "And you'll like the perks." With that, he gave me the car, a twenty percent raise, and a five thousand dollar bonus. I smiled and shut up. "That's a good deal, I couldn't come close," said Harry, when I'd told him. "And don't worry. Your day will come. Take the promotion and get yourself out of hock."

The first thing I did was meet my dad for lunch and hand-deliver a three-thousand dollar check, the balance of what I owed him.

"Wow," said Dad, "You're turning out to be quite a success."

"As God is my witness," I said.

"I'm *so* proud of you."

I'd waited thirty years to hear those words. "More importantly, Dad," I said. "I'm proud of myself."

In the year since Dan had lost his money, he'd flitted around searching for opportunities. He had already launched two businesses. Each time he claimed he'd be earning hundreds of thousands of dollars within the year. Each time something went wrong. The business start-ups included investments related to second mortgages and irrevocable trusts for tax protection. But the mortgage company was underfunded, and the irrevocable trusts attracted unpleasant attention from the IRS. At the same time, Dan was receiving $3,500 cash each month from a friend of Johnny's who was having Dan review his business contracts. With my salary, that was more than enough to pay the bills.

Meanwhile, Dan was still fighting the battle to recoup a settlement from the development project. With Richard on the lam, the partnership filed a lawsuit that kept the property tied up while they strategized other options. Since I'd stopped believing he'd see real money anytime soon, I learned to live with all activity on that front as one would live with any eccentric hobby of one's spouse—like poker or hunting for lost pirates' treasure. It cost him time and money, but he got to hang out with his friends and seemed energized by the highs and lows, seduced by a possible payoff. Meanwhile, I excelled at work and got more involved with Rachel's school, running the public relations committee for the PTA fundraisers, an activity that made me feel like a normal mom.

"Did you guys grab some cassettes? You should hear these speakers." My old Toyota didn't even have a working radio.

"Show Mama what we have," said Dan, playfully.

Rachel yanked a small, plastic cassette out of her jacket pocket and yelled, "ABBA!"

I groaned. Rachel had recently discovered that whenever Dan heard "Dancing Queen," he couldn't restrain his urge to boogie. Now she regularly inserted the cassette into our stereo, to watch disco gyrations that resembled John Travolta having a seizure.

Rachel climbed into the front seat and inserted the cassette. "Papa. Listen!"

Much to his delight, Rachel had recently been calling Dan, "Papa." After our wedding, Dan had told me that he wished she didn't call him "Dan." "It doesn't capture the depth of our relationship," he'd said. We were both aware that this could be a delicate subject with Kevin, so we started referring to ourselves as "the three bears"—Mama Bear, Papa Bear, and Baby Bear. And then Dan asked Rachel to skip adding the "bear" part to "Papa," since she didn't do it with "Mama." I knew we'd tricked her into it, but with Kevin happily coupled with a steady, sober music store manager, even he seemed comfortable with Dan's new title.

I backed out of the driveway. The spring sunshine streamed through the open skylight as ABBA blared, *"You can dance, you can jive…Having the time of your life…"*

Dan winced as he buckled his seatbelt.

"Are you okay?" I said.

"Yeah. Give me a second. My back's gone out."

"Well, you've got to go to the doctor anyway," I said. "You have your physical for life insurance Monday. And please—don't cancel it again. You've rescheduled it ten thousand times."

"I've rescheduled it twice. Both times for good reason," he said. Whenever Dan didn't want to do something, he claimed to be in the middle of a critical negotiation regarding the phantom settlement.

We dropped Rachel at her piano lesson and wound through the tree-lined streets of Oakland, eventually entering the gates of Mt. View Cemetery.

"The day of your big promotion and you're driving me into a cemetery?" said Dan. "I hope it's a round trip."

I laughed. Dan knew how much I loved this place. To him all cemeteries were reminders of his parents' obsession with the family plot. But for me, the Mt. View Cemetery was a magical garden, an oasis of peace in the center of a noisy urban jungle. Inside these walls the distant freeway traffic sounded like ocean waves, and the train whistle drifted up from the waterfront, blending harmoniously with the ubiquitous birdsong. The grass smelled sweet and there was always something colorful in bloom.

I parked the new car behind a screen of eucalyptus trees and nuzzled into Dan, kissing his neck. He smelled like spiced soap.

"Are you making a pass in front of the dead people?" he said.

"Not exactly." I straightened up.

"I'm not complaining." Dan pulled me back toward him. "Powerful women turn me on."

"Dan, there's something I want to talk about."

"Shhh." He put a finger over my lips. "I bet I can nail your T-spot and N-spot without doing any further harm to my back." He started to unbutton my blouse.

"Dan. I want to talk."

Dan shut his eyes, the smile fading from his mouth.

"You know how you've been saying you had a way to sort out the IRS thing? You promised me you'd tell me the plan."

"This isn't the time or the place," he said.

"Okay, I give up. What is the time and place?"

"Honey, please. My back hurts." He turned his head toward me and opened his eyes. "And you know it's been put off because of the delayed settlement. After that, it'll all be handled."

I was determined not to let the issue drop this time. "Dan, we have to sort out this IRS mess right now. I was looking at my tax form. It asks you to report if you have more than $10,000 deposited in a foreign account. If you put the settlement money in the Panama account, I'll have to show it on my tax returns."

"No. That's the last thing we need. As soon as we transfer the money into the account, we'll add me to the account, then your name will be removed. I told you that. You won't get into any trouble."

"It's not just that. I don't want *you* in trouble. I keep picturing the IRS busting down our door and throwing cuffs on you in front of me and Rachel."

"That's because you have an overactive imagination." Dan's tone was brusque. "It doesn't happen that way."

"If you get a settlement shouldn't my name be on the account, too? I mean a legal account. What about a house? I'm finally getting my credit rating together and, with the raise, you know, eventually I'll qualify for a loan. But I want a co-signer. A partner. A *husband*."

"Honey, between the settlement and the new business, I'll hand you enough money to buy a house, free and clear. You just need to be patient."

"I'm willing to be patient," I said. "I just don't want to be stupid. I'm sure you could make more money in one year than you got in that settlement, if you'd just come clean."

No response.

"Dan, I was talking to Jamie about this. She thinks we need couples counseling."

Dan straightened up, his eyes ablaze. "You talked to Jamie about my private business? Jesus Christ, what were you thinking? This is none of her business and I don't see why you need to bring it up with her."

"That's not what you said when we needed her to sign the marriage certificate."

"That was different. We were asking her help for a decision we'd made—as a couple. Not soliciting her ongoing advice."

"Well who am I supposed to talk to about this? You won't talk to me. I'm worried sick half the time. We can't have a normal financial life. Can't you please negotiate something with the IRS?"

"You don't know what I know. They won't be fair." Dan winced again. "I'd rather drop dead than hand over anything to them." He pointed his finger as he spoke. "I'm starting over. I've already applied for an Irish Passport. They offer them to anyone whose parent or grandparent was a citizen, and I've got my grandmother, Bridget."

Minnie's mother was straight off the boat from county Galway. After her husband was murdered on the streets of San Francisco, she had supported Minnie and her brother through a thriving bootlegging business during prohibition. Dan had worshipped her, admiring her spunk and irreverence;

her skill at finding a lucrative way to beat the system seemed to have become the model for his own life.

"I'm looking into changing my name in Ireland. I've outlined a whole plan. I have notes about it at home," he said. "I'm more than willing to share the details with you; let's set aside some time to do it."

I was speechless. I had started a file with advertisements for legal services that specialized in tax problems. I was sure none of them advised creating a new identity in a foreign country, then returning as an immigrant.

"Don't you think when you're stuck in a hole it's best to stop digging?"

Dan closed his eyes and leaned against the headrest.

"Why does everything have to be so convoluted?" I said.

"Is this how you want to spend the afternoon?" he said. "We should be celebrating your success. Let's enjoy that for a second." Dan took my hand. "And if you would be so kind, you could offer me some support—and trust—so we can celebrate my success next. Do you think you can just give it a chance to work?"

Neither of us spoke for a few minutes. Dan's face looked drawn, his skin pale. He closed his eyes and pinched the bridge of his nose. "You know? Other than you, Rachel, and maybe Johnny, I don't think there's anyone I can trust. Sometimes I wish I could throw in the towel, go live out my days in a monastery."

"Without us?" I was alarmed. He was getting an Irish passport, after all.

"God no. That's not what I meant." Dan stroked my hair. "I'm just tired." He shut his eyes. "Come on. Put the spotlight back where it belongs. This is your big day. Let's get Rachel and go get us some chocolate mint ice cream."

One evening, three weeks later, Rachel and I arrived home to a dark house. Goody was snoozing on the welcome mat next to a disemboweled mouse.

"Ew, Mommy. Get rid of it." Rachel picked up the cat, looked away.

Grabbing the limp rodent by the tail, I tossed it into the big rosemary bush.

Inside the house, I flipped on the lights, trying to remember where Dan said he'd be. On the table in the entry, he'd left an envelope full of cash and a pile of unopened mail for me. Since he didn't have a checking account, I paid the miscellaneous bills he received at his P.O. box. In the pile, there was an unfamiliar sealed brown envelope with a post-it note that said, "Please file with bank statements." It was our quarterly statement from Banco Panama. When we'd received the first one, I told Dan there was no more file space in my desk, hoping I'd get access to his files. "Let's keep our household stuff in your filing cabinet. Just get the key copied for me." Without looking up, Dan said, "I can't even get my own stuff in there. Better work something else out."

I hadn't seen one of these statements since, and opened it distractedly as Rachel knocked around the kitchen, getting herself a snack.

"Don't eat too much, sweetie. I'm going to make dinner soon." I glanced at the statement and set it down. *Wait.* I looked at it again. It showed an initial deposit of $1,000. Then there was a July withdrawal in the amount of $367. Wasn't that the exact amount of our lunch with Dudley Blanco? Did Dan pay him back? *Wait.* How could he have paid him back? It was my account. Did Dudley have access to our account? I stared at the statement until my eyes burned.

"How can that be?" I muttered. First Richard distracts us from his heist by purchasing second-rate gifts. Now Dudley robs us for lunch money? Goddammit, was every thief Dan did business with also a cheapskate?

I slammed around the kitchen, pulling out pots and pans, spaghetti and tomatoes. I wanted Dan to be home *now.*

The doorbell rang. Rachel and I both responded.

It was Josh Varinsky, the boy across the street.

"Is Dan here?" While Josh's father was recovering from heart surgery, Dan had been attending Boy Scout meetings with him.

"No, honey—but I'm expecting him. Do you need his help?"

"He needs to sign off on my archery badge."

I never understood Dan's passionate commitment to all things Boy Scout. His Scout stories and memories had a cult-like quality to them, especially since Dan seemed to lose his sense of humor whenever he reminisced. A few years ago at dinner with a rowdy couple, Dan started recounting the difficult initiation process for the Scout's Order of the Arrow. "I had to stay up all night, keeping a fire burning in the woods." Our friends made a few sexual cracks about burning fires but Dan didn't laugh. "I'm telling you, this was a brutal, difficult deal." He launched into a detailed description of all the dark forces that worked against him as he "fought to keep the flames going." Everyone smiled politely and made comments like, "I had no idea it was so strenuous," and "It's a wonder you survived the night."

At the front door, Rachel stood mute. At ten, Josh was the heartthrob of every girl who ever laid eyes on him. His droopy blue eyes were framed by lashes so thick, they occasionally stuck together until he stretched his cheeks down and blinked a few times.

"Can I wait?" Josh looked at Rachel. "We could build another fort."

Rachel looked like she'd won the lottery.

"Sure, honey. Come on in," I said.

Josh and Rachel ran into her room, and I returned to the kitchen to make supper. What were the chances of someone having money embezzled from a bank account two times in two years by two different people? We were cursed, that was the only explanation.

Taking a few deep breaths, I filled a pot full of water, and covered it. I turned to get the Parmesan and jumped. Dan was standing in the kitchen.

"Dan. You scared me."

"Well, we have plenty to be scared about." Dan was glassy eyed.

"You know?" I picked up the bank statement.

"About the cancer? How did you know?" He took the statement from my hands. "What's this?"

"There's a withdrawal for the exact amount of our lunch. Did you say cancer?"

Dan stared at the statement, looking shocked.

"Goddamn him, I know what this is," he said.

"Dan, what cancer?"

"Just give me a minute. " Dan walked stiffly to the flowery blue couch. "I need to sit. You want to sit?"

"No I don't want to sit. Tell me what you're talking about?"

"Unbelievable." Dan stared at the statement, deep in thought. "Dudley's pissed because we didn't present any investors. Can you believe he can get away with this?"

"Dammit, Dan," I screeched. "Who has cancer?"

"Are you ready for this?" Dan eyed me for a moment. "I do."

"You do not. You just had a physical."

No response. An icy sensation spread through me.

"Dan, they said your cholesterol and blood pressure looked great."

"For a second, I thought you knew," he said, seeming disoriented. "They're so screwed up down there, I told them not to call the house—get you upset over nothing."

"So it's nothing?" My heart drummed in my chest, causing my voice to shake. "It's not serious, then."

"That's the point, they weren't sure. The doctor shoved a finger up my ass and felt something hard. Said he was pretty sure it was prostate cancer." Dan's face was grim. "I was so goddamn angry. 'You think you want to confirm that,' I said, 'before you scare the hell out of me?'"

"So, it's not confirmed?"

There were no outward signs of cancer. Dan had once told me that an old secretary used to call him a crisis junkie. He had to be exaggerating. Or it was a mistake.

Dan paused, pulled a folded piece of paper from his pocket, and handed it to me.

"They did the biopsy last week. Prostate cancer. Here's the results."

I unfolded the paper and stared at the black and white letters and numbers, blinking like little Josh, stretching my cheeks down so I could see through my lashes, or whatever it was that was blurring my vision, making it all unreadable.

Shrieks and giggles erupted from Rachel's room.

I closed my eyes. "But prostate cancer isn't serious, right? I mean, they can cure it?"

"Sit down honey. Please." Dan pulled on my hand. "He said he's been doing this a long time, and was pretty sure that because he could feel the lump, it was bad news. My back pain could mean the worst."

"The worst?"

All of the pieces I'd been stacking in place for our future crumbled in the face of this news. The IRS we could deal with. We'd set up a payment plan, pay a fine maybe. But cancer?

"He said he felt a tumor the size of a small rock—that it was hard, and that didn't bode well. Then he referred me to the urologist for the biopsy." Dan's laugh sounded like a dry cough. "The urologist wants me to have some incapacitating operation and I won't do it. *Never.*"

"But surgery may be the best cure," I said.

"If I want to be impotent. *And* incontinent, with no guarantee they'd even get it all." Dan stood and began to pace. "Honey, believe it or not, there's as much bullshit and corruption in our medical system as there is in our government. You know why? Because it's controlled by the government. There are many treatment options available that we don't even hear about because the FDA prevents them from ever making it to market. I'm going to find an alternative treatment. I've just got to make some calls."

I wanted to call my mother; or my father. One of them would know what to do. At least Dad could send some tranquilizers, or did we have any wine? I hadn't touched any alcohol since Panama, but some red wine would be good with spaghetti.

"Let's call my dad. He's a doctor. He'll know what to do." I grabbed the phone.

"No, don't call anyone! If this gets out, it's the end of my professional career. I'll be a pariah—this thing scares the hell out of people, makes them think you're damaged goods."

Now he wanted to add cancer to the list of things we couldn't talk about?

"Dan, this isn't business—it's family. Two of Dad's brothers had cancer, he'll be able to help."

"Two of his brothers *died* from cancer." Dan looked angry. "I'm not dying with this."

I was stunned. Of course Dan wouldn't die from this. He couldn't die. We'd just gotten married. I wanted to curl up like a pill bug and roll under the sofa.

What had Dan said?

I'd rather drop dead than hand over anything to the IRS.

I started to cry.

"Don't worry, sweetheart. I'm going to obliterate it."

Dan's words were familiar. He had been using war terms from the second this Richard fiasco happened. "I've got to mobilize the troops," "We're going to infiltrate enemy lines," and "I'm going to blow them away." But so far, there didn't appear to be an impending victory. Harry was right. This thing was eating Dan alive.

Chapter 18

October 1992

Dan and I drove across the Bay Bridge to visit his parents. On the way, we passed St. Brendan's Church with its tidy green lawn, yellow, pink, and purple pansies, and cobalt blue bell tower. Years ago, when Dan was in grade school, there had been forty-four kids living on this block and the streets were always filled with noise and laughter. But today the hill was gray and the cul-de-sac quiet, as if the neighborhood was suffocating under the weight of the pervasive fog.

We parked in front of the house. Dan slammed the car door. He looked tense, somber, like he was heading into battle.

"Hey, lighten up, soldier," I said. "We're here; we might as well have some fun." I slapped his rear.

Dan smiled, said nothing. This was the first time he'd visited his parents since he'd learned about his cancer a month earlier, and he'd come only on the condition that no one mention it, even though I knew he'd called his mother with each test result that confirmed the disease, always insisting that removal of the prostate was an unacceptable option. She would then call me in tears asking, "Why won't he get the operation? Why, Mary, why?" This conversation always turned into a painful rant about what a disappointment Dan was, considering how much potential he had, and did I have any idea how hard it was for a mother who had tried her best? "I'm only telling this to you," she'd wail, "because I know you love him too, honey."

One night, lying in bed reading the book *Illness as Metaphor*, I shook Dan awake and said, "If you don't want to talk about the cancer, would you please quit calling your mother with alarming news? It's sadistic. It ends up hurting me, not her. Is that what you want?"

"Why would I want to hurt you or my mother?" he said, leaving the question unanswered.

On this first in-person visit since the diagnosis, we'd agreed to take them to their favored—virtually their only—destination, the cemetery. We walked up the stairs and rang the doorbell.

"I'll take your mom, you take your dad," I said.

Minnie and Ralph were high maintenance passengers. Since they both craved attention, a lone escort was fought over like a bone.

We entered to kisses, hugs, smiles, compliments, Minnie's flowery shirt and sweet perfume, Ralph's faded woolen cap and scuffed white loafers, moving from odorless fog into the familiar musty smell of the house.

Dan and his mom discussed Joe Montana and his sizzling success with the San Francisco Forty Niners. There had never been a quarterback like Joe, they agreed.

"And those tight buns." Minnie slapped Dan on his rear and winked at me.

"My wife and my mother can't keep their hands off my ass today," Dan said.

"What a day we have ahead!" Minnie looked like an excited and earnest seven-year-old girl, hiding behind a mask of loose skin and powdery, pink make-up. "Time to go see Ralph's first little family. Let's get moving." She picked up her house keys and took hold of Dan's arm for help down the front stairs.

Ralph pulled me back and whispered loudly, "I need to talk to you."

"I know," I whispered. "But today's not the day to discuss cancer—"

"No. Not that. I need to show you something downstairs and I don't want her to see." Ralph thrust his chin in the direction of Minnie. "She's so goddamn nosy." Then he nodded his head toward Dan and said, "I don't want him to know either."

I paused, not knowing what to say. I was sure they could hear, but they remained immersed in football talk.

"Okay?" He whispered loudly.

Ralph grabbed my arm to lead me down the back stairs to the basement. I gently resisted. Once he trapped me in the basement I'd never get out. When Ralph got talking he never, ever reached the end of the story. Even if we were interrupted by one of his angina attacks, which he had more frequently now—unless it killed him—it was still no guarantee that he'd stop talking. At least when Minnie spoke, I knew her story would have a punch line. It might take an hour to tell, but there was always a wrap. With Ralph, it was a life story, and like life, it was sometimes fascinating but also excruciating and tedious and repetitive.

"They're already in the car, Ralph. I promise. We'll do it right when we get back."

He nodded, turned away from me, and shot out the front door before I could get in front of him. It was amazing how fast he could move for a half-blind octogenarian. He could barely see past his old cap, and when he kicked into high gear he always looked on the verge of falling face first over a cliff.

I sat next to Minnie in the backseat. Dan claimed his mom was never affectionate, but she was all handholding and touching with me. I loved having her close to me. She was dusted in face powder and soaked in Magic Noire perfume. Her breath smelled of lemon-lime Alka-Seltzer or the peppermint Pepto Bismol tablets that kept her tongue stained a permanent pinkish-black. It was minty or smoky or sour or somewhere in between, but whatever it was, it never offended me. My mother-in-law and I apparently had good body chemistry.

"Honey, have you tried those Pringles?" she said, swallowing a big gulp of air, "I can't decide what's better with a sandwich. Pringles or a nice, crunchy dill pickle—"

"Wouldjewshuddupforgodsakes Minnie, Jezusssss," said Ralph. "I was saying something." Ralph turned to Dan and said, "It'd be easier to cut off her head than to shut her mouth."

If my eyes fired darts, Ralph would be headed to the cemetery, permanently. But Minnie ignored him.

"I love those Pringles. I have an extra at home I'll give you. You get more for your money with the Pringles because there isn't wasted space. The way they shape them lets you get more in the package. And I love the way they fit so snugly into the can." Minnie snuggled into me as she said this.

I nodded and smiled. The packaging of Pringles reminded me of the jokes Minnie made about packing the Murphy family plot full of urns. The plot was originally intended to house four corpses in standard-size-coffins. Jimmy was the first one in. A few years later the family buried Jimmy's mother— Ralph's first wife—in the plot. That was okay with Minnie. She was friendly with Jimmy's mom. She even made her godmother of Dan. Jimmy's mom drank a lot after he died, but who could blame her? One night as she dozed with the TV blaring, hot embers of her Lucky Strike set fire to the mattress. It seemed Mary the First may have been burned alive; that was why no one liked to think or talk about the exact details.

Once the Catholic Church started allowing cremations, the plot had room for more remains. Though Dan would never allow it, there was plenty of space for him, Rachel, and me—and Minnie and Ralph had taken steps to insure our legal entry. They'd even signed papers to allow a few of my family members into the plot. When Minnie heard Aunt Maggie talking about spreading her ashes on Mt. Tamalpais, she was appalled. "Up on that mountaintop all alone? Don't be silly, honey," she'd said. "You'll come in with us." Fearing Aunt Maggie wouldn't want to be dead without her sister, Minnie and Ralph also hoped to include my mother and stepfather, but wanted to be sure to do it in a way that didn't make my father and his new wife feel less than welcome.

When I escorted the Murphys to the cemetery without Dan, we often talked about this. Who was in, who was out. At no time did we discuss Dan's extreme aversion to being buried alongside the controversial Milton/Mike. Conversation centered more on business-related topics. Cremation urns took up less space and Holy Cross got to charge a nice fee every time they opened the grave. They made more money; the family got more slots. It was a win/win—or a win/win-when-you-lose—situation, we always joked. Today, however, there was no mention of the subject.

Dan stopped at the K-Mart to buy a fresh bouquet of plastic flowers to deposit at the plot. Before he had the engine turned off, Ralph bolted from the car. Minnie started to open her door, but I pulled her back. "Let the boys do this errand." The truth was, if Minnie found her way into K-Mart, we'd all be goners. She could meander for hours amongst the clothes, greeting cards, and cosmetics.

We entered the cemetery gates and Ralph stared out of the passenger-side window. Colma's endless green hills were covered with plots, many of which were neglected, littered with dead flower arrangements or dirty plastic bouquets. There were always a few scattered sites that displayed fresh flowers, announcing fresh grief. The car wound through the deserted streets, passing Celtic crosses, statues of the Virgin Mother, Jesus covered with blood and thorns, and countless versions of St. Francis draped in loose robes and surrounded by adoring forest animals. I could never get enough of the Virgin or St. Francis, but lately the Jesus statues made me want to scream. That poor guy, why had he been so relentlessly picked on? I wanted to gently remove each version of his ravaged body off the cross and lay it on the soft cemetery grass—for God's sake, let him rest in peace.

The Murphy plot was located on a prime piece of real estate. It was in an older section of the cemetery where the stones rose above the ground, unlike the newer plaques that sat flat on the grass. We were on a hill under an oak, so there was shade. Dan's opinion notwithstanding, I was both proud and grateful that I had married into such a nice plot.

Dan parked on the curb next to the plot. I unbuckled Minnie and opened her side of the car. Ralph fumbled with the lock until he realized it was open, then pushed at the heavy car door. In one hand he held a tangled clump of yellow plastic daffodils, their foil tags still dangling.

Minnie kept her eyes on Ralph, clucking and sighing because she was afraid he would fall. Ralph had heart trouble and Minnie was terrified that he might drop dead and then what would she do? Sometimes if she didn't hear him snoring through the wall that separated their rooms, she tiptoed through his door with her flashlight and shined it on his chest to see if it was rising and falling.

The cemetery grass was uneven and damp from the morning dew. The stubborn gray fog still hovered. Ralph made a beeline for the grave, wobbling slightly as he walked.

"Mary, why don't you drive me to see my papa's grave?" said Minnie.

"Ma, we can all go," said Dan. "Just wait for my father."

"Dan, let him be. He needs time. Mary will take me."

Minnie had been only eight when her father was buried in this cemetery in 1920. Returning home from a Sunday ballgame, he had just gotten off the streetcar when he was hit over the head, dealt a fatal concussion. Like the mystery surrounding Jimmy's death, the murder was never solved.

"Dan, let Mary have your keys. I want to visit Papa's grave."

Dan didn't budge. He kept his eyes on his father. Ralph shuddered and cried as he slumped over the water-stained tombstone, brushing off the grass and dead bugs that had accumulated since our last visit—slowly rubbing his hands over the engraved letters. He was standing by the stone, blessing himself when he teetered slightly.

"Get your father, Dan. Help him," Minnie said sharply.

"He's fine Ma, he's fine."

"He's NOT fine, Dan. You don't know what it's like for me. He never listens, he just runs away and he falls. Sometimes he climbs up a ladder to weed the hill or to paint the ceiling and I don't know if he's going to break his neck and he…"

Minnie's forehead was furrowed with horizontal creases and her voice was shrill. Dan handed me his car keys and was gone before she took her next breath. He would rather be with his crying, genuflecting father than listening to his mother wail. Unlike me, he'd lost sympathy for her incessant worrying long ago. I held her hand; rubbed circles on her soft, hunched back as I helped her into the car. I could feel her bumpy bra strap under the polyester shirt splayed with bright flowers that resembled those sticking out of the vases at each headstone.

Dan stared at me as I started the car. Our eyes locked and I smiled to let him know I was aware of him, that he was not alone.

"Let's make a break for it," said Minnie. "We'll be like—what's the movie? *Thelma and Louise.*"

I laughed, patted her thigh. "How are you? *Really.*"

"Honey, I'm too polite to answer that truthfully. I'm just so happy I have you. That's maybe the only thing Ralph and I agree on. Just yesterday, Ralph says to me, 'I'd trust that girl with my life.'" Minnie clasped my hand, and gave it a squeeze.

"Is this the spot?" I glanced at Minnie. In her free hand she held a cigarette and a lighter. "Oh, I should have known. We're off for a smoke, are we? Let me have one." I unbuckled her seatbelt, helped her out of the car.

Minnie rummaged around her purse and pulled out a crushed pack of Merit Menthols. "Does Dan know you smoke?"

"Dan knows everything, doesn't he?"

Minnie chuckled.

"Anyway, he has his alternative treatments, I have mine." I lit two cigarettes, handing one to Minnie. We smoked in silence. I was thinking about Harry's advice, that I should just ask her about why Mike had changed his name. As much as I wanted to let this go, my mind returned to that question the way a tongue keeps running over a chipped tooth. And it was growing just as annoying. All I had to do was tell her about Walter's slip up at my brother's wedding, and how I'd punched his name in the computer for fun.

"Minnie, can I ask you a delicate question? And if I'm out of line, I'm requesting forgiveness in advance."

We leaned against Dan's car, holding hands and smoking, as I told her what I'd discovered. "I know it's none of my business, but I keep wondering about it."

She didn't even flinch. "Honey, does Dan know all this?"

"Actually, no. He gets so worked up whenever Mike's name comes up, I haven't mentioned it."

"Good." Minnie paused thoughtfully.

"You'd have to give me your word that you'd keep this between us." She held my gaze.

"I promise." *Dammit*, I thought. Now I couldn't even tell Jamie.

"It's not a big deal this day and age." Minnie sighed, blowing out a long stream of smoke. "And it's really Mike's business to share, not mine. But I trust you."

I was amazed at how well this was going. Harry was really onto something with this direct "Ask and You Shall Receive" approach. Outwardly I remained nonchalant, but inside the bells and whistles were going off like I'd hit the jackpot.

Minnie explained that Milton was the son of Maureen McDonough, one of Ralph's distant Pennsylvania relatives.

"No one knew who his father was, and Maureen kept that quiet. It was a terrible burden to him having grown up a bastard, if you'll forgive the expression. But the times were different then." Minnie, well aware I'd given birth to Rachel while unmarried, smiled and gave my hand a reassuring squeeze. "Ralph, being of that generation, felt just awful for him. Terrible. He wanted to help. To offer him a new name and a fresh start here in California. So that's what he did. Then that awful business happened with Jimmy."

Minnie was now crying. Like an infant, she could move from smiles to tears in the space of seconds.

"Mary," she said, taking a sharp detour from the topic. "How could he possibly have cancer? How? And saying he won't get an operation! After what his father went through with Jimmy? Is he trying to kill himself, too?" said Minnie.

"Jimmy didn't kill himself." My shoulders tensed. *"Did he?"*

"What? I never said that! What are you talking about? My God, I never said such a thing." Minnie crossed herself, and reflexively, I mirrored her. "Please don't say such things. My God, that death was a terrible accident. It should have never happened. No one meant it to happen." The tears were streaming again. Minnie clutched her chest and started to cough through the tears. I took the cigarette out of her hand, and gently stroked her back while waiting for her to catch her breath. She looked gray.

"Shhh. It's okay. I'm sorry, Minnie. I misunderstood."

The cigarette smoke was making me sick. I crushed both hers and mine under my shoe. So much for asking direct questions, I thought.

"Why can't we let Jimmy rest? None of the awful stories are true. People make things up to suit their own ideas. No one knows the truth about anyone's life anyway, do they Mary? Do they?" Minnie looked at me pleadingly.

"No. No one knows." She was right. Truth was relative. And speaking of relatives, Mike, Milton, and Jimmy were not safe topics of conversation with anyone in this family. That was it. I was retiring my curiosity on the subject. I quit.

"Oh, why won't Dan get the operation?" she wailed.

I pulled her into a hug and started to move her back toward the car.

"He never did anything the way we wanted," she sniffed. "He works with these crazy friends of Jimmy's, almost as if to spite us. And why won't he buy a house, Mary? Why doesn't he use his talent instead of squander it away?" I avoided her gaze. I agreed with almost everything she said, but thinking how desperately I'd craved my father's approval, I wanted to scream, "You're his mother. Shut up and be proud of him."

"Not to worry," I said. "I'm working round the clock on it. Trust me. Dan's going to be okay." More and more I found myself speaking like Dan, painting rosy pictures with little basis in reality. Soon I'd probably start believing in them, too. "If it makes sense for him to have an operation, I'll make sure he does."

"If anyone could convince him, honey, you could."

The truth was, no one could get Dan to do anything he didn't want to do. Lately I'd tried to get him to read *You Can Heal Your Life*, and *Mind As Healer, Mind As Slayer.* If he'd just clean up his past, quit hiding from the IRS, "fighting the wars," and focus on something positive—like getting the cancer removed from his body—he'd be a lot healthier. His response to my theories ranged from condescension to fury as the books gathered dust on his desk.

Minnie and I squirted ourselves with Magic Noire and Listerine breath spray. I resettled her into the backseat, got in myself, and then rolled down the windows: We both smelled a bit too flowery.

Dan was helping Ralph replace the frayed plastic flowers in the plot-side vase. He stood close to his father as they returned to the car. Ralph looked at me again, raising his spiky gray eyebrows, staring hard. For a second I thought he knew I'd been smoking, and then I realized it was to remind me he had something to show me at home.

Dan was apparently in no hurry. He suggested that after we shopped, instead of going to Red Lobster or the Olive Garden, we could have dinner at their favorite restaurant, Original Joe's in South City. Dan had to be in an especially good mood to agree to a dinner at Joe's, which meant a thirty-minute wait, cocktails, appetizers, salads, entrees, and dessert. I couldn't tell if Dan sensed that his dad didn't want to linger and was choosing Joe's just to stick it to him or if he was making an effort to please his parents. There was no backing away from the suggestion, however, because Minnie was thrilled.

At Original Joe's, Ralph was uncharacteristically quiet as we waited for our table in the crowded foyer. I accompanied Dan to the bar, where he ordered Manhattans for his parents.

"Get me a white wine," I said.

"Seems like you're drinking a lot these days," said Dan. "Think that's a good idea?"

"Apparently," I said. "Are you having a drink?"

Dan sighed. "I'm taking tonight off from all healthy behavior." He ordered three cocktails and my wine, and pulled out his chunky roll of money. No matter how many people robbed him blind, Dan always had a big wad of cash in his pocket.

"I wish you wouldn't smoke with my mother," he said.

"I wish you'd get your prostate removed." I glared at him. Lately my feelings around Dan ranged between two extremes: fury or desolation. I was either snapping at him, or curled up somewhere private, sobbing inconsolably. My mother said if I was to be any good to my marriage or myself I needed to learn how to operate an emotional dimmer switch.

Dan picked up our drink tray, and I followed.

Immediately after Dan was diagnosed, we'd switched to a fat free, vegetarian, organic diet. I quickly learned that when food wasn't cooked in oil or butter, it squeaked when you chewed it. Something about it was a little too clean. But nothing in this meal squeaked. We ate jumbo prawns with thick cocktail sauce, salads dripping with Thousand Island dressing, veal soaked in butter, lemon, and capers, and spaghetti covered with oily marinara and gooey lumps of parmesan. The heavy meal tasted great going in, but I had such a sinking feeling by the end of it, I understood how this kind of food could kill you.

Minnie monopolized the conversation, reminiscing about a party Jimmy had held at the bar here. Minnie and Ralph loved to talk about the good times with Jimmy. Minnie said he wasn't handsome like Ralph or Dan, but he was funny, charming, and made big promises that he often couldn't keep. This attracted a large following of both men and women. Jimmy insisted on buying rounds of drinks even if he had to spend his rent money, and no matter how often he asked his father to give him a financial bail out, Ralph did it and never stayed angry too long. They told me that Jimmy was so likeable, he could talk you out of your last dollar, and you'd thank him for it.

Jamie was right. No wonder Dan felt so brotherly toward con men and crooks.

Dan asked for the check before the spumoni arrived, kicking off a brief argument over who was going to pay.

"Dan, be a good boy," said Minnie. "Don't deny your father this one simple pleasure."

Dan relented, and handed his father the bill. Still sullen, Ralph paid and left the restaurant. When Dan remarked on his odd manner, I didn't mention that he'd asked to see me alone in the basement. Ralph's proclivity for secrets was a sore point for the family, especially since he had a history of philandering. He was too old for that now, but still, his behavior toward me made me feel like we were starting an affair.

Dan and Minnie laughed and chatted as they brought up the last bags of groceries from the car, set them on the counter, and started to unload. From behind, I wrapped my arms around Dan's waist. "I'll be trapped downstairs with your father," I whispered. It barely registered, so I poked him hard. "If I'm not back by sun-up, send the blood hounds."

Dan interrupted the story he was telling his mother. "Don't take a lot of junk from my father today, okay? I don't want you two packing all that crap from the basement into my car."

Mostly it was crap: rusty camp stoves and 1950s flashlights that dripped with cruddy battery acid, lamps with asparagus green shades, his hotel ashtray collection, a moldy set of red and navy plaid suitcases, and a drill set he'd bought around the time I was born. All the stuff smelled musty like Ralph, or Ralph smelled musty like all the stuff—it was hard to tell where it started and ended. Dan didn't want the junk, but my philosophy was to take what was given with love and appreciation and then throw it away when we got home. This gave Ralph the illusion that his old possessions lived on, and it gave me a chance to start cleaning out their house. Dan's parents couldn't continue living there independently for much longer, and to me it seemed inevitable that we would soon have to help them purge and move. This way we did it in secret—and this family certainly loved secrets.

Ralph shuffled me to the basement. In a conspiratorial tone, he said, "I know I can trust you, Mary. I know I can trust you because you married Dan even though he lost all that money."

"I didn't know he had that much money, Ralph. If I knew he'd had that money I would have married him for it." If Ralph only knew how frustrated I was with Dan for letting someone else squander his money, while I scrimped and saved to get out of debt and build a measly savings account. There were so many things I wanted for the family and myself: clothes, classes, vacations, property, a housecleaner and a manicure/pedicure once in awhile. If I'd had the chance to spend his hidden money right under his nose, at least he'd have something to show for it.

Ralph wasn't paying attention to my remarks; he was clearly on a mission. I was ambivalent, wondering if he was going to give me something I might like or instead offer something that came wrapped in a revelation about the past that would only reignite my compulsive curiosity. He'd always had a clandestine life outside his marriage. Mostly I only heard those stories when he cornered me at dinner parties after he drank too much. But today Ralph wasn't talking. He moved me rapidly into the back of the basement where he had hidden a pudgy canvas envelope that was closed with a zipper and small padlock. Silly, I thought, to lock a bag that anyone could cut open with kitchen scissors.

We stood by his workbench, where he set the bag. Ralph was slightly breathy from moving aside the toolbox, rags, and oil cans he had strategically placed to hide the bag. He sat on a little stool by the bench, his face ashy and tight. He started to whisper something but stopped speaking and held up one hand, his crooked index finger bent into the shape of a comma.

Here we go again. Be calm, I thought, be calm. I inhaled deeply because I knew he couldn't.

Ralph searched for the miniature caramel colored glass bottle of nitroglycerin tablets in his pants pocket. When they weren't there his eyes grew big and watery. He panicked, and I panicked. He groped wildly through his shirt and then sweater pockets where he pulled out some tiny keys but no pills and then, thank God, there they were.

Even though I was getting used to the frequent angina attacks, I shook as Ralph fumbled to get the lid off the tiny bottle and dump a little pill into his wrinkled palm. I didn't help because once before, when I'd tried, we'd wasted valuable time as he insisted on doing it himself. I took his left hand in my right hand as we waited for the tiny tablet to dissolve under his tongue. I stared at the skin on his hands. It was old and loose and speckled, like snakeskin due to molt. Even though the skin looked old, it didn't feel dry. It was smooth and soft and warm. His hands were handsome and strong, like Dan's. But the fingers were thicker and crooked. Ralph squeezed my hand, not because he seemed afraid, but to assure me that the icy pain in his heart was melting. He patted his chest with his free hand and then picked up the small keys on the workbench. Still pale and quiet, Ralph unlocked then slowly unzipped the canvas bag. He pushed it over to me and I peered in.

It was crammed full of money. There were hundreds of fives, tens, twenties, fifties, even a few one hundred dollar bills. I looked from the bag back to Ralph, then back to the bag again.

"Twelve thousand, six hundred and forty-two bucks. I've been saving it." He was still pale and raspy. "She don't know, so don't tell her," he added, jerking his head toward the stairs.

I looked back at all the money. I had never seen so much cash. I wanted to reach into the bag, pull it to my face and smell it. What if there was a fire in the house? All the money would burn. I didn't realize how much I craved money, how I was starving for it, until I had the insane urge to eat it.

Ralph was solemn. He held my upper arm tight and said, "Don't tell Dan either. I just want you to have it, to keep it, in case something happens to me. I want you to keep it, because I know I can trust you. Next time you come—without him—I'll pack it in your car."

I stared at the cash.

"You're giving it to me?"

I'll be damned. I really am *a money magnet.*

"There's not enough yet, but I have some ideas on how you can get a house—for you and Dan and the baby. I mean even with all his legal problems and now this goddamn disease." Ralph's eyes blurred with tears. "You're his wife—a good wife."

"Oh, Ralph." I sat on a dusty box. "I have to tell you something." I paused. "I'd never deny the fact that I'm Dan's wife, but— Ralph, there's something you don't know."

Ralph stared at me, frowning.

"Dan and I aren't legally married. With his big tax problems—I guess, it just didn't seem wise. He's my husband, but—Ralph, even my own father doesn't know." My heart raced, but I felt somehow lighter.

Ralph slowly stood up, nodding. He almost looked pleased. "This is it—this is the answer."

"Answer to what?"

"I need some time to think."

"About *what?*"

"Everything I've built will be flushed down the toilet if I leave it to him. Goddamn him, he's made it impossible. But you—you love him. You'd never turn him out of his own house. You'd always take care of him. I knew you were God sent—even *she* likes you." Ralph pointed up, referring to Minnie. "You're the answer."

"What's the question?"

"I'm going to name *you* in my trust."

Part Two

Chapter 19

September 1998

I dried the last dinner dishes in a hurry. I wanted to get the shopping bags I'd hidden in the trunk of my car stashed into the closet before Dan came upstairs. Rachel was sitting on the family room couch with my laptop. She was still in her school clothes, a turquoise cotton dress over black leggings. Her darkening curls were flecked with black and yellow paint from her latest mural project for art class. She had rings on every other finger, and a flat black filigree choker circled her neck like a tattoo. I wasn't sure what I thought of twelve-year-old fashion in general, but at least my daughter had a unique sense of style.

"No Internet until homework is done," I said.

"I'm *doing* homework," said Rachel, without looking up.

Rachel often used homework as an excuse to get online and check out the latest photos and gossip about a dark-haired, blue-eyed, twenty-something MTV host named Carson Daly, with whom she'd recently become obsessed. She'd been begging us to get cable so she could watch him every day.

"Well, no instant messaging, or MTV chat rooms. Got it?" I grabbed my car keys.

"I'm doing research about the writer of *The Dumb Bunnies* for my art class." While playing with her young cousins recently, Rachel had discovered a series of children's books about a well meaning but idiotic bunny family who made inane life decisions, often unconsciously wreaking havoc for everyone involved. She'd used her own money to buy me a copy for my last birthday. We both found them hysterically funny.

"Who are the dumb bunnies?" My sister Jamie appeared, a backpack flung over her shoulders.

"Aunt Jamie!" Rachel looked up and grinned. "I'm writing a report on kids' books that are funny for grown-ups too."

"I didn't hear you come in." I gave Jamie a quick hug. "What are you doing here? Don't you have class?" Jamie was now in a graduate program at UC Berkeley. Alison had purchased them a small home near campus, and they were planning to have a commitment ceremony sometime shortly after Jamie graduated.

"You look like you've been crying. What's wrong?"

"Nothing," she said. "Everything. I don't want to talk about it. Can I hang out?"

"Sure. What happened?"

Jamie glanced at Rachel, forcing a smile. "I knew if I could only see my niece, everything would be okay again."

Rachel tilted her head and focused on Jamie, her expression rearranging into one of concern. "Come here, Aunt Jamie, I want to show you something." She moved the laptop onto the floor and grabbed one of the books in a pile next to her. "Meet *The Dumb Bunnies*. These guys will cheer you up."

Jamie and Rachel snickered over the picture of the Dumb Bunny family swimming in the rain, holding umbrellas so they wouldn't get wet. I slipped out of the house, popped my trunk, and grabbed two large Nordstrom's bags full of new clothes. In that instant, a bright light hit me like a police spotlight. I dropped the bags and froze, half expecting to hear: "Step away from the vehicle. You're under arrest." Heart banging, I turned around, held a shaky hand over my eyes, and squinted into headlights. A silver Chevrolet Malibu idled at an odd angle across the street. The driver appeared to be an old man, hunched over and clutching the wheel. I let out a sigh of relief. "Step away from your paranoia," I mumbled. It occurred to me that the old guy might be lost or need help. I waved and started toward the car, but before I made it to the end of the driveway, he screeched off. I made a mental note of the crushed back bumper and a broken left taillight. Harry had once suggested that I might be a bit dim to make it as a private investigator, unless I learned to pay closer attention to details. "You really get some things," he'd said. "But you have some major blind spots. "

The detail I needed to focus on right now was getting the Nordstrom's booty into the house. I made it back to my bedroom and closed the door just as Dan's footsteps thudded up the stairs. Again, my heart pounded wildly. Then the footsteps turned toward the family room. There was time.

All this hiding and sneaking was making me feel as if I was on speed. I considered taking a tranquilizer, but I'd been using them so often for insomnia that I wondered if the pills were starting to eat up key brain cells. At the office the other day, our receptionist, Bob, had said, "Good morning, Mary." In that instant, I couldn't remember his name. "Good morning, you," I'd replied, feeling a jolt of terror. I'd worked with him for years.

Dan's voice sounded happily surprised as he greeted Jamie in the other room. Their singsong conversation and gentle laughter calmed me slightly, allowing me time to examine the loot from the shopping binge I'd had after Dan and I quarreled. He was adamantly opposed to my plan to quit my job and go into business for myself, insisting it would be better for me to wait until one of his countless deals closed and we were "set." "All we do is wait," I complained. "Wait until the deal pays off, wait to buy a house, wait to clear the tax mess, wait to take a vacation, wait until the cancer's cured. You're making more now, we've got money in the bank, and your cancer is under control, right?"

Dan assured me constantly that he would be fine, and he'd made so many positive changes in his health and lifestyle, his body had never looked stronger. He ate fresh food, exercised, meditated, and took countless supplements and herbal potions. Johnny Curtain had given him a three-week all-expense-paid treatment at an alternative clinic in the Dominican Republic, where he drank wheat grass juice and had a technician work daily with him, using a magnetic machine that was purported to destroy cancer cells. I thought the whole thing sounded like hocus-pocus, but prayed I was wrong. Now Dan was taking an herbal hormonal supplement that he said was having the same effect as one of the pharmaceuticals he was supposed to take, without all the chemicals. For all the crying and beseeching I'd done trying to get him to have the operation, maybe I was wrong. The standard tests that measured activity in his prostate looked good, he reported. The cancer was in remission.

"Come on, Dan. I'm sick of waiting for things to change before I can make a change."

"Bear with me. Now is *not* the time," he'd said.

The next thing I knew, I was speeding to the Walnut Creek mall, where I raided Nordstrom's like a bandit, pulling everything and anything interesting off the rack and into the dressing room. I figured if I had to stay at a job that no longer felt good, I sure as hell deserved to look good doing it.

The problem was, I hadn't spent my own money.

Pulling the clothes out of the bag piece by piece, I caressed the blue and white silk suits, cashmere sweater set, sheer pastel blouses, designer jeans, and suede pumps in both camel and chocolate. I loved the sweet peppery scent of new clothes, and inhaled deeply as I pulled off the crackling tissue paper that wrapped each item like a gift. I removed the price tags and neatly refolded and packed the clothes into a worn GAP bag. I ripped the tags into little pieces and flushed them down the toilet.

In the family room, Rachel was back at the computer, typing intensely. Dan was in the process of telling Jamie a joke. His entire body was involved; he paced and waved his arms. He was wearing a tattered camel hair jacket; it draped elegantly over his slimming body, but the color accentuated an odd new tea-toned pallor that made me want to force him out of his office and into the sunshine. At Nordstrom's I'd found two sports coats I wanted to buy him—one dark blue, one charcoal gray. He never wanted to spend money on new clothes, so after my spree, I'd purchased a five hundred dollar gift certificate. I planned to tell him I'd won it at one of the rubber chicken business lunches I attended regularly to promote the fire investigation business. I spent half my work life at these affairs; it wouldn't be implausible that I'd scored one of their door prizes.

Dan reached the punch line of a joke and Jamie groaned.

"Ah, come on. That was a good one," laughed Dan, gently pinching my chin. "It made your big sister laugh, didn't it honey?"

I nodded vigorously.

"She'll say anything to get laid," said Jamie.

"I'm leaving you ladies now. I'm up to my eyeballs in work downstairs."

"He's always up to his eyeballs," I said, rolling mine. "But this is good work. Dan's putting together a lesson plan for Rachel's civics class."

"I'm the teacher's helper," Dan beamed. "Wait until you see what I've done—it's a lesson on law and order. I've created a mock conflict between two neighbors and we're taking the class down to the civil courts to show them how it'd play out. I'll let you read it. Hey, maybe you can even join us. They need a few more chaperones."

"Rachel won't let me go," I said. "Dan's presentable, but I'm too embarrassing. Right Rachel?"

"Whatever." Rachel's eyes remained pinned to the screen.

"He's teaching them about settling disputes lawfully?" whispered Jamie. "That man is the most upstanding tax evader I've ever met."

"And the attentive father we always wanted," I smiled.

A familiar ring burst from the computer and Rachel stiffened.

"Are you using instant messaging?" I said.

Her eyes grew wide. "I'm not. Someone wrote me."

"Let me see what you're doing, young lady."

"I couldn't help it, they wrote *me*." Rachel quickly punched some buttons on the computer, putting it into shut down mode.

"You know you aren't supposed to be using that," I said, raising my voice.

"I was doing homework. We were chatting about homework." She slapped the laptop closed, jumped up. "I'm going to get ready for bed. Good night, Aunt Jamie. Good night, Mommy."

"Oh come on. She was only trying to get tickets to see Carson Daly live, in New York City." Jamie smiled mischievously.

"What?"

"Once she gets the tickets, she's *so sure* you'll take her there, she's planning on writing a persuasive paper about it."

"Oh really? I don't care. I told her in no uncertain terms that she couldn't use the Internet for that. What a sneak."

"'*No uncertain terms?*' Who talks like that?" said Jamie.

"I don't get the deal with Carson Daly," I said. "He looks like an altar boy."

"He looks like Dan. And speaking of inexplicable passions, remember Reid Remmington? You *loved* him." Jamie burst into song, doing her best imitation of the way I sang The Carpenter's "Close to You" when I thought no one else was listening.

I laughed. "Hey. Come here. If you're—as usual—not going to tell me what's up, I need your help."

Jamie followed me to my bedroom.

"How do you like my new suit?" I quickly undressed and slipped on the white suit, checking myself in the full-length mirror. The jacket was flowing silk and closed with mother-of-pearl buttons, dropping just below the hip to cover sleek pants.

"Va-va voom," said Jamie. "You look great. Grown up and very femme."

"Can I say it's yours?" I adjusted the jacket in the full-length mirror.

"Why?" She folded her arms and stared at me. Her blond spikes had been replaced with mellow highlights on a strategically mussed pageboy. "Did you spend more of the old man's money on clothes?"

"*Shhhh.* Yes. I'm dying of guilt. I was at the mall. I promised myself I wouldn't do it again, but couldn't stop. I've got a new work wardrobe stuffed in that GAP bag." I looked at Jamie sheepishly. "I was going to say you gave them to me—that you couldn't wear them anymore."

"Say anything you want. But we're not the same size and I wouldn't be caught dead in most of the outfits you wear. If you're going to embezzle money from your father-in-law and say the stuff is mine," Jamie lectured, "why not buy something I'd like?"

"Embezzle? Shut-up." I sank onto the bed. "Ralph wants me to save up for a house, which I would love, but there's no way we can get a house—

ever—with Dan's tax situation. Besides, they've left me their San Francisco house. That's probably the only way we'll get property, anyway."

Jamie looked skeptical. "They *say* they've left you the house. Have you seen the paperwork?"

"Seen it? I wrote it." I told Jamie how Dan had pitched a fit at the idea of Walter's family law firm doing any more work for his parents, when he was perfectly capable. Then he dragged his feet for so long that Minnie pulled me aside and begged me to take action. "Please, honey," she'd said. "Don't deny us the pleasure of knowing our family is cared for." When I told her I'd figure out a strategy she said, "If it were me, I wouldn't take a long time thinking about it."

After that, I ran out and bought the book *Make Your Own Living Trust*, from a legal self-help publisher, Nolo Press. Rather than being upset, Dan was thrilled. "Nolo? I love them. Did you know they've cracked open the legal profession—made it possible for anyone to get affordable legal advice, without the rip-off prices or the ungodly arrogance of big firm practices?" With the help of Nolo, I drew up the trust. Dan reviewed it, and Minnie, Ralph, and I went to City Hall to transfer the title.

"Doesn't it freak Dan out? That they're giving you the house?"

"Nope. He said he 'didn't want the goddamn thing,' so it might as well go to the woman he loved."

"What's that saying you have? 'I magnetize money'?"

"No. It's, *I am a money magnet*. But I don't say that so much anymore. What good is the house and money if something happens to Dan? I've shifted my focus to affirmations about health."

"I can't believe how things have turned around for you. I'm going to start doing these affirmations."

"It's amazing, isn't it? " I picked up my new cardigan, held it to my face, and inhaled deeply.

"Not to change the subject," Jamie grimaced, "but I need to tell you something."

"I'm all ears." I held my hands behind my head like rabbit ears.

"It's serious." Jamie's face flushed. "Just let me get it out."

I waited.

"Speak Jamie. Speak."

"Remember the day of the earthquake? I called you with news?"

I thought hard, but couldn't remember. But that was around the time she became so oddly private about her personal life, something I'd assumed was punishment for my history of snoopiness.

"Remember the day I read you our horoscope that said we'd have a life of cloaks and daggers, gowns and flowers, with someone from our past?"

"Yes. Hey. Wow. That was *exactly* what happened." I had to sit down. How did the stars know that I would be sneaking around, getting married with no license, hiding money from the IRS, from Minnie, now even lying to my husband about expenditures?

"That's when it started."

"What?"

"I had a fling."

"Really?" I was shocked. Intrigued. "With who?"

"My first lover after high school. Someone already in another committed relationship—like me. And I couldn't tell you then. Jesus, especially while I watched your life fall apart after Kevin's affair." Jamie rambled about how even though she loved Alison, she was miserable thinking of a life with her, and they never had sex, and she didn't even want to, and now she was having another affair. "With the same person. And this time we're serious."

"Serious how? Gowns and flowers?"

"I feel like such a liar," she said.

"Does Alison know?"

"I haven't even told you the worst part." Jamie looked like she was about to confess to a murder. I sat next to her on the bed.

"He's a *man*," she blurted, and started to cry.

"What?"

"Right. Can you believe it? I think I might be hetero." She wiped her nose on a sleeve.

I almost laughed, but Jamie's miserable expression stopped me.

"Oh come on, Jamie. Would that be such a tragedy?"

"Are you joking? It makes me such a cliché," she looked up, eyes panicked. "Not to mention, hello? I have a girlfriend. She supports me. How do I tell her?"

"I don't know, Jamie. But you have to. You can't keep living a lie."

"I can't believe I'm just another LUG."

"What's that?"

"Lesbian Until Graduation. It's a big insult."

"It's more insulting to pretend everything is fine while sneaking around, isn't it? All that cloak and dagger crap? Just tell her the truth."

"Look who's talking?" Jamie whacked me on the arm, her face twisted into an expression of disgust. "You're committing financial infidelity."

"Infidelity? You're nuts. It's not even in the same category. It's a little bout of compulsive shopping. I'm just doing like Dad suggests: upgrading my addictions. It beats binge drinking or drugs. Or snooping. And affairs are much worse than any of those—there's so much lying involved. And goddammit Jamie, we are not talking about me, we are talking about you. You have to tell Alison *something*."

"Well, if I tell her she'll throw me out. And I *do* love her. *Shit.* But I also appreciate that she has money. How else would I afford grad school? I don't want to leave—even though she deserves someone who wants *her* at least as much as wanting the security she offers." Jamie wiped her eyes.

I flopped next to her on the bed. "Why are we so fucked up in the love and money departments?"

"I can answer that in three words," said Jamie. "Mom and Dad."

She was right. Family relationships in our formative years had kept us on a roller coaster ride in the love, money, and security departments. But we were each getting to the age where the statute of limitations for blaming mom and dad had run out. In my financial planning class we had to recall our earliest experience with money. I thought about the time I was seven and my dad handed me a crisp one hundred dollar bill. I clutched it greedily, thinking of all the things I could buy. I'd take my best friend to Disneyland, eat all the chocolate mint ice cream I wanted; buy new dresses, make-up, patent leather shoes, and still have money left for a case of Mystic Mints, which I would never share with Hank. I thought of many things I could do with the money, and none of them included saving it. My dad cheered at all my ideas, then said, "Okay, honey. Give it back." *What?* I clung to the bill. "You didn't really think I was serious?" he said. Since then, I'd spent money faster than I got it.

"Now I want to confess." I shot Jamie a dubious look. "I know this will sound evil. But since I've been spending Ralph's money, I've been almost hoping he'd die before I get caught." My stomach tightened as I gauged her expression.

"Come on. Even Minnie jokes about wanting him dead," said Jamie.

"It's not like that," I said. "When Dan rants and raves about how broke he is, I think how helpful it'll be when his parents die. He won't have to worry, he can focus on his health, spend more time with Rachel and me. I can quit my job, build a little company. We'll be able to go on vacations."

"Interesting." Jamie looked thoughtful. "I'm in a relationship with someone who's the wrong gender, but at least I don't want her dead."

"*Jamie.*" I pinched her arm. "I don't *really* want him dead. It's not like I'm replacing his heart pills with saccharine tablets."

"Sorry. That's not what I meant."

"Besides, Minnie is more like a best friend than a mother-in-law. I don't know what I'd do without her. Sometimes I wish Ralph would go first, so she could spend her final years kicking up her heels, without Ralph harassing or hiding things from her." My words felt empty. Confessing wasn't making me feel better.

"Here's the worst part," I said. "Every time I'm at their house I'm distracted—thinking about how I want to fix it up for Dan, Rachel, and me."

"Like the wolf in the story about the three pigs," said Jamie. "Every time the big bad wolf looks at a little piggie, it morphs into a sizzling platter of bacon."

We both laughed.

"I don't know why I keep buying all this crap behind Dan's back. It makes me feel like Richard." I sat up abruptly. "That whole time he was robbing us, I bet Richard wished we were all dead."

"Where is that guy, anyway?" said Jamie.

"Who knows? I think they last tracked him somewhere in Arizona. But Dan doesn't want to pay anymore private investigators, even when I suggested he use his dad's secret money."

"Well, here's a revolutionary idea. Why don't you just let the money sit?" said Jamie. "In case something happens that you need it?"

"That would make sense." I bit my lip harder than I'd meant to.

"Dan's health is improving, right?"

"Yeah. Of course." Even as I said this, I worried about his odd skin tone, the dark circles under his eyes. But I didn't say anything. I rarely allowed myself to discuss Dan's cancer—even with Jamie. Too much discussion caused everyone to chime in with questions and advice and opinions, until I felt flattened defending Dan and his choices. Especially since I didn't agree with them.

Why won't he get the operation? Impotence and incontinence aren't death sentences. There's more to life than sex. You've got to get Dan in for a second opinion. Here's a list of clinical trials. Has Dan tried a detox? Energy work? Acupuncture? Qigong? Shark cartilage?

At least the cancer helped me understand why Dan kept secrets. If you told people what you were up to, you invited incessant input. Aunt Maggie had recently called and told me that people thought Dan and I were in severe denial. "Really?" I'd said. "Just because we don't want to talk to everyone about it, doesn't mean we're in denial. It just means we don't want to talk to everybody about it. Besides, Dan feels great." I'd wanted to hurl the phone through the sliding glass door.

"His health is improving," I told Jamie. "At least it's not getting worse. Besides, you know I hate to talk about it. I just wish he'd get a normal job, normal medical treatment, and let us have a normal life."

"You used to say the exact same thing about Kevin."

"I did?"

"More or less." Jamie stretched, sat straighter. "The point is, you love him and want to be with him, right? I wish I had it so easy. Look around. You own matching furniture, your kid goes to a great school, you've got medical insurance, you're a PTA member for Chrissakes. And one of these days, you'll even have your own business. This is about as normal as it gets."

"Can you do me this one favor?" I handed Jamie the GAP bag. "I'm going to keep the white suit on. When Dan comes up, give the rest to me in front of him, like you'd just cleaned out your closet. Better yet, say they came from Alison's closet. She wears my size and can afford nicer stuff. Chances are we won't be socializing much with her, right?"

Jamie shook her head. "Ah, the tangled webs we weave," she said, taking the bag out to her car.

She was right. Over the past few years, Ralph had given me over twenty thousand dollars in cash, and advised me to deposit it in two accounts, to escape the IRS requirement that banks report cash deposits of $10,000 or more. He insisted I not tell Minnie or Dan; all they had to know was that I was the trustee of the legal estate. I didn't tell Minnie but did tell Dan, making him promise not to tell Ralph that I'd told him. Dan thought it was funny, and encouraged me to keep taking the money, telling me we'd figure out what to do with it later. Almost every time we visited, Ralph pulled me aside and handed over small sandwich bags stuffed with the cash. He always asked me what the total deposit was, and reminded me to keep it secret.

Ralph's whispered inquiries seemed so obvious, I was sure Minnie suspected something. I had a strong urge to confess, but instead used some of the money to buy her expensive Lancôme perfume, Godiva chocolates, blue rhinestone earrings, and a regular supply of true-crime novels. Once when I gave her a box a mint truffles, she said, "Honey, if there were an encyclopedia of generous people, you'd be the centerfold." I squeezed my toes so tight, my left foot went into a spasm.

I kept double books, praying neither Ralph nor Dan would ask to see bank statements, always shocked that they didn't. I wondered how, exactly, Richard had altered the statements he presented to Dan when he was stealing money. According to the doctored books, Ralph and I had saved close to $24,500, but the amount I had in the bank after various shopping sprees was less than $15,000.

An hour later, Jamie and I were reading in the family room.

"Listen to this," I said, reading from F. Scott Fitzgerald's essay, "The Crack Up." "'The test of a first-rate intelligence is the ability to hold two opposed ideas in the mind at the same time and still retain the ability to function. One should, for example, be able to see that things are hopeless and yet be determined to make them otherwise.'"

"That's not first-rate intelligence, you Dumb Bunny," said Jamie, guffawing. "That's first-class denial. Ask me how I know."

Dan came in and flopped next to me on the couch. "You women look cozy. You staying the night, Jamie?"

Jamie eyed me slyly, then marked the page of her book. "No. I'd better get going. Oh wait! Let me get the rest of the stuff I brought you, Mary. Dan, you should see the great hand-me-downs I brought your wife."

"Yeah, check out this outfit, honey. Jamie gave it to me." As I modeled my new white suit, Dan's phone rang downstairs. He moved to answer it.

"Dan, can't you give work a rest?" I said. "It's almost eleven. Whoever is calling should wait until morning."

"Be right back." Dan left Jamie and me standing, mid-scheme.

Jamie returned with the bag. "I can't believe you spent all that money on clothes," she whispered. "If you're going to blow so much cash, why not give it to a public library? Or Noam Chomsky? Or me?"

"FYI, after my last binge, I gave a pile of it to Glide Memorial Church—an anonymous donation in honor of Ralph. They do amazing things for homeless people."

Dan ran up the stairs. "My father's in the hospital. They're not sure he'll make it through the night." Dan seemed upset, but filled with nervous energy. "I've got to get on this, now."

Jamie's eyes widened. She covered her mouth with her hand and murmured, "*Bacon.*"

I ignored her remark, but still felt unreasonably guilty. "What should I do?" I said. "You need me to come?"

"My mother's down there, hysterical," he said. "Maybe you should."

"Jamie, can you stay? Watch Rachel?"

"Of course. Go."

The emergency room doors opened automatically. I squinted into the bright lights and scanned the dingy waiting room, littered with newspapers and soda cans.

"Mary! Dan!" Minnie pulled herself up from the hard plastic chair. The skin under her eyes sagged like melted wax. "They took Ralph. They said to wait. Oh my God, they made me take St. Christopher off him. Dan, please make them put it back on."

The place was almost empty; just a few scattered people slumped in chairs, staring like zombies, waiting their turn for news of life or death. Back by the vending machine there was a large man staring in our direction, his hands full of snacks. I noticed his ears first: They protruded like small red wings. Reluctantly, Milton/Mike began to stroll towards us.

"What the hell is he doing here?" Dan glared.

"Dan, please!" Minnie pursed her lips. "How do you think we got here? Mike took your father and I out to the Lyon's for dinner. Your dad loves the liver and onions. But it was too rich, I think. He had an attack."

"You told me he moved back to Pennsylvania with his mother." Dan spoke as if Mike wasn't within earshot.

Minnie ignored him. With a shaking hand, she reached into the hospital-issued plastic bag that held Ralph's wallet and reading glasses. She pulled out Ralph's heavy St. Christopher medal on its thick gold chain. "He always wears this. They wouldn't let me go in. The nurse told me to wait." With each sentence, Minnie's pitch rose higher. Her gaze bounced between Dan and Mike, who now hovered a few feet behind us.

Turning sharply toward Mike, Dan said, "Thanks for poisoning my father with fat, Mike. Good work. Want to let me take it from here?"

"Dan, stop it," Minnie snapped, embarrassed.

"Ma, I don't want that bastard anywhere near my father."

Bastard? Unfortunate word choice, Dan.

"Enough!" Minnie hurled the St. Christopher medal, sending it flying right into Dan's cheek. On its slide downward, the chain linked to a button on his blazer and dangled awkwardly.

Minnie stood straighter and set a hand on Mike's arm. "Mike's poor mother died last month. He was right by her side, taking care of her. Now he's helping us. After all he's been through."

Dan's eyes twitched, and he calmed slightly, as if the guilt subdued him. Minnie's expression remained haughty, her jaw clenched and trembling. Dan coolly unhooked the gold medal and slid it into a side pocket before striding off to get information.

"It's okay, Minnie, I should be going." Mike set the chips and cookies on a chair and embraced her. "I'm so sorry about Ralph. Keep me posted," he added, nodding in my direction.

As Milton/Mike lumbered away, I again had an urge to chase after him to give him a hug. Something about that man seemed so innately sweet, or tragic—I wasn't sure which, but it was no wonder Minnie couldn't resist him.

"Oh honey," whimpered Minnie. "I just couldn't help it. What Dan doesn't know could fill an ocean. Sometimes he gets me so angry."

I knew just what she meant, but still.

"Mike looks pretty good," I said. I'd noticed that he seemed more fit, less red and swollen.

"Honey, that man hasn't touched a drop of alcohol since he went home to see his mother. And with all he's been through? That's no small feat."

Dan was engaged in a deep discussion with the triage nurse. I took Minnie back to her seat.

"God forbid this is the end, but if it is—" She looked at me, pleading. "I've been thinking of something. Not just because of this, but—maybe you and Dan and Rachel—if something happens with Ralph, maybe you could move in with me? There's plenty of room in that big house— " Minnie abruptly stopped, hit my arm. "How can I even talk about that now? God forgive me."

My jaw dropped slightly. *What a great idea.* On top of being practical, it immediately transmuted my desire for the house from something selfish and evil into something charitable and loving. We would move in *before* she died, and take care of her. But would Minnie mind if I did some remodeling? Ripped out the tired old shags to display hardwood? Painted it top to bottom? Without having to pay a mortgage we could really make that place shine. I could quit my job, go to work for myself, and be at home to greet Rachel after school. We could have nice family dinners every night, and Minnie would never have to live alone, or age fearfully like Grandma Mary.

What's wrong with me? My father-in-law is in crisis and I'm redecorating.

My fingers were entwined with Minnie's, like roots. She trembled and cried against my shoulder, a dark smudge of mascara staining the front of my new white suit.

"Oh honey, now look what I've done."

I took the crumpled tissue from Minnie and dabbed the tears streaming down the creases of her face. "Don't even think about that." I pulled her closer, almost grateful that she'd stained my illicit new outfit. Especially since she had practically paid for it.

Chapter 20

September 1998

We gathered around the hospital bed, thankful to be in a private room. Ralph's haggard face poked from the thin gown, his unshaven skin resembling worn sandpaper. Hanging bags of fluid fed him through an IV, and a ventilator tube snaked down his throat, forcing the breath in and out of his lungs. A low hum vibrated from the fluorescent lights above where Minnie and I sat. Dan stood in the corner frowning, arms folded, conferring with the doctor about whether to remove life support.

A handmade sign, printed neatly in bright blue ink, was taped on the wall above the nightstand, next to a large bowl of Snickers and Milky Way bars. It read:

Hi! My name is Ralph.
Next week I turn 90.
I've been married to my beautiful wife, Mary, for 53 years.
I am father to Dan and Jimmy.
I ran Fort Mason during World War II.
I managed Lachman Brothers' Furniture Store.
I'm quite a ladies' man.

Help yourself to candy!

The sign and candy were my mother's idea. "Those nurses and aides are so overworked they can barely see the old people who are rolled in and out of there," she'd said. "This'll let them know he's not just another cadaver-in-waiting—that there is a person and family to consider. And the candy will get him extra visits from the staff."

She was right. Before, nurses had floated through the room like passing clouds. Today, when we were standing in the hall, Darcy, a sweet-faced aide with skin the color of vanilla bean, had entered his room and said, "Am I the kind of woman you like? I like *you*." She returned to the nurses' station and announced, "That cute old guy in 107 is giving away candy bars."

Harry had dropped by and laughed at the sign.

"Go ahead, laugh," I said. "But a wise man once told me that everything in life—and I assume that includes death—benefits from a good marketing and public relations plan."

"I know," he said. "I think it's great."

After the doctor left the room, Dan scraped a metal chair across the shiny linoleum and set it next to his mother. Minnie turned away and dropped her head, burying it in her hands. "Don't say it," she said. Dan and I each put an arm around her shoulders, forming a tight support as she crumpled forward, her head falling on Ralph's bed.

"We don't have to do it right now, Ma," he said, rubbing her back. "We can have some lunch, talk it over, get used to the idea."

"Lunch?" Minnie drilled Dan with a pained look. "I can't believe it's come to this." She cried and shook, releasing squeaks and groans like a vintage car shut off after a long drive.

"Dan, look at your father." Minnie's nose was wet and pink, the whites of her eyes stained red. "He never goes a day without shaving. Do you Ralph?" Minnie slid her fingers under Ralph's large, speckled hand, latching on. "Oh, Ralph." She dropped her head back to the bed, sobbing.

The beeps from Ralph's heart monitor quickened, and zig-zagging lines on the screen appeared closer together. His mouth was forced open by the breathing tube, his lips dry and cracking. I took a small tube of Vaseline and dabbed some around his mouth. His eyes squeezed slightly, and he twitched, startling me.

After a moment, Minnie sat up and asked me to get the priest on duty to deliver last rites. The nurse's station was crowded with a group of young interns who were reviewing a chart. I asked for the charge nurse.

"I'll page Father O'Leary, right away," she said.

"Father O'Bleary," whispered one of the interns.

"Have you seen him?" whispered another. "They ought to call in another priest to give *him* last rites." I could hear their muffled laughter as I returned to the room.

But they were right. Father O'Leary was so old and feeble, I wondered if assigning elderly priests hospital duty was one of the Church's new cost saving measures. Lord knows, they needed all their funds to settle the mounting crush of child molestation suits. There'd be no need to squander money on expensive ambulance rides if the priests who were near death already worked right here.

Father O'Leary slurred his words, and given the smell of his breath, I suspected he had a great thirst for the blood of Christ—or a close facsimile. The priest started to mutter and anoint Ralph. We stepped away from the bed, relocating to the corner by the window, where we spoke in hushed tones.

"What's he saying?" said Minnie. "Are you getting that?"

"He must be speaking Latin," I said.

"I know Latin," said Dan. "That's not Latin."

The Father's hands shook so much that he spilled holy oil down the front of Ralph's gown. His heart monitor went crazy, as if he knew. Finally the priest turned around. He looked disoriented, and surprised to see us. We all blessed ourselves, offering our thanks to God, and reluctantly, to the soused Father O'Bleary.

"Dan, don't you have something for the Father?" said Minnie, sweetly.

Dan guided the priest out, pressing a few bills into his palm.

Ralph's aide entered the room. "Mrs. Murphy, as soon as they take the tubes out, I'm gonna shave your husband," said Darcy. "You hear that Ralph? I know you like to look good for the ladies—and your wife, she's a good-looking lady! You know," she said, lowering her voice. "The patients? They're in a coma but they can hear us."

Leaning close to Ralph's ear, I whispered, "Sorry about that priest," and kissed him on the cheek.

Minnie absently reached her free hand behind her and searched for Darcy's, holding it in a tight squeeze. Her breathing sounded like a distant door opening and closing on a rusty hinge. Earlier in the day, when I'd picked her up, she begged me to stop for cigarettes, even though her doctor suspected she had early signs of emphysema and implored her to quit.

"You want me to get 100s?"

"Honey, get 200s if they have them."

"Can you hear me Ralph?" Minnie sniffled. "Oh, Ralph. You lived a good life. I'm so proud of you." She turned to Dan, her voice suddenly defiant. "Tell your father how proud you are, Dan."

"My father knows I love him." Dan's tone was curt, steely.

Minnie held his gaze a moment, and let it drop.

A sharp throbbing in my brain set off a vicious headache. Weren't the dead as omniscient as God? Once Ralph died, he'd know for sure what I'd done. How could I have gone on all those shopping sprees, imagined moving in, remodeling his home, when Ralph was like a grandfather to me? Then something hit me: Was I so different from Richard? What if Richard *had* really loved Dan like a brother all through the time he'd been a low-life embezzler? He must feel horrid. Pathetic. Like a piece of scum on a clod of dirt. I gnawed on the inflamed skin around my fingernails, thanking God that Minnie, at least, remained clueless about my betrayal.

Darcy rubbed Minnie's shoulders while the medical team prepared to disconnect Ralph's life support.

A doctor explained each step of the process, warning us that Ralph might pass immediately, or linger for a number of hours—there was no way to predict. The doctor and an intern flipped switches and removed the IVs. Dan remained stern, arms folded, as if bracing himself. Minnie and I relocated to the foot of the bed, where I held and slowly rocked her as she quivered, releasing continuous high-pitched wails.

Darcy pulled a chair behind Minnie. "Mrs. Murphy, be careful not to fall. Maybe you need to sit."

As the doctor reeled in the long, plastic breathing tube, Ralph's face and body contorted.

"Oh no," squealed Minnie. She dropped into the chair and covered her face. "Don't make me watch."

Dan was by his father's side stroking his arm when a loud, wet rattle gurgled through Ralph's lungs. We all stood frozen as Ralph began to cough.

"Suction!" said the doctor. "Clear the airway."

There was a rush of movement, and Ralph's body settled into a quiet silence.

I closed my eyes and rested my hand on Ralph's feet. *I'm sorry, Ralph. Please forgive me.*

"Okay," said the doctor. "He's looking pretty good. Can you hear me buddy?"

My eyes popped open, shocked at the sight of Ralph looking at the doctor, alert. His lips moved, but no sound escaped. A slight wheeze accompanied each labored breath. "Mmmm," squeaked Ralph.

"Don't talk yet, buddy. I bet you feel like you've been gargling broken glass. Am I right or am I right?" The doctor smiled and turned to Darcy. "Let's get him a drink. That'll help."

I stared at Dan, confused. He shrugged his shoulders.

"Sometimes they surprise you," said the doctor.

"Ma," said Dan. "Come on over. He's trying to talk to us."

Ralph's lips were still moving. He lifted his left hand, finger up, as if he desperately needed to tell us something. "Mmmm—"

Was he finally going to tell Dan about Mike? Would it make any difference?

Darcy returned quickly with water, and held a long straw to Ralph's lips. "Drink first, talk next," she said, rubbing his head. He winced as the liquid worked its way down his raw throat.

Ralph pushed the water away. His murky eyes widened, squeezed tight, then reopened. "Maaaaaa—ree," he gasped. "Maaa-reee."

Minnie slid her hand into mine. "Is he talking to me? Or you?" she said. Ralph always called her "Mary," and we couldn't tell who he was looking at.

"We're all here, Dad. Ma, Mary, and I—we're all here," said Dan.

Ralph's hand lifted again. He appeared to be pointing up. Maybe he was seeing angels. Or his first wife, Mary. My heart pounded. I'd always known that there was something outside of this human experience, something celestial and pure, that one experienced at the brink of death. We had been deprived of glimpsing this when my sister was taken off life support; because she never regained consciousness, she never had any last words for her family.

"Maaaa—ree," Ralph gasped, took another breath. We leaned around him, in a huddle, faces so close our breath was mingling.

"Look, look—" Ralph wheezed in a painfully long inhale and closed his eyes, his left hand banging on the bed like a gavel. "There's ... there's—"

"Ralph! What? There's what? What do you see?" Minnie grasped his hand in both of hers, steadying it.

Ralph's eyes popped open and he rasped, *There's two-hundred-and-fifty-bucks in the sock drawer.*" After the words scraped out, his body went slack, his left hand dropping onto the bed.

"Ralph! Ralph?" Minnie, shrill and panicked, shook Ralph's shoulder. "Are you gone?"

"It's okay, Mrs. Murphy. He's resting." Darcy pointed to the heart monitor, which showed erratic activity. "Don't push and shake him, huh? Let him rest."

Everyone remained silent for what seemed an eternity. Minnie sat in the chair, her eyes panning the room like two cameras, then zooming in on Dan and me.

"Did he say there was two-hundred-and-fifty-bucks in his sock drawer?" said Minnie.

My nose grew hot.

"Is that what he just said?"

"Ah," said Dan, pausing for a few seconds. "I think he did." He glanced in my direction. I couldn't tell for sure, but I thought he was squelching a smile.

"Why would he say that?" Minnie looked perplexed and fidgeted in her chair.

"I don't know," I whispered, shrugging my shoulders.

Liar, liar, liar!

"After fifty-three years, that's what he tells me?" Minnie shook her head, looking pitiful. My toes cramped in my shoes.

"Ma, let me get you something to eat," said Dan.

"Dan, I can't leave your father. You go, find us a decent deli sandwich." Minnie stared at me, eyebrows raised. "We'll stay here. Okay, honey?"

I could tell that Minnie was craving a cigarette. When Dan left, we would sneak a smoke—maybe talk about living together. The idea had taken permanent hold in my imagination. "But Dan might not go for it," I'd whispered to her that morning. "We're just the gals to convince him. You and me—Arsenic and Old Lace," she'd said, nudging me with a smile, followed by a torrent of tears over Ralph.

As Dan stood to leave, Ralph's eyes popped open. He wrinkled his nose, grit his teeth, and groaned like a woman with labor pains. I grabbed Ralph's hand.

"Dad?" Dan ran to the other side of the bed, pulling Minnie with him.

Ralph's watery blue eyes looked up. His hand went limp in mine, sending a jolt, a powerful pulse of energy, bursting through me as life escaped his old, tired body. A piercing metallic shriek blared from the heart monitor, which glowed with a long, red line.

"Oh no, Mary," squealed Minnie, reaching for my arm.

I felt dirty, but relieved, like I'd just been airlifted out of quicksand.

Chapter 21

October 1998

For the ninth anniversary of the 1989 Loma Prieta earthquake, Dan and I made a plan to spend a night at the Pelican Inn, an old English-style bed and breakfast tucked between the ocean and the redwoods on the Marin Coast. I'd convinced him it was the perfect time for a romantic getaway, given it was the event that seemed to have catapulted me into his arms. We were also belatedly celebrating our birthdays, which had been overshadowed by Ralph's death.

"This year Mom is 3-5 and Papa is 5-3," said Rachel. "You guys can celebrate that you're exact opposites."

Dan pulled into the Inn's driveway and parked facing the beach. As he slowly got out of the car, his father's thick gold St. Christopher medal dangled in front of him, glimmering in the sunlight. Minnie had given it to him after Ralph's funeral last month, and he never took it off. Seeing Dan wear something that Ralph had treasured gave me an odd sense of pleasure on Ralph's behalf.

I was leaning to pick up my bag when something caught my eye. A silver Chevy Malibu crunched across the gravel driveway, pulling out onto Highway 1. It had a crushed back bumper with a broken left taillight.

"Dan, that's so weird. That car that just left? I swear it's the same one I saw parked in front of our house a few months ago with some old man inside."

"Oh, here we go." Dan stiffened, squinting toward the roadway. "You're not starting up with the tax stuff again, are you?"

I'd gone through a phase where I was sure the IRS was sending operatives out to track Dan's whereabouts, until Harry explained to me that they were not in the habit of stalking folks with unpaid tax liens.

"I'm just saying it's an odd coincidence."

We checked in at the front desk, where the clerk perked up at the sound of our names.

"Mary and Dan Patric? A gentleman was just asking about you."

"Who?" Dan's eyes widened. "Where is he?"

"He had an envelope, but he didn't want to leave it." She smiled. "He said he'd catch up with you."

"What did he look like?"

"Older. Thin. Gray hair. No. Brown? Geez, I'm sorry. He said he'd find you."

The only people who knew we were here were Minnie, Rachel, and the parents of Rachel's best friend, with whom she was spending the night.

"Who was in that car, Dan?"

"How would I know?" Dan looked stressed.

"I've seen that car by our house. I know you told someone we're here." I glared at him.

"What are you accusing me of now?" Dan frowned, momentarily distracted. "It couldn't have been Johnny. But he knows we're here." Dan pulled out a pen and paper and made a note. "Hope it wasn't some goddamn process server."

Annoyed, I decided to drop it. But I made a mental note that if I ever saw that car again, I'd get the license and have Harry run a check.

After settling in the room, we walked along the shore, where the autumn sunset cast a coppery glow on the water. Gulls yelped and dove, sending the smaller sandpipers scattering off, leaving trails of pronged footprints in the wet sand.

"What do you say we go for some red meat and Yorkshire pudding?" said Dan, gesturing toward the inn.

I tried not to think of what I'd read about the murderous effects of ignoring fresh-squeezed, low-fat, high-fiber, organic, hormone-free, vegetarian, whole food, macrobiotic diets. Given how Dan had already beat the odds, an occasional steak shouldn't kill him. And cancer or not, he ought to be able to eat whatever he wanted for our belated birthday celebration.

The dining room was lit by candles and a blazing fireplace. The waiter arrived, and I asked for a bottle of cabernet.

"We don't need a bottle. Give us two by the glass," said Dan.

217

"No. We'll take the bottle," I said, handing the waiter my menu.

The waiter stood there for a moment.

"Guess my wife knows what she wants." Dan kept his eyes on me, and frowned. The waiter took Dan's menu and scurried away.

"You're drinking a lot more these days," said Dan.

"Is it causing a problem for you?

"No—"

"Then I'd appreciate it if you'd quit acting like my father." Actually, he wasn't acting much like *my* father. Dad had allowed us to start drinking from the time I was eight years old, when he instituted "Wednesday night wine tasting." We were each allowed a small glass of wine with the idea that we would learn to drink responsibly, like European kids. I have a picture of one of these family events, where four-year-old Jamie is raising her empty wine glass in a toast, glassy eyed and giddy, red wine staining her baby teeth a dingy purple. It was taken right before she threw up.

"Why don't we talk about the move to San Francisco?" I said after the waiter had delivered the wine and prime rib. "You never want to take the time to talk when you're working. Now is the perfect time."

"Now is not the perfect time. Given your unemployment, I should be working harder," he said.

"I am not exactly unemployed."

After Ralph died, I'd asked my boss, Kent, if I could have a more flexible schedule, offering to take a pay cut in exchange for more time at home. He said it wasn't convenient, and given how much I'd been gone lately, I should be putting in more hours, not fewer. When I'd called Harry for advice, he had said, "If we worked together, you'd make your own hours." Soon after, I typed out a resignation letter and left.

"Listen, Dan, I know you're furious that I quit my job. But I have a plan."

Laughter and conversation filled the restaurant, making the awkward silence between Dan and I more pronounced. He stabbed his fork into the bloody slice of prime rib, sawed off another piece, dipped it in horseradish, and shoved it into his mouth.

"Quit ignoring me," I said.

"I'm not ignoring you. I just don't know what to say." Dan chewed silently. "I'm up to my eyeballs in paperwork for this new deal, can't even think about anything else. We agreed we'd set this issue aside until a few other things have settled."

"We didn't 'agree.' As I recall, you insisted." Dan's latest venture had him advising a group of investors who'd put money in a penny stock company that held mineral mines. "And this mining company may never take off."

"You need to have more faith. I've overcome betrayal and cancer, so you'd think my wife would have a little more confidence." Dan's voice was tense. At times, his expression now seemed to resemble Ralph's.

"I don't know what to think. You don't let me in on your medical decisions. If you're better, what are we waiting for? The cancer was diagnosed six years ago. It's like we're living in purgatory." I drained my wine glass and filled it again. "I have to tell you, Dan—you don't look like the picture of health."

Dan was paler and thinner with each passing month. Dr. Lowe, the urologist, said that short of removing his prostate—which he still refused to consider—he couldn't help Dan eliminate the growing pain in his groin. He believed it was caused by pressure from the tumor.

"If we moved in with your mom, we'd be consolidated in one place. That way if anything ever happened—"

"Nothing's going to happen. And I have to tell you, I can't fight cancer and you too."

"Then let's not fight. Let's talk." I took a deep breath to cool my rising temper. "First of all, I'm the one taking care of your mother all the time." The past few months, I'd banked hundreds of hours with Minnie, cleaning closets, paying bills, taking her shopping, to hair appointments, doctor appointments, the cemetery, and listening to her reminisce about the past and wail about every minute detail of her life—all of which would be a lot easier to cope with if we lived together.

"You won't clean up the IRS mess. I've accepted that. You won't come out of hiding; you won't get a normal job. Why can't you do this one thing?"

"Why do you keep insisting on bringing this up?"

"Because I think this craziness is keeping you sick."

"I'm doing the best that I can. Let's drop it."

More and more often, I was lying awake at night, worrying about everyone's health. I'd stare at the ceiling, where some years earlier, Rachel had placed glow-in-the-dark plastic stars. Now they barely registered light. Over and over, I ran through the same list of thoughts. Who would take care of Minnie if Dan got sick? Who would take care of Dan and Rachel if I had to work to support us? How would Rachel handle it if Dan died? What if both Minnie *and* Dan got sick? How would I take care of everyone? I'd been having a recurring nightmare about an IRS agent wearing surgical scrubs coming to the door, slapping handcuffs on Dan, and dragging him to a cement tomb. On the nights I didn't take tranquilizers, my worries got so stirred up, it felt like my brain might liquefy and soak into the fabric of the bed.

"What would happen if we needed money to take care of you? At least we'd all be together, sharing resources."

Dan dropped his knife and fork. It made a loud clang that silenced chatter from neighboring diners. "I cannot fight for my life if I think I'm going to lose. I won't even think about that because it doesn't help."

Dan's increased volume caught the attention of a tanned, silver-haired couple sitting next to us. "Why can't you stick to our agreement?"

"Agreement?" I whispered, but the words hissed like ice cubes tossed into a fire. "You want to discuss agreements? You said you were going to show me the world. I practically had to twist your arm to get you to leave your desk this weekend, to celebrate birthdays that happened a month ago. You were going to include me in your health decisions, but I have no idea what the hell all these herbs and concoctions are doing to you. You said we'd own our own home, and now you won't even let us move into a house that's sitting there waiting for us."

Dan pounded a fist on the table, causing a loud bang.

"Why do you have to keep harping on moving or buying a house when you know right now that I hate the idea?" His skin was shiny, a sign he was having a hot flash from the hormone supplements he was taking.

"Why do you hate the idea of something that would make me happy *and* make our lives easier?" I stared back, furious.

Dan turned up his volume. "You're just using this sad situation with my mother as an excuse to get what you want."

Before I could respond, the silver-haired man bolted up, shoved his napkin on the table, and glowered at Dan. "Do you mind? We're *trying* to have a nice evening out. Would you *please* keep your voice down?" He looked disgusted.

Dan jumped up, sloshing red wine onto the white tablecloth. He shoved his napkin onto his chair, and faced the man, who towered at least six inches above him. "You want me to keep my voice down?"

"If you think you're capable, yes," he said.

It looked like a confrontation between a groomed poodle and a scrappy barnyard rooster. Dan faced down this humiliation, like all others, primed to fight, which—as far as I could tell—always made things worse. I glanced at the silver-haired woman, who kept her eyes locked on her lap.

"Dan. Please, sit down," I whispered, desperate.

A waiter appeared. "Is there a problem here?"

"We are *trying* to have a nice, private dinner," said the poodle.

"The only problem is him," said Dan. "Come on. Let's go." He pulled me from my seat and turned to the waiter. "I'll pay up front. I can't eat this crap anyway."

Dan slapped a pile of bills on the hostess counter, leaving her stuttering and bewildered, and stormed out the front door. He race-walked across the gravelly parking lot, toward the beach. "Are you coming?"

"Dan, that was so embarrassing."

"Pompous bastard. If I'd had a gun, I'd have shot him."

The blue night air was wet and chilly. Waves crashed like thunder. I marched behind him on the sand dunes, the tune to *Happy Birthday to You* drumming through my mind like an elegy.

"It's freezing." I was wearing a sundress. "Hang on. I'll get our jackets and we can walk by the water."

"He's trying to have a nice meal?" muttered Dan, who escaped across the sand at a breakneck pace. "What the hell does he think we're doing? He ought to try to deal with cancer and the relentless betrayal—"

"That's it." I stopped cold. "If you're lumping me with your slimy list of people who betrayed you, just because I quit my job—"

"Well, what would you call that? You're just like the other ones."

"Other what? Wives? Have you ever stopped to consider that *you're* the common denominator in your failed marriages?" I was yelling. "Do I have any input in these crazy businesses you get involved with? Or these crazy people? Who the hell knows we are here, Dan?"

Dan ignored my question. "What about you?" he said. "Jesus, I'm not the only one with failed relationships here. Did you ever consider that the reason that you and Kevin couldn't make it was because you kept insisting he give up the things he loved to be some kind of Ken doll husband? I never lied to you about who I was or what I did, but it's not good enough, is it? You just can't accept anyone the way they are."

It felt as if he'd punched me. I did want Dan to be different. But come to think of it, Dan didn't accept me either. Why couldn't he support any of my ideas?

"I only want you to get a regular job because I don't even know what the hell you do half the time," I said.

"I'm fighting for my goddamn life—fighting to stay afloat, to sock enough away to take care of my family, have a future."

"Why don't you quit fighting then? Relax, spend some time with your family? You don't need to sock money away; your mom and dad have left us enough to give you a secure retirement. We just need enough to pay the bills now."

"I don't care about their money and their house."

"Then take an interest in my business. I already have two potential clients lined up, and Harry has an excellent reputation. I think it's a really great idea—"

"Well, I think it's a stupid idea. Especially because I don't see you doing anything to get it going—all you do is run around with my mother. And how do you expect to get approved for a mortgage if you can't show a salary? Did you think of that?"

Actually, I hadn't. Somehow I figured that by having all these fat bank accounts in my name—fifteen thousand dollars from Ralph, the investment account I'd accrued working with the fire investigators, and savings Dan and I regularly contributed to—I would be considered a good risk.

"You walked away from a good salary, and with this guy—Harry—there are no guarantees."

"I can guarantee you that Harry doesn't have a criminal history."

"What the hell is that supposed to mean?"

"It means, I'm a hell of a better judge of character in business partners than you are. Look at the people you've picked to associate with."

"Well, if I have such terrible taste in people, why don't you explain why I picked you?" he said.

I felt stung. All I could think about was my secretive spending behavior.

"Maybe I'm just the wrong guy for you," said Dan. "Maybe it's as simple as that."

"You know what? Maybe you are."

I stormed away across the sandy dunes. Maybe he was right. Maybe the time had come where I had to give Dan an ultimatum, and mean it: Counseling or separation. Come out of hiding or get out of my life. Then I pictured Rachel's face. She adored Dan. With her dad on the road with his band half the time, she counted on Dan to be the steady father who showed up at every soccer game and field trip, not to mention at the dinner table every night. How could I take her away from that? The truth was, I didn't want to be away from it either. And maybe Dan was right. On some level, I was no better than the liars and thugs he had done business with. I'd misused funds given to me by a blind old man, secretly plotted our living situation with Minnie, and hidden more and more from Dan. I remembered how I'd told him on our first date that I'd refused to shoplift with the gang of thieves I'd met in high school. Perhaps my character had been no better than theirs all along.

Wispy, black-streaked clouds bruised the face of the full moon. Kicking up sand with every step, I rushed to the inn to get to my pillbox, where I had one last tranquilizer, mixed in with a pile of painkillers.

Dan's breath grew louder behind me, until his hand reached for mine. I wanted to throw it off, but when I glanced at him, he wore the saddest expression I'd ever seen. I held his hand and kept walking, keeping my eyes fixed on the dim light stabbing through the inn's leaded glass windows.

Once we were inside, the inn's dark antiques and faded tapestries began to spook me. The atmosphere seemed to be sucking up whatever humor and romance was left in our marriage. Dan and I were exceedingly polite, taking turns in the bathroom, reading quietly in the canopy bed, saying "excuse me" after the slightest gurgle, "sorry" if a movement made the bed squeak. He snapped off his reading light and turned away from me. I turned off my light and slid onto my back, staring into the darkness.

It was just as well that we'd had a fight. Sex was difficult and awkward these last few months. Dan had refused the operation to remove his prostate for fear of becoming impotent and incontinent, but the cumulative effect of this herbal treatment had killed his sex drive and atrophied his muscles, and the pain in his groin only worsened during intercourse. Lately, I'd noticed that he made more comments laced with sexual innuendo when we were socializing with friends: "Sorry, gotta leave. We have business in the bedroom," or, "I need to get my rest, Mary kept me up all night." Though we never discussed it, I always backed him up—winking, flirting, doing whatever I could to maintain the illusion of sexual connection, even if just for show. It occurred to me that the passionate couples I used to envy when I was with Kevin—the ones who offered steamy displays of affection or made regular reference to their great sex lives—might have been overcompensating in public for what wasn't happening in private.

We drove home the next morning in silence. As we emerged from the gray coastal fog of the Richmond Bay Bridge onto the sunny East Bay freeway, Dan surprised me by taking the first exit, driving a short distance along the choppy water, pulling into a vista point and shutting off the engine.

"Why are we stopping?"

He put his hand on mine. "I'm sorry our weekend turned out this way. I really am." He looked at me, eyes moist. "I gotta tell you, honey. I just don't feel good. I want to be more of a lover, more of a man. I just can't stand the thought of you with anyone else." Dan's nose started to run and he pulled a white handkerchief out of his pocket.

"Anyone else? How could there be anyone else?" I touched his wrist. "I don't care that much about sex, as long as we—"

He pulled away, shoving the handkerchief back in his pocket. "I do. I care about it."

"What if we got help?"

"Will you stop with that? I don't want to talk to some counselor about our personal problems. That's why we have each other."

The truth was, I missed our sex life, too. Lately just about everything reminded me of sex —from the crashing ocean waves to the ripe melons, figs and bananas depicted in the still life painting hanging on the wall of the inn. More and more often I had daydreams where I inserted unsuspecting men *and* women into steamy fantasies that left me guilty and frustrated.

"I'm so sick of this fucking cancer," said Dan. "One miserable loss after another, like accelerated aging. I can't eat what I want, I can't drink, I've got indigestion all the time. My arm hurts, I can't get work because I have to remember to take this pill or boil some concoction, or deal with a hot flash like a middle-aged woman. Jesus, honey, I can't satisfy you, and now I can't even get a good night's sleep because of the pain."

"Pain? Why didn't you tell me it was so bad? I hate that you keep so much to yourself. There's always something you can do for pain. Here, I've got codeine and Vicodin in my bag." I unbuckled the seatbelt, and turned to get my purse from the back. "I wish you'd let me make you a doctor's appointment tomorrow."

"Okay," he said.

"Okay?" Dan never wanted to see the doctor. My eyes locked on the St. Christopher medal hanging like a weight on his chest.

"I'm turning into a big problem for you, aren't I?" he said.

"Yes." I stopped digging through my purse for the pills, turned his head toward me, looked him straight in the eyes. "But you're a problem I want to have. Okay?"

"Let's not worry. I'll go to the doctor. I know it's all okay. I'm just tired. I want to tell you something. And before I say this, I beg you, please don't take it personally."

"Okay." My chest tightened. Usually remarks like this ended up in comments that upset me.

"I'm sick of taking care of other people. I'm not talking about you or Rachel. I just can't take one more responsibility right now. Besides you, Rachel, and Johnny, there's really no one else I want to interact with right now. This thing with my mother, it's just too much. Sorry I've left so much of it to you. It just seems like nothing is coming together. It would mean so much if you could just accept things—accept me. As I am."

"I'm sorry, Dan. Maybe we just need to talk like this more often. I shouldn't have put so much pressure on you—"

"Shhhh." Dan pressed his finger on my lips. "Here's my thought. We'll call my mother, go over for a visit. And I'll take that pill, what is it?"

"Try the Vicodin—I take two when I get cramps." Even though Motrin worked just as well, lately I took narcotics whenever I had an ache, knowing it would dull more than just physical pain.

"I'm heavier than you. Maybe I'll take an extra."

At first I handed him three tablets, which he washed down with the dregs of a soda left in the car. Seeing him still wincing with pain, I handed him another tablet. It was the least I could do after deceiving him all this time—spending Ralph's money, nosing into his family history, fantasizing about sex with others.

"Trade places with me, honey," I said. "You relax, I'll drive."

Chapter 22

October 1998

Minnie opened the door of the Rockaway house and threw her arms open. "What a wonderful surprise. You left a romantic weekend to see your old Ma!" She'd dropped so much weight this past month, her dentures no longer fit properly, causing a slight lisp. "I was just going through more of Ralph's boxes. You wouldn't believe it. Papers, papers, papers. I'm so happy to have a nice break with you kids. Maybe we can go get some Chinese?"

"Ma, you smell so, well, what is that—a new cologne?"

"Oh, honey, I went to set my hair and realized I was spraying it with the air freshener." She whacked Dan on the arm. "I'm wearing Glade Country Peach!"

Dan laughed and staggered back. "Sorry. Mary gave me some pain pills. I feel a little off."

"Mary has painkillers?" Minnie looked at me, pointing a finger. "You've been holding out on me. You know I've got that sciatica pain—it's been giving me a lot of trouble."

"We've got an appointment for you next week," I said. "Let's wait and hear what the doctor says."

Minnie sighed. "Come in. Get something to drink. I've got to go put in my bottom teeth. And maybe dress up a bit." She ushered us in, and leaned toward my ear, whispering, "I've got your smokes in the drawer by the phone. I'll keep him busy for awhile if you need to slip away." She winked.

Dan wandered into the kitchen and sat down, leaning back in the chair smiling. The kitchen table was strewn with papers, letters, bills, a box of photos, and a small metal safe, about the size of a shoebox. Dan flipped through some of the photos, then slapped them down, an expression of pure joy spreading across his face.

"This is unbelievable. I've been to half the specialists at Kaiser, and my own little woman had the cure to my pain, right in her purse. I gotta tell you, honey. I feel great."

"I never could understand why you haven't taken drugs when you were in pain." Taking pills was such a knee-jerk reaction in my family.

Dan pulled me onto his lap. "I can't explain it. It's like I've been listening to a car alarm shrieking twenty-four hours a day, and someone just shut it off. This is the best birthday present I've ever had." He pulled my face down, kissed me playfully. "If we get out of here early, I might even be up for some dancing."

I laughed. Dan looked elated. I might have imagined it, but he appeared to have more color in his face and the dark circles were absent.

"Jesus, what a difference this makes!" Dan patted my back, and gently shifted sideways, knocking me off his lap. "Sorry, honey. The pills might make me a little loopy."

Dan absent-mindedly picked up a faded manila envelope and pulled out a thin pile of yellowing letters. They were attached to what looked like legal documents. He was distractedly thumbing through the letters, when his expression shifted into one of urgent concentration.

"What the hell?" He handed me the top letter. It was dated January 1952, about a year before Jimmy had died. It was a request to an orphanage in Allentown, Pennsylvania for information about the whereabouts of any known family members of Ralph Murphy, son of the late Maude Murphy. It also wanted to know the whereabouts of Maureen McDonough, daughter of the late Raymond and Abagail McDonough. It stated that both Ralph and Maureen had both been residents of the orphanage in the mid-1920s. The letter was penned in Minnie's handwriting.

"Wait. Your dad was an orphan?" I said.

"I know his mother died when he was sixteen," Dan frowned. "His dad died much earlier."

Reading through the next letter, Dan looked distraught. He handed it to me, and started skimming through the legal papers, all of which I could see were on Davidson, Riley & Sons letterhead—Walter's family's law firm.

The letter he'd given me was from Maureen McDonough. In it she thanked Ralph for contacting her, and apologized for refusing his earlier communications, but had thought it best to leave her past behind her. She admitted that, yes, she had given birth to Ralph's son, Milton McDonough, shortly after they had been together in Allentown.

Milton was Ralph's son?

"Look at this." Dan shoved the name change documents into my hands. "It's Mike—this kid Milton is Mike. Did you know about this?"

"How would I know all this?" I knew I was skirting the truth. But I'd only known about the name change. Minnie had obviously left out some of the juicier facts.

I continued reading Maureen's letter. She explained that Milton was then twenty-five years old, that he had always been a happy child and had never outwardly complained about not having a father. But he was single, lonely, and still seeking a steady profession. After some "prayerful thought" and a long conversation with her priest, she decided it would be best to accept Ralph's offer. She ended the letter by saying she would indeed appreciate anything he could do to help Milton—maybe even give him a fresh start in California. "Milton always dreamed of being a police officer. If you could truly help him, I'm sure he would be thrilled. Mostly he's excited to hear he has two brothers."

Dan set down the legal documents, and put the heel of his hands on his eyes. He was quiet for a few long seconds.

"That sonofabitch Mike—he's my father's son?"

"More than that, Dan. He's your brother."

Dan squinted at the last document in the pile. Peering over his shoulder, I saw that it was Jimmy's death certificate. There was a fading handwritten note that read, "All official documents will say it's an accident. Terribly, terribly sorry for your loss. Captain Dean."

Minnie entered the room smiling.

"Ma, what do you know about these papers?" Dan demanded. "Mike is my father's son? And what the hell is this?" He stood and waved the death certificate so that it missed slapping Minnie across the face by a few centimeters. "I goddamn *knew* Jimmy's death wasn't an accident. Was my father covering it up because Mike was his *son*? Was that his way of making up to him for being a bastard? To sacrifice Jimmy in the process?"

Minnie looked like she'd just walked into a wall. Tears filled her eyes; she backed up and stood behind the chair farthest from Dan. She looked at me pleadingly, but there was no way to save her. And I was also dying to know the truth.

"Oh no, no, no." She buried her face in her hands. "Your father *never* would have wanted you to see these Dan. I wouldn't have left them out if I'd known you were coming. Then I got so excited—oh why did this have to happen?"

"Dammit Ma. You'd better sit down and explain this to me." Dan looked wild, livid.

"Dan, give her a chance. Just give her a second." I moved between them, turning the chair so Minnie could sit.

"These papers. I'd forgotten all about them. I just came across them this morning." Minnie shook her head, made a few *tsk tsk* noises, and fumbled with her cigarettes, making very little eye contact as she searched for a match. "Dan, your father was embarrassed by this. It's not something he wanted anyone to know."

"Ma, I have a right to know. No one is leaving this room until you tell me what happened to my brother. I don't care if it takes a goddamn month." Dan's voice sounded slurry; his eyelids drooped like a lizard's.

My hand shook as I lit his mother's cigarette. She exhaled a stream of smoke, and paused for what seemed a long time.

"Ma, tell me what happened."

"You might as well know," she said, sounding feeble. "Jimmy killed himself."

No one spoke. The only perceptible sound was the low rumble of the refrigerator. I checked Dan's expression; he looked stunned.

"Oh, Dan. I'm sure he didn't even realize what he was doing," Minnie cried. "He was just overwhelmed, depressed. He'd lost his girl. He owed so much money. You know, the gambling. Your dad tried so hard to help, but he refused. So stubborn, just like Ralph. And there was no such thing as Prozac back then. I'm sure that would have helped. So in that sense it was an accident, Dan. It was. I know he never would have hurt us all otherwise."

I kept my eyes on Dan. I expected him to cry or explode but his eyes stayed fixed on his mother.

In between smoking and crying and blowing her nose, Minnie unraveled bits and pieces of the story. During Ralph's brief stint at the Allentown orphanage, he'd had a few encounters with a sixteen-year-old girl named Maureen McDonough before he ran away to California a few months before his eighteenth birthday. Once he'd settled, he made countless attempts to locate Maureen, even sending along some cash so that she could join him in California after she was emancipated. His letters were always returned unopened—the last one with a scribbled note that read, "Leave me alone." But in the early 1950s, when his relationship with Jimmy began to sour, Ralph started to pursue the matter again. He had a feeling that he'd let Maureen down, that there might be a child somewhere, and that he was being punished by God for not living up to his responsibilities.

"See, your father was superstitious. He had a bad premonition. And he felt that nothing would go right for Jimmy or you until he took full responsibility for his past. At the time, honey, Jimmy was so depressed. Ralph knew he was in trouble, running with the wrong crowd, drinking and gambling. When Mike came out here, Jimmy was excited. He was happy to have a big brother. Maybe even a little happy to know his father wasn't so perfect."

"Jimmy knew Mike was his brother?" said Dan.

"Jimmy knew. But we kept the details private. It was painful to Ralph, and he made it up to Milton in other ways. He gave him his name. Helped him financially. He loved Mike."

"But Jimmy hated him."

"That's not true! He loved having a brother his age. Jimmy hated himself. The last straw came when Rusty left him."

Minnie explained that a few nights after Rusty caught Jimmy fooling around and broke up with him, Mike—then a rookie cop—had returned home to their shared apartment and found his gun missing. He accused Jimmy of taking it to intimidate some of his gambling associates and the two had a loud argument. Just after Mike left, Jimmy had shot himself in the head. Mike heard the noise and returned home to find Jimmy dead.

"Wait," said Dan. "Maybe Mike was lying."

"Jimmy left a note, honey. And there was a mark on his hand. Gunpowder, or something, I don't know. Listen to me, Dan. It wasn't Mike's fault! How many hundreds of times do we have to tell you?"

"Why say it was an accident? Why would everyone lie?" Dan looked on the verge of tears.

"How else could we get Jimmy into Holy Cross?" When Jimmy died, Minnie explained, the Church still wouldn't allow suicides a Catholic burial. But Ralph was a big shot in the Diocese, the downtown merchant's society, and known in the police department. They'd agreed to call the suicide an accident so that Ralph's son could have the decent burial he deserved. Mike was also in some trouble for not taking proper care of his service weapon, so the powers-that-be agreed that he would quietly resign.

"My whole life is based on a lie." Dan looked glassy-eyed. His tone was flat. All of this was so overwhelming, maybe it was a lucky thing I had him doped up.

"My mother, my father, everyone has been lying to me. And all these years, I've been accusing that poor bastard Mike—"

"Dan *stop* calling him a bastard! You weren't told about all of this because your father wanted to *protect* you. Even in his note, Jimmy wrote, 'don't tell Danny.' *Don't tell Danny*, he said! Jimmy didn't want you to know he'd fallen so low. And your father had so much shame about this. Can't you understand? No one wanted you to have that terrible example." By now Minnie was rambling breathlessly. "Ralph had so much to be proud of in his life. He raised two boys, and always tried to find the other. Never in the world would he have abandoned any of you. Even when things were at their worst between us. No. After what he'd been through, losing his father and mother? Your father wanted you to have a home, two parents, to know you were wanted. And he eventually did the same for Milton. He even helped him buy a house—gave him an inheritance long before he died."

Minnie snatched the death certificate from Dan's hands. "Why can't you ever see how well your father did for himself? He may not have been perfect, but he had a good job. A good heart. He provided for two families. He would've helped Maureen too, if she'd have let him. He bought and paid for this house and Milton's. No matter what you think about him, your father was an excellent provider."

"I want to see the note." Dan started to rifle through the rest of the papers. "The note and…what else is hidden in here, Ma?" He tore through photos, scattered letters and papers, grabbed the metal safe and popped open its lid.

"Leave that," said Minnie. "That's your father's gun. We need to get rid of it."

Dan held the gun, turning it over in his hand, popping out the carriage and seeing it was loaded. It looked like the kind of gun they carried on old TV shows, like "Dragnet" or "Perry Mason."

"Fine, I'll take it."

"You will not," I said.

"Leave it, Dan. Dave down the street said he'd take care of it. You know, he's a firefighter," said Minnie. "They'll dispose of it properly."

"Why would you give my father's gun to Dave?" said Dan. "I want it."

"No. It's not coming into our house," I said. "We've got a child there!"

"I'll keep it locked up," said Dan.

I glared at him. "If you take that gun, you'll be living alone."

"Oh, look what I've started," wailed Minnie, throwing her hands up.

"Are you telling me I don't have the right to take my father's gun? After I find out he's been lying to me for years? Even my own mother never told me. Now my own wife is telling me I can't have his gun?"

"Dan, last night you threatened to shoot someone. Now you want a gun?" I said.

Sitting there, jaw tight, waving the gun around, Dan looked just like Ralph when he was drunk and angry.

"Oh, look what I've done. Look what I've done." Minnie was like a frightened hostage, cowering, her hands across her face. "This is all because of me."

"Put that gun away!" I said.

"Fine." Dan stood, wobbled backwards and knocked the chair over. He attempted to grab it, tripped and stumbled, crashing onto the linoleum floor. The gun went off with a deafening crack, followed by loud shrieks—Minnie's and mine—and glass shattering into sharp, silvery shards and splashing against the floor.

Dan's moan rose through a smoky, sulfuric odor of burnt gunpowder. Minnie trembled in the chair, releasing tight, squeaky sounds, like air being let slowly out of a balloon.

Chapter 23

October 1998

In the emergency room, each bed was separated by a thin curtain, offering only illusory privacy. A young child to our right wheezed, and doctors shot out orders while nurses, orderlies, and aides ricocheted around the ward. A few curtains away, a metal tray crashed to the floor, sounding like another gunshot cracking the air. I jumped from my chair.

This frantic energy was a far cry from the laconic greeting we received from the security guard at the entrance of the ER. He'd directed us to a long line of haggard people, waiting to state their complaints to a receptionist who screened people with the urgency of a hotel desk clerk. Dan's symptoms allowed him to move directly to triage, where—for convenience—they also agreed to get Minnie seen.

Dan lay on the gurney, eyes closed, as we waited for news from the doctor. I ran my fingers through his hair, taking advantage of his surrender to my touch. I still couldn't understand how his hair was so black and his sideburns pure white, and sometimes teased him about it. "Are you and Goody using the same hair color?" I'd asked. "I'm telling you, I do *not* dye my hair," he'd said, "I'll prove it. See?" he separated a part in his hair, revealing roots and a bluish white scalp. Sure enough, there were dull gray strands sprinkled throughout.

The nurse insisted I remove Dan's wedding ring and St. Christopher medal. I strung his ring on the chain and put it around my neck.

"Don't they know that the Saint promises safe passage?" I mumbled.

"Not anymore," rasped Dan. "The pope demoted him. Now he's just tacky jewelry." Dan smiled half-heartedly; I remained grim.

"Jesus honey," he said. "I'm so goddamn sorry about this."

"I know," I said. "Me too."

For a long time, Dan stared at the ceiling. I was taken aback by how much he resembled photographs I'd seen of him as a child—eyes appearing at once lost and hopeful.

"Remember that Mark Twain quote?" said Dan. "Something about how when he was a kid he could hardly stand to have his father around because he was so ignorant? But when he got to be twenty-one, he was astonished by how much he'd learned in a few short years. Have you heard that one?"

I smiled. "You're awfully forgiving."

"Yeah," he said, looking wistful. "Maybe I'm glad I didn't know Jimmy did that to himself until now. But my God, all these years I've hated Mike. Falsely accusing him. I feel so—I don't know. I wish there was something I could do, or say." He looked stricken.

"Dan, there's time. We'll figure something out."

Dan tightened his grip, rested his eyes closed. The crowded public space was unnerving, but at least he wasn't installed in the same room as Minnie. She had been given a small, private exam room on the other side of the nurses' station. I left Dan to check on her, and met the doctor in the hall.

"Mrs. Murphy, we're moving your husband to the transitional ward for observation. He's scheduled for an angiogram tomorrow morning. We need to take a look at his heart," said the doctor.

"Was it from the gunshot?" I said. "Did it kick this off?"

I should have never given him drugs.

"I can't answer those questions, ma'am. Just be happy the bullet didn't hit anyone." The doctor smelled like body odor and iodine. "Not to worry. These things are routine now—like plumbing. Worst case, we'll clean out his arteries, send him home."

"What about my mother-in-law?"

"That's a pretty bad wheeze she's got. We'll need to take a look. We're trying to get her into x-ray. You might want to give her a hand. She's not a happy camper."

I walked down the glaring corridors, suddenly touched by the trouble someone went to in order to clean and polish worn-out linoleum to such a shiny gleam. Turning a corner, I almost walked into Dan's urologist, Dr. Lowe.

"Mrs. Murphy? What are you doing here?"

Relieved to see a familiar face, I had to restrain myself from hugging him, an odd reaction considering his tactless bedside manner. When Dan had invited me to a consultation regarding the side effects of surgery, such as impotence and incontinence, Dr. Lowe had winked and said, "I'm sure you'd prefer to have a husband with wet pants than one six feet under, right hon'?" He also had an annoying habit of filling conversational gaps with tuneless whistling.

I told Dr. Lowe how Dan had accidentally sent a bullet through the glass door at his mother's house. He'd fallen, which sent a sharp pain racing through his left arm and chest, while Minnie launched into a coughing fit that left her gasping for over ten minutes. I'd run for Dave, Minnie's firefighter neighbor. He checked everyone over and suggested I get them looked at right away, so I'd driven them to Kaiser's Oakland emergency room, despite Minnie's repeated comments about how she *always* went to Kaiser in San Francisco. "Ma, please. Give it a rest. We need to be close to Rachel," said Dan, his only words on the ride over.

"Mr. Murphy's having chest pains?" said Dr. Lowe.

"From the scare. Or, Doctor, I gave him some painkillers, maybe one too many. He's been in so much pain that—"

"I'll be goddamned. He's having chest pains? Isn't he taking that alternative crap, ProstaCure? The natural hormone?" Dr. Lowe looked excited, his face flushing a meaty pink.

"Yes, he is."

"Mrs. Murphy, it can't be coincidence. I've had two, count 'em, two other patients in the emergency room this week with chest pains. They're taking that same damn supplement. I'll go talk to the attending. I'll be damned."

I went behind the curtain where Dan lay on a gurney. "You're not going to believe this," I said. "Dr. Lowe is here. He's had two other patients with heart pain, and they both are taking ProstaCure."

"You didn't tell him I was here, did you?"

"Of course I did."

Dan looked as if he might cry. Then we heard the familiar tuneless whistling.

The curtain flew open and Dr. Lowe grabbed the chart. "Mr. Murphy. Didn't you know? Guns are dangerous—about as bad as some of this junk you're putting in your body."

"I appreciate your concern, Doc, but I think we've got things handled around here."

"Suit yourself. I guess the wife told you? You're not the only one on ProstaCure who's visited us this week. Just thought you should know." He dropped the chart back into the slot and left whistling.

"Goddammit, I don't need the ER doctors to know about the cancer," said Dan.

"What are you talking about? How are they supposed to help you if they don't have the whole story? And Dan, this is Kaiser. They *have* your medical records."

"Not in here, they don't. You think they'll spend a dime fixing my heart if they think I'm a lost cause?"

"Of course." I stroked his forehead. "Honey, they're just people. They want to help."

"People in a fucked up system where they want to either save dough or cover their asses." Dan put a hand across his eyes, releasing a soundless stream of tears. He looked like a five-year-old abandoning all attempts at being brave. "Why did I drop that goddamn gun? So goddamn *stupid.*"

"You said you wanted to see the doctor. The good news is, now I don't have to wait on hold for an appointment." I rubbed my hand on his forehead. "They're taking you upstairs. I'll see what's going on with your mother and be up soon."

"What about Rachel?"

"Kevin's keeping her until I call."

"Honey, do me a favor. Call Johnny, get him over here."

I kissed him. "I'll be back."

I had no intention of calling Johnny. He'd arrive with a briefcase full of useless ideas for the next business battle plan, or some new miracle cure consisting of a lotion, potion, herbal tincture, electromagnetic signal, air filter, or yoga posture. I was a big believer in alternative treatment, but a month earlier Johnny had taken Dan to a weekend retreat in Santa Fe where he was wrapped in an oxygen suit, and fed purified water and organic vegetables that were unique to the area. Dan returned home weak and nauseated, insisting it was due to toxins leaving his system. I wanted him to relax and, for once in his life, cooperate with the doctors.

I knew something had been wrong lately: It turned out it wasn't the cancer after all. It was this heart thing. No wonder he was pale and having indigestion all the time. The news actually cheered me. Maybe this would be the wake up call he needed.

I entered the gloomy cell where Minnie waited. Her gray head drooped over her thin body like a dying rose.

"Dan's going to be fine," I said, meaning it. Minnie slowly looked up, eyes vacant. I smiled and patted her thin shoulder. "We're all fine, okay? They're keeping him for observation. Whatever it is, it's not going to kill him."

"Why did we have to come here? I have my *own* doctor."

My chest constricted. "Better safe than sorry, right? Now let's take off your clothes, put on this gown."

"Do I have to?"

I gently pulled off her green sweater and unhooked her bra. Her breasts flowed like fleshy rivers of taffy, stopping only when her thighs dammed them. She looked down, embarrassed, and whispered, "Look at me, honey. Just look at me."

"It's just me, Minnie. And I think you're beautiful."

Minnie stared at the wall behind me, quiet, as I slipped the gown over her gray hair, crunchy and fragrant from sweat and spray. She leaned on me and sobbed.

I was exhausted to the point that my eyes were drooping and my neck bobbing. I pulled her into a sitting position. I wanted to offer some kind of consolation, but all I could feel was the burden of her.

The doctor burst into the room, startling us. "We're about to change shifts. Sounds like there's some fluid saturation in her lungs, but we've got to run a few more tests. I think it's safe to say we're looking at emphysema."

"Oh no!" wailed Minnie. "No, no, no."

"Mrs. Murphy, listen up, you're gonna have to give up your smoking habit. Or you're going to have a lot more trouble than you're having today."

Minnie sucked in her sobs, and stared at the gleaming floor.

"Is there something you can give her for her anxiety?" I asked.

"Just sit tight. Wait to see what's going on." He turned and left the room.

"What a terrible, *terrible* way to spend a Sunday," she whined.

One more complaint from her and I thought my earrings would blow out. I slipped out the door, stopping the doctor in the hall.

"Doctor, she's a wreck. Can you give her something to calm her?" I whispered.

"Nerves are natural. She shouldn't be here much—"

"Listen: A bullet blew past my face; my husband is upstairs with heart attack pains. Give her something to calm *me*. Please."

"Fine." He scribbled a prescription for Xanax. "It'll make her sleepy. Hold off giving it to her until you get her home."

"Home? You're not keeping her?"

"Unless it's more serious, I'm guessing we'll get her on an inhaler and send her home."

The exam room door creaked open behind me. Minnie stood shivering in her loose gown. "Where did you go?" she squeaked. "I just got left here."

"The doctor prescribed something for your anxiety. I'll go fill it now."

Minnie perked up.

I dashed to the pharmacy and had the prescription filled. Checking to make sure the doctor was gone, I shook two Xanax out of the vial, and gave one to her with a paper cup full of water.

"One for you, one for me," I said. "Don't tell."

"Don't worry." She placed the small pill on the back of her tongue, and tossed the water back like it was a shot of whiskey. "It's too bad Dan doesn't want us all living together," she sighed. "It would be much easier on all of us."

I said nothing. We sat under the dull buzz of the fluorescent lights, lost in our individual thoughts, until Minnie broke into the silence.

"I'm loaded, you know that?" she smiled coyly.

"That's because the pill is kicking in."

A muscular male nurse entered, and I quickly shoved the prescription bottle in my bag.

"Hey Señora Murphy. How'd you like to take a ride with me?" he said.

Minnie responded with a coy, pharmaceutically induced smile, and said, "Now you're talking, cowboy."

The man rifled through notes on her chart. "You also have acute angina?"

"Why thank you. Yours is pretty cute, too." Minnie batted her lashes, making him laugh.

I grabbed Minnie's stuff and headed outside to sit on the bench under the glowing red Emergency sign, to make a list. That Xanax had helped me focus. I needed to call Aunt Maggie, see if she could stay with Minnie a few days, help her get settled. If Minnie was going to need even more care in the future, maybe we should check out the retirement home that had opened a half a mile away from us. Minnie had a decent retirement income, but the place in Oakland was expensive. We'd get someone to rent her house; Harry had told me crowds of well-paid yuppies were desperate to find rentals in San Francisco. I had to call Harry anyway, tell him I was ready to hammer out a contract, order stationery, and get him to quiz me on the P.I. test. I rifled through my calendar. The test was in ten days. If Dan was in the hospital, I could sit with him and study. I'd ask Mom to stay with us, help with Rachel. I wanted to clean out the empty storeroom next to Dan's study, set up a home office there. I'd show Dan; I was going to make us a fortune, I could feel it. Dan and I would work at home, Minnie would live up the street, and everyone would go to the same Kaiser. Consolidation without cohabitation. It was the most efficient answer. Maybe we'd even invite Mike over for regular Sunday dinners.

The next morning, I arrived at the hospital and Dan was on the phone. He saw me, dropped his voice, and said, "No, don't come now. Wait a little."

"Oh my God, are you *working*?" I said.

"You didn't call Johnny," said Dan, hanging up.

"Did you know that the Chinese word for 'busy' translates to 'heart killer'? A wise man told me that last night in the pharmacy." I was sluggish, fueled only by two hours sleep and a triple latte.

"It's these busy people who'll kill me. Honey, you can't believe this. They woke me up at 4:30 to take my vitals. And they weighed me. *Weighed me!* My IV popped out and it took five attempts to get it back in. I'm lying here in a puddle of my own dried sweat."

I kissed him. "Look what I brought." I pulled Dan's shredded baby blanket from my bag. "To keep the light off your face when you sleep."

He smiled, kissed me again.

"How's my mother taking the diagnosis?" said Dan. "Jesus, she loves her cigarettes more than she loved my father."

"They were around when she needed them. He wasn't."

"Where is she now?" he said.

"Back at her house. Aunt Maggie took over—saved the day. Your mom is being incredibly brave and cooperative. She's actually relieved that you finally know the truth about Mike, but she doesn't want to cause you any excess stress. Aunt Maggie is cleaning the place of cigarette paraphernalia and teaching her how to use inhalers. And listen to this—Harry already thinks he has someone to rent your mom's house."

"Harry works fast." Dan looked pleased, as he always did when positive cash flow was involved.

"Uh-huh," I said. "And we're getting serious about working together, too. I've already outlined a new client proposal. When you get home, maybe we could discuss it."

Dan sat up, interested. "Let's do it now."

"Hey, hey, hey! Am I interrupting something?" Johnny Curtain breezed through the room in a sweatsuit, a large brown satchel over his shoulder. He mussed my hair with his hand, and leaned over Dan, giving him a kiss on the lips.

"How'd you get here so fast?" I said.

"What do you mean?" said Johnny.

Dan shifted nervously.

"Honey," he said. "Johnny's here to go over easy stuff."

"Wait. Johnny, I've been meaning to ask you: Do we have you to thank for our visitor at the Pelican Inn?"

"What?" Johnny looked perplexed. He looked at Dan.

"I was going to ask you about that," said Dan. "Someone dropped by looking for us, but other than family, you were the only one who knew we were there. Mary thinks it was a guy driving an old Chevy Malibu?"

"Odd as hell, isn't it?" Johnny didn't miss a beat, shift an eye, squirm or even twitch. But he never did, even while lying; I'd seen that enough when I'd worked with him.

"Is someone having a party in here?" A middle-aged nurse with an Irish accent stood at the end of Dan's bed, hands on hips.

"Nurse Angie, tell my wife what good care I'm getting. And," Dan added with a brogue, "that a brief bit-o-business won't be ending the likes of me."

"Oh, darlin'." Angie turned toward me. "He'll be fine."

"Johnny—where's that cash?" said Dan. "Shoot it over to Mary."

"We should quit shooting anything at Mary," said Johnny, laughing.

I remained expressionless. Johnny rustled through his satchel, pulling out an envelope with the monthly retainer Dan received from one of Johnny's clients for contract review. It was the only work Dan did that I understood.

"Go ahead and get the rent out today, okay?"

"Am I being excused?" I was simultaneously annoyed and relieved. My list was long.

"Not without me telling you, in front of all these people, that I think you are the most wonderful wife in the world." He pulled me forward, slapped my fanny. "If only she'd stop wearing me out in the bedroom, I wouldn't have to endure these long hospital stays."

Everyone chuckled—me the loudest.

I went home and rummaged through the medicine cabinet for tranquilizers. The one I'd taken the night before seemed to help me focus. But all I had was Vicodin. I gave this some thought. I knew I was flirting with addiction by taking painkillers when I wasn't really suffering. But when I stopped to think about it, my chest felt tight and I had a slight headache. I took two tablets, just to help me get through the work day. Most people got lethargic from Vicodin, but on me it had an opposite effect. Within twenty minutes, I felt my energy soar.

I went right to work in the storeroom next to Dan's office, scrubbing caked dirt and bugs off the windows, amazed at how the afternoon sunlight changed the atmosphere of the dingy, unfinished space. If I looked from the right angle, I could even see a slice of the bay. Once I moved the boxes Dan had stored here, I'd cover the concrete floor with a rug, set up a desk, computer, and bookshelves, and be in business.

I swept the dust and hundreds of wispy cobwebs, and turned on the vacuum.

"Mama."

I jumped. "Whoa, you scared me."

Rachel and Jamie stood in the doorway.

I smiled, waved, and shut off the vacuum.

"How's Papa?" said Rachel. "Does he have heart cancer?"

"Good news. This is nothing to do with cancer," I assured Rachel. "This is something they can fix."

"What in God's name are you doing down here?" said Jamie.

"Setting up my office," I said.

"Now?"

"I love cleaning huge messes. It's therapeutic."

"Are you sure you're okay? You seem a little chipper."

"For the first time since his cancer diagnosis, it looks like Dan's going to do what the doctor says. And it's not the cancer. I *am* chipper."

"Me too," said Rachel, smiling.

"Just thought I'd let you know. Some woman from the PTA called. She said they sent flowers to the hospital, but they were returned. No Dan Patric registered." She raised her eyebrows.

"Great." All our new friends knew only Dan's fake name, but his medical records were still under his legal name. "What did you say?"

"I said aren't hospitals pathetic, considering what we pay for healthcare? She's having them redirected here. By the way, she said she always envied you two—you seemed like such a perfect couple."

I thought of that couple—that family—I used to envy when I walked by their white Spanish-style bungalow years ago, when I was still with Kevin. God only knows what madness they may have had brewing underneath their pretty red tile roof.

Jamie walked down the hall and into Dan's office. "You ought to clean in here, it's disgusting," she yelled.

"Men are messy," said Rachel.

"In more ways than you know," said Jamie.

"They only clean up for women," said Rachel. She had her hands on her hips and shook her head as she surveyed the mess, her wispy curls swarming around her rosy face.

Jamie ran a finger along the top of Dan's black file cabinet and collected a wad of dust so large it resembled a cocoon. She moved a book with her foot. "Look at this carpet!" It was an entirely different color from the dusty, exposed areas. "Let's pick up all this crap; you've got to vacuum in here."

"No way," I said. "That would give him a real heart attack. I promised I'd learn to accept him just the way he was."

"Accept him after you vacuum," said Jamie.

"Papa will be mad. But it'll be a nice homecoming present."

241

"Alright. Jamie, first help me move Dan's boxes to the garage." I returned to the storeroom, and reached for the first box, setting one arm on the side and one underneath. The box was moist; I lifted it. Before Jamie could get to the other side, the contents collapsed through the bottom, sending books and papers crashing onto the freshly vacuumed concrete. Some of the piles were moving.

Jamie screamed, ran out the door.

I looked down in horror. Moist, worm-like bugs writhed in a pile of pulpy cardboard. They had eaten through the box and much of its contents, turning it into mush.

"Ew, Mommy. What are those?"

"Maggots. Baby flies."

"You're shaking," said Rachel.

It occurred to me I hadn't had anything all day besides coffee, cigarettes, and Vicodin.

"I'm shaking too." Jamie hovered at the door, eyes averted. "I'd say cleaning is long overdue."

Sitting on the top of the undulating heap was Dan's framed law school degree, but it wasn't from the school he'd told me he attended. If this was correct, Dan had graduated from a smaller, less prestigious law school. I knew Dan had lied to protect his identity, but I didn't think he had ever lied to me. Suddenly embarrassed for him, I shook away the broken glass, set aside the framed degree so Jamie wouldn't see it.

"Mommy, can I put some of these in a jar?"

"No, I'm killing them," I said.

"That's mean," said Rachel, frowning.

"Try pouring salt on them," said Jamie.

"No. This is out of control. Jamie, grab the Raid from the garage."

"Oh-oh," said Jamie. "Chemotherapy. Rachel, let's get out of here."

Wearing rubber gloves, I moved the boxes, dumping out all the contents to check for infestation. I filled two hefty trash bags with maggot-gnawed books and files, salvaging what I could, throwing away the rest.

In the book *Illness as Metaphor*, I vaguely recalled, the author had chastised the medical profession for using language that blamed the patient for causing the illness. But our life was literally crawling with health metaphors, the most obvious of which was that Dan's messes were eating our household alive. I interpreted the timing of this discovery as a sign from God that I should clean everything. My headache was gone, but I popped two more Vicodin, hoping to obscure a rising sense of doom. Moving on to Dan's office, I wiped, scrubbed, and dusted the furniture. I set up an "Idea file," and filled it with hundreds of scattered paper scraps; I emptied boxes, filed papers, and arranged knick-knacks and law books on the shelves. I polished the black file cabinet, testing each drawer to see if it remained locked.

Goody hid under the office chair, her unblinking yellow eyes watching me as if I were committing a crime. Three hours later I dragged Rachel and Jamie downstairs to admire my work.

"You sure are energetic today, Mom," said Rachel.

"Yeah," I sighed, scratching my arms. On top of causing constipation, too much Vicodin made me itchy.

"I've got wine open and dinner waiting upstairs," said Jamie. "I'd say you deserve it."

"No. I've got to get this done before Dan is released, and I still have the closet."

The phone rang; it was an internist calling from Kaiser.

"Is it Papa?" Rachel lit up. "Let me talk!"

"Shhh. It's his doctor," I whispered.

"Mrs. Murphy? We need you down here first thing in the morning for a meeting with the oncologist."

"Oncologist? I thought this was cardiac?"

"Cardiac?" The doctor sounded young, confused.

"Can I speak with my husband? Is he there?"

"No, ma'am. He's heavily sedated—probably out for the night. They're trying to manage the bone pain."

"Bone pain?"

"From the metastases."

"What are you talking about?" Under the prickly veneer of itchy skin, my blood crawled as if the maggot infestation had made its way into my veins, the first ones arriving and chewing straight into my heart.

Chapter 24

November 1998

"Mrs. Murphy, I can tell by your expression that this news is coming as a surprise." The oncologist squinted at me through concerned blue eyes. "Considering he was diagnosed over six years ago and opted not to have surgery or even radiation, I'd say he's done well."

"But the PSA tests were coming back fine."

"As I explained to your husband: The cancer dedifferentiated, which means that it altered its form. It wasn't being picked up by the tests he was taking."

"Shouldn't you know that could happen? Why weren't you testing for that?"

Dr. Peters' young face was etched with a few comforting lines. His white jacket was crisp and he smelled clean, like fragrance free soap. He cleared his throat, remaining even-tempered and kind as he explained that Dan had been managing his own health care, and "had not reported any alarming symptoms that would trigger a recommendation to seek more conclusive testing or directive advice."

Dan appeared distant and distracted, and made a slight grunt with each exhale. His glassy eyes and skin were tinged a dull yellow.

"This doesn't make sense. Dan's cancer was fine when he checked in. He was fine when I saw him yesterday. I thought this was his heart? What did you do to him?" I tried not to panic.

"Mrs. Murphy, your husband was not—*is not*—fine. The cancer is in his bones. X-rays reveal evidence of something in his lower tailbone, which explains the searing pain he felt radiating through his back and groin last night. Frankly, I don't know how he's tolerated such levels of pain for so long. What you are seeing now is a side effect of the morphine drip. He's sedated, and very tired. It's been a long night."

"Are you saying he doesn't have long to live?" I lowered my voice, and turned so Dan couldn't see my face.

"I can't answer that," said the doctor. "But he is eligible for hospice."

"But hospice is for people who don't have long to live," I whispered.

"The cancer has also moved into the liver and right kidney. That's not good." Dr. Peters faced Dan. "Right now, Mr. Murphy, I'd suggest we keep you here, get your pain stabilized. If you decide to start the chemotherapy, there's a combined treatment—a chemotherapy cocktail, so to speak, that's had excellent results. I can get you into the infusion suite tomorrow morning."

Cocktails. In a suite? It sounded like we were going on a cruise.

"We were told prostate cancer couldn't be treated with chemotherapy," I said.

"The chemo is just a palliative—comfort care. It might buy some time—reduce the mass in the liver, some of the pain. Mr. Murphy, I know you have strong opinions about your cancer care, and I'll support any choice you make. The downside of modern medicine is that we've mastered the ability to prolong disease. Fighting for your life becomes your life. That may or may not be worth it to you."

No one said a word.

"I'll give you as much or as little input as you request," said Dr. Peters. "It's a very personal decision. It's okay to do this your way."

No. We always do things Dan's way. Why couldn't we do it my way?

That song—"I Did It My Way"—wasn't it supposed to be the final thoughts of a dying man? I felt dizzy, disoriented.

"Take your time discussing this. I'll make myself available whenever you're ready." The doctor shook our hands, and gave us a stack of literature about hospice care, chemotherapy, and pain management. I glanced at the list of hospice benefits. It included a hospital bed, commode, oxygen, a walker, all delivered at no charge; we got free visiting nurses, free prescriptions, and from now on, free parking at all Kaiser medical facilities. There were volunteers willing to do massage, housework, and childcare. Dan had said so many times that he wanted someone else to take care of him. *Be careful what you wish for.* Round the clock help and no more co-pay on anything. Under any other circumstance, this was just the kind of deal we'd get excited about.

The doctor left the room, taking with him my last delusions of a future with my husband. We would never work together, buy a house on a tree-lined street, or travel the world. He would not organize any more field trips for Rachel's class, grill her young suitors on their intentions, or work on Boy Scout badges with the little boy across the street. He wouldn't ever get a settlement on his unending development fiasco, despite all these years of work. Would he even get a chance to make up with Mike? I clutched the paperwork, not knowing what to do, to say, to think—even what to feel.

A nurse appeared with a small cup of pills and a paper cup full of water. Dan thanked her and took the drugs. Neither of us even asked what they were. I tapped my foot involuntarily to the pulsing buzz of the ambient electrical noise, amazed at how closely its beat matched the Sinatra tune, which I couldn't seem to shake.

And now, the end is near, and so I face, the final curtain...

I sat glued to the metal visitors' chair crammed between the sink and Dan's bed, my eyes burning, wondering if I could remember all the lyrics. But I couldn't think of the next line. It was the last line—*I did it my way*—that marched in circles through my mind. It could be the theme song to the movie of Dan's life.

We sat silently and I stared at Dan; his skin appeared to be yellowing faster than old newsprint.

"You think I'm going to die, don't you?" said Dan.

I looked away. There was no way to organize my thoughts around that question.

"I don't need hospice," said Dan. "I'm not giving up that easily."

And more, much more than this, I did it my way...

Maybe I'd heard this song at Minnie's, during one of the countless times we sat in her kitchen smoking cigarettes, while KABL radio played Oldies But Goodies in the background.

Minnie.

I started to cry.

Who would tell Minnie? I'd been saying he had it under control, to her, to Rachel, and to everyone else. I'd lied even though the knowledge of this had been gradually simmering through me, like the story Dan told me years ago about the live lobster that was eased in a pot of tepid water, the heat going up slowly—so by the time it started to feel uncomfortable, it was already half cooked.

Lying to protect one another was a pointless proposition, and not because the truth will set us free. One way or another, truth finds its own freedom, and it doesn't always have the best timing.

My vision blurred as Sinatra hummed through me.

Or is that me humming? Dan can't hear me hum this song… I don't want him to know that I know the most absurd secret: Death is inevitable. Not just any death, either. Dan's death. And it's coming soon, to a theater near me.

"Let's get this goddamn pain stabilized, then I'll be able to think clearly," said Dan. "I know it's a long shot, but people beat these things all the time."

How would I explain this to Rachel? Our happy family life? I'm sorry honey, it's over.

"Dan?" I slowed my breath, tried to pull thoughts together. "You've wanted to relax and travel for as long as I've known you. Maybe we can get your pain stabilized and take a trip? A family vacation like we keep talking about?"

I blew my nose. Dan looked drawn. When he finally spoke, his normally resonant voice was small and flat, like he'd been unplugged from the main sound system.

"Is that what you think I want?" Dan shook his head, and slipped into a weary version of his radio announcer voice. "'Hey, Dan! Now that you've won entry into hospice, what do you want to do next? Go to Disneyland?'" He sunk further into the bed and grimaced. "If anything, it makes me want to work harder, start that foundation I told you about. Something to honor the real heroes of the world, the ones making a difference. But I can't. I'm in the middle of three deals, there's still work to be done. I don't have time to run away and take a vacation."

He was right. There wasn't enough time.

"We'll get a handle on this thing, honey." Dan winced, grabbing his back and groaning. "I'm going to get the chemo. Go tell the doc."

Returning home for some of Dan's things, I entered the living room, and stared at the distant view of San Francisco Bay. The sun had collapsed into its own fiery pool, shooting sharp rays of yellow-red light through our scattered trees like flaming spears. There was so much to do—phone calls to make, work to delegate. But first I had to pack a bag for Dan.

I descended the brown-carpeted stairs to his office. At the bottom I stared into the disheveled walk-in closet, the one place I hadn't feverishly cleaned while waiting for news from the hospital. The left side held a row of crisp dress shirts, a long line of dark business suits, and a wardrobe of polished shoes placed neatly on shelves. The rest of it was crammed with sweats, t-shirts, yellowed newspapers, magazines, and old business files—much of it covered with thick dust and the skeletons of insects that didn't make it out alive. I picked up a note off the dresser dated a week earlier: "Mary's Christmas gift—pick up Tuesday."

My legs went rubbery.

Would Dan be here for Christmas?

I wrapped my arms around a row of shirts, breathing into the soft, familiar scent, when something shiny caught the corner of my eye. I pushed the hangers aside, causing a shrill metallic scrape. There, on the back wall of the closet, a silver key dangled from a tiny hook.

My heart backfired, making me dizzy.

It can't be.

Grabbing it, I ambled out of the closet like a drunk, lightheaded, excited. I carried the key into Dan's office, where the large black, three-drawer file cabinet was wedged in the back corner. With shaking hands, I slid the key into the little lock, turned it, and the lock popped up.

The first drawer was long and rectangular and stuffed full of legal files, each marked with a typed or hand-scribbled label. Only one drawer opened at a time so I shut the top, and opened the second, scanning the contents. The thought of Dan catching me in this invasion made my face flush with heat.

I pushed the second drawer closed, reaching to open the bottom drawer, which felt light and slippery as it rolled open.

What the hell?

I stared for a moment, blinked, and stared some more.

The drawer was filled with cash. Neat piles of twenty, fifty, and hundred-dollar bills organized in clear Ziploc bags. Hands shaking, I reached inside to haul out the contents.

My head floated up as if it were full of helium.

"Son-of-a-bitch," I whispered.

I felt sick. I knew Dan was hiding money from the government. But he was hiding it from me, too?

A door slammed upstairs and footsteps clapped down the hall.

Jesus.

I froze, then shoved the drawer closed.

Clack. Click.

I looked for a place to stash the cash.

"Hey. Anyone home?"

It was Jamie. I hustled into my new office, and tried to stuff the chunky bags in my bottom desk drawer. It wouldn't close. Dan's bags of money were nothing like the small wilted sandwich bags Ralph had used for cash.

"I'll be right up," I yelled.

Jamie met me at the bottom of the stairs.

"What's wrong?" she said. "You look awful."

I sat on the dingy brown carpet and started to cry. Moments later she was sitting next to me on the floor, counting money, while I went through the rest of the bottom drawer.

There was over fifty-seven thousand dollars in cash; a ring that had twelve stones missing—the exact number of small diamonds Dan had given me when we got engaged; a file containing letters from the IRS threatening his ex-wife with a lien for Dan's unpaid taxes; an Irish passport; a tube of erection enhancement cream; a bottle of Grecian Hair Formula for Men; and a sealed manila envelope that was thick with papers.

"Such a liar." I snatched the hair formula from the drawer. "I knew he dyed his hair."

Jamie reached for the bottle. "Grecian really isn't a dye." She read the label. "'It's a gradual change to natural color.' What's this?"

Jamie pulled out a varnished wood box with a small plaque saying, "Daniel Murphy: The Best Hired Gun Money Can Buy."

She opened it and gasped. "It's a pistol."

"Put it away!" I snapped. "It might be loaded." I stared at the dark box. "We got into a fight about him bringing a gun home, and he already had one here?" I snatched the tiny box holding the plundered ring. "He gave me diamonds from a hand-me-down ring? And *kept* the evidence?"

"Is he Irish?" Jamie thumbed through the passport pages. "It's not even stamped."

"Put that down!" I shouted.

She carefully tucked it back into the drawer, eying me like I was a mental patient.

A gun, a passport, and cash? Was he planning on leaving town?

"Is he a crook? I never really understood what he did," said Jamie.

"No. I don't know. Maybe. But not the way you're thinking—it's not like he robs liquor stores."

Jamie studied one of the letters. "From the looks of the IRS papers, he sure screwed his ex-wife."

We sat in silence, staring at the money.

"You want to go through the other files?" said Jamie.

"No, not now." My eyes wouldn't focus on anything.

"But you're my sister, the private-eye, right?"

"And this is a private matter, okay?" The lump in my throat felt like a pinecone. "Oh God, Jamie. They said he's going to die." I burst into tears. "And all I can think when I see all this is how much I want to kill him."

Jamie touched me delicately, as if the glue that held me together wasn't yet dry. I shrank back. Goody ran down the stairs, sounding hungry and mad.

"What are you going to do?" she said.

"I don't know. Feed the cat. Smoke cigarettes. Drink scotch. Have a really expensive dinner. And Dan's picking up the tab." I grabbed some bills from the pile and then carefully rearranged everything back in the file drawer—give or take a few hundred dollars—and slammed it closed. I tucked the key in its hiding place so he'd never suspect I'd been anywhere in the vicinity.

"Wake up. Wake up, Mary." Someone jostled my shoulders. "Shouldn't you be at the hospital?"

"Whah?" My eyes fluttered open. My mother was sitting at the edge of the bed, clear eyed and perfumed, her frosted red lips blaring commands.

"Get up, honey. Get in the shower. Let's get this bed made. Dan's chemotherapy appointment is in forty-five minutes—don't you want to be there?"

I attempted to answer. My tongue was mossy, my lungs ached, and the best I could do was groan.

"It smells like a bar in here," said Mom.

I tried to lift my head but it was dead weight. My mother yanked open the shades, sending light screaming into the room.

"Too bright." My eyes felt like hot lead balls. How had I gotten home from the bar? "Where's Jamie?" I bolted upright, seized by dizziness. "Where's Rachel!"

"Rachel was with Kevin last night, remember? I assume he took her to school? Jamie's passed out on Rachel's bed." My mother sighed, felt my forehead. "Where on earth were you two last night? Minnie was desperate to speak with you. I had to fight to get her not to call Dan—to just let him rest."

"Jamie and I went to dinner. Obvioiusly I drank too much. God, Mom, how is Minnie?"

"How do you think? Hysterical. Thank God Maggie's with her. But you need to call."

I bolted to the bathroom and leaned over the toilet, heaving into the bowl. Every cell in my body was punishing me, and I deserved it. What kind of shopaholic, drug using, binge drinking, chain smoking wife and mother was I? With this track record, what would I abuse next? Sex? Gambling? Krispy Kremes?

I needed Dan. Jointly we had built one container for our lives—as individuals, as a couple, and as a family. Depending on the day or how well we were getting along, this container was filled with love or exasperation or inertia or acceptance, but whatever it held, we were both in it together.

Without him, the container would crack and all I could see outside of it was a bottomless free fall.

Mom's heels thudded across the carpet as she patted pillows, shook blankets, and transformed my disheveled crash site into a neatly made bed. I emerged from the bathroom, a tranquilizer melting under my tongue, my water cup fizzing with an extra-strength Alka Seltzer.

"My God, look at you." My mother folded her arms. "You're going to have to pull yourself together. I'll sit with Dan. And before you pick up Rachel, get some healthy food in this house—make things nice for Dan."

I could afford to make things nice for Dan, I thought, now that I had access to thousands of dollars in unexplained cash. I could hire an attendant and have all of our meals catered. I'd have put a housecleaner and masseuse on staff, too, if they hadn't come free with hospice.

Aunt Maggie answered the phone when I called to check on Minnie.

"She spent most of yesterday locked in her room tearing up old papers." Maggie's hushed voice sounded muffled, like she was cupping her hand over her mouth. "Then she insisted on burning them in the fireplace."

"Did you let her?" I said.

"You think *I* could stop her? And listen, I don't think that thing's been used since the Stone Age. We were inhaling so much smoke last night, she might as well have been back on cigarettes. She kept saying that when she died, no one was going to be snooping through her past."

Later that morning, I left the grocery store with bags and bags of organic foods that Dan loved, and anything I could think of that might calm his stomach after chemotherapy. Once the groceries were put away, I couldn't sit still. I drove to Rachel's school forty-five minutes early and went over and over what I needed to tell her, occasionally muttering aloud to myself. As soon as she saw me, she said, "What's wrong, Mom? You look bad."

I drove around the corner, parked under a tall magnolia tree, and shut off the car. I had to do this, and do it now. I was sick of telling lies to everyone, especially Rachel.

"I have some very sad news. Take a deep breath and brace yourself." I stroked her hair.

"I don't want to take a breath." Rachel pulled away, leaning against the door. "Just tell me."

"Honey, Papa's not doing well."

"What do you mean? Is it his heart?"

"You need to prepare yourself, okay?"

"Mama!" The pulse in Rachel's pale neck was visible, like something desperate to get out. "Just tell me."

"There is no easy way to say this. Papa is very, very sick. He can't be cured."

"That's not true."

"Honey, I'm just going to say it. Papa is going to die from his cancer."

"No he isn't." Rachel's expression contorted. "I want to talk to *him.*"

"He's resting. They've given him lots of drugs."

"That's not what he told me. You're wrong," she said.

"I wish I were wrong. I wish there were some other news. This is just too terrible. Too unbelievable."

"Where is he? Let me talk to him."

"He's coming home soon. Nurses and doctors have to come to the house to help take care of him." I rambled on for a few moments, explaining the progression of the cancer, how chemotherapy could only slow it, what hospice was, while Rachel's face flushed from pink to red and then drained so pale her freckles seemed to darken. "Do you have any questions for me?"

"You said it wasn't serious." A few quiet tears rolled down her cheeks; she swiped at them like bugs. "You *just* said that."

"We didn't know, honey. I'm sorry. Everything's changed now."

She looked everywhere, except at me. "He said he'd get better."

"I know. He tried. He really did."

"He promised me." Rachel shook her head.

"It's not his fault. He tried so hard." Even as I said this, the ache in my heart stung with anger. Like he was doing this on purpose, hiding money and passports and dedifferentiated cancer so he could leave us. Leave us so he wouldn't have any more responsibilities.

"He can have a bone marrow transplant. Like Sammie's mom."

"The cancer has spread too much. It's in his liver and kidney. There's nothing they can do to stop it."

"No. A bone marrow transplant works." Rachel's voice quivered. "Call and talk to Sammie's mom. She had one for breast cancer and it *worked.*"

"It's not an option for Papa. It won't work."

Tears, but no sounds, came from Rachel.

"Honey, are you okay? Do you want to go sit somewhere? Go to Fenton's, get an ice cream?"

Rachel looked at me like I was insane. It was the same expression Dan had when I suggested we take a vacation. I leaned in to hug her, feeling her limp body shift uncomfortably.

"I'm tired," she mumbled. "I wanna go home."

"Do you have any questions?"

"No."

"I'll tell you anything you want to—"

"I want to go home."

I waited a second, then started the car.

We drove silently, her head turned away from me, gazing at passing houses and trees along the drive. I wanted to apologize—tell her I was sorry I couldn't seem to land us inside one of these well groomed homes, insulated by the structure of a normal, healthy, law abiding, legally married, nuclear family who deposited money at the bank and didn't require fake names, P.O. boxes, or chemotherapy.

"It's a good thing Goody doesn't understand," Rachel said softly. "This would kill her."

The afternoon sun dropped as I drove higher into the Oakland hills. The sky was streaked violently red, with veins of violet-blue. An oxygen truck passed us as we pulled into the driveway. Before I shut the motor, my mother jogged up the walkway.

"You just missed Johnny Curtain. He had to get into Dan's files."

"You let him in Dan's office?"

"Dan asked me to. He's going to take over some files. He took quite a bit of work home with him." Mom opened the passenger side door. "How's my girl?"

Mom pulled Rachel against her cushioned body, where she buried her head. I jogged down the walkway, heading straight for the file cabinet.

The drawers were unlocked. Each slid forward effortlessly, unburdened by any contents. I knelt on the carpet and stared into the bottom drawer. The gun and the money were gone, along with most of the files. Johnny had even taken the Grecian Formula and the erection cream. The only thing remaining was a sealed manila envelope. I grabbed the envelope and ripped it open. I didn't care what Dan said when he got home; he had no right to let Johnny rob us right under my nose. I turned the envelope upside down and shook, scattering about twenty greeting cards, and a handful of scribbled notes into a messy pile in front of me. They all looked vaguely familiar. The first one I picked up was the card asking him to marry me.

"I've never felt so safe, secure, sane and loved... Will you be my spouse?"

I'd signed it, "Your Best and Last Wife..."

There were notes and pictures from Rachel and her classmates, thanking Dan for taking them on the field trip to court to learn about "law and order," and for his involvement in two mock trials the following year. There was a coupon book I'd given him on our first anniversary, promising a different erotic activity on each page. And there was a sketch of two hands that he had scribbled on a paper tablecloth one night in an Italian bistro—Dan's vision of what our matching wedding bands would look like. "Twelve shiny diamonds," he'd said. "One for each month of the year that I love you." Did he design the ring this way because he already had the diamonds, or had he meant it? I shuffled the cards and papers into a neat pile, tucked them into the torn envelope, and held it to my chest.

My mother's rapid footsteps banged down the stairway. "Mary? What on earth are you doing? You look like you've seen a ghost."

I stared blankly, searching for an answer that didn't expose my invasion or Dan's willingness to hide so much. "Nothing. Look, Mama. Dan saved all of our love notes." I held out the envelope, and started to cry.

"Honey, honest to God, you need to get yourself together. Get back to the hospital immediately. Dan's having a bad reaction to the chemo."

I pulled into the Kaiser garage, and scanned for an empty spot. As I turned to the second level, I stopped the car with a screech. There it was, *again*. The silver Chevy Malibu with a broken left taillight. If this car didn't belong to someone Johnny knew, what was going on? It couldn't be here by coincidence. It was at home the night before Ralph died; it was at the inn the night before the gunshot; and now at the hospital? It was stalking us like the Angel of Death. I scribbled the license plate number on my business card. Someone honked at me from behind, forcing me to move.

After parking, I ran straight to the chemotherapy suite, appalled by its dismal atmosphere. I had pictured it to be like a day spa, an oasis of calm in the middle of the chaotic hospital, filled with pastel colors and soothing music. But it was a harshly lit room, scattered with mismatched vinyl recliners holding exhausted-looking people with varying amounts of hair, each attached to an IV bag that dripped fluids into their veins. A TV blared in the corner. Dan was nowhere in sight.

"He's been taken to intensive care," said the nurse on duty. "The doctor is waiting to speak with you."

"Was anyone with him?"

"No, but his friend was looking for him about ten minutes ago."

"What'd he look like?"

"Skinny guy. Older. You'd better get over there, they're waiting on you."

At the intensive care unit, I gave my name and was told the doctor would be with me immediately. I scanned the faces in the waiting room. An electrifying jolt ran up my spine when my eyes landed on a thin, balding man slumped in a plastic chair. The emaciated, pale, unshaven face of Richard Harding stared back at me. His name, his face, his legacy in our family drama loomed much larger than this withered figure. It looked like he'd spent the last six years fasting in the desert. Why was he following Dan? Was he planning to rob him? Hurt him? What kind of sick plan did he have? Then it came to me: *Richard is the Angel of Death.*

I wanted to attack him, fight him off, but my legs were cement blocks. Before I could speak, Richard stood up and ducked out a side door into the hospital maze.

A doctor appeared at my side, her round brown eyes moist, full of compassion. "Are you Mr. Murphy's wife?"

"Yes." It occurred to me how lucky I was they didn't make me prove it. "Where's Dan? I need to see him."

"He's unconscious. We need to talk."

"No, I need to see him now. Did anyone else visit him?" My voice was shrill; the doctor remained calm.

"Peek in for a second."

I followed her to the corner of the ward. She pulled back the curtain where Dan was hiccoughing in his sleep, his complexion jaundiced.

"He needs his baby blanket. He likes it over his eyes. Where is his baby blanket? *Get him his blanket!*"

"Okay. Okay, Mrs. Murphy." She firmly grasped my shoulder. "I'll make sure we find it. I promise. Right now you have some decisions to make." She led me back into the corridor. My heart flapped wildly. I scanned the area for more signs of Richard.

The doctor sat me in an empty exam room and told me that Dan's potassium level was dangerously high. It was likely he would go into cardiac arrest unless he was treated in the next few hours. The only way to prevent this, she said, was to force-feed him some kind of fast working laxative that would detoxify him, give him another chance. "I know your husband has final stage prostate cancer. I know, so well, how hard it is," she said, her hand landing gently over mine. "My father recently died of prostate cancer. What you may not know is that it is a long and painful death. I hope you don't mind me being so frank, but I thought you might want that information as you decide on treatment."

She watched me meaningfully. I was confused, mute. She squeezed my hands, her eyes brimming with tears.

"I'm so sorry you have to go through this," she said. "Take a few minutes, tell me how you want to proceed." She patted my hand. "Decide what you think would be most compassionate, even if—hard as it is—that means you have to let him go."

Let him go?

Dan can't die now. He promised Rachel he'd get better. He is in the middle of three big deals. He has to tell me what law school he attended.

I sped outside to the pay phone to call my mother. "The doctor told me if I didn't treat him now he'd die of a heart attack. If he lives, he'll have a long and painful death. She said she just went through it so she *knows*. Mama, I don't know what to do." A new wave of nausea gathered in my gut.

"The arrogance of these damn doctors!" snapped my mother. "She doesn't *know* Dan."

"You think *I* know Dan?" I cried.

"Calm down, now. Calm down."

I held the phone with shaky hands. My eyes swept the hallway, sure that the Angel of Death lurked close by.

"You know, Mary," Mom paused. "It's not his fault he has cancer."

"I know." Did I know that?

"And it won't be your fault if he dies."

"I don't want him to die, Mom," I whispered.

"I know, sweetheart. I know."

"It can't be time."

"Tell that doctor to call Dan's regular physician. He'll know what to do."

I shivered on the metal chair next to Dan's gurney. The scent of blood, alcohol, and disinfectant filled the eerie hospital ward, making my eyes sting. Anxiety clawed inside me and my sobs were strangled. I couldn't get enough oxygen in or out. Dan slowly opened his eyes, and his hands stumbled along the cold metal safety rod at the side of the bed, searching.

"Dan? Are you awake?"

Dan's eyes searched my face. His finger pointed weakly. I threaded my fingers between his.

"Dan? Please say something."

"I've got it handled," he rasped. "You're all set." His eyes fell closed.

"DAN?"

The moon-faced doctor reappeared. "Dr. Peters said to treat him immediately," she said.

Lightness lifted me from the chair. "Thank God."

"He wants to speak with you," she said, making no eye contact. I left her poking and prodding Dan.

"Mrs. Murphy, I'm sorry for any confusion they put you through. I know he wants a fighting chance, or he wouldn't have tried the chemo. After they stabilize him, I'll be by. We'll probably release him to hospice by morning. Hang in there. We'll hope for the best."

I leaned over Dan's face and told him they were going to fix this. He groaned slightly. A tall muscular nurse entered, sweeping the curtain aside as if he was appearing on stage. He held a bottle of green liquid and his face opened into a friendly smile. He was the same nurse who had cared for Minnie. "Hey, don't I know you?" he said.

"I'm here a lot."

The nurse raised Dan's bed. "Okay, buddy, wake up. This is serious. We need you to drink this now." He shoved the bottle into Dan's mouth and poured it in. Dan hiccoughed and gurgled.

"Hey, easy," slurred Dan, his face contorting.

"Can't go easy. You need to drink this. You need to drink all of this, *now.*" Dan pushed the nurse's arm; green goop splattered across my face and t-shirt. Suddenly lucid and glaring, Dan said, "How can you let them do this to me? This is exactly what I *didn't* want!"

"How am I supposed to know what you want? You don't tell me anything. *Anything!*" I shrieked.

"Mrs. Murphy, you've got to get out of here," bellowed the nurse. "I've got to get this down him. I know it looks cruel, but it's all he has between life and death. Step out, please. You're not helping."

Stumbling outside, I stared into the darkness. A block away a luminous billboard marked the site of the Albert Brown Mortuary. It seemed in bad taste to have a mortuary with an operating crematorium situated within eyeshot of the emergency room. Thin trails of purplish-gray smoke curled from its chimney, bruising the sky with harsh streaks of embers and ash.

I bolted to the phone to call my mother.

"I don't know if it was the right thing," I said, voice trembling. "He was furious."

"That's not anger," said Mom. "Just fear. And you're the only one he can show it to. Welcome to the wonderful world of marriage."

"Mama, what should I do?"

"Don't *do* anything," she said. "Just love him."

Chapter 25

November 1998

On the morning Dan was scheduled to come home, I paced up and down the hallway. When the doorbell rang, I ran to answer it.

Harry stood at the door holding a platter of homemade cookies.

"Don't worry, I didn't bake them. They're from my secretary." Harry put the cookies on the entry table. I was having a hard time getting used to how he looked since he'd permanently removed his toupee. He'd told me that a strange odor started emanating from it, especially on days when he did a lot of sweating. "Sooner or later," he'd said, "everything needs airing out."

"Did you get a chance to run the DMV on the Chevy Malibu?" I said.

"I traced the Malibu to Rent-a-Relic. The owner confirmed it was leased to a Richard Harding, who is apparently at some cheap motel in the neighborhood."

"I *knew* it. I also need a home address for Johnny Curtain. Can you believe it? In all these years, he's never had me to dinner? He might be listed under James Curtain. He's got Dan's money. He won't return my calls." I'd left three messages with Johnny's answering service; the last time they had informed me he was out of town on an emergency. "I think Richard and Johnny are in on it together."

"In on *what*?"

"I don't know. But Johnny stole Dan's money. And Richard's back in town. It can't be coincidence." Had Johnny sent Richard to find us at the

Pelican Inn? Had he been planning to hurt us? "Something's going on, and I have to figure it out."

"Listen, Mary," Harry paused, his expression full of compassion. "Dan is really sick. Trying to sort out all of this business isn't going to change that."

"What else am I supposed to do? Dan is unconscious. These guys are taking advantage of him—of me." My voice became shaky. "He can't speak, or even defend himself. I have to take care of things now. I have to find Johnny Curtain."

"Okay, okay. Settle down. I assume Dan keeps an address book of some kind. You've checked that already, right?"

"Oh," I said, embarrassed. *Duh.* "Sorry. I'll do my homework. But I may need your help again, okay?"

"Anything. Just call."

After Harry left, I went into Dan's office and located his black leather address book in the side pocket of his brief case. *Jackpot.* If the information was accurate, Johnny had a P.O. box in San Francisco, but lived right through the tunnel in Orinda. There was a street address scribbled in pencil. What was I going to do, put surveillance on him? No. I needed to get his attention without taking time away from Dan.

I dialed Johnny's answering service again. "When he checks in, tell him an agent for the IRS asked me to confirm his home address." I read the street address to the woman. "Ask him to let me know if this one's still current."

Later that afternoon, Dan was moved by ambulance to a hospital bed in our living room. His liver was too chewed up by cancer to process more chemotherapy, or anything else for that matter. The doctor said toxins were backing up in his system, and it wouldn't be long. Hospice staff helped rearrange our furniture to accommodate the hospital bed and oxygen machine, setting it up so I could sleep next to him on the couch. We both faced the window that looked out over the bay, but Dan couldn't open his eyes.

For the first three days I stayed with him around the clock: moistened his lips, massaged his feet, shifted him so he wouldn't get bedsores. In the late afternoon, when the winter sun beat into the living room, I draped his baby blanket over his eyes and played his favorite music. Though he couldn't speak, he made a soft humming sound when he was comfortable, a low guttural moan when he was in pain and needed morphine. Every afternoon, after school, Rachel sat by the bed telling Dan about her day. This always made him hum.

Five days passed and I still hadn't heard from Johnny. I thought about sending Jamie to look for him. I even considered calling Milton/Mike. After all, he was a private investigator. But as Dan shrunk before my eyes, so did my interest in recovering the contents of his file drawers. Everything seemed so pointless. The most I could do was look out the window once in a while to check whether Richard's car was lurking around the house. Friends, relatives, and business associates dropped by daily, armed with casseroles, relaxation tapes, cakes, wine, and flowers. The house took on the atmosphere of a festive community center that was open twenty-four hours a day. This was fine, at first. What else would I do with so many casseroles except share them?

One night, about a week after Dan came home, Jamie, Mom, Dad, Aunt Maggie, and a neighbor were in the kitchen, chopping food, pouring wine, and examining the array of casseroles available for consumption. Kevin and his new girlfriend arrived to pick up Rachel. Kevin had been so helpful, running errands, spending extra time with Rachel, even sitting with Dan, holding his hand, tearfully thanking him for being a loving stepfather. My mother insisted he stay for dinner.

Someone had recently delivered taco salad and chicken enchiladas, and the group settled on a Mexican meal theme. I heard Mom ask Maggie to find some tequila, and within minutes the blender whirred as margaritas were prepared. Laughter and chatter erupted in the kitchen. I wrapped the baby blanket around Dan's head to muffle the party noise. He was heavy and still, like a wax replica of himself. The oxygen machine rumbled, feeding Dan's shallow breaths. I moved around the room, organizing medication, tossing old tissues, straightening Dan's blankets, and wondering if anyone was going to check up on us. In the kitchen, Jamie recounted a story about getting caught by Mom in a Tijuana strip club.

Laughter exploded, and more margaritas were poured. Clutching the small trashcan from Dan's bedside, I stomped down the hall and into the kitchen. "Could you all please shut the fuck up while my husband dies in the next room?"

Talk stopped. Smiles faded and eyes dropped.

I dumped the contents into the trash compactor, turned on my heel, and walked out. Back on the couch, I curled into a ball and cried into the flattened pillow. I was barely conscious of the kitchen being emptied, the murmured goodbyes, my mom settling next to me.

"It was like this when I was a nurse," she said, rubbing my feet. "People would be going through terrible crises and we nurses would sit at the station, talking and laughing about our plans for the weekend." She sighed. "People forget where they are, honey."

It was agreed that from that moment, Mom and Dad would stay to help. Aunt Maggie would stay at Minnie's, keeping her company and bringing her to visit when she felt strong enough. Everyone else would go home. I didn't hide my gratitude that my mother and father, both married to others, were taking care of me under the same roof for the first time since I was eight.

The next day my mother convinced me to leave the house, run some errands. "You've got to take a break. Do something nice for yourself," she said.

I had my nails done, bought a pack of cigarettes and a bottle of scotch, and went to Whole Foods for organic milk and produce. It took all the energy I had to push the cart up and down the aisles—and really, what was the point? The casserole crusaders arrived at our house daily; more food was superfluous. I parked my cart in the cosmetic aisle to sample scented lotions, using them to camouflage the scent of cigarettes on my hands and face. Ceiling speakers blared Whitney Houston's version of *Have Yourself A Merry Little Christmas.* Her voice was clear and pure. She must have recorded it before she became a crack addict, I thought.

"*Through the years, we all will be together...*" she sang, "*If the fates allow...*"

For the first time, I registered the viciousness of the lyrics. This song was a musical version of those visual optical illusions, like the one that appeared at first glance to be a beautiful young woman in a hat and fur, but at another angle, was a decrepit old hag. It took mental dexterity to slide from one interpretation to the next, and at this point, I could no longer make out the beautiful version of this song.

We hadn't even celebrated Thanksgiving yet, but a fake Christmas tree already towered above a display of supplements. The tree's lights flashed in nonsensical patterns that made me think life had no clear meaning or purpose. *For godsakes just pull the plug,* I wanted to yell. Instead I picked a bottle from the display. It was labeled "Positive Thoughts," and cost $19.95.

"What a rip off," I said aloud. Two passing shoppers glanced at me, then quickly looked away. This was the same alternative therapy advertising bullshit that would tell a dying man that oxygen cleanses or wheat grass enemas or alkaline water diets or a combination of the above would do everything from reverse aging to cure cancer.

I felt my rage simmer. I believed in taking common sense good care of yourself: you should eat fresh food, exercise, get check-ups, live in the open, and pay the damn taxes. But I hated the ridiculous promises made by the American marketing machine. These blood suckers were also behind get-rich-quick schemes and the promotion of the biggest lie on the planet: the one that claimed if we had the right kind of wedding, house, spouse, job, kid, and mini-van, we'd live happily ever after. With their incessant messages, these liars sold pipe dreams for a profit. How could they live with themselves? They took advantage of the vulnerable and the desperate and could guarantee *nothing* because in the end every one of us was going to have big problems—the biggest of which was that we were all going to die.

Still, I tossed a bottle of Positive Thoughts into the cart hoping it might get me off the Ativan and Vicodin. And if it wound up generating even one upbeat brain wave, it was worth the risk of being bamboozled once again. Before leaving the parking lot, I took two tablets and washed them down with a furtive swig of scotch. No noticeable positive thoughts erupted while driving, but the scotch kicked up a craving for a cigarette. I passed the house, looking for a place to smoke, when I glimpsed something that sent a shock up my spine and made me slam the brakes. The silver Malibu was parked on the side street by our house.

Richard was HERE.

My heart battered my ribcage; there was a sudden metallic taste in my mouth. Was he here to rob us again? Did he think there was still money in the file cabinet? Or had Johnny sent him for hidden cash I didn't even know about? Was he here to hurt Dan? Or me? Oh my God, where was Rachel? Maybe he thought Dan's gun was still here. I had to call Harry. No—the police.

I made a screeching U-turn and sped down the hill to the pay phone at the corner gas station. Harry wasn't there, so I left a message: "Something's wrong. Richard's at my house. I'm calling the police."

The 9-1-1 operator asked me twice if I was safe, or anyone's life was at risk. "I don't know what this guy wants with us. He might want to hurt my husband." She promised to dispatch a unit immediately and told me to "rest tight," and not to enter the house until they arrived.

It was a bright winter day; the white sun burned high in the sky. Trees blurred past as I raced home. I parked a distance away, behind a drooping acacia. Squinting through the windshield, I tried to see into the front window, but the glare made it impossible. Blood banged in my temples. I checked my watch. What did she mean, *rest tight*? I couldn't wait endlessly for the police to check on the family. What if someone was hurt?

I slipped out of the car, hunkered down, and scooted up the road, darting from tree to shrub to parked car. Reaching the corner of our wooded property, I made a dash to the side stairway that led to the deck. Every twig and pine needle cracked under my shoes; the redwood stairs squeaked. Right before I made it to the back window, I heard car tires screech, a door slam, and footsteps running toward our front door.

Please, please, please, let it be the police.

I scooted quickly up the stairs, turned the corner on the deck toward the front door and yelped. Johnny was facing me holding a gun.

"Mother of God, you scared me," he said.

"Don't kill me," I threw my hands up. "I'll give you everything we own. Don't hurt us."

"Jesus Christ," Johnny whispered. His right arm dropped, the gun now pointing at the ground. He held a fat brown grocery bag in the other. "What the hell are you doing?"

"Richard's in there." Keeping my hands in the air, I nodded my head toward the house.

"I know Richard is in there," he whispered. "That's why *I'm* here. Put your hands down and tell me what's going on."

"You tell *me* what's going on," I said, terrified. "Why did you steal Dan's money?"

"You don't know what you're talking about." Johnny pulled me around the corner, and in hushed rapid-fire tones, told me that he had called earlier and learned from my mother that Richard was at the door. This set off an alarm, because the last he'd heard, Richard was driving around Arizona in an RV. "We'd offered to give him some cash if he'd return, give a deposition, do whatever he had to do to end this lawsuit. Enough to get him back on his feet."

"You guys were bribing him?"

"More or less. We wanted him back. But then he just shows up on his own? That wasn't part of the plan. Maybe he decided to just take the money and run, the bastard. But I've got it right here." Johnny patted the bag with his gun hand. After a few seconds of silence, he handed it to me.

"Wait." I clutched the bag protectively against my chest. "How did Richard find us at the Pelican Inn if you didn't send him?"

"Honest to God, Mary darlin,' I have no idea." Johnny looked sincere—which of course meant nothing.

"I'm going in," he said.

"NO," I hissed. "You're not bringing a gun in there."

"It's not even loaded." Johnny popped the chamber and gave it a spin. It was empty. "I brought it to scare that fucker."

"NO. This is my family; I don't want you to set him off. I'll go around the back and see what's up. You wait for the police."

"The police?" Johnny looked startled.

Scrambling back down the stairs, I tiptoed onto the deck and peeked into the living room. My heart froze. Richard was alone with Dan. He was slumped in the chair, sobbing. Dan was still as stone. *Was he dead?*

I pictured the rest of the family upstairs, tied up, with duct tape across their mouths. Richard, it seemed, was weeping with guilt over what he'd done. My knees weakened; and my mouth watered. Why did I have to leave the house *today*?

Struggling to breathe, I ducked and shuffled over to the window by the family room. Rachel and my parents were sitting at the table. Dad was dealing cards to the three of them, and a fourth hand to an empty chair. Mom saw my face pressed against the glass and shrieked.

She jumped up and opened the sliding door. "What are you doing? I thought you were some kind of lunatic."

"She is a lunatic," said Rachel, deadpan.

"Yes, but she's our lunatic," said Dad, smiling. "Put down your things." He pointed to the empty seat. "We're playing gin rummy."

Setting the bag on the table, I spoke in a harsh whisper. "What is Richard doing inside this house?"

"I brought him over." Milton/Mike emerged from the bathroom like an unexpected character arriving in a dream. "I brought Richard as a gift for my little brother."

"What are you doing here?"

"Honey, did you know that Mike was a private investigator? He tracked down Richard for Dan. As a surprise." Mom wore an apron dusted with flour. The house smelled like fresh-baked bread. She put one arm around me, and whispered, "Richard was *desperate* to see Dan. He had no idea he was so sick. And after seeing your expression in the hospital—he was certain you'd never let him in."

"He was right!" I said.

"We didn't just let him barge in," said Dad. "Mike called first. Told us the whole story. Amazing."

"And I asked Dan," said Mom.

"Papa made his happy sound, Mom. He *wanted* to see Richard," said Rachel. "And Uncle Mike," she grinned over at Dan's newfound half-brother.

I stood silent for a moment, utterly confused.

"Honey, relax. That man is in there begging for forgiveness," said Mom.

"Begging for money, more likely. Dan and Johnny had to bribe him to return. Just go ask Johnny. He's out front."

"Johnny's out front?" Mike clomped down the hall and opened the front door. I heard police sirens.

"Bribe him?" said Mom. "All I know is Richard feels awful about taking Dan's money, and messing up the work project. He specifically waited for you to leave so he could see Dan. You terrify him."

I terrify *him*? I sat on the couch.

Mike returned. "Johnny left," he said. "I saw him drive off."

Dad picked up the grocery bag from the table and looked inside. His eyes gleamed. "Do you know what's in here?" he whispered.

The doorbell rang. "Oh God." I jumped up. "I called the cops."

"Really?" Rachel ran for the door.

"Dad. Quick. Hide the cash," I said.

"Why?"

"Mike, get Richard out of here—send him out the back."

"They're not looking for Richard," said Mike.

"Or money, right?" said Dad, reemerging from my bedroom, where I assumed he'd left the cash.

Rachel reappeared. "Mom, they want you."

"They do?" My palms moistened, and I started to shake.

"Well, *you* called them," said Dad, patting my head. "I'll take care of it."

Dad invited two officers in, explained it was a misunderstanding. Mom offered them food. Quiet, somber chatter emerged from the kitchen. I stayed in the family room near Mike, who had a soothing effect on me.

"I am so confused," I said.

"Come with me," said Mike.

Mike and I went into the living room. Richard was sitting next to Dan, looking nervous, wary. There was a framed copy of the Prayer of St. Francis sitting on the coffee table. Without looking me in the eye, he pointed to it and shrugged. "I was reading it to him. He's not making much sound, but he seemed to like it."

"It was nice of you," I said, stiffly.

Richard smelled like stale cigarette smoke; his hands shook. It occurred to me that he and I were in the same condition.

Other than his low, gurgling breaths, Dan was quiet. I was never sure what he could hear. I approached the bed, rested my hand on his forehead.

"Let's go on the deck, Mike." I let out a sigh. "Help me understand all of this."

The afternoon sun was warm, pleasant. Mom delivered us hot tea and sandwiches, then moved to the living room. Through the window I saw her fussing around Richard and Dan, straightening the room.

Mike explained that he knew a lot more about Dan's life and the failed development project than anyone realized.

"Ralph—my dad—kept me up to speed on Dan. I knew that Richard stole his money, destroyed his deal. That it all started when Dan tried to hide his money because of the IRS mess. I kept up with family business. As you may imagine, I'm a gifted listener." He pointed to his enormous ears.

I smiled. "Makes sense."

"A few days after my dad died, just to get my mind working on something positive, I decided to track down Richard Harding. And I've got to tell you—it didn't take too long. In less than ten days, I located him outside of Sacramento." Mike explained that he'd called Richard's ex-wife and simply asked her where he was. Harry's straightforward approach to witness interviews, I thought. *Ask and you shall receive.* She was hesitant, he said, but he explained that he meant Richard no harm. "And it was true. I wanted to help him."

Perhaps there was something about Mike's sincerity that prompted her to trust him. She gave him a cell phone number. Mike called Richard and offered to do what he could to facilitate a mutually acceptable reunion—get him back on track with Dan, with his son, even with his ex-wife, who didn't want her son going much longer without seeing his father. "I know how damn hard that can be," said Mike.

"Wait, Johnny said Richard was in Arizona. And that he and Dan were going to pay him money to return."

"Could be." Mike looked skeptical. "I don't know about anything Johnny says. He was a liar when I met him, and I doubt he's changed. I hold him partly responsible for Jimmy's death. Jimmy owed him money; did you know that? Johnny knew Jimmy's gambling was out of control, but he didn't put a stop to it. Just kept pressuring him for the money. Wouldn't let him quit his job until he got paid."

"What do you mean, wouldn't *let* him leave?"

"I mean it would have cost Jimmy his knee caps."

"Johnny would do that?"

"No, Johnny was too nice. He'd outsource it. I don't know, maybe he's mellowed over the years."

"Mike, Johnny came here the other day and took thousands of dollars Dan had locked in his file cabinet. He implied they were going to give it to Richard."

"Maybe that's true. But Dan never said anything about it to me. And as far as I know, Richard didn't put a price on his help. You can ask him yourself."

"What do you mean, Dan never *said…* when did you speak with Dan?"

"He called me. From the hospital after he shot off that gun. Said Minnie told him everything about Jimmy—the suicide. Me. I couldn't believe it. Danny said he was *sorry.* After all these years, he said he needed his brother." Mike's eyes teared-up. "I was so happy. I wanted to pick up Richard, drive right down, get the whole mess settled for him."

I suddenly remembered walking in on Dan in the hospital when he was on the phone—how when he saw me, he had dropped his voice and said to the caller, "Don't come now. Wait a little."

"Why didn't Dan tell me he was in touch with you?"

"He wanted to get this deal all straightened out first. He said he'd been disappointing you for years."

"Disappointing me?" That news made my heart hurt. "That's *not* true." I stared into the living room where Dan slept. The skin under his eyes was dark. His arms poked like twigs from sunken shoulders. Even as he withered before my eyes, he looked proud, defiant. Dan never shied away from a fight; that wasn't going to change now. How I wished I could shake him awake and tell him it was all going to be different now. How much I appreciated how hard he worked, and what a devoted husband and father he was.

"Here's the best part. When Dan called for help, I already knew where Richard was! Can you believe that? Can you believe the timing of it all? Now Richard's back, and if we can keep Johnny in line, you girls ought to see a nice profit."

Mike grinned, looked up, and pointed to the sky. "If you ask me, I think the big guy had something to do with it."

"You mean, God?"

"No. My father. Ralph." Mike blessed himself.

I mirrored him, and then sighed. When I'd gotten the sign back in that Panama hotel room, that God was going to "open the windows of heaven and pour out a blessing that there would not be room enough to receive," I'd always assumed that meant more money. But I was starting to think it was much more complicated than that.

"How could you stand it all these years, Mike? Being accused of something you didn't do? The irony is, false accusations were the one thing that used to make Dan crazy."

"I didn't mind. I wanted to protect my brothers. Both of them. And I knew Ralph loved me. He was the greatest."

"Dan's always been so desperate for a brother."

"Being able to help Danny? This is like a dream." Mike flushed, and gazed at his half-brother through the window. "All I ever wanted was family."

His nose started to run, and he pulled a handkerchief from his pocket.

"I can't believe you convinced Richard to return," I said.

"People don't want to end their lives going down in flames. Richard felt so bad about taking off on Dan and on his kid. He told me he'd even thought about killing himself. Like Jimmy. He thought he'd let everyone down. Like the rest of us, he's getting old. He just wants to make good, and needed a way to do it. When Minnie told me you guys were spending your birthdays at that inn, Richard thought it would be a hoot if part of the present was to leave a signed affidavit and a forwarding address at the front desk."

"*You* sent him there?" I was dumbfounded.

"But he got cold feet. Thought it might mess up your weekend—that Dan would run off to chase him. Then all of that happened with the gunshot and the hospital. But it's all sorted out now. I'm on the job." Mike pinched my chin. "Until it's done."

"Did Johnny know you'd tracked down Richard?"

"No. Dan wanted to make sure he had a slam dunk before throwing any more celebration parties. Johnny was as surprised as you today."

I told Mike that after Johnny had raided Dan's file cabinet, I hadn't heard from him since, until today. "I thought he was trying to steal it, so I called and threatened to turn him in to the tax man."

"You did?" Mike cracked up. "I like the way you work, sister."

I wondered how much he'd like me if he knew how squirrelly I'd been with Ralph's hidden stash. For a second I thought of confessing, but stopped short. He was such a sweet man. I didn't want him to lump me in with the criminal crowd Dan seemed to attract.

"Hey, I understand why you changed your last name to Murphy. But why Mike?"

"I wanted something more macho than Milton, like Chuck or Hercules," he grinned. "But I didn't want to change the my initials." He spread out his handkerchief, displaying the hand embroidered *MM*. "My mother makes— or made—these for me every year for Christmas and my birthday. I didn't want to make a big deal about telling her I changed the name she gave me. She was everything to me." His eyes moistened again.

"Then why change it at all?"

"It was hard being a bastard with big ears. I thought if I changed my name I wouldn't have the same problems."

"Your little brother thought a name change would help him, too," I said. "But it doesn't work that way, does it?"

The sun was setting and the air turned chilly. We moved into the warm glow of the living room, where Richard dozed in the chair next to Dan's bed.

"We better get moving, buddy," said Mike, jostling him. "Let me just say goodbye to the family." He went into the kitchen.

Richard stood by the bedside, lifted Dan's hand, and gave it a squeeze. "I know. I'm such a prick. But the way he treated me? Closest thing I ever had to a brother. I just hope he'll forgive me." He looked up at me, red-nosed, and choked out the words. "That you'll all forgive me."

I looked away, unable to make eye contact. It occurred to me that maybe I should offer him my bottle of Positive Thoughts, but I wasn't ready to give them up.

"Okay, let's go," said Mike, reappearing in the living room. "Richard's moving out of his motel, staying with me for awhile." Mike took out a card and handed it to me. "I'll call you tomorrow. And don't worry about Minnie, I'm going over there in the morning."

"She's having a hard time. My Aunt Maggie's with her."

"I know. I talked to Maggie this morning. What a nice lady."

With Mike leading the way, Richard slumped out of the house and climbed into his injured car. We sent them home with two donated casseroles and a loaf of mom's home-baked bread.

I returned to the living room, where my dad was sitting next to Dan.

"Dad," I whispered. "Dan kept so much from me. He even lied to me about where he went to law school. Why would he do that?"

Dad shrugged. "People are always lying to be loved or accepted," he said, holding my hand. "Over the years I've learned that the only proper response is to just forgive them. And myself, for that matter."

Wise words, I thought, from a guy who had once furiously pelted me with socks.

The next night, as the rest of the household slept, I lay wide-awake on the couch, alone in the company of Dan, missing him desperately. "I'm so proud of you," I whispered, stroking his forehead. "I don't want you to die, Dan."

I knew this was the wrong thing to say. All the hospice literature encouraged family members to tell their loved one it was all right to go—to assure them that you would be able to carry on alone. But I was sick of lying. I didn't want Dan to go anywhere. I'd wasted so much time fighting with him, trying to get him to be different. He'd wasted so much time hiding, being angry with his parents, and hating Mike. And Rachel was too young for this kind of loss. How could it be over so quickly, just when things were starting to make sense? Why couldn't we have a miracle? A few years where I could stop focusing so much on what was wrong and just have some fun with him?

Just love him.

My eyes swept the room, taking in the small details. Dan's worn baby blanket. A murky glass of water where we dipped the peppermint sponges used to cleanse Dan's mouth, flecks of skin floating on top. Colorful crayon drawings of dancing queens that Rachel and her friends had taped around the room. A package of adult diapers and a box of Latex gloves, next to a tidy stack of washcloths, threadbare and stained from wiping endless bodily fluids. Room freshener. Chapstick. Enemas. And drugs, drugs, drugs. Liquid morphine. Tablet morphine. Pain patches and tranquilizers. Vicodin. Restoral. Enough narcotics to obliterate a broken heart.

While everyone else slept, the house hummed with quiet activity. Goody curled between Dan's legs, sleeping silently until something awakened her—a drop in Dan's pulse? A twitch from pain? I sat up. The house hissed and groaned, releasing moisture and heat from the day. Outside, tree branches scraped against the roof. Spam arrived uninvited on the downstairs computer with a high-pitched *ping*. Upstairs, Rachel slept, taking a desperately needed break from the worry and chaos. Through all of this she managed to rest, rejuvenate, and grow up, while my parents rested, rejuvenated, and grew older. I stared at the clock on the mantle, wishing desperately I could pull out the batteries and make time stop.

Gray fog pressed against the windows, blocking streetlights and starlight and muffling outside noise. A votive candle had burnt to a miniscule blue flicker, close to being extinguished by its own liquefied remains. Dan labored to breathe, his lungs wet and raspy. I imagined Dan's organs and systems shutting down, second by interminable second, cell by poisoned cell. I curled next to him and sang The Carpenter's "Close to You" until it seemed each of us breathed easier.

I awoke suddenly as Dan let out a long guttural moan truncated by a strangled wheeze. Then nothing.

No inhale. No exhale.

No rise. No fall.

It was an eerie and impossible silence, as if the earth itself had stopped moving.

I jumped up and ran to the family room to wake my father. Dad rushed to Dan's side, wrapped his fingers around his wrist, searching for a pulse.

"He's gone, honey," Dad whispered. "He's gone."

"No, Daddy." I couldn't move. "Not yet."

We both sat on the couch and silently watched Dan's still body for the longest time. I was afraid to say anything, do anything, or call anyone who would move him away from me, or me closer to my life without him.

The first morning light filtered into the room.

Chapter 26

January 1999

The day after Dan's memorial, Minnie stepped out of bed and her hip snapped like a dried twig. Hip replacement surgery was yet another blow. If there was any good news, it was that the hospital had her transferred to a rehabilitation center in Oakland, very close to me.

The lobby of the Oakland rehab center was sunny and bright, but Minnie's room was dark and claustrophobic. She was hunched on her side in bed, the orange paisley bedspread fanning out behind her, making her look like a squashed butterfly. I opened the draperies, exposing the stuffy room to gray light from the overcast day. I tried opening a window, but it was jammed.

"Oh honey," she said, shaking her head, eyes wet with tears. "Finally, you're here. No one has checked on me since breakfast."

Pulling a cosmetic bag from my purse, I brushed her hair and applied blush on her cheeks.

"You get better service if you look alive." I gave her tiny, wrinkled hand a squeeze, and she held on so tight that her rings bit into my flesh.

"They give me all kinds of pills but none do any good. And I can't go to the bathroom alone so I need someone around all the time. And I don't want someone around all the time, especially then."

"I guess it keeps you from feeling lonely."

"No it doesn't. I'm always lonely," she said weakly.

I sat beside Minnie all morning, reading excerpts from *The Star* and *The Enquirer*, because she couldn't see due to worsening cataracts. Now all of her favorite pastimes—smoking, reading, and television—were ruined. She couldn't walk, she was in constant pain, and her only child was dead. Though we didn't discuss it, she probably couldn't return to her house ever again, especially since I'd lost all interest in living there without Dan.

"Honey, turn on the radio and just relax on the empty bed. You look so tired. Take just a minute to rest."

"I have to get Rachel. I'll be back after I get her settled with Mom. Okay?"

I leaned to kiss her, but Minnie turned away and stared at the putty colored wall. I turned the radio to her favorite station and the sterile, empty room filled with an old Dean Martin love song. Minnie's pale, skinny shoulder poked out of the colorless cotton gown. Her fading green eyes sat flat against a drooping gray face, making the pink smudges on her cheeks appear fluorescent, ridiculous. While she stared, and Dean crooned on, I had an urge to tear the radio out of the wall, throw it across the room, send it smashing through the window. That way, at least we'd get some fresh air in here.

A nurse in a starched white coat sashayed in, smiling big. Her skin was black, smooth and shiny, like polished granite. She stood almost six feet tall. Her plastic nametag said, "Dee." Even though it stank in here, this nurse stirred a clean breeze, and I breathed deeply. Dee filled the room with activity, unjamming the window, washing her hands, shaking and fluttering them dry, clearing off a chair where she sat and examined Minnie's chart with a cocked eyebrow.

She looked up, winked at me, and said, "Sister, I am Dee-Dee, the visiting nurse from Kaiser. I am looking after your mother-in-law and she told me *allll* about you. I think it's so nice you two look after each other. I'm a recent widow too, sister, so I know." She shook her head solemnly, and repeated, looking into my eyes: "I *know*."

I kept my eyes on Dee. She was a widow? But she looked strong and beautiful—even happy.

Out came the wiggling rubber stethoscope and Dee aimed its cold metal part on Minnie's chest. Minnie stiffened. Dee stopped, rubbed the metal fast against her hand to warm it.

"It's okay sister-girl, let Dee-Dee listen and oh yes," she exhaled, "Minnie, you are breathing so fine today."

Dee smiled, warm and wide. She took Minnie's head in her strong hands, leaned over, struck a kiss on her cheek and hummed, "Mmm-hmm."

Minnie ignited, briefly, like a firefly. They looked at each other, Dee's black almond eyes twinkling into Minnie's rheumy green. Minnie put her small, wrinkled hand on Dee's head, where the hair was cropped tight, in an elegant cap of singed curls.

Oh, what I would give for an infusion of her energy.

Kiss me too, Dee. Mmm-hmm. Kiss me too.

Dee swirled around, talking, touching, taking pulses, and explaining what Minnie needed. For a moment it seemed that Dee was breathing life back into this room, into Minnie, into me, and I was so absorbed in this resuscitation, that I didn't hear any clear words until she said, "That's why, sister, you should take your husband's little mama home with you until she gets back on her feet again. She can't go back to her house alone."

I flashed on a cartoon scene where Road Runner dug his heels into the hard desert terrain and was forced—*screeeeeeeech*—to an abrupt halt that left him disoriented and suffocating in a swirling dirt cloud.

"What?"

Dee explained that Minnie could stay at the rehab center for one more week, but then she was on her own, as far as coverage went. "When your little Minnie told Dee-Dee how close you two were—how you two wished you could live together even before your husband passed? Well, I realized that the perfect solution was to send her home with you." Dee looked pleased. "Minnie told me how much you have in common, and I thought, that's *right*. That's right. Folks say opposites attract. But the truth is, likes do. How nice you two are so much alike, including having the deep love of Minnie's only son. You're birds of a feather; you *must* stick together."

"Maybe God gave Mary *me* to take care of so she could keep her mind off her grief. I don't know what I'd do without this girl." Dee and Minnie smiled over at me, as if they'd just witnessed me sprout gossamer wings.

Pain stabbed through my skull and I thought my eyes might start to bleed. I certainly owed it to her. I'd deceived her, taken money from her husband, spent it behind everyone's back, and constantly told her Dan was going to be okay, when somehow, deep down, I'd known that wasn't the truth.

As Dee fluttered around, talking and marking the chart, I remembered a story Harry had told me about his Aunt Annie, the family saint who was always there for everyone who needed her, especially her mom, Harry's diabetic grandmother. After Granny had her leg removed, she moved in with Annie, who fed her, bathed her, helped her with her prosthesis, changed her adult diapers, and listened to her thoughts, stories, complaints, and orders. Lots of friends offered help, but Granny always interrupted the offers with, "No, no, no. My Annie will do it, it's easier this way." The family was shocked when Saint Annie told them that she often fantasized ripping off Granny's prosthesis and beating her to death with it.

"Girlfriend, are you okay?" Dee pushed my arm, bringing me back.

I motioned Dee into the hall and with a shaky voice I told her, yes, I loved Minnie. Deeply. And, yes, we were very close and I once thought we should live together. "But, Dee, I can't bring her home now. She wears me out. No matter what I do she's unhappy, no matter how long I sit with her, it's not enough. She whines and cries. It makes me feel terrible when I leave. I'm afraid it won't be for a short time. I won't have anyplace to get away."

"*No*, sister, *no!*" said Dee, pushing my shoulders. As I spoke, her eyes and mouth bloomed wide, her expression incredulous. She thought I was heartless. Tears swelled in my eyes.

"No, no, *no*. Now, that's *no* good, girl." Dee pulled me against her strong, warm body, cradling my head into her soft chest. She smelled like clean earth and flowers and I inhaled her.

"Listen little sister. It's gonna be okay. I see the one you have to care for now is *you*. You have got to tell Mama you are stressed out and you have got to get on with your own life. And when you talk? No, no, *no*. She doesn't get to act like the *mother* with you as her *daughter*. It's time for you two to talk *girlfriend* to *girlfriend*."

I started to cry.

"That's right. Let it out now. You've got to feel it to heal it." Dee wagged a long, graceful index finger in my face. "Now go. Give me some time with the little mama. Go on. Go breathe and be back in a little while."

I returned to the room and, without looking up, grabbed my purse. "Minnie, I'm going to get a soda. I'll be back," I said, whisking in and out quickly.

My head throbbed, enough to warrant painkillers. I rummaged through my purse and found two Vicodin. They barely affected me anymore, and I was tempted to take something stronger—to try morphine, which I had vowed never to do, even though I maintained an amazing stockpile of it. The hospice nurse had asked me to return any unused drugs after Dan had died, but I told her—apologizing profusely—that I'd already flushed them down the toilet because I couldn't stand having them around one more second to remind me of Dan's death. I waited for her to scream, *liar liar liar!* Instead she replied, "Perfect. Thanks."

In the lounge I got some water to wash down my pills. I sat at an empty table and stared at the television, which was running a hospital soap opera where an actress with long, golden hair wept while a strong, handsome doctor comforted her in a tender, sensual embrace. I hated soap operas. Like life, they were crisis after crisis with no resolution in sight. Except on TV, everyone looked great.

I walked to the bathroom and checked myself in the mirror. I was gaunt and splotchy. My face was thin and my clothes hung loosely. The only explanation for the five pounds I'd gained since Dan died was the weight of a heavy heart. I turned from the mirror. My looks, my duplicity, my dead husband's sneaky activities, illness, and death—they were just not glamorous.

Back in the room, Minnie and Dee were still together, relaxed, talking and laughing. Minnie saw me and beamed. "Honey, what did the old patient say when the doctor told her she had cancer *and* Alzheimer's?"

I sat on the empty bed. "I give up."

Minnie lowered her voice. "'Well, Doc, at least I don't have cancer.'"

We giggled and nudged each other, Dee joining in our laughter.

I turned to Dee. "What'd you give her?"

"Girl, I gave her a shot of Demerol. There's something wrong with the way she's been feeling. Nobody needs to be in that kind of pain."

This was the first smile I'd seen from Minnie in months. Times like this, I wasn't sure why drugs got such a bad rap. It was no longer in vogue to insist women experience natural childbirth, so why did we have to endure death and all the attendant pain and loss without the help medical science has to offer? Why not install grievers in nicely appointed hotels that allowed us to remain under the influence of pharmaceutical quality narcotics until we emerged from the visceral anguish of this gruesome experience? We could pool resources, hire sober people to drive and cook for our children, and use drugs to bypass this unbearable period when angry, depressing thoughts played like a soundtrack of blood-curdling screams—twenty-four-hours a day.

"Oh honey," said Minnie. "I'm sorry. I don't mean to forget all you're going through. You'll be no good to me or anyone if you don't take care of yourself. And Rachel! How is she doing in her new school?"

"I guess middle school never changes. She's having her ups and downs—pre-teen stuff. It'll take some adjusting."

"Tell her I know *just* how she feels." Minnie reached her hand out, wiggling her fingers for me to grasp. "My God, I don't know what I'd do without you and all you do."

"Minnie wants to help *you* now, sister, help you with *your* stresses," said Dee, "And I'm going to help her more with her pain. Something's just not right. We're going to do a full work up on her tomorrow morning—get to the bottom of this."

"That's right." Minnie smiled, winked.

Pain free with the Demerol shot, she resembled her old, charming self. I stared at Dee in amazement as she sailed out of the room.

"And we won't worry about it if you have to stay a little longer here, Min. There's plenty of money to cover it." I was relieved that I'd have to spend Ralph's hidden booty on Minnie's recovery.

"I don't worry about money," slurred Minnie, eyeing me slyly. "I know there's plenty."

"You do?" My heart picked up a beat.

"Honey, Ralph had nothing on me."

"He didn't?" My toes cramped in my shoes.

"Ralph thought he was so clever." She shot me a quick sideways glance. "I didn't just fall off the potato truck."

"Oh God Minnie," I said, blushing hot. "So you knew?"

"Knew what?" She looked at me, confused.

"About the money," I said.

"You know about the money?" she asked.

My mouth tasted like a moldy rag.

"Wait," she said. "What are you saying, honey?"

"Ralph was hiding money from you, Min."

"I *know*. He hid it from me for years. I don't think he stopped until he finally retired."

"I don't think he stopped at all, Minnie."

"What?" she said.

"There may be some hidden money you didn't know about."

"You think there's more?"

"No. Yes. Minnie, there is more." My voice cracked. "This is so awkward. Ralph was hiding money," I looked down. "And giving it to me." I rambled nervously, explaining that he had insisted I keep it a secret, that he'd given it to me because of Dan's tax troubles, and that I'd told Dan and sworn him to secrecy. "As far as I'm concerned, the money is yours."

Minnie fidgeted with a balled tissue. Her face was drained of emotion.

"Minnie, please. Say something."

Minnie waved her hand, like she was clearing cobwebs. "Oh, honey. What a terrible position to be in. Ralph loved you. He trusted you." She shook her head. "How much was it?"

According to which records, I thought? But this was my chance to clear the slates, to extricate myself from the quagmire of lies that had muddied my money dealings with this family.

"Over twenty-five thousand dollars." I held my breath.

"Twenty-five thousand?" Minnie's lips pursed like a pouch pulled closed with a string. "Ralph had twenty-five thousand dollars stashed? Now you have it?"

"I only have about fifteen." My tongue felt like rubber. "I kept spending it on stupid stuff."

Minnie cut me off, shaking her little fist skyward. "Ralph! You handed away all those thousands? Without even mentioning it? Who do you think you are?"

"I'm so sorry—"

Minnie latched her green eyes onto me. "Don't get me wrong, honey. I don't begrudge you the money. But you, Ralph?" She looked up. "Why couldn't we talk things over, like a normal couple? Didn't he think *I'd* want you kids to have money for a house? Why the secrets, why always the secrets! And for godsakes, we're old. What if we needed the money?"

"That's what I'm saying, Minnie. I want to give it all back. Or we could get you a more appropriate place to live—closer to me."

"That's not it. Honey, can't you see? I would have *wanted* you and Dan to have the money. And you know what? I'm glad you told Dan. I *am*. If I have any pleasure in life, it's in knowing I raised a man who a woman can talk things over with."

"I don't want to burst your bubble," I said, "but it turns out Dan was hiding money from me, too."

"What?" Minnie's mottled hands tightened into fists.

"Dan had thousands hidden. I have no idea if he ever planned on mentioning it. I found it right before he died. How do you think I paid for that nice memorial?"

Minnie pursed her lips, making a clucking sound. We stared at each other, silent, for a long moment.

"Well to *hell* with them." Minnie shook her head and looked heavenward again. "Just so you know, Dan and Ralph Murphy, I have a few secrets of my own," she slurred, smiling. "Ralph was having his affairs, hiding his money. Who did he think he was kidding?" Minnie giggled, loopy from the drugs. "Did I tell you how I stockpiled it?"

"Stockpiled what?" I said.

"Honey, are you listening to me?" slurred Minnie. "I'm telling you, you're loaded."

"I think *you're* loaded, Minnie." I brushed her coarse curls away from her face.

"Check the zipper compartment in my purse. You might as well know now." Her voice was weak, barely fueled by emphysemic lungs. "I wanted it to be a surprise for Dan, after, you know—after I died. Prove to him his old ma knew a thing or two. Oh, what I'd've given to see the look on his face!" Minnie's Demerol smile relaxed into a thin, flat line. "Come on, get it out. It's all for you, now."

I sat up in the hard plastic chair and opened her purse, unzipping the inside pocket to find three thin black passbooks from various banks. I opened one, rifling to the last page. I blinked hard when I saw the number. "You saved fifty thousand dollars and Ralph didn't know about it?"

"Fifty thousand! No, honey. That's just Bank of America. Keep looking. There's over two hundred and fifty thousand!" Minnie's chin tilted up, in a proud expression that reminded me of Ralph. "Been at it almost as long as we were married."

"Two hundred and fifty thousand dollars?" If I were a cartoon, my eyeballs would have been bouncing at the end of long, springy coils. I grabbed the other two books, thumbed through all the pages.

I stared at Minnie, flabbergasted. She, Ralph, Dan, and I were nothing but a gang of hard-drinking, pill-popping, two-timing, lying Irish thieves. We deserved one another.

"How in God's name did you save this much without Ralph knowing?"

"Easy." Minnie smiled, her eyelids drooping closed. "I stole it from places he hid it, and he hid it all over the place."

At least Dan came by his deception honestly.

"Too bad I didn't know about Ralph's stash in the basement, that rascal. But at least you've got that." Minnie patted my hand and offered a sly smile. "Or what's left of it, seeing as you tried to eat the evidence."

I flushed with shame.

Minnie snatched the passbooks from my hand, and waved them like a delicate fan. "Ralph's gift was chump change compared to this." She attempted a wink, but her entire face stumbled awkwardly. "We paid taxes on all of it, too—unlike You Know Who. And Ralph! All these years I expected him to catch on, to ask. But you know, for the last twenty years he was blind as a bat. It was right there on the tax forms—every year I had to claim the interest, and honey, there were years we were earning nine, ten percent, and he couldn't even see it! He'd have been so mad. And so proud we were rich."

"Why did you hide it from him?"

"What else could I do, with all his carrying on? How would I take care of myself if he left?" Minnie looked up and shook her tiny fist. "I gotcha, Ralph. I gotcha good!"

I had to laugh—at her chutzpa, Ralph's cluelessness, and our sudden largesse.

We would now inherit a house in San Francisco *and* over two hundred fifty thousand dollars—years and years of chump change that Dan's mother had skimmed from his father supplemented by the miracle of compounding interest. Just what I'd always dreamed of—a house and enough money for my family to enjoy a sprinting start toward financial security. Wait until I told Dan. This would crack him up.

My heart drained as I remembered.

I returned to Minnie's room the next day at lunchtime. Dee had assisted her through a battery of tests, and she looked exhausted. I pulled up a chair, and with a magician's flair, lifted the beige plastic cover off the lunch plate. "Ta-daa!" I smiled.

"I just wish God would take me," said Minnie, flatly. "Ralph used to say that. I'd get so mad at him. You never know about a man until you walk a mile in his shoes. Now I know."

She had a point. Lately I'd been walking a mile in Richard's shoes, and thinking about how he'd convinced himself he'd pay back Dan. I used to imagine ways to put Ralph's housing fund to heroic use—open a thriving investigative business, send Dan to the nation's top cancer specialists, discover a lucrative investment that would generate enough interest to reimburse all I'd pilfered. But ideas are cheap, and what I ended up with was a closet full of clothes I no longer wore.

Nurse Dee appeared at the door, frowning. With a graceful flick of her long finger, she motioned me over. In the doorway, Dee draped her arm around my shoulder, squeezed tight, and whispered, "Sister-girl, there's no other way to say it. I'm afraid we got some devastating news today." She pressed her lips onto the side of my head. "*Devastating* news."

Minnie's radio played "You Keep Coming Back Like a Song," one of Grandma Mary's favorites. She stared blankly in our direction as I learned of her spreading lung cancer, something that had gone undiagnosed during our countless trips to the doctor—until now, when it was too late to do anything to stop it because it was in her bones.

"Oh, Dee. I *knew* something else was wrong." I thought about how the doctors had dismissed the odd appearance of the x-ray at the emergency room, how stingy they had been with pain medication, how we'd all insisted she have a better attitude about her hip replacement and exercising. It made me want to smash something.

Dee and I moved to the front lobby, where she reviewed the end-of-life care options, all of which I already knew about. "Hospice can deliver their services right here at this rehab center, which may be the best bet," said Dee.

"Why did the doctors take so long to figure this out? I should've been more assertive when they found something in her lungs months ago."

"Girl, right or wrong, you did your best."

"Dee, why couldn't they have found this out before they did her hip? My God, to put her through that surgery for *nothing*."

"It's natural to look for someone to blame, sister. I see it all the time." Dee patted my back. "I guess you could even sue. A lot do. But people see what they want to see, when it's time to see it. God never gives you more than you can handle. That might've been just a little too much information at once."

In a corner of the lobby, a parrot in a sterile white cage screeched incessantly as it flitted from perch to perch. Dee ushered me down the hall. "Sister—I can't hear myself think with that bird making itself miserable, fighting against its fate. Such a useless waste of time."

Dee and I returned to the room. Minnie stared at me quizzically.

"Dee, call hospice," I whispered. "I'm bringing Minnie home."

Epilogue

October 1999

The tenth anniversary of the Loma Prieta earthquake fell on a Sunday. The anniversary had become symbolic for its ability to jolt my life into some wild new direction, and this time I planned to mark it—literally—by unveiling the three new names now carved into the headstone at the Murphy family plot. There was a small cemetery service planned for three the next afternoon, and I'd invited a few friends and family members to attend.

It was Saturday morning, the day before the ceremony. I lingered in bed, as I often had these past months, puzzling over how I'd ended up as a death midwife to three Murphys as they were delivered to—*to where?* I couldn't wrap my mind around the fact that they were all gone, let alone figure out *where* they'd gone.

As I showered that morning, I heard the phone ring. There was a voice message from my new pal, Nurse Dee. "I'm calling to get directions to the cemetery service, Ms. Mary." After a long pause, she said, "Girl, I know you miss your husband, but get that dead man's voice off the answering machine. He's got better things to do than creep out your friends."

Recently I'd read that Sir Walter Raleigh's wife kept his head in a leather bag for twenty-nine years after he was executed. Extreme, yes. But she had my complete sympathies. Since meeting the Murphys, I'd inherited one house, one cemetery plot, countless cash baggies and bank accounts, one half brother-in-law by fake marriage, a legal settlement from the coast project,

281

and a cauldron of family secrets. After all the death, I'd spent hundreds of hours purging two houses, on the lookout for more surprises. But there were just meaningless papers and paraphernalia: law books, notes, ties, dentures, and pictures, pictures, pictures—of ex-loves, ex-lives, unidentified relatives and forgotten holidays. Still, no one understood how often I felt I'd betrayed Ralph, Minnie and Dan, just by getting rid of one of their *things*.

I replayed Dee's message, a sick feeling gathering in my gut. This wasn't the first time a caring friend or relative had suggested I update the message. But somehow hearing it from her—a widow, too—had greater impact.

Goody jumped next to me on the bed, rolled on her back, aimed her yellow eyes at me and cried. I stroked her belly, causing her to settle into a steady vibrating purr. As soon as I stopped, she slapped me with her paw, leaving a slash that looked like a thin red thread.

"Dammit Goody."

But I knew just how she felt. The loss of Dan's physical presence made me hungry—no, *starving*—for touch. Lately what I craved as much as the numbing effect of alcohol and narcotics was heart racing, gasping, panting and sweaty carnal contact of the most desperate kind. I rifled through the self-help sections in bookstores, paging through the manuals for widows, but none of them mentioned this embarrassing symptom. I had no idea how much love, comfort, and attention Goody also must have received from Dan, but since he'd died she didn't eat much, often moped around the house crying, and never even killed anything.

Worried, I took Goody to the vet; he told me that it was "just grief."

Just grief.

After that I regularly settled her on Dan's side of the bed, turned on the speakerphone, and dialed our voicemail. The two of us would stare at the boxy black receiver while Dan cheerfully declared: "You've reached the home of Dan, Mary, and Rachel. Leave us a message and we'll call you back."

I stared at my cat: Her shining eyes, two full moons of anxiety, glowed back at me from a furry black face.

"Sorry, little one," I said. "It's time."

I set Goody in the hallway and closed the door. Dialing the number for the message center, I braced to hear Dan's friendly radio announcer voice.

To continue to play this greeting, press pound. To erase this greeting, and leave a new one, press one and record after the beep.

My finger hovered over the keypad. I couldn't breathe. The computerized voice repeated, this time sounding impatient.

To continue to play this greeting, press pound now! To erase this greeting, press one!

I pressed the "1" key and—*wait!* I grabbed the phone cradle and pressed the pound key once, twice, three times—hands shaking, waiting for the voice to tell me how to get it back. But Dan was gone.

Again.

Poof.

A sudden drowsiness flattened me on the bed. I imagined a full-blown migraine was on its way, and I got up and rummaged through my top dresser drawer, where I'd stashed a large Ziploc bag of all the remaining drugs in the house. I hadn't touched them in months, but had kept them around just in case.

In case of what?

I placed the drugs in my purse and looped the strap over my shoulder. Aunt Maggie had agreed to meet me at the cemetery to make sure everything was ready for the ceremony.

The pale morning sky was layered with an ashy-lilac haze that pressed against the horizon. The pervasive grays made me think of a remark Minnie had made a few weeks after I'd complained about my changing hair color. "Honey, the more gray you get, the more gray you'll see," she'd sighed. "Get used to it."

Driving through the cemetery gates, I passed the chapel, the fountains and the duck pond. I parked along the side of the road and slowly inhaled the scent of freshly mowed lawn, while scanning the sea of gray looking for our plot. I found the marker directly below the old Oak tree. The Murphy name was centered in large lettering on the front of the stone, out of my line of vision. Jimmy and his mother, Mary, had their names on the top, the inscriptions softened by age. But now, even from this distance, I could see the bright new letters etched along the side.

Ralph Edward 1908-1998
Daniel Patrick 1945-1998
Mary Francis 1912 -1999

It amazed me how clichés took on such meaning in times of great crisis or sadness. Now that I could see their names set in stone, I was gripped by the sickening fact that it was really over. I searched my purse for a tissue, and wrapped my hand around the bag of pills. How simple it would be if I could just permanently drug the pain and fury of being left behind.

I stared at Dan's name for a long time. I had decided to add the "k" back to "Patric," mostly out of respect for Ralph and Minnie. They'd never understood why we'd taken his middle name and lopped off a letter. And the reasons no longer made sense to me, either. With his middle name restored, I decided I'd better add the "k" back onto my name, too. I didn't want to be buried next to him with a different name. And the process had been even easier than before. I'd simply called customer service lines and haughtily complained that they had misspelled "Patrick" by leaving off the "k." Thinking they were in the wrong, no one even stopped to consider the legitimacy of my complaint.

Dan's old Lincoln Town Car pulled behind me on the road, and I jumped as if I'd seen his ghost. I'd given Dan's car to Mike; did he think the ceremony was today? Someone was with him, but I couldn't see because of the glare. The passenger door opened and Aunt Maggie emerged, looking vibrant in a pink tunic and bright gypsy skirt. I met them by the curb. Aunt Maggie, noticing my reddened eyes, wrapped her arms around me and gave me a long hug.

"Hope you don't mind that I joined you two," said Mike, kindly.

Mike looked good, fit and dressed in crisp new clothes, and seemed relaxed and comfortable, as if chauffeuring my aunt to her cemetery appointment was nothing out of the ordinary. I looked back and forth between the two of them.

"I had some business here, too," he said.

"Yes," said Maggie, fluffing her hair against the dampness. "Mike was at the house fixing the water heater and he offered me a ride over." Aunt Maggie was staying in the empty house in San Francisco. It made much more sense than putting her on our couch or in a hotel this weekend.

"Honey, Mike needs to find a spot for his mother's ashes. He wants her to be close to him," she smiled toward Mike. "And of course, he's going to be resting right on top of me."

"Maggie and I figured since we'd be spending an eternity together, we might as well get acquainted," said Mike, winking at Maggie.

My aunt giggled and batted her lashes like a teenager. And now that I thought of it, she smelled pretty flowery. I wanted to dash over to the headstone and tell Dan about this. In another circumstance, he'd die laughing.

"Mike, you're shopping for a plot?"

"I thought I'd get Mom a nice crypt, just over there," he pointed. "By the duck pond."

"Don't be silly." I blew my nose. "She'll come in with us."

"No. You don't have to do that."

"Of course I do. She's family."

"At least let me pay the additional fee. I already planned on—"

"Mike, please." I waved him away. "Don't deprive me of this pleasure." I started walking toward the cemetery office.

In the distance, I heard Maggie laughing while reciting the list of characters that would ultimately wind up in our family plot. Turning around, I stared at the distant cemetery marker, remembering how I'd once mentioned to Minnie that if all the invited guests were interred together, it would be almost impossible to make sense of the relationships.

"Someone would have to write a book," she'd said.

As I walked through the cemetery grounds, I felt it twittering with life: Geese and ravens fought over bits of food, squirrels darted between stones and trees, and a family of deer lingered against a fence, stealing bites of the overgrown grass.

The sprinkler system sputtered on, spraying colliding arcs of water that sounded like a chorus of crickets. Despite the ambiguity of the weather, the dull sunshine warmed my back. The longer I walked, the stronger I felt. Hundreds, maybe thousands of tombstones checkered the rolling green landscape in endless shades of gray.

The main service road was lined with plum trees. Reddish-black leaves, the color of dried blood, dropped from the branches, leaving them bare and stretching toward the sky. Feeling inside my sack, I grabbed the bag of painkillers and lobbed it into a concrete trashcan. It landed dead center, with a thud.

Glancing behind me, I caught sight of Aunt Maggie and Mike playfully dancing under the Oak tree that shaded our family plot. More than once Maggie had asked Dan to fix her up; watching them, I couldn't help but think this was a heavenly sign from my husband, the King of the Dancing Queens. Humming "Dancing Queen," I felt the upbeat rhythm lift my spirit and wondered how it was that I had never, until this moment, appreciated the finer qualities of ABBA.

About the Author

Mary Patrick Kavanaugh has a checkered professional past that includes time served in a wide range of professions, ranging from private investigator to Avon Lady. Recently, after a series of crushing disappointments, Mary redirected a lifelong dream of becoming bestselling author into a new goal of being the most successful failure possible. In this role, she offers workshops, products, and cheap advice that assist the downtrodden to reframe difficult experiences in a positive way. Her website, www.mydreamisdeadbutimnot.com, serves as a gateway to a virtual cemetery that invites visitors to bury the failed dreams that have morphed into obstacles to light-hearted living.

Because no life is only about its flops, the author admits to having one perfect daughter, one happy marriage with a loving (but now dead) husband, one well-adjusted cat that prefers to live with her aunt, and a confusing, yet fun, personal life. She has an MFA in Creative Writing from University of San Francisco (2003), a BA in History from San Francisco State University (1988), good teeth, and an excellent credit rating.

Printed in the United States
128348LV00004B/1/P

9 781440 104664